W9-ARU-258

THE
LION PIT

THE
LION PIT

A NOVEL BY

Frank Harvey

Boston · Toronto

LITTLE, BROWN AND COMPANY

LIBRARY OF CONGRESS CATALOG CARD NO. 61-9294

FIRST EDITION

Published simultaneously in Canada
by Little, Brown & Company (Canada) Limited

PRINTED IN THE UNITED STATES OF AMERICA

This book is dedicated to my beloved wife, Christine Holzer Harvey, without whose patience, encouragement and help it would never have been finished.

THE
LION PIT

Saturday

THE coal train came before dawn. Archie Saunders heard it before anyone else in Carey Furnace (he could hear things others could not, like flies walking on the ceiling in the dark, or the purring inside a match flame), and he heard the coal train forty miles away, on the river above Kittanning, a faint and distant murmur in the hot August night. Archie lay very still in bed and after a while the sound of the train grew more distinct: a mutter, a rumble, a roar. Archie smiled. A vision had come to him. The sound was no longer a train. It was a man — the same man he'd seen in the horror movie at the Empire two weeks ago, with a hairy face and hot eyes, running through the hills with a piece of iron pipe in his hands, chasing a girl. In the movie, the chase had been made suspenseful by flashing from the savage staring eyes of the hunter to the desperate gasping face of the victim. Finally, in a patch of bushes, the monster had caught her. The camera had held on his face, glaring down, smiling. And then the hand holding the pipe had lifted and begun to strike, furiously, hysterically, and the madman had begun to make a queer roaring sound. . . .

Archie could bear the thought no longer. He shivered, deliciously, and chuckled — very softly — and then slid out of bed in his shorts and moved to the window quickly, quietly, like a cat. He was a thin boy of thirteen, with a round head clipped all over to save money on haircuts, now grown out into a thatch that resembled a fur cap. His eyes were round and wide open and some people said Archie's eyes gave them the willies: they looked like the glowing eyes of a cat — which wasn't true, of course. Archie's eyes did not glow. They were merely excited and bright, and his lips were usually parted slightly, and moist, like the lips of a pretty little girl waiting to be kissed.

Archie leaned out of the window of the rickety house. An average person might have seen nothing but darkness, smelled nothing but the pervading chemical stench of the Carey Furnace steel mills. But for Archie the night was alive with all kinds of sensory excitement. He could smell the odor from the outhouse in the elderberry bushes under the railroad embankment, the faint sweetish musk of his own body, the dying richness of last night's boiled cabbage from the kitchen below, the sultry, almost overpowering sweetness of overripe grapes from the nearby arbor, and the warm comforting smell of the dry lumber in the house. The darkness was full of wonderful sounds. There was the giant nighttime hum of the steel mill, half a mile downriver; a lonely haze of crickets; the soft snoring of his mother in the next room; the ripsaw chittering of some insect in the horseweeds which choked the city dump above the tracks. Through this maze of sound, Archie heard, with exquisite clearness, the tiny perfect voice of an unknown creature in the grass: *pip-pip . . . pip-pip . . . pip-pip. . . .*

Archie's eyes moistened.

"Pip-pip," he whispered, in reply. "Pip-pip. Pip-pip."

He yearned to see the baby insect, which, out there in the grass, was testing its voice cautiously, hopefully. He could see the mite in his mind: wistful, microscopic, with tiny eager beads for eyes and hairlike feet clinging to the monster underside of a burdock leaf, big, for it, as a circus tent.

"Pip-pip," he whispered again, his eyes prickling with unshed tears. "Pip-pip. Pip-pip."

He could make out the loom of the embankment above the house, where the train would come by, the black tower of the hillside above it against the sky, which was only slightly less black, pricked with stars. The train was coming now. He could hear the rail joints humming. The headlight burst around the curve — a dazzling eye which cast its whiteness ahead along the right-of-way, glittering on the rails, whitening the crushed rock of the roadbed, drawing out delicate shadows behind each spike-head and bit of waste. The mutter of the diesel engine which pulled a hundred loaded coal cars was guttural and unhurried, curiously deliberate in comparison to the headlong rush of the train. As the headlight hurtled toward him, Archie's fingers tightened on the window sill and his soft girl's mouth opened expectantly. The glaring eye towered high above him for a heartbeat, like the burst of a flashbulb, and the air horn went off — hoarse, fierce — like the shout of a madman, and then the light was gone and the night was filled with the rocking roar of the cars. . . .

Archie's thin body was rigid. It strained against the window. Those wheels up there were big whirling knives, in the dark, and the hot wind-of-passage of the train made a smoky swirling in the bedroom. And then the roar snapped off short and the two red eyes of the caboose fled away down the track past the blast furnaces, and Archie's body slowly relaxed. The excitement was over. Behind the blast furnaces, there was the beginning of a faint lightness in the sky. Dawn was coming. In a little while he would have to get dressed and go to work for Mr. Brothers in the River Avenue Market, which everybody said was the largest and best-stocked market in Carey Furnace. He would have to listen to the lecture about putting the canned goods on the bottom of the cardboard carton and the potato chips on top, and he would have to smell Miss Van Sant's perfume as she stood there sweating in the heat, checking out orders on her cash register. To Archie's sensitive nose, Miss Van Sant smelled equally of onions and violets, and Mr. Brothers smelled of toilet water and tobacco, and sometimes of whisky. He hated Mr. Brothers and Miss Van Sant. Some day, after he was able to patent one of his inventions and got a million dollars, he would get even with them for laughing at him and calling him a little moron. He did not know exactly what moron meant, but he knew it was something ugly, or they wouldn't say it. But right now he might as well go back and lie down on the bed until daylight. This was Saturday, and there was going to be a great big party up at the John Carey mansion on the hill, and there would be a lot of stuff to be delivered up there — which meant a lot of stuff for Archie Saunders to pack.

The dawn crept from the east over the town of Carey Furnace, sullen, red-eyed, like a hungover drunk. For five weeks, since early July, there had been no break in the heat wave. There had been promises of rain. Thunderheads had boiled up from the south, over Pittsburgh; the sky had gone black, low on the horizon; there had been flickers of heat lightning and the moist rumble of thunder, but there had been no real rain. Just a flurry of scattered drops in the dust before the sun flared down again, shrinking the Allegheny between its banks, withering the leaves of the forest trees into folded yellow curls, burning the goldenrod, thistle, sumac, and Queen Anne's lace along the roadside. In Carey Furnace, Pennsylvania, on this Saturday morning in the first week in August, there was a quiet, confined quality to the heat, like the inside of a pit, where hot stones are lying. . . .

High above the town, on a sweep of lawn in front of a massive house built out of cut stone, darkened by years of mill smoke but partly redeemed by a cloak of ivy, a man sat in a canvas lawn chair. He had wide shoulders and the blocky torso of a football player, a lion's mane of gray hair, parted on the side, a large powerful nose, and light blue eyes. His face, in repose, gave him the disarming appearance of a schoolboy. He wore leather sandals on his bare feet, a terry-cloth bathrobe, and he leaned forward as the sun crept over the rim of the mountain. The dawn was his favorite time of day, and the valley below, which was being flooded by the low pink sunlight, was his — or at least it had been his, almost like a kingdom, before the unions had risen to power — and still was essentially his, in spite of the unions. He was John P. Carey, principal stockholder, president, and chairman of the board of Carey Furnace Steel Company.

"John . . ."

John Carey turned to see his wife Eva standing behind him on the sunburned lawn. His eyes crinkled approvingly. Still, at fifty-two, his wife was one of the most attractive women he knew. Her hair was done in a poodle cut, tinted faintly blue at the moment by the rinse she used, and she carried herself as erect as a young girl in her white linen dress and high-heeled white shoes. She was tanned a yellow cream: face, neck, arms, and bare legs. Looking closer, of course, one saw the signs of age that must inevitably be there: the blue veins under the tan, the spidery network of lines on her hands, the pale shadows under her brown eyes. She looked at her husband, smiling. "Still love me?"

"Yep."

"That's the right answer, dear. You're well trained." Her gaze turned slightly and went past him to the dawn-lit valley. "It's lovely, John — right now."

He followed her stare. The sunlight painted the sides of the grimy houses, lay in luminous stripes across the mill-town streets where an intersection let it through, and embossed the edges of the mill stacks with vivid pink enamel. Jets of steam, pluming from the labyrinth of pipes and girders, were transformed by the low sunlight to flamingo mist — and the sun glare, catching the façade of windows of the main office building, created the illusion that the structure was being gutted by a raging fire. Sounds of the mill, miniaturized by distance, rose to them: the tortured grinding of a ladle-train around some curve inside the plant; the hoarse snoring of a snort valve in the blast furnaces; the measured, sullen rhythm of a drop forge.

"Eve — I thought you were going to sleep late and build up your strength for the party this afternoon."

"I woke up and you were gone. So I came out to find you."

He started to rise, but she pressed her fingers on his shoulders. "No, John. I'll sit beside you. I want to."

She curled her legs under her, and he could see the slim brown knees at the hem of the linen, and the curve of the calves against the grass. He spoke, in his peculiar soft husky voice. "I don't know if I've mentioned it lately, Mrs. Carey, but you have very nice legs."

"You're a very bad boy," she said, smiling at him. Her smile faded. "John —"

"Yes?"

"How do you feel?"

"Fine."

"No — really."

"I'm all right, Eve. It's just the heat. It's been going on so long. Four weeks — five — I don't know —"

"Have you seen Pop yet?"

"Saw him at the plant yesterday."

"Oh, John, you know what I mean. Have you gone in and let him give you that check-up?"

"I'm going to — as soon as I have a free minute."

"Oh, darling — please! Monday morning go in and let Pop look you over."

"All right. Not Monday, though. I have to be in New York Monday. Stanley Sucek has called a little meeting on the export situation in South America."

"My God, John — Stanley's a big boy now. He's your vice president in charge of export. Does he need you to hold his hand every time he calls a little meeting?"

"I guess I used the wrong word. It's not a little meeting, really. As you well know, our whole position in South America has become increasingly touchy ever since this fellow Castro made his revolution stick. There's more anti-American feeling down there now than the newspapers are letting on. And the Communists aren't helping it any with these offers of second-hand Migs. An American is being pictured — even to the little kids — as a pot-bellied capitalist out to squeeze them dry like a bunch of lemons."

Eva Carey smiled. "Thank heaven you've never grown a pot, John. And I'm sure you'd never squeeze anybody like a lemon — unless he tried to squeeze you first. But you must admit you aren't selling steel in South America for your health."

"Of course I'm not. I'm there to make a profit. There's nothing wrong with a profit — in South America or anywhere else. It burns me up the way people seem to be ashamed of making a profit any more. They act as if it was a dirty word. Well, I can say this: when you pull the carrot out from in front of the donkey's nose, the donkey slows down considerably — and the only way to make him move is to belt his rear end with a stick. These people who think Communism is so wonderful are new in the game. Wait until they feel the stick —"

He broke off, and she glanced at him quickly.

"What is it, John?"

"Nothing."

"You stopped talking, all of a sudden."

"It's nothing. Say, look down there on the main drag. That's Maggie Fiori's red Pontiac, isn't it?"

She looked down from the hill to see the red shape moving like a toy along Main Street. "Can't tell from here — but it could be."

"Maggie coming to your party?"

"No. Bert's suffering in the heat. I guess she doesn't want to leave him."

He shook his head gently. "Poor bastard. Will he ever walk again?"

"Nobody seems to know for sure," Eva said. "But it's been four months now since the accident, and he's still in the cast."

John Carey was silent, thinking of Umberto Fiori's fall from his horse — and then, by automatic chain of thought, back to Fiori's whirlwind courtship of Margaret Hunter, belle of Carey Furnace and heiress to one of the largest fortunes in western Pennsylvania. Fiori had been a fortune hunter, and old Amos Hunter had done his best to break up the romance. John Carey could still remember the visit Amos had made to the house on the hill to ask John Carey Sr.'s advice. Old John told him to pay the young Italian off, and Amos had tried to do this — but had failed. Umberto Fiori was a horse-beater and a woman-chaser — but he had a cool head where money was concerned. He told old Amos to keep his $50,000, and when Amos upped it to $100,000, he told him to keep that too. Young Fiori was very sure of Maggie. He became highly indignant when her father offered him money to go back to Italy. There was no price on love, he said, and Mr. Hunter should know it. Amos had been worth almost three million dollars at that point, and Fiori had been playing for the jack-pot.

"What are you thinking about?" Eva Carey said.

"Nothing much. Maggie and her big horseman. The mess she made by marrying him."

"It was her own fault," Eva said. "Nobody could tell her anything"

"No, I guess they couldn't."

"Fiori has certainly led poor Maggie a terrible life," Eva said. "But I guess he's getting it back now — with interest."

"He's getting it back," John Carey said. "I have to pity the guy, fortune hunter or not."

Eva Carey rose then, lithely, in a single motion, and stood looking down at her husband. "I'm going in and get some breakfast, John. There won't be much chance to eat after the stampede of caterers begins. Want to join me?"

"No, thanks. I'm going to stay here and soak up some sunshine."

"Can I bring you coffee or toast or anything?"

"No, thanks. I'm not very hungry."

She bent, quickly, and kissed him on the mouth. He put up his right hand and held her shoulder and kissed her again. She straightened and they looked at each other a moment. It was a look of affection and regard, troubled by a slight frown of worry on Eva's face. Then she turned and walked away across the lawn and John Carey let his weight sink back into the chair and stared down at the mills.

The pink flush of dawn was gone. The sun was well up above the river hills and lit the valley with a white glare. The mill stretched along the riverbank for five miles. On the steep slope above it, a welter of cramped ugly houses crept upward like a blight. This was the tough section of town, known as the Strip. It had not changed, except in the density and degree of its ugliness, since John Carey's father, old John, had built his first crude cupola furnaces and beehive coke ovens in the valley so many years ago. There had been no attempt at city planning. In those days, a man could build his house out of old packing cases if he felt like it. He could burn rubbish in his yard, keep coal in his bathtub, and locate his privy on the edge of his property within ten feet of his neighbor's pump. One family, according to legend, had even kept pigs in the backyard until neighbors, infuriated by the stench on a hot summer night, had killed them. The slaughter had not been any clandestine use of poison; it had been a fusillade of deer-rifle fire, accompanied by high-pitched squeals of agony on the part of the pigs, curses and screams on the part of the killers and the owners. According to legend, all had ended happily. The pigs had been butchered on the spot, cooked on a fire made of stolen railroad ties, and washed down with two kegs of beer brought up from the old River Avenue Tavern (now burned down). The pig killing could have gone either of two ways: a roast-pig party — or an interfamily massacre. In those days many of the people on the Strip spoke completely different languages, and very little English, and did not let little things like the law of the land deter them from acts of violence. Why this particular incident ended amicably nobody remembered now — but the party had gone on for two days, the railroad never heard about the stolen ties, and the neighbors had remained friends.

The blight of the Strip stopped abruptly at the crest of the slope — at Highland Avenue. Here stood Carey Furnace proper — a conventional middle-class Pennsylvania town with a main street, a public square, a hospital (John Carey Memorial), a hotel (the Carey House), and well-kept houses along streets lined with maple trees, in which lived the merchants, doctors, dentists, real-estate men, and car salesmen upon whom the area depended for its various services. This section of town, like the Strip, had changed little since old John Carey had founded his Iron Works, as the company was then called. The old folks still rocked on their verandahs behind the kudzu trellises in summer, and complained of the heat, and the taxes, and the downtown parking situation. Some businesses went to the wall. Others blossomed forth with streamlined fronts and neon signs. Buckminster's and Wetherholt's, two big Pittsburgh department stores, built modern suburban annexes on opposite sides of the town square — which forced old Horace Foyle to modernize Foyle and Sons — but many old-timers were still loyal, as long as old Horace kept his prices in line with the city boys.

The big changes had taken place in the company itself. It was no longer a local Iron Works. Under John Carey Jr. it had expanded steadily until it was an industrial empire with outlying plants, warehouses, and sales offices in principal cities. Its annual business ran into multiple millions, its stock was listed on the Big Board, and its products were used around the world. John Carey Jr. was one of the last of the big independent steel producers, and he ran his company — with the help of his directors — by personal supervision. Times were changing rapidly, however. Bigness and the complexity of operations — the continuous demands of the unions, the intricacies of taxation — these had now gone up in geometric progression, and it was becoming increasingly difficult for one man — even a man like John Carey — to keep abreast of the details which must be fully understood if disastrous mistakes were to be avoided. He'd told Eva his trouble was the heat, but it was more than that. He was tired — mentally, physically, bone-deep — and yet he had no wish to relax. He loved the company, and he loved the business. As long as he was able to sit at the head of the board-room table, he would never step down. . . .

Sitting on the lawn of his mansion, John Carey let his gaze move up from the mills and the town proper and turn westward. The mansion stood on a freakish peak, like a tree-clothed chocolate drop, which dominated the area on all sides. He turned his back on the river smog and looked into the smiling countryside on the other side of the mountain — the side shut away from the stench and fury of the mills — the side which old Amos Hunter had purchased many years ago when it was scrub growth, and later subdivided and sold for huge and relatively untaxed profits. Hunter's Valley, this sequestered paradise was now called. In it lived the top executives of Carey Furnace Steel Company, in their Tudor mansions behind their broad lawns, stake-and-rider fences and spike-iron gates. The only plebeian touch in this remote neighborhood of wealth and power were the mailboxes, ordinary galvanized products such as might be found in front of any farmhouse, except, of course, for the names painted neatly on their sides: J. P. Detweiler, Four Oaks Farm . . . David B. Ross, Smokerise . . . William T. Caldwell, Sunset Hills. . . .

From his chair on the lawn, John Carey caught a glint moving in the distant valley, a blood-red speck on the curving ribbon of road. He watched it disappear behind a grove of trees, then reappear along the border of the golf course, turn into a lane, and lose itself. John Carey knew that lane well, knew the name on the mailbox which had once stood at its mouth: Amos Hunter, Horizon's End. Since Amos's death, the name had been changed. It was now Umberto Fiori. John Carey felt a small inner twitch of laughter. Maggie Fiori's gigolo husband hadn't stopped at being big, dark and handsome, and a heller on horseback. He'd gone the whole way. He even had the name to fit all of it: Umberto Fiori — you could almost see it in lights on a theatre marquee.

Umberto Fiori lay on the Hollywood bed which he had ordered placed in the room he called his den, on the ground floor of the old

Hunter mansion. He had been in the master bedroom upstairs for several weeks after leaving the hospital, but the place had finally bored him so much he'd ordered himself brought downstairs. It was noisier here, what with the kitchen clatter, the man who clipped the hedges around the house, and the traffic in the driveway. But it was better. He could scream at the cook, if he felt bad, or curse the man with the clippers, or turn on the television. It had been nearly five months now since his horse had refused the water jump in the exercise field and had stumbled through it and fallen with Fiori underneath. He had been unconscious when they found him. It was a miracle, the doctor said, that he had escaped with his life. He was a very lucky man.

At first, before he realized how serious his spinal injury was, Fiori was inclined to agree with the doctor. But as the weeks dragged on, he began to get very irritable. He had never cared much for books — he often said that life was something you lived, not something you read about. And he had gone about living it in the manner which he felt would bring him the most enjoyment: riding, drinking, lounging in the sun, lifting the skirts of a pretty woman when he had the chance. He had met Maggie Hunter on the beach at Rimini, on the shores of the Adriatic, the summer of John Carey's marriage to Eva Peck. Maggie, then nineteen, had fancied herself heartbroken by the marriage and her mother had taken her abroad "to forget." Mrs. Hunter's idea of forgetting involved a steady diet of museums, cathedrals, and other stock tourist attractions, and by the time Maggie reached Rimini she was thoroughly bored and looking for a little excitement. Nobody could deny that Umberto Fiori, whatever his other faults, was a very exciting young man. He was, as Maggie's distraught mother later described him to Maggie's father, "a black-headed young beast who made me want to slap his face every time he looked at me."

Fiori's stare had had quite a different effect upon Maggie. When he looked at her she felt her wrists get weak and had a warm sickish feeling in her stomach. When he kissed her (the first night after they met on the beach) she felt it go all through her. Fiori was the younger son of a well-to-do Italian family. He spoke English with an intriguing accent, swam like an Olympic champion, danced magnificently, rode a horse brutally and recklessly, and made love far better than Maggie had ever had it made in America. He had some money of his own, but not enough, not nearly enough, to implement the plans he had for himself — plans, of course, which Maggie knew nothing about. . . .

Maggie and the young Italian spent every waking moment together. They danced, swam, rode, drank, and made increasingly passionate love. Maggie's mother, usually not one to worry about casual romances, finally realized things were getting beyond the casual stage and tried to break it up by snatching Maggie home. "We've been in Europe nearly two months, dear," Mrs. Hunter said. "Frankly, I'm getting bored with it, and I'm sure you are too. I guess it's time we booked passage back."

"Oh Mums, you couldn't be more wrong! I'm having a perfectly marvelous time!"

The older woman was then forced to reveal her true motive: Fiori. Mrs. Hunter was willing to admit that he was handsome, and no doubt he rode a horse superbly, but he was not the sort of person a girl like Margaret Hunter could consider, even for a moment, in any serious manner.

"Oh Mother, for heaven's sake — I'm a big girl now — and I'm having fun for the first time since we left the States! You can't deny me a little fun after all those horrible art galleries you dragged me through. I want to stay two more weeks. . . ."

Maggie stayed her two weeks.

The marriage did not take place in Italy. Maggie came home to Carey Furnace: an impassioned correspondence ensued, and finally, in the spring, young Umberto Fiori arrived in town. Maggie wanted to invite him to the house, but her father flatly refused. So young Fiori took a room in the Carey House and laid siege to the heart of his beloved Maggie. Old Amos was utterly without tact. By his heavy-handed opposition to the handsome young Italian, he drove his headstrong young daughter straight into his arms. Finally, he actually called his daughter to him and forbade her to see "that young gigolo" ever again. It was the final straw. Maggie and Umberto ran off to New York and were married, spent their honeymoon in Bermuda, and returned to Carey Furnace as man and wife. Maggie was deeply in love with Fiori at the time. She was quick to come to his defense over any real or fancied slight. She was determined to show her father, and the rest of the critics in Carey Furnace, that they were wrong about "Bert." He was not a fortune hunter. He was a fine, talented young man, and his motives were of the highest. . . .

He had been unfaithful to her in the first year, with a maid — an incident she never discovered. But in the middle of the second year, when she was pregnant with Enid, she surprised him, quite naked and quite drunk, lying on top of an old college chum, Helen French, who was also naked and drunk, and who had come down from Buffalo to spend two weeks with her dear friend Margaret. Helen French departed with deep scratches on her right cheek and some of her hair pulled out by the roots, threatening to sue for atrocious assault (she never sued), and Fiori spent a long time beating his chest, blaming liquor and Helen French for a situation which he swore would never happen again. It was not in Maggie Hunter's heart to cheat on a person she loved. But it was also not in her heart to forgive when that person cheated on her. She was too proud to divorce Fiori. Enid was coming. She did not dissolve the marriage, and later, after Enid was born and the image of Helen French, lying naked under the loins of her husband, had blurred with time, she had relations with Fiori again. But she had ceased to love him. And, of course, he did not change. There were other women, from time to time, after Helen French. Finally, he was brutally specific about his philosophy on the subject. "I don't put one book in my library and read it over and over," he told her. "I read different books. It's the same with women. I need different women — and I intend to have them — so you might as well shut up and get used to it."

Lying in his cast now, in the old Hunter mansion, Umberto Fiori was impotent; spiritually, mentally, and physically. He had no resources to fall back on: not patience (he had none); not music or the arts (they did not interest him); not God (Fiori prayed wildly at first, but when nothing came of it, he stopped). Perhaps the doctor had been wrong: escaping with his life had not been lucky. If he was going to be paralyzed from now on, he would be better off dead.

As the weeks passed, Fiori gradually alienated the people who came to help him or to try to cheer him up. The bone specialist from Pittsburgh was one of the first to go.

"When will I be up?" Fiori had yelled at the man one morning during his examination. "No more of your pussyfooting! When? Tell me!"

"It depends, Mr. Fiori," the doctor said stiffly. "The X-rays show —"

"Shove the X-rays up your ass!" Fiori shouted. "Just answer my question!"

The doctor's eyes had flickered, but his voice had remained calm. "Since you ask me this way, sir, I'll be perfectly glad to tell you. Your spine is involved. It is possible you will be in bed a year, maybe even longer." The doctor rose. "Now, sir, there are many competent men in Pittsburgh who will be happy to handle your case. Personally, my work load makes it impossible for me to attend you here in Carey Furnace any more. Good day, sir."

Fiori had cursed the doctor out of the house. When Maggie came in to see what the matter was, he cursed her. The doctor had been trying to scare him out of his mind, that's what he'd been doing, and Margaret had probably put him up to it. But they were mistaken! Neither she nor the doctor nor anyone else was going to succeed, because Fiori was going to show them! He was going to be out of bed in two weeks and walking around with a cane in a month and back to the stables soon thereafter! And the first thing he was going to do when he got out to the barn was find the horse that had thrown him — it had survived without any broken bones — and beat it. He would beat it until it fell down in its stall, and he would keep on beating it until it was dead. He would use a ball bat. It was the horse's fault he was lying there now. If it had not refused the jump at the last moment, nothing would have happened. Maggie heard him out, staring at him impersonally with her bright blue eyes. "Are you finished now, Bert?"

" 'Are you finished now, Bert?' " he mocked her, in a thin yell. " 'Are you finished now, Bert?' Yeah, yeah, I'm finished now, Bert!"

"Shouting won't change anything," she said. "You can shout yourself hoarse and it won't change a thing."

"You bitch!" he yelled. "Don't tell me what to do! When I'm back on my feet again, I'll show you and a lot of other people a thing or two."

"I'm sure you will, Bert. You've already shown me and a lot of other people a thing or two."

She stared at him without love or pity. Her face was still beautiful — but the years of pride, too much money, lust, indolence, boredom, despair, and yearning had left their mark. And yet, in one way, the marks of life did not wholly detract. Her face had a hardness, and yet it also had a vulnerability which the thoughtless face of the innocent girl had not possessed. Her lips were expressionless at this moment, but they could quiver like the lips of a young girl when she was in the arms of Ken Carpenter. With him she was unsure of herself, nervous, eager to please, yet quick to anger if offended. Sometimes, when she thought of her son-in-law, she pressed her fingernails into her palms. She was a silly old woman, an utter fool, a cradle snatcher, and she vowed never to see Ken alone again — never, never, never! Except, of course, even while she clenched her hands, she knew she was kidding herself. When she saw Ken Carpenter get out of his car on the drive, or suddenly appear in a doorway, or when she heard his voice on the telephone, she had a feeling so intense she was sometimes close to tears. She wanted to hold him in her arms and whisper to him, like a baby. She wanted to give him everything in the world he ever wanted. She dreamed of him sometimes, and they were walking in the woods and it was early spring and she could smell the wet leaves and the arbutus underneath the leaves, and they did not even kiss. They just walked through the leaves, hand in hand, and she knew that they were completely one. They were one person against the world, self-sufficient, close, untouchable in their love. It was like a foolish sentimental story in a magazine.

Now, standing beside her husband's bed, none of these emotions showed in Margaret Fiori's face. Her lips were swollen-looking under their bright lipstick. There were dissipation creases, like blue scars, under her eyes, and the swollen mouth retained a trace of mockery, of dissatisfaction, even when she smiled. She held herself erect with the grace of a dancer on her still beautiful legs. She was forty-six years old, but she was still a very desirable woman, for her body and her passion — aside from the fact that she controlled close to three millions of dollars. On the bed, Umberto Fiori felt physical desire for his wife for the first time in months. If he were on his feet, he thought, he would grab her and throw her down — not on the bed — on the floor, and rip that expensive dress and those expensive panties and stockings and the rest of it into a pile of rags, and then, when she was naked and furious, trying to reach his face with her nails, he would shove her face flatside against the rug, and catch both her hands in one of his, and force her legs wide apart, and go into her — and if she screamed, and if the cook came in from the kitchen and saw it, well, why not? He knew that the girl he had married, the girl who had loved him long ago, would not have minded particularly. That girl had been as wild — wilder, truly, when fully aroused, than Fiori himself. But when he saw her eyes, now, looking at him as if he were a stranger, the lust in his head turned, suddenly, to rage, and he said, "Where have you been? Out in the barn making love to one of your boy friends?"

"You know I have no boy friends."

"Hell, that's a lie! You're nuts about young Ken Carpenter. Your own daughter's husband! It's a town scandal."

"I like Ken. Why shouldn't I?"

"Like him? Oh yes, my dear, I know you like him. You like him so much you roll him in the hay every chance you get. Well, I've had all of it I'm going to stand. You hear? I'm going to tell Enid! I'm going to tell that her dear old mother is laying her handsome young husband! I'm going to —"

"Please, Bert. The cook can hear every word you're saying."

"Fuck the cook! Wait until I tell Enid. She'll put a stop to all this whoring around. She'll get me a new doctor. She's my baby girl, and she loves me . . ."

And then, suddenly, his bluster evaporated, as she had known it would, and he shut his eyes tightly. "Oh, Margo, Margo — I'm sorry, my darling. It's just that I'm hurt and I'm scared. Oh, Margo, I'm so scared. Forgive me my darling. Forgive me. . . ."

He turned his face away, and she saw that he was weeping, and, against her will, she felt a grudging sympathy. He lived by what people said, not by what they meant. He thought Enid loved him because she was always saying she loved him. He prized the little gifts Enid brought, when she happened to think of it, far more than the sustained day-to-day routine of the care which his wife must supervise: the day and night nurses, the medicines, the meals. Enid, who breezed in in her newest Paris gown, modeled it briefly for her father, brushed his forehead with a kiss, and was gone — Enid was his strength, his baby girl, his salvation. He turned on his pillow and looked up, and he might have been reading her thoughts, for he said: "Where's Enid now?"

"In Pittsburgh, shopping."

"When is she coming home?"

"Do you mean here — or to their home?"

"Here."

"I don't know, Bert. Maybe tomorrow. Why?"

"I want to see her," the man said. "I want to talk to my little baby."

"I'll try to get hold of her," Margaret said, "as soon as she gets back. I'll tell her you want to see her."

"All right. Thank you."

Margaret had a sudden impulse to bend down and kiss him, but she did not. She turned and walked out of the room. She went through the dining room to the kitchen, and was relieved. The cook was not there. Margaret could see her through the window, out by the garage, talking to the yard man. A small smile tugged at her lips. The cook hadn't overheard Umberto's tirade over sex. The cook had a little sex matter of her own to attend to. . . .

For a man who did not drink at all, Ken Carpenter was occupying an improbable position on that Saturday morning in August; he was sitting on a stool in the Linger Awhile, a small bar-and-grill on the blacktop road which provided access to the big estates in Hunter's Valley. The blacktop was known among the natives as Veep Row. Its real name was Old Mine Creek Road. Old Mine Creek was the waterway which meandered through the woods and pastures of Hunter's Valley, and land upon its banks was the most exclusive of all. The Linger Awhile was a very old establishment, serving beer and sandwiches back before the days of John L. Lewis and his Committee for Industrial Organization brought sweeping changes to Carey Furnace.

The establishment owed its continuity of tenure to that shadowy but all-powerful group, the Hunter's Valley Steering Committee. J. P. Detweiler, vice president and treasurer of Carey Furnace Steel Company, was one of the most influential members of the committee. J.P. liked a cold glass of beer, a ham sandwich, and a plate of clams on the halfshell in season. He liked a host who could provide these things at their best — who respected the privacy of his guests — who operated a clean, orderly establishment. Dutch Huber, the big-bellied, close-mouthed proprietor of the Linger Awhile, measured up on all counts. Dutch bought his ham from a secret source out in the country. It was so tender you could cut it with a fork, sweet as honey, and he sliced it a quarter of an inch thick for the sandwiches. When you sat down at Dutch's bar he did not move up in front of you, plant his elbows, and blow the smell of onions in your face. He nodded and smiled. If you wanted to talk, he would talk — but you had to start it. But nobody got away with loud or obscene language in Dutch's place. He weighed two hundred and sixty pounds and it was doubtful if he could have run a hundred yards. But when Dutch's brows met in a furry ridge over his black eyes, and he bent over the bar and spoke to a man earnestly, that was usually the end of it. If not, Dutch had a short piece of iron pipe on a ledge near the beer tap. He had only had to bring it up once. He had not had to actually use it.

Dutch had no family except Skipper, his fourteen-year-old fox terrier, who occupied a special basket fitted with a blanket, which the little dog dragged around on the inlaid linoleum floor, to suit his changing desires for sun or shade. Skipper was probably the most pampered dog in Hunter's Valley if not in the entire state of Pennsylvania. Steel Company vice presidents fed him jumbo shrimp or bits of ham from their plates, and most of them greeted the dog by name when they entered the Linger Awhile, even before speaking to Dutch himself. Now, on the floor beside Ken Carpenter's stool, Skipper was peering up with his age-milky eyes as Ken removed a cheese curl from its cellophane bag and held it down to him. The little dog sniffed delicately, then took the cheese bit with dainty deliberation, as if he were conferring a favor upon a rather shabby donor (after all, this might have been a jumbo shrimp!) and dropped it on the floor for further examination before risking the ultimate commitment — actually eating it. Two stools away, Frank Hewitt, J. P. Detweiler's farm manager, chuckled. "Damn little bugger's doin' you a favor, Mr. Carpenter! Ain't it?"

Ken Carpenter smiled along the bar at Frank Hewitt. "Skipper is a friend of mine, Frank. Right, Skipper?"

The dog glanced up at mention of his name, picked up his prize, and retired to his basket, chewing. Behind the bar, Dutch Huber polished his beer glasses with the steady industry of the Pennsylvania Dutch, wishing the heat would break — wondering if he should not, after all, order an air conditioner. Dutch had once made a public announcement in his bar condemning air conditioners as a prime cause of summer colds. But that had been before this marathon heat wave. He would gladly install a conditioner now — and he could easily afford it — but he shrank from losing face. Having announced against air conditioning — a silly thing to have done, and much against his usual policy of keeping his mouth shut and quietly doing whatever it was he had in mind — Dutch could not now bring himself to install air conditioning, no matter how much he suffered with the heat.

"Oh, Dutch," Ken Carpenter said. "Give Frank another of whatever he's drinking, will you?"

Dutch looked inquiringly at Hewitt. He was glad to serve treats from one customer to another, but the treatee had to consent, first. "Another Budweiser, Mr. Hewitt?"

"No, thanks, Dutch — and thanks a lot, Mr. Carpenter. But one's my limit in the morning, on a work day."

"Work, Frank — in this heat?" Ken Carpenter said.

"Hot weather, cold weather," Frank Hewitt said, "what's the difference? The cattle got to be looked after."

Ken Carpenter looked at the man. Hewitt, like Dutch, was of Pennsylvania German extraction. He had the sad-hound look in the eyes, the straight-line neck from the collar to the top of the back of his head, the insect-like instinct to keep busy, at something, anything — just so it wasn't sitting around. Ken had never cared much for the Pennsylvania Dutch, as a group. He had come into contact with them in Bethlehem, Pennsylvania, when he had gone to Lehigh to study mechanical engineering. He had seen them out in their yards pruning the clean natural limbs off their maples, so that hideous knobs, which sprouted branches like Medusa's hair, were left. Once he had stopped and asked one of them why he was doing this. The man had stared at him a moment, and said, "Efrybody does it. Dot's why. Efrybody trims his trees, Mister." And the man had returned to his work. Frank Hewitt, however, was only part Pennsylvania Dutch — on his mother's side — and there was no argument about his ability with beef cattle. He was one of the best Black Angus men in the business, which was why J. P. Detweiler had put him in charge of his prize herd. It was no secret in Carey Furnace that old man Detweiler was very interested in his cattle. He was more interested in his cattle, some people said, than he was in the steel company which paid him a salary that, with bonuses and stock options and whatnot, came to about $190,000 a year.

Ken Carpenter said, "You know something, Frank? You think too much about cattle. You should relax. With your boss in Scotland, why break your neck?"

Frank Hewitt looked up from his beer. It was a small gesture, but it was not lost on Carpenter. Ken knew that very few people knew J. P. Detweiler's whereabouts at any given time. Ken didn't know it himself. The Scotland remark had been a guess — an attempt to get exact information — and for an instant he thought it had misfired. Then Frank Hewitt said, "I guess Mr. Detweiler told you, eh?"

"Told me what — about his being in Scotland? Oh, that's common knowledge down at the plant."

"Oh?"

"So you'll have your work cut out for you, Frank," Ken Carpenter laughed. "You better save your strength for when the boss ships over those new cows."

"Not cows this time," Frank Hewitt said. "A couple of good bulls. Mr. Detweiler wanted artificial insemination, but I told him no — get a bull. Take it off the income tax, give the cows a break, eh?" Frank Hewitt's sad-hound face smiled briefly, showing gold teeth. "Christamighty, Mr. Carpenter, a cow's gotta have a little fun, too."

"Frank, you're a romantic, under that tough exterior."

"Oh, no, I ain't. I guess I got a little theory. I can't prove it, but I think a bull gives a cow a better calf than a goddamn test tube can!"

Polishing his beer glasses behind the bar, Dutch Huber smiled.

"Frank . . ." Ken Carpenter said.

"Yeah, Mr. Carpenter?"

"Would you think I was completely out of my mind if I got hold of a young beef calf and fattened it up in my back pasture?"

"Why would I think that, Mr. Carpenter?"

"Well, I know there's a lot of pretty silly do-it-yourself stuff going on these days. One man I know has a woodworking shop in his basement fancy enough to turn out anything under the sun, but all he ever did with it was to play with the turning lathe a couple of times. I've been hearing you talk about cattle, Frank, and it's obvious you really care about them, and I figured maybe you'd think I was goofy if I tried to be a rancher — with one little cow."

Frank Hewitt had forgotten his beer and was leaning on the bar. A look of eagerness, almost akin to love, shone in his sad eyes. "Ah, Mr. Carpenter — not goofy. Never goofy. You could have a fine cow. Easy. It's nothing."

"Nothing to you, maybe, Frank. But for me — what would I feed it? Where would it sleep? And first of all, where would I get a good one?"

"Get a good one? Why, that's simple. You want a good heifer? Look, I'll be glad to go down to the auction market and pick one out for you. And it wouldn't cost much, neither. Not with me buying."

"You serious, Frank?"

"It will be a pleasure, Mr. Carpenter."

"Okay, Frank, you got yourself a job. When's the next auction?"

"Well, it's Monday — day after tomorrow. I guess you wouldn't want to move that fast."

"Why not? When I decide to move, I move. Want a check now?"

"No — I'll pay myself, and you can pay me back."

"Fine, Frank." Ken paused and his face clouded. "There's only one thing. How about after I have my heifer? Are you going to turn me loose — or keep a fatherly hand on my shoulder until I learn the ropes?"

Frank Hewitt's eyes now glowed. "Don't worry about that, Mr. Carpenter. I'm not going to run away and leave you. If you want, I'll bring you over to Four Oaks and show you how it's done — from start to finish." He rubbed his chin and winked at Dutch Huber. "Mr. Carpenter here has got nearly a hundred acres, most of it good grazing land. He starts with one cow — maybe he gets two cows, three, four — and maybe one of these days we have *two* Black Angus herds in Hunter's Valley. It's a good business deal, you know. If you make money on the cattle, it's in the bank. If you lose money on them, you can take it off the income tax."

Dutch Huber smiled silently, polishing his bar glasses. In the basket, the fox terrier, Skipper, lay sleeping.

"Sure you won't have a beer?" Ken Carpenter said to Frank Hewitt. "Bind the partnership?"

"Well, I shouldn't," Frank said. "But then I guess this is a special occasion. Another Bud, Dutch."

Twenty minutes later, after he had dropped Frank Hewitt at J. P. Detweiler's Four Oaks Farm, Ken drove back along Veep Row toward the house he and Enid had built on land old Amos Hunter had willed to his only granddaughter. The car moved over the blacktop road between two great estates: Detweiler's and Hunter's (now Fiori's). Detweiler's sleek Black Angus cattle were restrained in their wide meadows by ordinary electric fence: one strand of barbed wire strung on Carey Furnace steel fence posts. Detweiler was so far up the status ladder that he could afford to ignore the stake-and-rider tradition observed by lesser people in the valley.

Amos Hunter, on the other side, had far surpassed the stake-and-rider tradition. His land was fronted by a two-mile-long "dry wall" of hand-fitted field stones, twined, in season, with red rambler roses. The wall had been built at a time when the labor of an entire gang of immigrants could be had for the wages of two or three union men today. To replace the dry wall at current prices would cost at least $100,000. Behind it was a sun-dried hedge of boxwood, thick but somewhat in need of clipping, which completely walled out the sight of the Hunter mansion itself. Passing the stone pillars of the open front entrance, Ken Carpenter got a fleeting glimpse of red behind the shrubbery, and knew that Maggie was home. In summer, she spent much of her time in whatever car she happened to be driving that year: this year it was a red Pontiac convertible. She could have afforded a Rolls-Royce or a Mercedes, or any other car she chose, but she had liked the low flat lines of the Pontiac and had seen in an ad that it was the leading car in the stock-car racing circuits, and had bought it. Maggie, like J. P. Detweiler, was beyond the point where she bought anything—

or avoided buying anything — because of what the status-seekers were doing.

Ken Carpenter drove past the Fiori residence without slackening his speed. He seldom went into the house if he could avoid it. He knew Fiori suspected him of sleeping with Maggie, and hated him for having married his only daughter. Of course there wasn't much the poor man could do, lying there in a cast with his back broken, but Ken was not a person to hit a man (or annoy him) when he was down.

He did not blame Fiori for hating him, but he had no intention of stopping his affair with Maggie. They met circumspectly, in their homes, or they met clandestinely, taking care to cover their movements, in hotels in distant cities. Ken knew Maggie was in love with him. And if he had been capable of love, after his divorce from Debbie, he might have returned it, despite the fact that Maggie was seven years older than he was. In bed, Maggie was far superior to any woman he had ever had — except Debbie, in the first wild tender nights of a marriage which he had believed would last as long as they both lived. That tenderness was dead now. It had died the day he came home from a trip to Dayton, ahead of schedule, and found Dick Remick's white Cadillac parked one block down the street from his house in Shaker Heights. Since that day, Ken had operated differently. Before Debbie, he had thought that you get what you give. Now he operated on the belief that you get what you take.

He had known exactly what he was getting when he married Enid. She was vividly beautiful, rich, socially prominent, dull, and incredibly vain. For example, she could never seem to obtain too many photographs of herself. She owned two Polaroid-Land cameras, complete with flash attachments. One was kept in the house and the other in the car. Enid never could tell when she would happen upon a sunset, a field of flowers, or some other exotic background against which her portrait could be obtained within sixty seconds after snapping the button.

At least, Ken thought, Enid did not waste any time worrying about the H-bomb. She was too busy investigating really urgent matters: her hair, her teeth, her nails, the merits of Royal Bee Jelly on skin tone. As for bed, sleeping with Enid was like sleeping with a dummy out of Foyle's window. Softer, more pliable, but just about as responsive otherwise. In fact, in some ways, a dummy might have been preferable. A dummy would not be wearing grease on its face, curlers in its hair, and would not complain about being crushed or smothered.

Ken, however, did not complain about Enid's deficiencies. He hadn't married her for love or companionship, and didn't expect them. He had married her because of his plan. Enid's mother was Margaret Hunter Fiori, who owned $2,300,000 worth of Carey Furnace common stock. Basic in Ken Carpenter's plan was this simple fact: he who controls a sufficient percentage of the common stock of a corporation automatically controls the corporation.

He drove off the highway, stopped his car beside his garage, and got out. Heat waves shimmered over the valley. The concrete pool behind his house was empty, drained because of the water shortage, so he could not swim. He entered the cabana beside the pool, stripped, and quickly put on his running shorts and track shoes.

He looked at himself briefly in the full-length mirror which Enid had installed in the casual room off the dressing rooms. He was in good shape, considering the sedentary nature of his job in the office. He had a small pot, but his legs were well-muscled and his arms were not flabby. He was not a handsome man. He had blond hair which he combed straight back. His face was ruggedly boned, with a big nose, and very sharp blue eyes. His eye sockets looked dissipated. They always had, even when he was a baby. As Debbie had said, when they were in love, "You have a sort of sad, sweet face, darling — like a passionate water buffalo." The dominant feature of the face was the eyes. They were intelligent and alert, and there was no film of boredom or indulgence to blur them.

The hardest thing you did, in this life, was look at it without kidding yourself — or so Ken Carpenter believed. The random clutch of circumstance was often so brainlessly savage that the opium of dreams was almost irresistible. The inclination to dull the pain or enhance the bliss with some chemical stimulus or mental self-delusion was great. Ken Carpenter had not succumbed to alcohol or Miltown; he had never lain on a psychiatrist's couch; he had, however, crouched in the cellar of the Cleveland house and wept like a little kid, and he had walked for miles, some nights, after he left Debbie, feeling as if his body were going to fly apart like an exploding bomb or turn into a mass of tiny writhing worms. Reality, for Ken Carpenter, was the only game worth playing. It was the roughest when it was rough, and the sweetest when it was sweet.

Now he dropped lightly on his belly on the floor of the bathhouse and began to do pushups. He did ten with relative ease, strained fairly hard with the next five — and pushed himself to twenty with a great effort. He turned over on his back, feeling his body lengthen and settle wonderfully on the flat hard surface, and lay there until his breathing subsided a little. Then, clasping his hands behind his neck, he did twenty sit-ups, giving each one a double bend toward his knees, after achieving the sitting position. When he stood up his tanned face was flushed with the exercise, and he felt better. In front of the mirror he assumed a boxing crouch and shot a couple of jabs, followed by a hook and a straight right-hand. He hit short and with skill — the result of working out, in the Army, with a professional middleweight who'd been a leading contender for the world title, before the war had put him inside a tank.

Ken had been a good boxer and he had been a good tank commander. In the tank corps he had learned lessons which worked as effectively in corporate combat as they had against the Nazis in Holland and Belgium. In tanks, you never tried to use "just enough" power to take a strong point. You tried to double or triple or quadruple whatever power would be "just enough" — and then you tried to bring it to bear suddenly, like the body snap of a left hook. That was how you won battles anywhere — that, plus the indispensable ingredient in any kind of battle since the beginning of time: courage. Once, in a village in Belgium, Captain Carpenter's tanks had been cut off from fuel and his men had taken to the houses to try to delay the enemy advance. They had been fairly successful with the Nazi infantry—and then a Nazi tiger tank with its stylized black-and-white crosses had clanked down the street with its 88 mm. gun moving slowly back and forth, as if daring anyone to fire from a window. Nobody had fired. To have done so would have invited instant death.

It was then that Ken Carpenter had seen his demonstration of the indispensable ingredient of battle. An American GI had scuttled out of a doorway with a milk bottle full of gasoline. He had dodged under the snout of the 88, and, as the tank driver saw him and pivoted frantically on one tread with a hooting blast of power, spinning the tank in place, trying to crush this rash little soldier, the GI had skipped aside, and the huge bulk had swung past him; and then he had stepped in close, awkward and ugly as a scarecrow, and smashed the bottle of gasoline down into the louvers of the tank's exhaust. There was an instant cloud of flame, followed by the tank's stopping suddenly, its lid opening, and the Germans popping out like panicky rats.

Ken Carpenter had talked to the GI later: he was a spindly little Jewish boy from the East side of New York named Eddie Weinstein, and he had obviously not been impressed by Ken Carpenter's rank, nor the favor Ken proposed to do him, namely, recommend him for the Silver Star. The ratty little character had merely grinned and said, "Ah, don't bother, Captain. After the war nobody is gonna give a shit for medals, anyhow. A Silver Star and a subway token will get me over to Brooklyn any time I wanta go." Ken Carpenter had grinned back, and the little GI had said, "I tellya what, Captain—I *will* take a cigarette, if yuh got one." Ken Carpenter had had a pack. It was the last pack he had. He gave it to Weinstein. And even now, when he was out on tank maneuvers with the National Guard (he still maintained his reserve commission, and was commander of the local battalion) he often thought of the little Jew and wondered what he was doing. He would like to run into him again, buy him a drink. Among all the things Ken Carpenter had seen men do in

Europe, the killing of a Nazi tank with a milk bottle was the thing he would rather have done himself, personally.

Now he stepped out of the cabana beside the pool, moving on his toes in the track shoes, and began running across the lawn. He left the yard and came out on a ridge covered with yellow sun-killed grass in which a few volunteer arbor vitae trees stood, dark and lonely, like travelers stranded in a desert. The ridge overlooked the estate of Ken Carpenter's neighbor, David B. Ross, vice president in charge of sales for the Carey Furnace Steel Company. Through a gap in the trees which bordered the Ross property, Carpenter could see two men playing tennis on the Ross court. Both were big, but both moved fast; even at this distance he knew who they were: Dave Sr. and his son, Dave Jr., known as Duke.

Carpenter stopped to watch them. He saw Dave Sr. move across the court to take a forehand drive from his son, saw the big man set himself with the coordination of the natural athlete, saw his tanned forearm slash savagely at the ball. It was a beautiful shot, deep and hard to his son's backhand. Duke got to it, but the best he could do was pop it up. Dave Sr. moved in and took the ball in the air, close to the net, and killed it with an overhand smash his son did not even attempt to return.

Carpenter felt a sudden tightness in his stomach. One day, perhaps soon, he was going to face Dave Ross — and the others — in a fight to the finish, a fight of his own making. No quarter would be asked on either side, and none would be given. Ross and the others would have entrenched power on their side, but Carpenter would have a potent weapon too: surprise. When he struck, it would be with all his strength, and without any warning at all.

Virginia Ross sat in the shade of a copper beech, watching her men play tennis. She was a small, trim woman in tennis shorts and short-sleeved tennis shirt, very brown from the sun. She cut her hair in bangs and so closely resembled the wife of General Douglas MacArthur that people sometimes came up to her on the street when she was shopping in Pittsburgh and asked if she was, indeed, Mrs. MacArthur.

"I'm afraid not," Ginny Ross would say, smiling. "My husband happens to be a steel salesman."

Which was not in any sense an apology. Virginia Ross had no strong feelings one way or the other about General MacArthur, but she had some very strong feelings indeed about David B. Ross, vice president in charge of sales for Carey Furnace Steel. She knew many top executives well. She knew the amalgam of intelligence, hard work, luck, ruthlessness, charm, and self-discipline it took to rise to the top of the corporate heap and stay there. And with the possible exception of John Carey, Dave Ross was the best-equipped man Ginny knew when it came to surviving in the corporate jungle. He always played to win. He was not an advocate of the Good Try. He used the precepts advocated by Dale Carnegie — but only when he was dealing with amateurs. The pros, Dave said, were rarely taken in by sweet talk. For the pros, Dave had a small oyster-colored book titled *Gracian's Manual,* which had been written by a tough-minded Spanish philosopher in the 1600's. Into 267 pages, Baltasar Gracian had packed enough worldly wisdom, Dave said, to chart a career by. He kept the manual in his bedroom and read it, from time to time, like a monk reading the Bible. Virginia had browsed through it herself, and some of the things she had read there had shocked her. Which wasn't surprising. Those things had shocked the Spaniards, too, back in 1650.

Out on the tennis court, Dave was playing much too hard for a man of his years, but Ginny made no attempt to stop him. There was a small poem in a silver frame on his dresser, one stanza of which stuck in her mind: *Let me go quickly, like a candle light . . . snuffed out just at the heyday of its glow . . . give me high noon . . . and let it then be night . . . thus would I go.* But Dave didn't expect to go with a heart attack, playing tennis. Heart attacks hit men with big bellies and flabby muscles who trained on four-course dinners and drank too much. Dave took regular exercise, without being a health crank. He sometimes ate four-course dinners, but he also ate small breakfasts and often no lunch at all. When he drank, he drank hard. "One shot just makes me woozy," he said. "I don't want to fool with it unless I have the time to drink ten." And with the pace he kept, Dave Ross seldom had that time.

On the court, Dave now dropped a shot just over the net. Duke came in fast and made a placement well out of his father's reach.

"Game and set!" Duke cried out triumphantly. "Want another, Dad?"

"Nope," Dave panted. "Not with the Carey party this afternoon. Buy you a beer, though, if we've got a cold one in the house."

"You've twisted my arm," Duke said, grinning as he wiped the sweat off his neck and cheeks with the back of his wrist. As he stood in the noontime glare, Virginia could see every detail of his face, thinner than his father's—partly her own face, of course—and, as always, the sight of the broken nose brought a quick twing to her stomach. It brought back that terrible day during the strike violence, when Dave had come up the front walk, bloody and in pain, with his left arm around the shoulder of his bloody-faced son. Duke had been in the summer of his last year at Carnegie Tech, Virginia remembered. He had driven his father to work to find the main office blocked by a mob of strikers. They had parked on a side street and watched while several executives approached the narrow passage between the strikers, hesitated, and turned back rather than run the gauntlet of shoving and catcalls.

"It looks rough, Dad," Duke Ross said. "You want me to drive you back home?"

Dave Ross got out. "I'm going in," he said. "You better take off. No use getting the car turned over and smashed."

Dave had almost pulled it, too. He had walked up to the narrow passage between the massed strikers without lagging or hurrying, without looking to right or left, holding his brief case in his left hand. He had started through the mob, had nearly reached the entrance to the office, when a big striker recognized him and stepped out and blocked his way. The man had had a lot to drink and he was very pleased with his luck.

"Hey, fellas," he shouted. "Look who we got here. Mr. Bigshot himself! The vice president of the sales department, the great man who hasta have his ass kissed by four secretaries inna morning before he can get a letter signed." The striker put out his hand and pressed it against the front of Dave Ross's chest. He smiled and fingered the fabric of the summer suit. "Mighty nice suit yuh got here, Mr. Ross, sir. Mighty nice goods. How much yuh pay for this suit, hey?"

Dave Ross said nothing.

"Whatsa matter?" the big man jeered. "Cantcha talk, Mr. Bigshot? Cat got ya tongue, hey?"

"Get out of my way," Dave Ross said then, keeping his voice down.

"Oh, he *can* talk! Mr. Bigshot can talk after all. And he's givin' orders yet! Get out of my way, he says! Just like he's talking to one of his flunkies. Well, you ain't talking to no flunky now, Mr. Bigshot! Understand?" When Ross stood still, meeting the striker's eyes, the man suddenly grabbed his jacket with both hands and twisted it, drawing Ross close. He looked at his face, grinning, and there was sudden laughter from the crowd, and the laughter and the drink spurred the striker to top his performance: he made a hawking sound in his throat and spat a gob of mucus in Dave Ross's face.

Dave dropped the brief case and hit the man with his right fist, a short chopping blow that sent him reeling back. Dave had no chance to strike again. They closed on him and began beating him.

Young Duke Ross had not gone home. He had stayed in the car and watched. Nobody was paying any attention to the side street, so they were not prepared for the young maniac who squirmed and shoved his way toward his father through the mob. He was almost there when they began to try to stop him. They broke his nose and one of them kicked at his groin and missed and hit his knee, and then he was beside his father against the brick wall of the office, white-faced, his mouth and chin bright with blood, a steel jack handle in his right hand.

"Come on," young Duke Ross panted. "Come on. Hit him again. Anybody. *Come on, you sons-of-bitches!*"

Nobody had moved in, and Duke Ross and his father had got up the steps and into the office. Al Greenewalt, the doorman, described it later. "Jesus," Al said. "You shoulda seen young Ross's eyes when he come up the steps with his old man. I never seen eyes like that on a kid. They looked like they was burned in his face with a blowtorch."

Now, on the tennis court, Virginia Ross saw her men start toward her. She stood up. Duke was grinning, and Dave, despite the fact he hated to lose, and had just lost, was smiling too.

"I hate to say this," Duke said, "but I'm afraid Pop is slipping. He looked a little decrepit out there today, didn't you think, Mom?"

"I let the boy win," Dave panted. "Didn't want to damage his ego. Head-shrinkers come too high these days."

Virginia laughed. "There's nothing wrong with Duke's ego," she said, "that chopping it in half wouldn't help."

"Look, Mom," Duke said as he reached her, "I don't want to change the subject — but could I beg off from the Carey party this afternoon? John and Eva won't miss me in all that mob, and I happen to have a date with the cutest little gal in Carey Furnace."

"Oh? And who is the cutest little gal in Carey Furnace?"

"Her name is Eleanor Keck. She works in George Hurd's department."

"I'm afraid I don't know her. What does she do?"

"Types."

"Duke . . ."

"Yes, Mom?"

"No hanky-panky now, you hear?"

"No hanky-panky, Mom," Duke said, laughing. "The fact is, I doubt if there could be any, even if I tried. Eleanor's goofy over some young copywriter in Hurd's shop. The dumb oaf apparently doesn't appreciate his chance. He's the guy who needs a head-shrinker — not me."

Dave Ross looked down at his wife. He put his arm around her and pulled her against him. "You've got it wrong, Duke," Dave Ross said. "The cutest little gal in Carey Furnace doesn't work for George

Hurd. She works for us, uncapping beer bottles. Now let's stop all this palaver and get into the kitchen."

The city of Carey Furnace had grown vastly since World War II, mainly by expanding outward along the ridges and highways. Layers of dwellings took shape around the basic city like contour lines on a map. There were slums: the trailer park on the Lundyville road, parts of the Strip, the rat's nest of shacks through which Paradise Creek (an open sewer) meandered on its way to Honeysuckle Pond in the middle of the Carey Furnace dump. Several sections were, of course, inviolate. Nobody could buy or build on the approaches to the chocolate-drop hill on which the Carey mansion stood, and which was known as Bonus Mountain. Nobody could buy or build in Hunter's Valley without the blessing of the all-powerful steering committee.

But elsewhere, buying and building were rampant. Climbing Route 81, on the way to Butler, a house-hunter passed through a gradation of developments whose prices were roughly proportional to their distance from the smog of the valley. First came Tuckaway Knolls, a group of pastel cracker boxes on 50-by-100-foot lots, garage under kitchen, Bendix washer included, starting at $13,999. A mile farther out was Blue Spruce Manor, which featured an ornate iron gate flanked by four blue spruces—brittle corpses now, in the August sun, surrounded by piles of rust-colored needles. Next came Cadwallader Village, featuring ranch types and split-levels, which started at $29,999.

It wasn't until the house-hunter reached Spook Hollow, where Route 81 turned and followed the rim of the valley overlooking the river, that he got into the real folding money. This area had once been an open-pit coal mine, but the unsightly piles of overburden had been flattened, topsoil brought in, and the name changed to River View Terrace. One acre was the smallest plot you could buy in River View Terrace, and the zoning regulations called for a minimum expenditure on the house of $40,000. Most people spent far more. Here the status war raged at its fiercest. Not just a gravel driveway — a paved driveway; and not just a paved driveway — a paved driveway with a photocell to open the garage door automatically as the car turned in from the street. Even such lowly items as the outdoor grill (nobody admitted it, of course) were pawns in the status struggle. Time was when a man could go out and start a simple fire with charcoal briquettes in a simple metal grill he bought at the hardware store for ten or fifteen dollars. Now, if he hoped to keep in the swim, he broiled his steaks in a stone structure, designed by an outdoor decorator, and fanned his coals by an electrically driven gadget embedded in the hearth. Competition in the homes themselves was limited only by the ingenuity, daring, and cash on hand of the owners. One family had scored a hit with a house which had a kitchen and library on the main floor, bedrooms in the basement, and a garage on the roof, reached by a spiral ramp. The trend in status warfare on the automobile front had changed somewhat with the coming of the compacts. Now a man wasn't judged by the size of his big car but rather by the number of his little ones.

The dwellers on the Strip, of course, had their own brand of status competition. They had a 21-inch TV — maybe with color — and maybe with remote tuning. They had the Deluxe Golden Jubilee bedroom suite from Kane's Furniture Mart, inlaid linoleum in the kitchen, a frost-free refrigerator with revolving trays, and an automatic washer and drier. It was inevitable that the washer would overload the cesspool and cause seepage on the neighbor's backyard down the hill — but the neighbor couldn't complain, really, because his washer was doing the same to his neighbor. Recently there had been some unpleasant rumblings about inflation, and rumors about old folks who had moved to Florida on fixed pensions, who were now fishing off the bridges for food to keep alive, but nobody worried too much. That stuff was up to Washington. Why worry? With the H-bomb and all, a person might not make it through to next Saturday night's beer party.

Most of the landmarks in town which had been familiar to pre-John L. Lewis residents were still there, but many of them had been buried or changed. TV had forced the closing of two movie houses: one was now a supermarket, the other a bowling alley. The majestic granite shaft which thrust up fifteen feet from the grave of one Morris Damlamian, placed there "In loving gratitude" by his wife, Sofia (which looked so much like an erect penis that little kids were always smirking around it on Decoration Day), was lost in a forest of stone angels, crypts, and mausoleums. The dilapidated wooden toll bridge across the Allegheny, which pedestrians had once been able to use for a penny, had been torn down to make way for the four-lane concrete bridge which carried Route 81 across the river on its way to join the Pennyslvania Turnpike east of Pittsburgh. Parking had become a great problem in Carey Furnace, as elsewhere. The annexes of several big Pittsburgh stores had foresightedly bought up enough adjoining real estate to build parking lots for their customers. Old Horace Foyle, usually one jump ahead of everybody, had been caught short on this gambit; and Ely Donovan, who owned a tumble-down boarding house behind the Foyle store, made enough on its sale for a parking lot to retire to Florida.

But some establishments stubbornly resisted change. The plumbing in the Carey House was still as subject to stoppage as it had been in the days of John Carey Sr. The murals in the bar of the hotel — furnaces belching molten steel and tended by huge half-naked men — remained the same through the years, except that the flames grew slightly dimmer with time and repeated cleanings. Old Kelly, who tended the bar, had looked ninety years old back in the days when John Lewis was riding high — and he still looked ninety years old.

One of the pleasantest residential pockets in town was the ravine at the foot of John Carey's mountain. On three sides it was embedded in virgin forest. John Carey Sr. had once planned to build guest quarters there, and had installed terraces behind stone retaining walls and planted them with lilac, syringa, roses, asters, and poppies. Old poplar trees shaded the walks, forming a casual canopy over the ravine.

But John Carey had died before he got around to building the guest quarters, and Judge Asa Packer had bought the ravine (with young John's blessing) and constructed a large brick house. Packer later suffered a heart attack, had a hard time making ends meet, and it became necessary to subdivide the rear of the property into building lots.

Two other houses subsequently had been built in the rear, and at the moment all three homes were being occupied by employees of the steel company. The Judge Packer house was being rented by Howard and Ethyl Snyder, their eight-year-old daughter Carole, and their Pekinese dog Hubie. Howard was a technical writer in the advertising department of "the Steel," as the company was called in local parlance; Ethyl was an ex-schoolteacher whose principal claims to fame were her interest in refinishing antiques, improving herself and her family in a cultural way, and the fact that she had the largest and best-formed breasts in town (at least according to men who considered themselves to be experts in these matters). Carole was, in her mother's mind, a delicate and talented little girl of uncertain health, and in the opinion of her neighbor Trixie McHugh an insufferably spoiled little brat. Hubie barked: he barked at anything — bees, clouds, grass blades quivering in the wind, or, as Trixie McHugh often said to Jack, he barked just to be barking.

Jack and Trixie lived in a tall, old-fashioned wooden house, the one farthest up the hill. They were childless. Jack was space buyer for the company, a heavy-set man with a horse face, cleft chin, and long iron-gray hair which he combed straight back and which had a natural wave in it. Jack drank hard upon occasion, but he held his liquor well, and was not in any sense a drunk, or even a problem drinker. To Ethyl Snyder, however, he was a debauched old horror who pinched fannies and who, she predicted to her husband, would one day be carried off in a strait jacket, kicking and screaming, by men in white. Jack McHugh understood perfectly how Ethyl Snyder felt, and, with deadpan delight, often went out of his way to confirm her worst suspicions. On evenings when he'd been out with space salesmen having a few highballs on some trade-paper expense account, he might spy Ethyl Snyder's face at the kitchen window as he walked through the common right-of-way toward his own house, and he might suddenly stagger, catch himself with difficulty, and mutter some pungent phrase which he knew would carry through the screens to the twitching ears of his neighbor's wife. But Jack McHugh would be steady as a rock and smiling his "aged horse smile," as Trixie called it, when he let himself into the kitchen where his wife was waiting.

Ethyl Snyder was wrong about Jack McHugh on most things. He did not pinch fannies, even though he had many an opportunity to do so on his various trips to media conventions. Space salesmen eager for Carey Furnace business had, in the beginning, offered to get him "fixed up with a cute little gal" in strange towns, but Jack had always declined, and now they didn't bother asking him any more. Several of them kidded him once or twice — but they didn't do it a third time. Jack McHugh almost always wore a relaxed smile, but he could be firm when he wanted to be. He loved his little bird-like wife Trixie, and although he was not a Holy Joe (he never tried to dissuade anybody else from anything), he could slow a wise-cracking salesman down in a hurry if he felt like it. The one thing Jack mourned — and so did Trixie — was their inability to have children. They could have adopted children, but neither of them wanted adopted children; they wanted their own.

Trixie McHugh weighed a hundred and eight pounds. She had been Kathleen McCrory, with red hair, and it was still red, thanks to Tintair; and Trixie was still as impulsive and suicidally daring as she had been as a kid, when she had jumped off the top of the old wooden bridge, a distance of forty feet, into the Allegheny River, on a dare from a juvenile companion. Trixie could still climb if the need for climbing arose. Jack had returned home from work one afternoon to find her clinging to the upper branches of a poplar tree, where she had ascended to rescue a baby bird, which, she shrilly explained from aloft, had been marooned up there. "A bird marooned in a tree?" Jack had called back, deadpan. "Jesus, Trixie, that musta been a helluva sight. What happened to it?"

"It flew," Trixie screamed down. "The poor little thing finally *flew*. It was a little bird, Jack. A little baby bird, all huddled up, kinda, and its mother was flying around frantic, so I climbed up and —"

"And it flew," Jack said. "Some little bird!"

He loved Trixie for climbing up after the bird. He loved her for not yelling at him when he came home slightly stiff, for not whining about the kids they couldn't have, for not pestering him to know if he still loved her, for saying what she meant, regardless of who was listening, but never really saying anything vicious, even when she was mad at Ethyl Snyder. Trixie's bark was truly ferocious, her bite usually quite feeble.

It was Jack McHugh's morning habit (because he had to get up anyhow, as he told Trixie) to bring her her first cup of coffee while she was still in bed. Trixie said of herself that she wasn't safe to live with until she'd downed that first cup of hot black coffee, and it was true that she could be exceedingly bitchy at that hour, particularly if Hubie had been barking in the night. But Jack didn't bring the coffee just to escape her temper (although this did figure at times). He brought it because he got a kick out of seeing one of Trixie's eyes open warily in the depths of the blankets and pillows, peer out suspiciously and combatively, focus on the steaming coffee, take on a reluctant interest, and then Trixie's whole face appear, and her voice say: "What time is it, hunh? What time — middle of the night?"

Whereupon Jack would solemnly, very deadpan, lift the covers from the foot of the bed and tickle Trixie's foot with his fingers, and she would jerk it back, bunch the covers protectively around her and yell, "You *bastard!*" Whereupon she would hold her lips up and Jack would kiss her.

On this particular Saturday morning in August, Jack was awakened by the barking of Hubie, the Snyders' Pekinese. The yapping came to him first in his dreams. He was, for some reason, out in the plant inspecting the blast furnaces. He was talking to Mr. Ralph Doane, the superintendent, something about running the molten iron through a long ceramic pipe, straight from the blast furnaces to the open hearth, thus eliminating handling it in ladle cars. The idea seemed brilliant to Jack, but Mr. Doane thought it was silly. He was giving the horse laugh, ya, ya, ya, ya, and Jack was getting burned up at him, and then he woke up and it was Hubie yapping.

Normally Jack would have lain in bed awhile on a Saturday morning, but today he had things to do. The annual picnic of the advertising department was coming up next week, and Jack had been put in charge of organizing the men's games by George Hurd, his boss and the advertising manager of Carey Furnace Steel. It would be necessary to drive to Mr. Hurd's cottage on Black River, where the picnics were always held, and make sure the brush was cleared off the softball field and the horseshoe pits were in order, and other details of that type. Jack had a date to play golf in the afternoon with Willie Martin (who wrote articles on steel products and placed them in the trade magazines), and he wanted to get the picnic chores out of the way first. He put on a pair of slacks and a polo shirt and went down to the kitchen in his bare feet to start Trixie's coffee. The sun had already topped the hillside across the river and was streaming into the kitchen and he could feel himself sweating. He turned on the electric stove, put on some city water, which had a faint odor of chlorine, and rummaged in Trixie's cabinets for something to eat while he waited for the water to heat. He found a fresh block of sticky buns with pecans on top, wrapped in cellophane, tore it open, and began eating one of the buns.

Then, through the open kitchen window, he heard a voice which he recognized as belonging to Ethyl Snyder, speaking in the adjoining yard. Mrs. Snyder, believing herself alone, was indulging in a little baby talk. McHugh stopped chewing his bun and listened. He heard Ethyl's voice, usually so refined and la-de-dah, now crooning behind the hedges. "Oooooo — mummy's Hubie! Ooooh — mummy's sweet ittle Hubie! And how was teensy ittle Hubiekins this morning? Was he dood boy? Did he seep dood? Him mummy brung him goodies — real real special goodies — for his ittle breakfuss!"

A smile touched the lips of Jack McHugh. He swallowed the last of the sticky bun and, moving silently in his bare feet, walked through the hall and out onto the screened porch which overlooked the Snyders' yard. Mrs. Snyder was kneeling, putting food in a pan in front of the little dog, which resembled a fat brown insect. Jack watched as the animal sniffed languidly at his special breakfuss him mummy had fetched, then began to nibble at it without enthusiasm. Ethyl was more than usually attractive this morning in a blue dressing gown which showed off her fabulous breasts, despite the fact that it covered them completely. Jack McHugh cleared his throat and Ethyl Snyder's head jerked upright and her normally pink skin grew pinker as she realized she must have been overheard.

Jack bowed grandly from the waist. "Good morning, Mrs. Snyder. Lovely day."

"Yes it is," Ethyl Snyder said shortly. She rose, pulling her gown about her, and Hubie, peering up with his bulgy eyes, saw McHugh dimly and gave a short and peevish bark.

"Little Hubert is well, I trust?" Jack said.

"Oh yes, he's fine," Ethyl Snyder said, and for an instant Jack McHugh thought he had broken through her sweet fourth-grade schoolteacher control and was about to get a really angry retort, but he was disappointed. Ethyl Snyder managed a smile, understanding and sweet, the smile she had once bestowed upon naughty little not-quite-bright boys who had been apprehended in some animal prank for which wiser grownups must excuse them. "Thank you so much for asking, Mr. McHugh." And then she turned and swept out of the yard and back into the house.

Jack went back to his kitchen, spooned instant coffee into a cup, and filled it with boiling water. On his way upstairs he called out in a crooning voice: "Oooooh — here comes Trixie's daddykins. Trixie's daddykins brung her big wunnerful cuppa coffee. Has Trixie been dood girlie? Did her seep dood?"

From the bedroom, Trixie's voice said hollowly, "Jesus Christ, Jack, it's too early in the morning for that stuff!" Jack reached the landing smiling, and headed for the open bedroom doorway.

Howard Snyder had been awake in his attic office bedroom since before dawn, lying in his shorts on top of the sheet in the hot draft of the ventilating fan which pulled air continuously from one end of the room under the eaves to the other. He had heard the coal train hoot in the darkness for the River Avenue crossing just before dawn, but it had not made him think of monsters running through the hills sniffing for victims — it had made him think, as nearly everything now did, of travel. This time next week he would not be in Carey Furnace. He would be in Tehuantepec, Mexico, on the shore of the Pacific Ocean, listening to the slopping of the sea. And Ethyl and Carole would be with him. The airline tickets to Mexico City had already been bought. They would rent a car and drive through the mountains down to the seacoast at Tehuantepec. Howard had investigated the condition of Mexican roads and the availability of roadside inns and eating places. He had made a study of the area in Mexico where he would spend his two weeks of vacation this year, down to the small details, just as he had always done in the past when planning a trip. This year, however, there would be an important difference. This year he would actually get a chance to utilize the results of his study: this year there would be no last-minute change of plans; they were actually going. They even had arranged for little Hubie to board in a dog hospital and had paid five dollars a week extra, in advance, to make sure he was fed in the manner to which he had become accustomed.

The rush of the ventilating fan, set in the window behind the bed, effectively masked many outside noises, even the yapping of Hubie in his yard below. Howard always felt comforted when he got into his room and shut the door behind him and turned on the fan. This room was his retreat, his castle. In it were all the things he prized: his Hallicrafter short-wave radio, which could pick up Hong Kong on good nights; his long shelves full of *National Geographic Magazines,* stretching in yellow rows under the eaves; his light reading — *The White Tower,* by James Ramsey Ullman, *Auntie Mame, Aku Aku, The Cruel Sea,* some Hemingway and Marquand and Irwin Shaw; and of course, his technical library

(*Strength of Materials,* Waggoner . . . *Empirical Design,* Smith and Turner . . . *The Behavior of Eutectic Alloys,* Tanner and Best). Howard did much of his work here, in the evenings, with the radio tuned in to some South American dance band, very low, bending over his drafting table with his glittering instruments and his freshly sharpened drafting pencils, his slide rule, logarithmic tables, and maybe a candy bar to munch on — he was partial to "Three Musketeers" or "O Henry." It did not bother him if Ethyl was absent from the house to attend PTA, bridge club, or one of Carole's many sessions with various types of teachers. Howard was happy to be alone after a day in the office of the steel company. He was not a joiner or a party-goer.

Now, as he thought of the upcoming party at the John Carey mansion, he felt some of the pleasure of contemplating the vacation drain away. Ethyl had been overjoyed, even triumphant, when the invitation came. It was due to the fact (Ethyl said) that Carole was a member of the Junior Water Color Association, a project sponsored by the Hunter's Valley Art League, of which Mrs. Paul Dana, wife of the vice president in charge of public relations for the steel company, was president. Ethyl had spoken to Mrs. Dana on a number of occasions, asking her advice about Carole's work in the Junior Water Color Association; and although Mrs. Dana had been a little vague, and her breath had smelled of liquor, or maybe it was wine, she must have remembered that Ethyl and Carole were kindred spirits, and had probably mentioned to Eva Carey that it would be nice to invite them to the annual party. At least, they had been invited this year and had not been invited last year, so something or other had taken place. Howard did not know what the reason was. Possibly Ethyl's contention was correct. Jack and Trixie McHugh had not been invited. In fact, Howard had felt embarrassed when Jack asked him to play golf and he declined, saying they were going to the Carey party. Jack had whistled. "Well — that's real fine, Howie. Have a ball. Trix and I didn't make it. I guess I'll just have to run down and buy me a crying towel or get sozzled or something."

"Between you and me, Jack, I wish we hadn't made it either. I've got some stuff I'd like to do to get ready for the trip."

"When you leaving, Howie?"

"The first of next week."

"No changes in plans this year, eh?"

"Nope. I've got the tickets all bought."

"Good. Have yourself a hell of a time."

"I will," Howard Snyder said. "And I'll bring back some color slides to prove it."

"Oh, God," Jack McHugh said. "Not color slides, Howie. I love you like a brother, but no color slides. Willie Martin took a camera with him to Maine one summer and brought back ten thousand color slides of Indian guides in canoes and big strings of dead fish and things like that, and he and Stephy had Trixie and me over and Willie took two hours flashing those goddamn slides on a screen. No slides, Howie — you hear!"

"Okay," Howard said. "I may take some — but I promise not to show them to you."

He had decided to go to Tehuantepec, Mexico, for a romantic or (as Ethyl said) a childish reason: a poem he had read by Wallace Stevens called "Sea Surface Full of Clouds." He had glanced at the poem casually, while leafing through a book, had read a little, and then had gone on to finish it. He couldn't seem to forget it. That night, when he lay in bed, he recalled the first lines and they kept going around and around in his head like the lyrics of a popular song: *In that November off Tehuantepec . . . the slopping of the sea grew still one night . . . and in the morning summer hued the deck . . . and made one think of rosy chocolate . . . and gilt umbrellas. . . .*

"You're joking," Ethyl had said, when he'd told her why he wanted to visit this far-off place.

"No, I'm not, honey. I mean it. I want to go there."

She had argued, but eventually she had given in. She was not in a strong position after the way she'd backed out of the Virgin Islands trip they'd planned, months ahead, for last year's vacation. She'd done it at the last minute, after Howard had bought swim-fins and an underwater mask and special fiberglass fishing rods — because of her mother's heart attack. At least that's what she had told Howard, and had added that neither one of them would ever forgive themselves if they went ahead on some pleasure trip and something happened to Ethyl's mother while they were gone. It had been quite a shock, therefore, at least to Howard, when they drove into the driveway of Ethyl's mother's place in New Jersey and found the older woman out in the garden hoeing peas.

"Mother!" Ethyl had cried out from the car. "Your heart, dear! What are you doing out in this broiling sun?"

"My heart?" Ethyl's mother had said, seemingly puzzled. "What's the matter with my heart?"

"In your letter," Ethyl cried, "you mentioned dizzy spells and black specks in front of your eyes! I knew it was your heart!"

"Oh heavens, Ethyl," her mother said, laying aside the hoe and coming out of the garden. "You're such a worrier. It was just something I ate, I guess. It went right away, after I wrote that letter, and never came back." She crossed the lawn, smiling. "Well, anyhow, I'm glad to see you and Howard and little Carole. I hope you can stay awhile."

"We can stay two weeks," Ethyl said. "Oh, Mother, I wish you hadn't written that letter. I asked Howie to cancel a trip to the Virgin Islands, and the lamb did it, because we were so worried over you."

Howard said nothing. The year before, Ethyl had ruined a proposed drive over the Alcan Highway because of a sprained ankle. At least Ethyl was in bed when he got home, a few days before they were due to drive north. The ankle was swathed in bandages and stayed that way for quite a while, so that Howard had to take her word for the horrible swelling and discoloration the bandages concealed.

He did not speak to Ethyl in her mother's yard. He helped her into the house with the suitcases and Carole's toys and then he left on foot and went down to a saloon in the little Jersey village where Ethyl's mother lived, and got good and drunk. After a couple of days he cooled off and took them to the shore and fished off a deep-sea fishing boat, jammed at the rail with a hundred other people. He caught two good-sized flounders and Ethyl cooked them for him. She was a marvelous cook, that he had to admit, and a good mother to Carole. You couldn't have everything. . . .

Trixie McHugh did not think Ethyl Snyder was marvelous at anything, and she had very little sympathy for Howard either. "I go by their kitchen window in the evening," Trixie said, "and there's your buddy in there, with an apron on, washing dishes. What kind of a man is that?"

"The same kind of a man that gets up early every morning, shaking with fear, and gets coffee for the little woman who's still in the sack."

"Oh, come on, Jack."

"Okay, sweetie," Jack said, grinning. "Howard's a poor soul and Ethyl's a wicked old slave-driver. What do you expect me to do about it?"

"Where does he imagine he's going on his vacation this year?"

"A place in Mexico. Some funny name — I forget."

"Want to bet he doesn't make it?"

"Oh, he'll make it this year. They've got the tickets all bought."

"What do you want to bet?"

"Ten bucks."

"All right, darling," Trixie said. "Ten bucks it is. You want to pay me now, or later?"

"You'll lose this one, Trix. Ethyl has pulled the rug out from under old Howie too many times. She's got to come through this summer, just by the law of averages."

"I'll believe it when I see it," Trixie said.

The third house in the ravine belonged to Jake and Frances Abbott and was set in the hillside below Jack McHugh's place. It was a sprawly white-clapboard place with a big sunporch, a music room where Frances kept her Steinway grand piano, and a downstairs bedroom where Jake and Fran slept — as far removed as possible from Hubie's chronic bark. The two upstairs bedrooms were occupied by eleven-year-old Henry and sixteen-year-old Nancy, the Abbotts' two children.

Jake Abbott was a tall, stooped man with a red face. He had been a Navy lieutenant in World War II, stationed at Tomoka River on the east coast of Florida, about eighty miles south of Jacksonville. He had worked for the company before the war as a copywriter. Now he had graduated to writing the monthly Confidential News Letter. He and Frances had met in New York while they were both staying at the International House on Riverside Drive. Jake had been a senior at Columbia, and Frances had been studying piano at the Juilliard School of Music.

Frances had been the belle of the House that year. She was a big-bodied, silky girl with a snug waist and a full, sullen mouth. The word beatnik had not been invented at the time, "Bohemian" being its closet counterpart, and Jake's friends were mostly Bohemians — or weirdies, if you took the conservative House view of them. One was a ragged fellow who never seemed to do anything except sit in the lobby and stare at the girls' legs, who smelled slightly because he never changed his clothes, and whose claim to fame was that he was a conscientious objector. No major wars were being fought at the moment for him to object to, but he stood ready to object violently as soon as somebody gave him a war. Another friend of Jake's was a lovable alcoholic who specialized in smashing plate-glass windows with his bare fists when under the influence, and making abortive efforts, at parties, to leap from high windows into the street below. There was a stupid and inscrutable Japanese, who never learned more than two or three words of English, who attended all the gin-and-grapefruit-juice binges in Jake's room, and of whom, later, Jake often wondered: had he really been inscrutable and stupid, or had he been a brilliant spy, gathering data for military use? And of course there were the usual number of budding geniuses: writers, painters, Communists, Socialists, fairies, Nazi bully-boys, and one coal-black son of a Zulu chieftain.

That most of the talk was spurious or obvious, or both, did not occur to Frances Whitehead, fresh from Carey Furnace via an exclusive Philadelphia finishing school. For her, this was Life, Art, Beauty. She sat, tempting and delicious as the cherry on a cake, in the midst of these self-styled intellectuals, listening to discussion of such great concepts as Human Love. What was it? A strong bond that conquered all, as she had always believed? Not a bit of it. It hung up behind the bathroom door, somebody said, and smelled of Lysol. (Frances had not read Hemingway and thought this remark was original and not very nice.) Somebody else thought Love was a Number, with a decimal point in front of it. He had a complicated explanation of this view, but he never got it completed. The conscientious objector made a loud hawking sound in his throat, and spat. He said nothing. But those who knew him realized he had just made his contribution to the definitions.

Jake Abbott fared well in these discussions. He was voluble, had read Hemingway and Thomas Wolfe, saw with terrible clarity exactly what was wrong with the world and had the exact prescription for fixing it up: he was for equality for all men, suppression of injustice everywhere, and he had very hot pants for Frances. In which, it must be stated, he was not alone. One of the young Nazis told her, at a dance, that she ought to come to Germany and inspire Hitler's Luftwaffe pilots (of which the Nazi was one) for the greater glory of the Third Reich. She had been flattered and pleased until, in the taxi coming back from a dinner date, the young Nazi birdman had tried to rape her in a more or less gentlemanly fashion. He had not succeeded, but it had been a very active experience. She was glad to get back to Jake, who, at the time, was writing a poem which was intended to immortalize her beauty. He never seemed to get it to suit him, however, and she never saw it in manuscript, but at the time it was something thrilling to contemplate.

Jake told Fran he intended to be a writer. He was studying

writing under James Warner Bellah, a famous contributor to the *Saturday Evening Post,* every Friday night, in a Columbia extension course. Once Jake took Frances to the class. He never took her again. Mr. Bellah, who was an ex-fighter-pilot, was a powerful, ruddy figure of a man who appeared at the class in a derby hat and an expensive topcoat and read some of his own *Post* stories to the class in a rich, exciting voice, and Frances sat and peered at him glassy-eyed. There was no sense in continuing that sort of thing, Jake decided.

At this point, Frances Whitehead was a virgin. At the tender age of thirteen, she had been so well-developed that grown men in Carey Furnace were stopping to peer at her interestedly on the street; and now, at nineteen, she was so ripe that the merest jiggle against the tree would almost certainly cause her to fall happily to the ground, or to the bed, as the case might be. Jake wanted Frances in bed, of course, but he also liked to hear himself talk about himself, and Frances being a good listener to the kind of talk he was then putting forth, their association tended automatically to be on a so-called intellectual plane. Which was just the sort of tricky business Frances was not prepared to cope with. Up to now she had been exposed to the conventional approaches — gifts, flattery, petting, attempts to get her dress up or her breasts out — and she was well able to deal with it. But this tall, untidy young man who wrote poetry (even though you couldn't get him to show it to you), who invited your opinion about books and ideas, who flattered your mind instead of your body, and never seemed to get around to asking for a date — this young man was a challenge. And then, unwittingly, Jake made the challenge irresistible by saying, during one of his extravagant flights of fantasy, that he could never stay married to one woman for long — too boring. He intended to remain single, rather than break some poor girl's heart, and then have to cast her off like a worn-out glove. All this he confided to Frances over a bottle of beer in Paddy's Shamrock Bar, on upper Broadway, where the Bohemians of International House were doing their drinking that year, as if Frances were another man, and not a luscious young girl whose desirability he was now unwittingly challenging. At this point, Jake's high-and-rare pronouncements ceased to be amusing. They had to be proved wrong. And Frances felt she was well equipped to do the proving.

It was, of course, an easy conquest. Jake was planning to do an article which he hoped to sell to *Esquire,* in which he would humorously explore the various techniques of kissing. Frances said she thought it would be a fine idea — but what about the research? Would he go around and interview people, or what? No, Jake said, he would not interview people. He would draw on his own experiences in the past.

"If you want to," Frances said lightly, "I might be able to help you there — on the up-to-date part of it."

"You mean, actually try various ways of kissing, ourselves?"

"For the sake of the article only," Frances said. "We wouldn't have to feel anything. Just for the sake of the article."

"All right," Jake said. "For the sake of the article, we'll go some place and practice. What about Riverside Park?"

"I guess that would be all right," Frances said. "It's secluded. I guess nobody will bother us there."

For the sake of the article, they sat in the park until nearly two o'clock in the morning, finally with Frances lying almost on top of him in the warm spring darkness with her tongue halfway down his throat, and it was impossible, through the light silk dress she was wearing, not to feel him hard and throbbing against her thigh, and Frances thought, passionately but happily, *worn-out glove my eye,* and Jake thought of rolling her over suddenly and pulling her dress up and trying to shove her legs apart, but he did not. He was still, in a swollen-groined, heroic, silly fashion, trying to do research on his proposed article on the technique of kissing, and he was not becoming emotionally involved.

The session inflamed Frances's passion and piqued her pride. She had not elicited a single ungentlemanly reaction, except the hard throbbing inside his pants, which obviously was not voluntary and was something he was probably burning with shame about — and she had used her most advanced technique. The tree upon which the apple so delicately hung was jiggling. Its frail grip on the bough was weakening. And then one Saturday night, when they had gone to the Old Algiers, a dine-dance place on upper Broadway, and both of them had quite a lot to drink, the grip on the limb finally broke and the ripe and luscious fruit fell into the arms of the waiting poet. It began on the dance floor, which was so crowded they had to stay in one place, shoved gently but persistently by other bodies, until Frances could again feel him through her dress. She became slightly dizzy and very hot and clutched him convulsively. He held her tightly — and then she moved her hips slightly, and he went rigid. He suggested they go where they could be alone.

"Where will we go?" she said. "The park?"

"Never mind the park," he said shortly. "Come on."

Somewhat breathlessly, she agreed. Here, at last, was action. He paid the bill. They stepped into the street. It had turned cold and a wind whipped her skirts around her full hips. Across the street was a red neon sign: Hotel Manchester. They both looked at it. Jake said: "Over there."

"Oh, we can't."

"We'll take a taxi up to the house and get some luggage."

"Oh, I couldn't do that."

"Why not?"

"I don't know. I just couldn't, darling."

"Goddamn it!" Jake said in a low furious voice. "Now come on — here's a cab!"

She would never forget that cab ride: the cold, unseasonable wind swirling in the side window of the cab, the reek of the cabbie's cigar, the dim glow of the lights in the little park in front of International House, the sickly light in the elevator going up to her room, the sitting on her bed looking at her burning cheeks in the mirror thinking, *I can stop now, here, by just staying in my room,* the sudden packing of her new green silk pajamas with the red dragon embroidered across the front and her toilet things, the changing of hats, from the pillbox to a more sophisticated cartwheel brim;

then the standing inside her door for a full two minutes before going back to the elevator, the knowing look of the old man who ran the elevator — and then, back into the dark of the park, where a tall, terrible figure waited for her, the Monster of the City she had been so often warned about back in Carey Furnace — Jake.

The night at the Hotel Manchester was full of nervous fear and misgivings and, at the end, exquisite delight for Frances. Later she remembered the oddest things about it, such as the fact that Jake had put textbooks in his suitcase to make it heavy when the bellboy lifted it — so it would seem they had traveled from a distant city. When Jake had been in the bathroom she had taken one of the books and looked at it: *The Theory of the Leisure Class* by Thorstein Veblen. Ever after that, she could not look at or think about this title without getting a small twinge of excitement. They were very modest when they finally got to bed. Jake had turned out the light and put on his pajamas, and Frances, when he kissed her, would not let him even put his arm around her. Later, they laughed about it. "It took me two hours to get the top button of those pajamas unfastened," Jake said. "I thought it would be broad daylight before I got them off — if I ever got them off at all." Frances always defended herself. "I was a sweet innocent girl," she said. "And you were a wild lecherous college man. It was the biggest mistake of my life." But she always said it with a smile. Sex had never been a bugaboo with Frances. Her family had walked around from bedroom to bathroom without a thought of clothing. The whole thing was treated perfectly casually. Frances's mother had her own private theory on the matter. "Sex isn't dirty," she'd told Frances once. "It's only the minds of people that are dirty. Sex can be dangerous, and it can be tragic — but never dirty — not if two people are in love."

The night at the Manchester wasn't dirty, certainly. It was a clean and shining night — and, after the fear and nervousness wore away, it was a night of increasing delight. The green silk pajamas with the embroidered dragon came off, at last, and Jake's pajamas came off, and they held each other closely. Jake smelled of shaving lotion, she remembered, and his heart was thudding so violently she could actually feel it against her breasts. He hurt her then, and she cried out, but presently the pain went away and the delicious first glimmerings began, spreading like a rose-colored glow through her flesh and nerves, and finally, lying under him, she went rigid and clutched at him with all her strength, and there was not a thought in her head, at this point, about poetry or literature. The luscious apple had finally fallen from the tree, glad and relieved to be down. . . .

They dated steadily from then on. They returned to the Manchester each Saturday night, Jake selling his radio and his camera and even some of his less-needed books to get the extra money. They made love in Riverside Park, on the stone stairways below Grant's Tomb. They kissed in front of the elevators on the women's side of the House until somebody complained and the director called Jake in and sternly warned him to stop this unseemly behavior or remove himself from residency. Jake's studies suffered. Frances tried to help him with his French, but only succeeded in distracting him. She walked from the House to the corner of 116th street and Broadway with him each morning, and kissed him goodbye, and he went into class with faint pink signs of lipstick on his mouth, which his handkerchief could not remove, to the great delight of his classmates.

Eventually Frances wrote home and announced she was in love with a wonderful young man named Abbott and Dr. Whitehead flew over to New York to have a look at the young paragon. The doctor made Jake very nervous. Those bright-blue eyes seemed to see everything that was going on inside Jake's head, including the abandoned writhings in the bedrooms of the Hotel Manchester and the consummations in Riverside Park (they managed it standing up in the dark on the lower stairways, each looking in opposite directions for approach of some midnight stroller). Jake had heard of horse-whippings and shotgun blasts at close range and other violent manifestations of parental wrath. He had also just finished reading *King's Row,* a novel in which a surgeon had whacked off the leg of one of his daughter's suitors following a minor injury to the luckless fellow's foot. Jake was very polite and respectful in Dr. Whitehead's presence — so much so, in fact, that the doctor, upon his return to Carey Furnace, told his wife that Fran had picked out a boyish nincompoop.

"I know it's supposed to be best to let these things alone," he said to Mary Whitehead, "but my instinct is to get in there and break it up. I don't want grandchildren like that."

"Don't worry," Mary Whitehead said. "You know Fran. She had the head coach of the high school, a man with a family, running after her like an old hound dog when she was fifteen. She's run through the pick of prep schools and colleges in the East. We've got a beautiful woman on our hands, Arthur, and — like all beautiful women — she's fickle. This Jake, whoever he is, will be past and forgotten by the end of the summer."

But Mary Whitehead, who was seldom wrong in her judgments of people, was wrong in this instance. After graduation, Jake got a job in the executive-training course of a big New York store and Frances came back to Carey Furnace to wait for him to get his "first raise" so he could call her to New York and they could be married. Jake, when he really wanted something, was more determined and dynamic than Dr. Whitehead gave him credit for being; and he really wanted Frances. He, too, realized that an entire summer was too long to wait without taking a very serious risk. He knew Frances was oversexed; she liked it, and now that she had been having it regularly, it was up to Jake to see to it that she got it permanently — from him.

He saw almost at once that there was very little future for him in the store. He did not like the work, and he had managed to alienate the buyer who was in charge of his department. He wasted no time. He went back up to Columbia and haunted the employment office, explaining he wanted to get married and had to get a good job, and fast. The mere desire to get married and to have a good job does not insure getting one, and the placement director at Columbia pointed this out. But the placement director was impressed with Jake's sincerity — which amounted to desperation — and entered into correspondence with the man from Carey Furnace Steel who made an annual trip through the college each spring in search of executive talent. The placement director mentioned Jake's name, said he was a good student, very eager to marry the daughter of a Dr. Whitehead, who lived in Carey Furnace, and was there anything at all the company might offer him? The employment office replied regretfully that there was not. The one opening young Abbott seemed best fitted for was in the advertising department, and it had been filled by a Dartmouth man who'd spent two summers working on a daily newspaper.

Now Jake was really worrying. Frances and he wrote every day, but he thought he detected a cooling in the ardor of her letters. The work in the bathing-suit department of the New York store was becoming depressing and aggravating. It was not the sort of job he had expected after spending $10,000 and four years in college. He was supposedly in the "pre-executive training group," which was, he soon discovered, a glorified title for clerk. He made $20 a week, was docked a half-hour's salary for every minute he was late in the morning, got half an hour for lunch (which he ate standing up at a Nedick's counter), and after a few weeks he realized he would never be able to marry Frances Whitehead if he held this job—even if he got a raise in salary, which wasn't likely. He lost fifteen pounds in the July heat. He stopped getting up in the subway after work to give his place to a woman. He saw another clerk go berserk behind his counter and be carried, kicking and screaming, off to the elevators by several New York policemen. He was disillusioned, and was seriously considering trying to get into the Navy Flight Cadet program, when the miracle happened: the young man from Dartmouth who had spent two summers on a daily newspaper backed out of his job with Carey Furnace several weeks before he was supposed to report for duty. The employment office, going through their files, saw Jake's name and wired the placement office at Columbia with the news that a job was now open if Abbott cared to come in for an interview.

"You can get a day off to run over to Pittsburgh, I guess," the placement director said to Jake.

Jake smiled. "I'm ready to quit the store anyhow. I'll not even ask for the time off. I'll just take it."

Jake flew to Pittsburgh that night and stayed at the William Penn Hotel. He rose early, skipped breakfast, being too nervous to eat, and was waiting for his interview with Mr. George Hurd, advertising manager for the company, at nine sharp. Mr. Hurd was a large placid-looking man who greeted Jake with a smile and listened politely while the young man answered his questions. Then Mr. Hurd called in his assistant, Mr. Al Bishop, who asked some more questions of his own. Both of them were most pleasant, but noncommittal. They told Jake to go back to his job in New York and wait for their decision. They did not want him to lose his present employment, if for some reason his application was not successful. Jake had it on the tip of his tongue to say that he was quitting his job in New York anyhow, and would stay in Pittsburgh and wait, but he did not speak. Green as he was, he realized that he was dealing from strength as long as he appeared to be holding a fairly good job, and that a show of too great eagerness would react against him.

He thanked Mr. Hurd and Mr. Bishop and went back to New York, but not without stopping to see Frances. She said he looked "very thin," and she did not seem enthusiastic about his interview. She drove him to the airport at Pittsburgh, but when she kissed him goodbye he thought he sensed a definite change in the warmth of her embrace: perhaps, already, she had found a new lover. When he got in his room at International House he lay down on the bed with his clothes on, completely exhausted and more discouraged about his future than he had ever been. All was lost — the job, Frances, everything. He might as well go back to the store and sell bathing suits. At least he could pay his own way. Finally he undressed and went to bed. The future looked dark.

The next day at the store his section manager stopped beside the bathing-suit counter. "Well, Abbott," he said, and the sarcasm in his voice was plain. "Your grandmother's funeral yesterday — or did you sit up with a sick friend?"

"It must have been something I ate," Jake lied. "I couldn't hold a thing down all day."

"Stay in your room, eh?"

"In bed," Jake said, and realized, too late, that the question had merely been a trap.

"Then why wasn't the girl at the desk able to find you when she sent a man to look?"

Jake felt his face flushing. He could not think of anything to say.

"You weren't sick, Abbott. You're lying."

"Well," Jake said, feeling a sort of relief. "All right — I was. I went to look for another job, to tell you the truth. In Pittsburgh."

"Oh, Pittsburgh, eh? Big deal! You get it?"

"They're going to let me know."

The section manager smiled. "I see — you didn't get it. Well, now, Abbott, let me give you a little advice. We don't stand for any foolishness around here. I'm going to let you off this time — dock you three days' pay and put you on probation — but if this happens again, you're through. Understand?"

"Three days' pay?" Jake said. "But I was only gone one day."

"You heard me! Three days' pay. And don't give me any trouble or I might decide to make it a week!"

Suddenly Jake saw it was over. He had never talked back to authority before — not seriously — and he didn't do it very dramatically now. He said, "I'm not going to give you any trouble. Frankly, I've been thinking of quitting for a long time. Now I'm going to do it."

He was surprised at the section manager's reaction. He had expected him to lose his temper and give him a tongue-lashing. Instead, the man seemed suddenly to be unsure of himself, almost frightened. "Let's not be hasty now, Abbott. You're in the college training program. Mr. Rogers will have to fire you if it ever becomes necessary. Now get back behind the counter and start working — and I'll just dock you the one day."

"I'm not quitting because of that," Jake said. "I'm quitting because I want too. I've got other plans."

"Well — I'm not firing you, Abbott. I want that understood. That would be up to Mr. Rogers."

Suddenly Jake felt sorry for him. He said, "Don't worry — I won't get you in wrong with Rogers."

"Look," the section manager said. "It's not that I'm scared of Mr. Rogers, you understand. It's just that I've got a wife and two kids and —"

"I know," Jake said. "You've got my word. Your name won't be mentioned."

Jake finished out the day and left the store for the last time, but not with any sense of hope or release. He rode the subway to 125th Street, came down the escalator and stopped at Paddy's for a beer. He had the beer, and then he had a whisky, and then the bartender set him up a second whisky, so he had to buy a third, to be polite. He wound up, three hours later, leaving the bar quite drunk and without a care in the world. He'd told them about quitting his job at the store, only he made himself much tougher than he had been. He said he'd told the section manager to take his job and shove it up his ass, and all the good Irishmen in the bar heartily approved. Paddy even offered him a job as a daytime bartender, at one point, and when he left the place he knew that there is no friend like an Irish friend, particularly after six shots of Four Roses all around.

He staggered going up Claremont Avenue, and did not stop, as usual, to gossip with his friends in the Waffle Wing of the House. He stopped at his mailbox on his way to his room to look for a letter from Frances. There was a letter, and a telegram. He started to open the letter, then tore open the telegram instead. It might be some emergency. It read: COPYWRITING JOB AVAILABLE ON TERMS DISCUSSED. PLEASE ADVISE SOONEST. HURD.

Jake Abbott and Frances Whitehead were married in the St. Bartholomew's Episcopal church in Carey Furnace two weeks later — and, except for a three-year leave of absence in the Navy, during World War II, Jake had been working in George Hurd's department ever since. It had not been too bad, working on copy. He still had time, in the evenings, for his "serious writing." He had never succeeded in finishing a novel, but he had sold articles to *Parents Magazine* and the *Farm Journal,* and once he had gotten a short personal rejection note from the *Saturday Evening Post,* saying that while the story he had submitted was not quite in their line, they would be happy to look at anything else Jake might wish to send them.

When the war came, Jake stuck it out in the steel company, writing institutional copy for a full year after Pearl Harbor. He was in a basic industry, and Al Bishop had assured him that he would never be called. But Jake finally could wait no longer. He went down to Pittsburgh and applied for a commission in the Naval Reserve, got it, and he and Frances spent three years in a cottage on the beach near the Naval Air Base at Tomoka River, Florida. He never fired a shot in combat — but he accumulated impressions and notes on what he hoped would be a best-selling first novel. Now the hope was growing dim. He had a thick stack of yellow manuscript in the shed below the house, which he had fixed up as a writing room, but he had stopped showing it to Frances. He felt that this was his last chance, and he could not bear to show it to anyone, lest the dream be shattered. When Frances asked him how his writing was coming, he said, "Okay, okay — it's coming."

"Let me read it."

"Not yet. I want to get it in one piece — polished up — and then I will."

"Oh, damn you, Jake — you haven't got forever!"

"Oh, sure I have," he said, feeling scared and angry. "I've got forever. Ten, twenty, thirty years. I'm going to live forever."

"All right," she said. "Be nasty. I'm only trying to help you."

"I know it," he said. "I'm trying, Fran. Believe me, I am. I'll show you that novel one of these days."

He had eleven hundred pages of rough manuscript — most of it revisions of revisions. He could never seem to get it on paper the way he saw it in his head. It came out awkward and trite on the paper, and when he tried to tighten it, it got telegraphic and lousy; when he tried to loosen it and give it body, it got dull. He was writing about young Navy fighter pilots training in Grumman F-6-F Hellcats at Tomoka River during the war. He called it, tentatively, *A Feather in the Wind,* using a T. S. Eliot quote: "My life is light, waiting for the death wind, Like a feather on the back of my hand." The title was intended to symbolize the lighthearted philosophy of the Navy student pilots who were flying high-performance fighters for the first time, and whose death rate was higher, per hours flown, then the death rate in actual combat in the Pacific. Parts of the book, Jake thought, were pretty good. But organizationally, it was all over the map, and many of the characters were paper dolls, and when he tried to fix it, the whole thing got like a rubber horse he had once seen in a Walt Disney movie. Donald Duck had been trying to push the entire rubber horse under water, but could not do it, because some portion always popped up. And when he turned his attention to that part, the part he had let go of popped up. It had been funny in the movie. But it wasn't funny in the novel. It had finally become a nightmare.

Now, on this Saturday morning in August, Frances Abbott sat up in her bed and stared across the room at her husband, who was lying on his stomach with a pillow partly over his head. "Honey," Frances called. "Hey, wake up — big day . . ."

Jake turned, sluggishly, shoved the pillow aside and peered at his wife. She smiled at him. "Good morning, Mr. Abbott."

"What's good about it?" Jake groaned. "It feels about a hundred and thirty already."

"It's Saturday," Fran said. "No office work. No News Letter approvals to get. That's what's good about it."

"Oh God . . ."

"Oh God, what?"

"The Carey party," Jake groaned. "We got to go to that goddamned party."

"Now, Jake, you'll have fun. You always do. Just don't drink too much and start giving out your own opinions on the H-bomb, juvenile delinquency, inflation, and other of your specialties."

"Oh, you don't like my ideas?"

"I love your ideas, pet. It's just that after you've had about four of Kelly's blockbusters, your *volume* gets a bit strong. You're enthusiastic, love, and I love you for it, but the vice president in charge of overly loud advertising writers might not." She sat up. "Come on, now. We have to hurry. I have to do some food shopping, and I want you to clip the hedge —"

"Clip the hedge? What in the name of Christ for? It's dry as a bone!"

"Take a look at it. Go ahead — go over to the window and take a look. It's eight feet high if it's an inch. It hasn't been clipped since spring."

"Then let's not spoil the record," Jake said. "Let's leave it alone until next spring —"

"All right — if you're going to be nasty about it, I'll get Archie Saunders —"

"Look," Jake interrupted, also sitting up. "I don't want that kid around here any more. He gives me the creeps. I don't know what he does to that goddamned dog of the Snyder's, but the little monster barks itself hoarse whenever the kid comes near. And not only that, the kid never does anything right. He'll mess your hedge up so bad you'll have to cut it down to the ground and let it start over."

"All right, I won't get Archie. I'll get old Mr. Schmidt."

"Old Mr. Schmidt my naked fanny!" Jake yelled. "Twelve dollars a day for pottering around oiling the shears. He's worse than Archie. Where are those clippers — I'll do the job myself!"

Frances smiled. "Oh, Jake, you're a doll baby. The clippers are in the garage, hanging on their peg on the wall. You're so sweet to do it for me in all this heat!"

Jake looked at her balefully. Then he rose, in his pajama top (he never wore the pants), pawed his hair down over his face, stiffened his legs, and began crossing the bedroom like a monster stalking a victim. Frances got out of the other side of her bed, crouching, like the heroine in an old-fashioned melodrama. "Ohh!" she screamed in a Betty Boop falsetto voice. "Ohh, Henry, Nancy! Come rescue me! Frankenstein's after me! Quick! Quick!"

From upstairs there were noises, then steps running down, and Henry's voice shouting. "I'm coming, Mummy! I'm coming! I'll get him for you!"

Jake made a sudden lunge across the bed. Frances eluded him and darted into the center of the room, and Henry hurtled in and threw himself on his father's back, securing a strangle hold from the rear. Frances took advantage of the diversion to slide past the struggling forms and make her escape to the bathroom at the end of the hallway.

The preparations for the Carey lawn party had been going on since eight o'clock in the morning. The caterers had brought in dozens of trays of tiny sandwiches: chicken, ham, cream cheese and olive, various kinds of lunch meats and fancy spreads, cut in small triangles and protected from the air by tight covers of waxed paper. There were platters of carved turkey, cold roast beef, baked ham, and assorted cold cuts; there were stuffed eggs, ripe and green olives, assorted nuts, potato chips, cheese flakes, iced boiled shrimp, potato salad, cucumber-and-tomato salad, black and red caviar, four kinds of cocktail crackers, anchovies wrapped in tight oily rings with capers, hearts of celery, sweet, sour, and dill pickles, cottage cheese, and all sorts of cake, pastry, and ice cream. The catering job came to almost a thousand dollars, all told, and Eva Carey rotated it each year, to be fair, from one firm to another. This year it was being handled by Thomas Cooper and Sons, and as far as Eva Carey could see, when she made a last-minute inspection before the guests began to arrive in the late afternoon, Cooper and Sons had done well enough. The food was set up on long tables on the lawn, carefully protected from flies by waxed paper or pliofilm sheets until the moment for consumption should draw near, and serving girls, hired for the occasion, moved about in their starched blue-and-white uniforms, faces pink and perspiring in the heat, waiting to assist the hungry guests.

The bar was set up on the verandah of the Carey mansion, and was presided over by Kelly, the venerable bartender at the Steel Room of the Carey House, assisted by his staff (the Steel Room had been shut for the afternoon). Kelly was an institution in Carey Furnace. He was very old — nobody knew exactly how old, possibly not Kelly himself: a wizened, red-faced, white-headed little vulture of a man with a peg-leg and thick glasses which made his eyes look like soft-boiled eggs. He had stocked the bar for an all-out attack — a high mound of cases of scotch, bourbon, gin, rum, vodka, blends, and the various mixes, vermouth, soda, ginger, ice water, and Seven-Up. Nobody, looking at Kelly's ammunition, could doubt that he would more than meet the challenge. He had ice cubes by the barrel and enough assorted glasses to stock a gift shop; and he had privately ordered his helpers: "Don't be afraid to load the drinks. Servin' doubles you kin get the job done twict as fast."

When Eva Carey paused at his newly set up bar, Kelly peered at her through his thick lenses with somewhat less belligerence than that with which he greeted the world in general. She smiled at him. He was John's pet, and she didn't really mind his rudenesses (they had become humorously acceptable over the years, if they were not directed against you personally). "Well, Kelly, do you think you'll be able to care for my thirsty guests?"

"We'll handle 'em Miz Carey. I'm ready for five hundred, every one dyin' of thirst."

"Oh, there won't be that many, Kelly. I've only invited two hundred and thirty."

"Two hundred and thirty," Kelly said. "Miz Carey, I could handle two hundred and thirty all by myself, I had to."

"I'll bet you could, Kelly."

"How's the mister?" Kelly said. "I ain't seen him lately — but I heard he ain't feeling so well. I hope it's nothin' serious."

"It's the heat, I guess. He's up in his room taking things easy."

"Yes, Miz Carey, probly the heat. You want me to fix a nice cool drink for Mr. Carey? A little gin and tonic, maybe?"

"I'll ask him when I see him, Kelly, and let you know."

"Anything!" Kelly said. "Anything, any time, for Mr. Carey!"

She smiled, feeling a twinge of liking for the old man with his soft-boiled-egg eyes and his arthritic worm-veined hands and the wooden leg which John Carey had provided for him, twenty years or more ago, when he had stepped backward into the hot top of an ingot and plunged his foot into molten steel up to the knee. There had been a company union in the plant at the time, which meant no union at all, and if John Carey had cared to, he could have paid Kelly's wages, given him a few extra dollars, and forgotten him. John had gone to see Kelly in the hospital, and after Kelly finished cussing, he'd asked him what he wanted.

"Want?" Kelly had yelled. "I want my goddamn leg back, is what I want!"

"If you can't have your goddamn leg back," John Carey had said, "what else do you want?"

"I want to get out of the son-of-a-bitching plant," Kelly had said. "I want to get a decent job for a change."

"What kind of a job?"

"Well, tending bar maybe."

"You ever tend a bar?"

"No, I din't — but it ain't hard. You just trow some booze in a glass and trow in some ice and some water or ginger ale or somethin' and there you are."

"How about the Steel Room at the Carey House, Kelly?"

"Jesus, Mr. Carey — you kidding?"

"No. You want it?"

"Yes, sir, Mr. Carey — Jesus H. Christ, of course I want it!"

That had been over twenty years ago, and Kelly was now as much of a fixture in the Steel Room as the spewing blast furnaces painted on the walls. He knew what anybody who was anybody in town drank, and when you came in he sloshed your specialty into a glass with a grand gesture, always heavy on the whisky, shoveled in some cracked ice, and pushed it carelessly across the bar. Kelly was as spoiled as an only baby. He could hardly help but be. For the past twenty years he'd been sitting in the shadow of the man on the mountaintop, a shadow which covered the whole valley in which the mill stood, and the valley on the other side of the mountain as well.

At this party, Kelly would be an automatic station stop for nearly every guest on their way through nervousness or boredom to exhilaration and enjoyment, and, for some, on through to reckless imprudence or outright drunkenness. Nearly everybody would come to see Kelly sooner or later, and from his years in the Steel Room, and at private parties like this one, Kelly could pretty well predict, in advance, who would do what. Mrs. Paul Dana, wife of the vice president in charge of public relations, was usually one of his first and most active customers, and this afternoon, after the party began to move, she was running true to form. She had arrived looking slim and elegant in her expensive clothes, her gray hair immaculately groomed, and she had asked Kelly for a stinger in a soft, polite voice. Kelly provided the stinger, and then, rather soon, another — and then a third. And he watched Mrs. Paul Dana gradually become transformed from the cool immaculate gentlewoman with every hair in place to something quite different. Her eyes began to squint, her face grew flushed, and her voice rose in volume and increased in positiveness. She was, at the moment, engaging in an argument with Dr. Arthur Whitehead, whom everybody in town referred to as "Pop." Mrs. Dana was jabbing a diamond-studded finger at Pop's ample belly and projecting her words into his pink, perspiring face.

"Personally," Adelaide Dana was saying, "I don't believe all this namby-pamby about fallout. It's just something the government has been playing up to scare us into higher taxes. Personally, I think we're a bunch of foolish sheep. We know there are six hundred million Chinamen over there working like a bunch of cockroaches to build atomic bombs, and what do we do? Nothing! We have the power to exterminate them, and we ought to do it — just like any mess of bugs. Then we'd be through with them."

Pop Whitehead smiled behind his rimless glasses. "Addie, my dear, it's too hot to be killing Red Chinese —"

"Go ahead!" Adelaide Dana said harshly. "Go ahead and laugh. You won't feel so much like laughing when those little yellow men start swarming over us like ants!"

"Ants, cockroaches," Pop Whitehead said. "Oh come on, Addie — let's get off insects. Tell me about your art class."

Adelaide Dana lifted her stinger, tossed it down deftly, like a man, and placed the empty glass on the bar. "Kelly — the same, please. Pop, you're like everybody else in America. You don't want to think about anything nasty or unpleasant. You want to sweep it under the rug and forget it. Communism, segregation, H-bombs, all those rough ones. We're like people who'd get sick to their stomachs if they went through a slaughterhouse, but eat steaks and lamb chops with no trouble at all. There are answers, you know, if we had the honesty and the guts to face up to them."

She looked past Dr. Whitehead, into the crowd, and he saw her eyes tighten. Then she looked back, and her eyes were the same as they had been, bright and drunken and angry. "My art class?" she said. "Between you and me, Pop, my art class is ridiculous. I'm a fool to go to it. I don't know why I bother. I guess it's because everything else in this ghastly town is either dead or about to be dead." She lifted the fresh stinger Kelly had made, and drank deeply from it. "One of these days you may wake up, Pop, but I doubt it. You won't wake up until you look up in the sky and see those white stripes the bombers make — or maybe you won't wake up at all. There'll just suddenly be a great big blast in this valley from one of those intercontinental missiles that nobody knew was on its way or heard coming, and that'll be the end of this whole silly business."

Then she was looking past him again, across the lawn, and he turned and followed her gaze. Paul Dana, vice president in charge of public relations, was bending over a small porcine woman with red hair — Dottie O'Brien, the widow of Jack O'Brien, who'd killed himself about a year ago in his Mercedes 300 SL. Dottie O'Brien was wearing a cocktail dress which showed most of her back and chest, including her plump little breasts: she was a red-gold-freckled little woman with a nose you could see into the nostrils of, a wide crimson mouth, and very white, even teeth. She did not seem to be mourning her dead husband (not that Pop particularly blamed her — O'Brien had been a spoiled young bum). She was leaning back tilting her vivid little face up in appreciation of what Dana was telling her.

Too bad Dana couldn't wear a monocle, Pop thought. He was a take-off on those swashbuckling Nazi tank drivers of Rommel's Pop had seen in the newsreels — arrogant and sharp-featured as grim birds of prey, somehow more impressive in defeat than their British and American captors in victory. Dana was a small, compact man with sunken Teutonic eyes, a taut mouth, and a jaw upon which muscles could be seen rippling when he spoke. Dr. Whitehead now saw Dana's hand fall on Dottie O'Brien's bare shoulder and remain there, Dottie making no attempt to remove it, and he saw Dana's Prussian profile bend close to the freckled glowing pink face of the widow, and then he looked at Adelaide Dana. She was watching her husband too, and Pop quickly turned away. The look in Addie Dana's eyes did not go with a mature and caustic sophisticate. It was the look of a frightened and bewildered child.

Across the lawn, Dr. Whitehead saw his daughter Frances standing with a group of people. He had not spoken to Frances yet today and he left the vicinity of Kelly's bar and made his way through the mob toward the group. Frances saw her father approaching and called out to him. "Hi, there, Daddy! How are you?"

"Fine," Pop said, and bent to kiss his daughter as he reached the group. "How are you, dumpling?"

"Daddy! Please! Idiot, trollop, moron — *anything but dumpling!* I've lost eight pounds on my raw-egg and grape-juice diet. I'll be size fourteen in a week!"

"On you," Pop said, "a size sixteen looks pretty good."

He put his arm around her waist and gave her a little hug. He never attempted to hide his affection for his family — in public, or anywhere else. She giggled. "Stop it now, Daddy. Where's Mummy?"

"I'm not exactly sure. I think she and Eve went off somewhere to look at mongoloid begonias."

"You know everybody here, don't you, Daddy?"

He looked around the group. There was Jake Abbott, his son-in-law, Herman Stegmeyer, president of the Carey Furnace First National Bank (with his silent wife and his big shy daughter), and young Father Boyer of St. Bartholemew's Episcopal church.

"I know most of them," he said. "I've heard Father Boyer speak from his pulpit, but I've not met him personally as yet. How are you, Father?"

"I'm fine, sir," Boyer said. He felt ill at ease at this gay — and sure to become much gayer — party. He felt embarrassed to have a man of such importance in the community, a man many years his senior, calling him Father. But at this point in the conversation, Boyer was glad to see help appearing. He and Jake Abbott were having a religious discussion which he might have welcomed at another time, when he and Jake were alone and Jake was sober, but which he now wished to terminate. But Jake Abbott, standing beside him, tall, red-faced, bright-eyed with four scotch-and-sodas, apparently had other ideas. Jake said, "I'm glad you came, Doctor. You can be the judge in a little argument the Reverend Father and I have been having —"

"Now, Jake," Frances cut in. "Remember what I told you —"

"No, Fran," Jake said. "This is just a friendly discussion between friends — nothing else — right, Father?"

Father Boyer nodded. He smiled resignedly at Dr. Whitehead. "Your son-in-law has been giving us his views on Judas Iscariot," Father Boyer said.

"I was just saying," Jake said loudly, feeling no inhibitions, feeling warm and reckless and glad to be here showing off his smarty-pants ideas, as Frances called them. "I was just saying that people ought to get off poor old Judas's back. I mean, somebody had to do the betraying, didn't they? It was written, as Christ said at the Last Supper, that one of his disciples was going to betray him. So God, or somebody, had set it up in advance. Poor old Judas was the finger man elected for the job. I can't see how people get so exercised about it. Actually, without old Judas playing the heavy, the show would have fallen a little flat. I think Judas got kind of a raw deal. He built things up, and then they shoved the whole thing onto him personally — just as if the script hadn't been written in advance —"

"Jake!" Frances cried. "For heaven's sake, will you *shut up!*"

Pop Whitehead put his hand on his son-in-law's arm. "Jake," he said, his eyes twinkling, "you should have been a minister, boy, instead of a writer."

"They'd have thrown him out of the seminary in two days," Frances said.

"Speaking of writing," Pop said, "how's the novel coming Jake?"

"In 1994," Frances said, "if we all live that long, Jake is going to let me read it."

"I hadn't heard about a novel," young Father Boyer said. "You writing a novel, Jake?"

Jake's happy mood was suddenly gone. The parson-baiting was spoiled. As sometimes happened to him, when he had had too much to drink, he was suddenly savage and ugly inside, wanting to hurt, offend, incite. He looked at Herman Stegmeyer, eating one sandwich and holding another in a fat pink hand: chewing, swallowing, his pink dewlaps moving steadily on his boiled collar. A pig, Jake thought; the man ought to carry a portable trough with him. Herman Stegmeyer smacked his lips and opened his mouth when he chewed, so Jake could see his tongue, with the sandwich mixed up in saliva on it, and when he finished chewing he actually licked one finger of the hand he had used to transport food to his mouth, and then, discreetly, he belched. King Henry VIII, Jake thought. Charles Laughton, playing Henry VIII. Well, fat Herman could afford to act this way. He wasn't involved in foolishness like novel writing. When he made a buck, there it was, in the till. And Herman made plenty of bucks. Regardless of his eating habits, he was a very shrewd and successful businessman. When it came to foreclosing a mortgage, Herman Stegmeyer was a master. He used the crying towel technique; you'd have thought he was selling up his own aged mother — but sell people up he did, and on the dot, when the mortgage came due. The pay scale at the First National Bank was notoriously low. As Clyde Simmons, the assistant teller, had put it to Jake, Herman Stegmeyer had to be rich — it took a wrecking bar to pry open his fat fingers, once he clutched a nickel.

"The thing I can't figure out," Clyde had said, "is why the old boy doesn't at least dress his womenfolks decently. They look as if they'd just come from a rummage sale. He could import their things from Paris if he felt like it."

Jake looked at the Stegmeyer women now. Vivian stood like a trained cow beside her fat husband. Louise looked pathetic in a pleated skirt and frilly blouse with her hair done awkwardly in a billowy mass around her ears. Louise had started working as the librarian in the steel company several months ago, and Jake had spoken to her frequently, since the library came under George Hurd's department. She'd been almost pathetic in her eagerness to please. She wasn't bad-looking, either, if she wouldn't hide that voluptuous figure with those dowdy clothes, and use that washed-out lipstick. She had a full, rather pouty mouth, a cute dimple in her chin, and nice eyes. Perversely, because he had an idea that Herman Stegmeyer wouldn't like it, Jake said, "Louise, I'm going after a fresh drink. Can I bring you a scotch and soda?"

She blushed, smiled embarrassedly, and said, "No, thank you, Mr. Abbott. I don't care for anything."

Herman Stegmeyer peered sharply at Jake. "Louise don't touch it."

"Maybe she ought to give it a whirl," Jake said. "She might find she enjoyed it."

"She won't give it a whirl while she's under my roof," the banker said grimly.

"Oh, come on, Herman," Jake said. "You sound like an old-fashioned novel."

The banker stopped chewing for a moment and scowled. Then he popped another sandwich into his mouth and his jaws began to work again. He looked directly at Jake Abbott, and his blue eyes were cold and without movement. "You're an expert on novels, Mr. Abbott," Herman Stegmeyer said. "I guess you should know." The man paused, "At least by 1994," he said, and his blue eyes did not flicker as they looked into Jake's.

Before coming to the Carey party, Ethyl Snyder had more or less briefed Howard on the best way to conduct himself. It wasn't that they were climbing socially or anything like that, Ethyl said. It was just common sense and good judgment to seek out people they wouldn't normally meet, in the ordinary daily round, and make themselves known. Not be pushy, of course. Just be friendly and natural. Everybody was lonely, Ethyl said, and if you were friendly and natural you could go up and speak to anybody and they'd be glad to talk to you. Often as not, the more important a person was, the lonelier they were likely to be. Now, if Howard would just play along and watch her lead, Ethyl said, she would show him what she meant. Well, Howard had tried to play along, but somehow it hadn't worked out quite as Ethyl had predicted. Ethyl had taken Howard over to introduce him to Mrs. Paul Dana, one of the sponsors of the Junior Water Color Association. "Hello, there," Ethyl had said, smiling and being friendly and natural. "I want you to meet my husband, Mrs. Dana. I've been telling him what an inspiration it's been to work under your leadership in the art projects for the youngsters."

Mrs. Dana had wheeled a little unsteadily, with a cocktail in her hand, peered at Ethyl's bright smile, and said vaguely, "Oh, it's you, Mrs. Simpson. For a moment there, I didn't recognize you."

"Mrs. Snyder," Ethyl corrected gently, her smile still intact. "Mrs. Howard Snyder, Mrs. Dana. May I present my husband?"

Mrs. Dana peered at Howard, seemed to remember she had a drink in her hand, and finished it. Then, as she looked for a place to set the empty glass, she noticed she hadn't introduced the Snyders to the people with her. She said, "Wantcha meet some very dear friends of mine, the Cudahays and the Marshalls. Cudahay's in wire rope, I think, and Marshall's retired — that right, Roger? Um. Retired, the lucky guy. Well, I wantcha meet the Cudahays and the Marshalls. Mrs. Simpson and her husband. Henry, was it?"

"Howard," Ethyl Snyder said, her smile stiff. "Howard Snyder."

The Cudahays and the Marshalls were polite. They murmured something, and Mrs. Dana said, "Mrs. Simpson's with the young peoples' art group," and turned toward the bar. "Kelly — Kelly — 'nother li'l drinkie, Kelly m'love —" She lurched and nearly fell. One of the men, Mr. Cudahay, or perhaps Mr. Marshall, caught her in time. Ethyl Snyder took her husband's hand, quite friendly and natural, and said, "Well, nice to have met you all — I've just seen some people I know. We must go over and speak to them."

"Goodbye, Mrs. Simpson!" Mrs. Dana called loudly after her. "Goodbye, Henry."

"Bitch," Ethyl Snyder said softly, as they departed through the press of people to spend the rest of the afternoon, safely, with Mr. and Mrs. Mortimer Kline, who would remember their names at least, even if Jerry Kline had been born Geraldine Houk of Lundyville, and her father had been a mailman, and Mort had the local Cadillac agency, and was a town councilman (all town councilmen were automatically invited to the Carey lawn party, regardless of their antecedents). Mrs. Dana wasn't so great, Ethyl thought. Couldn't even keep her own husband in line. Look at him right now, smelling around that little O'Brien widow like she was in heat. Well, she probably was, at that. At any rate, there were other fish in the sea besides Mrs. Adelaide High-and-mighty Dana, and Mrs. Dana could whistle her way through hell before Ethyl would speak to her again, regardless of what kind of social standing was at stake.

Howard Snyder, too, was aware of the rudeness he and his wife had just experienced, but he did not feel as strongly about it as she did. He knew Addie Dana was very drunk. If she forgot names, what did it matter? It didn't matter, really. He looked out over the smoky valley as Mort Kline began talking about his favorite subject, Cadillac cars, but he did not hear Mort's words and he did not see the smoke. He was, in fact, not there. He was in Tehuantepec, Mexico, listening to the slopping of the sea. . . .

John Carey was sitting in his bedroom on the second floor of the big house, looking down on the valley and sipping a scotch and soda. It was cooler in his room than it had been on the lawn, where he had made his greetings to Eva's guests, and he had had two other scotches while waiting for Pop Whitehead, whom Eva had said she'd send up to the room as soon as he arrived. The scotch had worked wonders. The low-back pain was gone, and John Carey felt better than he'd felt in months. In fact, by the time Pop actually appeared, the intention of asking for an impromptu examination, here in the bedroom, had been abandoned. John Carey stood up to greet his friend. "Pop, come in, boy. How are you?"

"Hot."

"What are you drinking?"

"Cold beer, if you happen to have any lying around."

"I don't — in the room here — but we'll have it in a jiffy. Any special brand?"

"Ballantine," Pop said. "If it isn't too much trouble."

"Sit down," John Carey said. "Take that chair by the window. There's no cool draft, but at least you can look out. I'll phone down to the kitchen for beer. They've got a new gimmick now — portable thermos-pack. Very nice for this kind of weather." He picked up the phone beside his bed and called the order downstairs.

Pop Whitehead let his heavy body down into the chair John Carey had indicated. "Nice little party," he said. "Active. Old Kelly loading the drinks as usual. Everybody happy."

"I did my bit," John Carey said. "I spoke my piece and quit while I was ahead."

"How're you feeling?"

"Good. Better right now than for quite a while."

"Eve said something about your coming in for a checkup next week."

"I thought of it, but as good as I feel now, maybe I won't have to bother you. I know you've got your hands full."

"Oh, it's not too bad — not since I got my new boy. I tell you about him?"

"I don't think so."

"Bright kid from Allegheny General named George Hudson. You ought to see him use a scalpel. Beautiful. Delicate, light, careful — but not afraid of the incision. If I ever get on that table I'll not bother going over to the city. I'll let George do it. Well, here comes my beer."

The servant uncapped a bottle of Ballantine, and Pop waved away the glass. "I drink out of the bottle," he said. "Put the box down and leave me an opener. How many have I got there?"

"Six, sir," the servant said.

"Six ought to hold me for a while," Pop said. He tilted the bottle against his lips, drank deeply, and brought it down. "Nothing like beer on a hot day. Look, John, with this heat and all, why don't you and Eve just duck and run some place — Colorado maybe, even Switzerland, and have some fun until we cool off around here?"

"I can't do it right now, Pop. We've got misery in South America — as who hasn't? — And I'm going to have to replace J. P. Detweiler. That's just between you and me, Pop, but Det's getting along and he's been pretty well wound up in his cows for two or three years. As a matter of fact, he's asked to be retired a couple of times, and I've talked him out of it."

"J.P.'s over seventy, isn't he, John?"

"Seventy-one."

"Then why don't you let him retire? Give the young blood a chance."

"Right now there's nobody to take Detweiler's place. Oh, there's George Donovan, of course, but George is just a rubber stamp for Det. Good rubber stamp. The best. But not the man for treasurer."

"How about young Ben Oliver? I've heard he's a wizard with figures."

"Ben's good, but he's too young. Not even forty."

Dr. Whitehead smiled. "How old were you when you took over the company, John?"

"Well, that was different. My daddy died, and I had no choice."

"You were thirty-six — and the first year you had it you very nearly doubled the gross sales, if I remember correctly. So don't come whining around about young people, John. Not to me."

"No, Pop, it's not just Oliver's age that worries me. He's good with figures, darned near a genius, I guess, but he's moody and touchy. You have to be more than a good adder and subtracter to sit on the Carey Furnace board of directors — and treasurer brings automatic board membership with it, has to. No, I'll have to worry along with Det through this summer at least. Then maybe I'll put one of these management recruiting services on the deal. Body snatchers, I guess they're called. They don't care how they get a man — he could be running a big outfit for somebody else — but if he's big enough and good enough, they'll try for him. Often as not, or so I hear, these pirates get him too."

The two friends sipped their drinks and looked at the gathering dusk through the casement windows. There was going to be a full moon tonight. A pale lemon-colored disc was edging up from behind the hills, but high above, in the vault of the sky, a faint pink flush still lingered. From the other side of the house the sound of the party came and went in a wash of conversation and laughter.

There had been no diminution of the heat. Suddenly, in the darkness, there was a tinsel flicker, like lightning. Pop turned and peered outside. "Hey, what's that — a storm?"

"I don't know," John Carey said. "I don't see any clouds."

"I thought I saw lightning."

"Heat lightning," John Carey said. "No rain in it."

"I'm afraid you're right," Pop Whitehead said.

He drank again from his bottle of beer. He felt good. His friend wasn't sick, after all; he had a crackerjack assistant at the hospital; the beer was cold and sharp. He'd really sleep this night, too, Pop thought — with his new air conditioner, and all this beer. Once he got in bed, he'd put everything out of his mind: Jake's novel, Addie Dana's dipsomania, Herman Stegmeyer's sad wife and dumpy daughter, J. P. Detweiler's cows, the dozens of big and little crises at the hospital . . . All of it would be lost, drowned happily in the gush of cool air from the conditioner and the drowsy aftermath of beer. It was a pretty good life, by and large; Pop Whitehead, personally, had no complaints.

Enid and Ken Carpenter were quarreling. She had returned late from shopping in Pittsburgh, had made the usual interminable preparations she always considered necessary before any appearance in public, and Ken had tried to hurry her, near the end, when they were running an hour late for the Carey party, with the result that she had begun to sulk. Enid seldom flared up when she was angry. She smoldered in silence, like a piece of wet wood. Sometimes it went on for hours, sometimes for days. At first it had bothered Ken, and he had tried to break her of the habit by appealing to her better nature, by jollying her, by logic and reason, none of which brought any results at all, except, perhaps, to intensify the sulks. So finally he had given up. When Enid began to sulk, Ken simply put her out of his mind, like some insoluble problem at the office which time alone could take care of, and upon which further thought or worry was wasted. This proved to be a good solution. Enid took his silence to mean that he was suffering — or perhaps sulking himself; in either case, her offensive was having an effect.

Enid had not spoken to Ken since they had left their house in Hunter's Valley for the drive up the mountain to the Careys'. Actually she had been thinking about the fittings she had gone through in the afternoon, at the Exclusive Shop, in Pittsburgh, and what these new clothes would do for her (she'd put on four or five pounds in the hot weather). She was also wondering whether she ought to try the wrap-around hairdo the woman at the beauty salon had recommended, which, as the woman had stated, would make her look like the newest young Italian sensation recently imported by Hollywood. Enid had inherited her father's black hair, and she was currently wearing it long in a spectacular mane that hung to her shoulders. She intended to leave her hair long, in any event, until she went to New York in the fall to start her dramatics course, and then, if the people at the school wanted her to change it, she would. Which reminded her, the school had written a letter a week or so ago, wanting to know if she was really going to enroll.

She'd have to answer that letter one of these days, if she decided to go. It would be a lot of work — and her mother had offered her a trip to Europe in the fall, all expenses paid. Why Maggie would do a thing like that Enid didn't know or care. But she didn't have to make up her mind right this minute. It was too hot, and as she could see from the confusion of the Carey lawn, under the strings of Chinese lanterns, the party had degenerated into the usual brawl. It was a shame, too; she'd put so much effort into her appearance, and now, because they were late, everybody would be too drunk to appreciate it.

"We don't have to stay long, do we?" Enid said, as Ken stopped the car in the lower driveway (being late, they could not park in the reserved area and would have to walk from the end of the line). "It looks like a terrible mess in there."

"Not long," Ken said. "Just speak to John and Eva, move around a little, and take off." At this point, he was disposed to agree with his wife. The party did look like a mess, and he had some overdue National Guard business to attend to which he'd been putting off for a month. He did, however, have one reason for wanting to attend the Careys' annual party. Ben Oliver, in J. P. Detweiler's office, should be here, and he had definite plans for Ben. He wanted to approach him on a casual, accidental-seeming basis, preferably after Ben had had a couple of drinks. This he intended to do as soon as Enid found her place in the midst of her usual admirers, and it became possible to slip away. It would not be the first time Ken Carpenter had cultivated Ben Oliver. He'd been doing it for months now, very low-key and at widely spaced intervals. This party, however, would, he hoped, be the setup for the business he hoped to transact with Ben, in the cold light of morning, in his office at the company.

"You'd think they'd make better provisions for parking," Enid complained as they made their way up the steep graveled drive past the line of cars. "I'm ruining my high heels."

Ken made no comment.

"I'm going to have to go to the powder room and freshen up," Enid said. "I'm beginning to perspire."

"All right, dear."

"Oh, look," Enid said. "Look at that."

"What?"

"There — Paul Dana and Dottie O'Brien — see them?"

He stopped and stared past the line of cars to the bridle path the Careys used when they took the horses out for a ride. A car was leaving early, and was backing, and its headlights were illuminating the path. Dana and the O'Brien woman were briefly exposed in the glare, as they walked up the bridle path in the direction of the blue spruce planting Carey had put in as a wind break.

"Revolting," Enid said. "No wonder poor Addie is drinking herself into the grave."

"Poor Addie doesn't have to drink herself into the grave," Ken said. "She could put a detective on lover boy's trail and have herself a divorce and a handsome income for life, if she —"

He broke off and she looked at him. "What's wrong?"

"I left my cigarettes in the car. You want to wait here while I get 'em?"

"No, I'll go on in. We're very late as it is."

"All right. I'll see you in a little while."

She did not reply. She turned and walked away from him, proud, lovely, sulky, childish, into the warm light of the Chinese lanterns, and then Ken turned in the other direction and began trotting down the drive. He found the Polaroid-Land camera, with its flash attachment, stowed in its usual place in the glove compartment of the car in the event that Enid wished to be photographed. He removed the camera and checked it in the utility light under the dash panel. It was loaded with film, ready for use. He focused it for twenty feet, set the shutter speed and lens opening correctly for a flash exposure at that distance, took the camera in his hand and hurried back up the driveway. When he reached the bridle path where he had seen Paul Dana and Dottie O'Brien, he paused to let his breathing settle down and his eyes become accustomed to the darkness. Then he began moving up the path, slowly and carefully, making as little sound as possible, listening as he went.

The annual lawn party was almost over — cars had been pulling out of the driveway for more than an hour — and the full moon rode high and serene over the valley above the smoke. Eva Carey was glad. She was very tired and the party had been more strenuous than usual. Adelaide Dana had gotten very drunk and become obnoxious with some of the guests, and had finally been taken to one of the bedrooms, where she had vomited all over herself and the bed. The maid had brought hot coffee, and Addie had taken a cold shower, so that she was now relatively sober. Which was just as well, since her husband seemed to have vanished, and she would probably have to drive the car herself.

The party, Eva Carey was thinking, had been about par for the course. One of the girls in the kitchen, trying to carve some additional ham, had cut herself and had to be given first aid by Dr. Whitehead. Old Mrs. Trimball, mother of Dexter Trimball in wire sales, one of the most garrulous old ladies Eva Carey had ever known, had gotten started on a marathon reminiscence of the Good Old Days before the country was spoiled by high taxes and TV and too many automobiles, and nobody had been able to get her stopped. Young Ruthie Delaney, daughter of Kevin Delaney, manager of structural steel sales, had dragged some poor young man all over the party introducing him as her fiancé. Mrs. Carey hadn't caught his name: Fernando or Nabisco, or something like that; but one thing she had to give Ruthie credit for, the boy was handsome. He'd make a nice trophy for the Delaney mantelpiece. Whether he'd stay put on the mantelpiece, Eva Carey had no way of knowing. Ruthie Delaney, even at the tender age of twenty, could talk the arm off a wooden Indian. She'd been babbling to Eva Carey about Proust in some new accent which she had apparently picked up in the Philadelphia finishing school she was attending. She used phrases like "simply divine" and "utterly fabulous," which she applied indiscriminately to the view from the Carey lawn, the cocktail sausage she was eating, and Marcel Proust himself.

"I'm afraid I'm getting a bit artsy-craftsy over theah," Ruthie Delaney had said, waving a languid hand toward the East, presumably toward Philadelphia. "Don deah, do you think I'm getting a bit artsy-craftsy? I mean, wouldn't you rahthah have me just my simple self, the way I used to be before I went to Miss Deane's?"

Young Don Francisco (who owed his presence at this top-level affair to his interest in Kevin Delaney's daughter) took his pipe gravely from his lips, stared solemnly at Ruthie and Mrs. Carey with his Greek-god profile, and said no, no, he did not really feel that Ruthie was getting too artsy-craftsy (whatever that might be). Eva Carey had had a hard time keeping from laughing.

But for the most part, the party had been a success. Those who liked to drink had certainly had plenty of opportunity, with Kelly supervising the pouring; those who had come to collect raw material upon which to base juicy stories about "those stuck-up bastards, the Careys" had no doubt been amply repaid for their afternoon's observation; real friends, Dave and Ginny Ross, Arthur and Mary Whitehead, Elwood and Dorothy Price, Horace Foyle, and others had appeared, paid their respects, and, in most cases, departed fairly early. It had been a great deal of work and had cost a great deal of money, but, tired as she was, Eva Carey considered the party was worth it.

She loved parties. She had been a gay, happy child, blessed with good looks and good health — and, of course, with plenty of money. Her father, Nathaniel Peck, had been senior partner in Peck and Osborne, a firm of investment bankers. He also had been a Quaker, and possessed the hard-headedness which frequently seemed to go with the persuasion. He indulged little Eva when he felt he could do so without spoiling her, but he was stern in his criticism when she failed to live up to the high standards he set for her. Eva's mother died when she was nine, and her father had raised Eva until his death, shortly before she married John Carey. Eva had not realized what a tremendous force her father was in her life until she looked down upon him as he lay, white and still, in the upstairs bedroom of the Peck house in Pittsburgh, and realized she would never hear his dry little chuckle again, or see the quick alert sharpness in his eyes when he was angry or suspicious. The pale form on the bed was that of a stranger. She wished she had not come in, as the undertaker had suggested, for a "last look at your dear father." She would rather have remembered him alive, carving Sunday's roast beef, or smacking a croquet ball cagily through a wicket (he had been a fiendish opponent at croquet), or sitting in his office at the bank, calm, serious, slightly smiling, as quiet and tough an adversary in a business deal as there was in Pittsburgh.

In a way, Eva's marriage to John Carey had been a transference from the protection of one strong man to another. It was before the psychological hocus-pocus about father images, and Eva Peck had never thought about John Carey as her father — certainly not when he made love to her — and the marriage had not merely been one in which the strong, capable husband shielded and pampered the weak, frivolous wife. Eva Carey had inherited business sense from her father, and frequently her advice was useful to John in the conduct of his affairs. He talked over most major decisions with Eva, partly to get them clear and complete in his own mind (which the talking automatically did), but also to give her a chance to pick up any flaws or loopholes which he might be too tired or too close to the subject to notice. They made a good team.

They had only one truly deep disappointment — John Carey III, their only child. The boy had a sunny disposition. He took after his maternal grandmother, the one who had died when Eva was still only a child. He was weak, pleasure-loving, charming, and not endowed with ambition or much common sense. His passion at the moment (he was twenty-nine years old) was rock-and-roll music, which he played on his $9,000 hi-fi system, which had four speakers, and was matched, he said, and blended for the entire spectrum of sounds audible to the human ear, and which filled most of one room of his New York apartment. He could not abide the steel business, and after a number of painful efforts at converting him, his father had given up. His son would not carry on the tradition. Some stranger would have to take over when he and Eva let go. The boy was known, in Carey Furnace social circles, and presumably in New York hi-fi circles as well, as "Junior."

But Eva Carey was not thinking of her son as she stood on the lawn saying good night to her departing guests. She was thinking of her husband, and feeling relief and gratitude for the news Pop Whitehead had given her a few minutes ago, when he and Mary had stopped to say goodbye before going down the hill to their house.

"John seemed better than he's been all summer, Eve," Dr. Whitehead had said. "Just like the old running buzz saw he usually is. I think you can stop worrying about him. As soon as this hot spell is over, he'll be back in high gear."

"But you are going to look him over, aren't you, Pop?"

"I'll look him over, if I can grab him going past and hold him down long enough," Dr. Whitehead said. "But I wouldn't worry."

"Oh, Pop, I'm glad!"

"So am I, Eve. Nice party, as usual."

"Thank you, Pop. Mary, do you want me to send those begonias down with the gardener?"

"I think we might better wait now, Eve, until the hot weather breaks. The flowerbeds are baked, and I feel guilty about using too much water. I'll let you know — and thanks for offering."

"All right. 'Night, Pop, Mary."

"Good night, Eve."

She watched them go away from her through the thinning crowd, solid and familiar, the dearest friends she and John would ever have. She felt her body relax. It was going to be all right. John wasn't seriously ill after all. It had only been the heat, as he himself had said. She breathed deeply of the night air and turned, her hostess smile now secure on her lips, to give her farewells to a new group of her departing guests.

Sunday

THERE was no break in the heat wave the next morning, when Archie Saunders awoke in the shack he shared with his mother below the tracks north of town. Archie's head ached. It had been aching for a long time — as long as he could remember. Maybe an hour, maybe a day, maybe years. The heat, he thought, had certainly gone on for years. Once there had been snow out there on the window sill, but that had been in another lifetime. Archie lay in bed, his head full of hot cottony pressure, listening to the ticking of the Big Ben alarm clock. He knew exactly what was going on inside that clock. He had taken it apart and he knew where all the gears were, and all the shafts, and which way they were turning, and how fast. He could see inside the clock in his mind as if it were a big room, like the River Avenue Market, full of gears as high as his head and shafts as thick as his body. It wasn't only clocks he could do this with. He could do it with tiny ladies' watches, no bigger than a quarter; his eyes could see the tiny gears as if they were as big as the machinery that drove the thundering mills inside the Carey Furnace plant. People brought watches for Archie to fix, and he was glad to fix them, just as he fixed old phonographs and old locks and other mechanical gadgets which people got tired of and threw on the dump above the tracks. Often as not, those things just needed a little oiling here and there, or an adjustment of some kind, or, if a part was missing, Archie could get it from Sam's Handy Repair Shop on River Avenue, in exchange for making deliveries or doing odd jobs. Sam was an easy-going man and he felt sorry for Archie and his mother. "The kid's a genius," Sam told his wife. "He can do things with gadgets that I can't do myself, and that's no lie. 'Course the little bugger's nuts — but so what? He wants to fix up old junk he finds on the dump, why not?"

Archie was also fast at adding figures. The numbers in a column were like little people to him, little friends. When he looked at a column of the little friends they all ran together, obediently, in his mind, and when he reached the bottom of the column, in maybe two seconds, he knew how many of them were there. He didn't know how he knew. But he knew — and when they checked it on the adding machines, in the River Avenue Market, they had to believe him. Maybe he was a moron, as Mr. Brothers said, but he could sure add a column of figures. Even Mr. Brothers had to admit that.

Archie rolled over on his side in bed and peered through the window. It was bright daylight, but it was Sunday, and he didn't have to worry about being late to work at the market. Through the branches of the red astrakhan apple tree, he saw the cinders of the railroad embankment, the rotten boards of the barn, sagging in a tangle of dried wild raspberry bushes, and above the barn roof, across the tracks, he saw the tawny wall of the horseweeds that hid the city dump. The weeds were eight feet high and he had made secret pathways through them, and he could run through these pathways like a rabbit to Honeysuckle Pond, a slimed mudhole now, in the continued heat, its uphill bank solid with orange crates, rusty bedsprings, smelly old mattresses, rotting fruit, and the spewed-out filth of the sewers from Little Italy, which bordered the dump on the south. The dump was infested with large brown rats. Archie threw rocks at them when he saw them, but, quick as he was, they were quicker, and he never hit one. He thought the rats were laughing at him, and he was very glad when he found one of the old-fashioned wire-meshed rattraps, shaped like a sugar loaf, with an opening in one end. The rats could get through the opening, trying to get Archie's bait inside the trap, but it was so constructed that they could not get out again, and when he arrived the rat would be racing around, its eyes glaring, making angry squealing sounds.

It was much better to catch the rats in the wire-mesh trap, rather than with a spring trap, which killed them when it snapped shut. This way Archie could have the fun of killing the rats himself, by poking them with a sharp stick. The sight of the bright beads of blood on their brown fur, and the sound of their squeals of pain and fury, made him feel dizzy and sick at his stomach — but good. So far, since he'd found the wire-mesh trap, he'd caught and killed twenty-three rats, first with a sharp stick, and then, to increase the excitement, with a hatpin taped to the end of a stick. The rats lasted longer when he used the hatpin. He could often jab them as many as ten or twelve times without killing them.

Then he hit upon the idea of saving the rats until he had three or four, and putting them in a big empty oil drum. When he poked them with the pin on the end of the stick, they raced and squealed and leaped frantically trying to get out of the drum, but they couldn't jump high enough, and always fell back, and then, in senseless fury, they sometimes began to rend and tear at each other. It was very amusing to watch. He would poke the rats and let them jump and fight, and then he would draw back from the rim of the barrel so they would think he had gone away, and would calm down; then, when they were quiet and at peace, he would reach in and poke them again.

Sometimes he varied the procedure. If he could steal some of the kerosene his mother used for her oil lamps, he would dash it into the drum, soaking the rats, then light a match and toss it in. The flame would ignite the kerosene with a butterfly rush of fire and the rats would become tiny leaping torches for several seconds before they died. But Archie hadn't burned any rats alive lately. Father Boyer, taking a short cut past the dump on his way to visit Archie's mother, who was a parishioner of St. Bartholomew's in addition to being the cleaning woman there, had spotted Archie pouring kerosene, and had come up behind him just in time to see him toss in the match. There had been no way to stop things then, of course, and Father Boyer had had to stand there and watch the rats leap and scream in their fiery death throes. He'd been very stern with Archie. He'd said that torturing God's dumb animals, even unpleasant ones like rats, was a sin — a very terrible sin — and Archie must never do it again. If he did it again, Father Boyer said, maybe God would remember it, and maybe later, when Archie died, there might be some fiery leaping and screaming in store for him personally. Father Boyer did not actually believe in a hell of fire and retribution, but he wanted to impress Archie, and threats of hell-fire seemed the only logical way to do it.

"Archie!"

In bed, Archie lay still, not answering.

"Archie!" his mother's voice called. "Time to get up! We don't want to be late for church!"

"Okay," he called. "Okay, *okay* . . ."

Church, he thought, what a place to spend a nice morning like this, when he could be enjoying himself up in the horseweeds instead of sitting and listening to Father Boyer ranting about God and Jesus and the Holy Ghost. If you were in trouble, Father Boyer said, and you prayed to Jesus, he would help you. Maybe Jesus would, but Archie had his doubts. How could a little tiny thing like Jesus help anybody? Father Boyer was always saying how Jesus sat on the right hand of God. If Jesus could do that, he must be about the size of a grapefruit. Archie had a mental image of what they all looked like. God, an old man with a heavy beard, who resembled Jake Kowalski, the junk man who brought loads of stuff to the Carey Furnace dump, holding this little grapefruit Jesus on his right hand, and the Holy Ghost, who had a sheet over his head and looked like a Ku Kluxer, sitting on God's lap. A pretty silly bunch of people to be praying to, Archie thought.

"Archie!" his mother's voice cried out below. "I won't call you again! I'll come up and get you with a switch!"

"All right, Mom," he yelled. "I'm coming!"

He knew his mother wouldn't come up for him with any switch. She was a bigger silly than Father Boyer. Since Archie's father had died, she'd spent every spare minute with the boy. If there was something he wanted, and she could get it for him, he knew she would. He loved her as much as he loved anybody. She was awful easy to lie to and to fool. Most people were hard to lie to and to fool, particularly Mr. Brothers, at the River Avenue Market.

Through the bedroom doorway he could smell the bacon and eggs his mother was cooking in the kitchen. He got out of bed and quickly dressed and went downstairs. His mother was standing in front of the stove, a small, worried-looking woman with false teeth and big brown eyes, and hair which was still as glossy and brown as that of a young girl. She had many jobs. She worked two days a week at St. Bartholomew's, cleaning both the church and the rectory; she helped at the steel company when any of the cleaning women were sick, or they wanted her to fill in; and she did babysitting in the evening, now that Archie was old enough to stay home alone.

She saw her son and held out her arms. "How are you this morning, honey? Come give Mommy a kiss."

He kissed her dutifully. "My eggs ready yet, Mom?"

"Sit down, dear, I'll serve them up."

"You got any sticky buns?"

"Not this morning, dear."

"Aw, heck! I wanted sticky buns!"

"I'm sorry, dear. I'll have them for you tomorrow for sure. All right?"

He sat down. His mother placed the bacon and eggs on his plate and poured him a glass of milk. She even salted and peppered the eggs for him. He relented about the sticky buns, and looked up and smiled at her. "You're a good mom," he said. But when she tried to kiss him again, he already had a mouthful of eggs.

Jake Abbott sat in front of his typewriter in the office he'd rigged for himself in the shed below the house. This morning, despite the nagging hangover from the Carey party, he felt remarkably good. The novel was going well. At least it seemed to Jake, at the moment, that it was going well. Where his writing was concerned, he suffered from acute Gestalt reactions. It was like looking at a skeleton cube drawn on a sheet of paper. One second the cube was pointed toward you; the next second it was reversed. His writing was the same way. He would finish a passage in a glow of enthusiasm, go into the house for a cup of coffee, come back, and find that the glow had died out and turned into a murk of discouragement.

This morning, however, he had the feel of it. He was working on a dramatic scene from his own experience as a lieutenant (jg) when he had been an instructor in fixed gunnery in the Ground School at Tomoka River. One morning he had been lecturing to a group of young student pilots on the theory of leading a fast-moving enemy fighter — in the manner you would lead a duck with a shotgun — based on the illuminated Mark 8 gunsight. He had been using information he had learned in Special Devices School, in Washington, D.C., and the students had been polite enough, listening to him with attention. Their instructor, however, had not. He was a red-faced lieutenant, just back from shooting Japanese planes in the Pacific, and he was smiling at Jake as Jake talked.

Finally he broke in. "Tell me, Lieutenant," he said, "where did you get all this red-hot dope? You been out shooting at the Japs, or what?"

"No, sir," Jake said. "I'm not a pilot."

"Not a pilot," the red-faced lieutenant had said. "Then how do you figure to teach pilots?"

"I took a course," Jake said, feeling his voice quiver, and hating himself, "in Washington, D.C., at the Special Devices School."

"I see," the lieutenant said, winking at the listening students. "They've got the word in Washington, D.C., on these matters, I guess."

The students tittered. Jake felt his knees get loose and his breathing deepen. He wanted to turn and run out of the room. The combat pilot smiled at him. "Go ahead," he said. "We got to kill this hour some way. Tell us how they shoot down Zeros at the Special Devices School in Washington, D.C."

Jake picked up a piece of chalk and turned to the blackboard. Something happened behind him, he never knew what it was, but the students all suddenly tittered again. He felt a twinge in his abdomen, and then, at last, he was angry. He had turned, still holding the chalk, and looked at the mocking face of the instructor pilot and his grinning students. He said, "Do you want to teach this class, sir?"

The pilot's eyes widened. "What's that?"

"Do you want to teach this class, instead of me?"

"Now, hell, Lieutenant," the pilot drawled. "I've got important things to do, like teaching these kids how to fly the airplane. I haven't got time to fool around with this fancy theory you Special Devices types put out."

"I'm sure you haven't, sir," Jake said, feeling his knees shaking, "but I wanted to ask you. I have asked you. You've declined." He paused, and met the mocking eyes. "Since you've declined, sir, I must ask you to keep your mouth shut while I'm trying to do the job myself — or take your kids and get the hell out of my classroom."

There had been a moment of complete silence. Jake had heard a Hellcat fighter, out on the line, rise to a high hard thunder, as some mechanic tested its engine, and die to a mutter. The veteran fighter pilot stared at him, unbelievingly, and then his tough red face broke in a smile. "Son-of-a-bitch," he said softly. "Son-of-a-bitch." He turned in his chair and faced his students. "Okay, men," he said. "We'll listen to what this jaygee has to say — every frigging word of it."

This morning, in Carey Furnace in August, Jake was finally getting it down on paper the way it had actually been. He'd broken through, that day in the Ground School at Tomaka River. From then on, it had been easier, and harder. The combat veteran had taken him up, from time to time, in the back seat of an SNJ, taught him how to fly straight and level, taught him acrobatics, gone on to gunnery runs: high-side, flat-side, low-side — the kind of runs they'd made in combat against the Japanese. Jake had blacked out, had vomited, had clutched the seat with his fingers, watching the wings of the SNJ wiggle and shimmy on hard pullouts, wondering if they would come off. But he had stuck with it, and finally, before the summer of 1944 was over, he had become a good back-seat flier, and a very good gunnery instructor. The word had gone out among the pilots at the base — the instructors and the students both — that Lieutenant (jg) Jake Abbott was an okay guy. He puked in the back seat, and he wiped it up, and the next day he was back for more. A good son-of-a-bitch, the pilots said. An old ground-pounder (Jake had been thirty at the time) but a good son-of-a-bitch.

This section of the novel ought to be all right. If nothing else, he could pull it out and turn it into a short story for the *Saturday Evening Post*. Except, of course, that he couldn't necessarily do that either. Selling to the *Post* was just as tough — maybe tougher in its own special way — as publishing a novel. The truth was, all writing was a bitch. Even the Confidential News Letter which he wrote for the steel company to earn his bread and butter. Every item in that letter had to be checked and double-checked and sometimes triple-checked. It had to be approved by sales managers, metallurgists, engineers, lawyers — until it finally read like a legal document, prepared by lawyers who fully expected to be sued for every penny they owned if one comma was out of place. The inevitable result was, of course, that the News Letter was dull to the point of being unreadable. Charley O'Dowd, the jovial Irishman who'd written it before Jake took it over, had entertained no illusions about his product. "It's a silly puff sheet," Charley had said cheerfully. "Waste of money, waste of time, waste of brain power. But they pay me $15,000 a year for putting the thing together, and as long as they can stand it, so can I."

Charley O'Dowd had been wrong, however. He hadn't been able to stand it quite as long as the company had. At first, when he could slap down four pages of copy and get it cleared through the circuit and send it off to the printer, all was roses. But then somebody decided it would be a good thing — just to make absolutely sure no mistakes sneaked through — for somebody in George Hurd's department to take a final over-all look at the copy. The man assigned to the job had been Al Bishop, assistant manager of publications, who, it was said by certain disgruntled individuals, could not bring himself to go to the john unless he cleared it with Hurd first. Al Bishop did not feel this way about himself — not at all. He was all in favor of speaking up, putting it on the line, and the hell with the consequences. He was fond of saying that he had no use for people who couldn't make up their own minds. He wasn't scared of his job, personally, and he had no respect for people who were. Life was too short to pussyfoot through it.

The truth of Al Bishop's case, however, was just the opposite of his public statements. Underneath all his bluster and his brave words, he was the most conservative and cautious man in a company where conservatism and caution were the order of the day. While it was doubtless untrue that he went in to ask George Hurd's permission to visit the toilet, he certainly consulted Hurd on just about everything else. When Hurd was out of town, therefore, or unavailable for a decision for some other reason, Al Bishop's production slowed to a halt. Which, in the case of the News Letter approval, meant that Charley O'Dowd's production also stopped dead. Al Bishop's frustrating spinelessness, coupled, as it was, with so much phony bluster, had given ulcers to more patient men than Charley O'Dowd. Two months of nitpicking under Al, and the Irishman came unglued in a spectacular manner. He chose a lunch hour, in the toilet off the executive dining room, when a number of department managers and other dignitaries were washing up for their noon meal. Charley was in one of the stall toilets. Nobody could see anything but his feet, but they could hear him quite plainly when he announced, in a loud, carrying voice, what he held in his hand, to wit, the current copy for the Carey Furnace Confidential News Letter, and what he intended to use it for, forthwith.

There ought to be a monument to men like Charley O'Dowd, Jake thought. How much more fitting to have Charley O'Dowd commemorated in living bronze in the Carey Furnace public square — not astride a charger with a sword in his hand, as was the case with the present Union cavalryman who occupied the spot, but astride the john with the remains of the Carey Furnace News Letter wadded in his clenched fist. Portrait of the Non-Organization Man in open revolt.

"I wish I had old Charley's guts," Jack McHugh had said, upon hearing of the dramatic exhibition in the executive washroom. "Where is he going now? What's he going to do?"

"I hear he got a job in Florida," Willie Martin said. "Promoting a monkey jungle or something."

"Monkey jungle," Jack McHugh said, grinning. "Jesus Christ!"

"Why don't you go down and help Charley promote monkeys?" Willie Martin said.

"I've already told you why I don't go with Charley," Jack McHugh said. "I haven't got the guts. I'm an Organization Man, and I'm bucking for my twenty-five-year watch."

Jack McHugh was an Organization Man — but with a difference. He admitted it. The fact that he bore the title of space buyer, Jack said, did not necessarily mean he bought space. The space reps might as well be talking to themselves in the mirror in the men's room, Jack said, as talking to the so-called space buyer. George Hurd, manager of advertising, bought the space. It was all handled in about ten minutes at the annual budget meeting in the fall. Mr. Hurd would ask for Jack McHugh's recommendation on which magazines they should use for the coming year, and how many times each, and if they should take single pages or spreads (Carey Furnace never took less than a full page) and Jack would give him the rundown he'd prepared for the occasion. George Hurd would take off his glasses and nibble the earpiece, then put them back on and glance at the facts and figures Jack McHugh had prepared, and then he would say that Jack had certainly done a fine job — thorough, intelligent, perceptive (George Hurd used encouraging words at all times in his budget meetings) — and Mr. Hurd was most grateful and happy to have Jack advise him, and now he would take the budget under advisement, and let Jack know. Then there would be some table discussion. Mr. Hurd would invite the opinions of Al Bishop and Jake Abbott and the heads of departments, and nod solemnly as they suggested this or that. Finally the budget meeting, so-called, would adjourn. In due course the ad schedule would be released — and any similarity between it and Jack McHugh's careful recommendations would be purely coincidental.

"I tell the boys the truth," Jack McHugh said to Jake Abbott. "I don't try to snow anybody. I tell them I got a sign on my desk says I'm space buyer — but don't knock themselves out with the hard sell. It's all going to be decided at the end of the hall anyhow. But don't try to pass my desk and go down the hall. I tell them that, too. Because if they do, and I hear about it, they'll never get past the reception desk downstairs as long as they live. And every so often, no crap, I actually get a word with Hurd at the department picnic — put in a plug for this or that magazine — and he pays attention. That's how we got six pages in *Wire Rope World* last year. I caught George at the picnic, and plugged WRW hard, and he put it on the list. George will listen to anybody, about anything, at the picnic."

Jake didn't need Jack McHugh to tell him about Mr. Hurd's feeling about the department picnic. Jake knew the picnic was Mr. Hurd's own private party. He was the good father to all his earnest loyal little workers, beaming, nodding, shaking hands, slapping on the back, giving the impression at all times that he might be about to reach into his pocket and bring forth an all-day sucker, recite a nursery rhyme, or perform some other happy little service on demand. At other times during the year, Mr. Hurd was inclined to be remote, passing you in the hall with a vague smile which made you doubt that he remembered your name, and there were extended periods when he was not seen at all. There were no criticisms of these absences, however, among the help, no speculations that the boss might be living it up in Jamaica or taking in a week of New York theatre. Nobody knew who had the boss's ear — or might, in the future, have it — and nobody was going to say anything which, if passed along, might cost him his job. Mr. George Hurd was a Great Guy, Wonderful to Work For, and all of them were Damned Lucky to Have Him. Pass that on, if you cared to, and the hell with you. Mr. Hurd might spot it for bullshit — but at least he wouldn't can anybody for saying it.

In the littered workshop below his house, Jake Abbott typed steadily, filling one yellow sheet after another, stopping, from time to time, to read what he had written, feeling warm and happy. If he could just hold this pace, through other scenes, other characters, he might eventually amass enough material to serve as a grab bag for a good novel. Thomas Wolfe had done it this way, more or less, at least according to the stories. He'd handwritten whole trunkfuls of stuff, much of it utter crap, and then that brilliant editor, Maxwell Perkins, had laboriously gone through it and sifted *Look Homeward Angel* out of it. If something like this happened to Jake Abbott, he would not go violently, as Charley O'Dowd had gone. He would go gently, but quickly — very, very quickly. If and when *A Feather in the Wind* became a certain success, Jake Abbott would fold his tents like the Arabs and, taking Fran and the kids, silently steal away. Not to Paris or Key West or the Italian Riviera, but to some remote farm where he could sit down in a back room and write. This novel was not an idle dream for Jake Abbott. It was the most important thing in his life. If he could write one good one, he could, and he damned well would, write a second, and a third, and a fourth. . . .

From his pulpit in St. Bartholomew's Episcopal Church, on Main Street in Carey Furnace, young Father William Boyer was preaching his Sunday morning sermon. He was a large untidy young man with a wide forehead, a thatch of brown hair which he parted on the side, and a thin, rather high-pitched voice. He had been vicar of St. Bartholomew's for less than a year, since the sudden death of old Father Garrigues, of a heart attack, and while he had been welcomed first with the enthusiasm born of novelty and change, there had been certain rumblings, lately, among the old guard, who did not wish the boat to be rocked. St. Bartholomew's had been a very "high" church under Father Garrigues, who delighted in dressing up in colorful robes, burning incense, and encouraging other matters of ritual and pageantry. Young Father Boyer retained these practices, but in a greatly modified form, and his sermon delivery was very different from the delivery of the former minister. Father Garrigues had confined himself almost wholly to Biblical themes, and had spoken for the most part in a sanctimonious singsong, letting his voice become deep and solemn when the subject matter appeared to call for deep and solemn tones, whispering when it appeared proper to whisper, but sounding at all times as if Father Garrigues felt that God, or at least one of God's helpers, was sitting in the audience waiting for some blasphemy or impropriety, or perhaps only a bit of bad taste or bad judgment, to snatch the minister from his pulpit and propel him downward into the place of fire and brimstone. Father Garrigues received very little criticism from his parishioners on the quality of his sermons. The sermons were uniformly innocuous, pious, and dull, and hence, from a conventional point of view, above reproach.

Not so with young Father Boyer's sermons. He often used a Bible quotation as a theme, or keynote, but he usually got quickly from there to practical applications in the present. He frequently picked out some newspaper headline or editorial as a jumping-off point, and sometimes he trod uncomfortably close to the private prejudices and somewhat dubious business practices of his parishioners. Father

Boyer spoke in a matter-of-fact manner, without any rhetorical flourishes or singsong religious rhythms. But the things he said sometimes caused dozing members of the congregation to sit up, suddenly wide awake, and stare at the pulpit.

This morning, Father Boyer was making use of some of the various discussions of the hydrogen bomb which he had overheard at the Carey lawn party the previous evening. He was not waving the bomb over the heads of the congregation like some awesome club. They were too sophisticated, in the main, for this. Neither was he touting the bomb as God's punishment to ungrateful and bloody-minded man. Father Boyer was developing the fanciful idea that God had given man the H-bomb as a supreme test of free will. When God was creating man, Father Boyer pointed out, He could have made him any way He liked (absolutely perfect, as a matter of fact — a walking paragon of love and charity without a violent thought in his head). But such a man, said Father Boyer, would have been a robot. Growth, for him, would have been out of the question. He would have started out in life as a perfect being and ended as a perfect being. The world would be a showcase full of pretty automatic dolls.

"If I can believe what I read," Father Boyer said, "we already have enough hydrogen bombs to wipe out mankind. Even if we and our enemies miss every target we aim at, the poison fallout will do the job. Maybe not so quickly, but just as surely." Father Boyer paused and stared down at his drowsy congregation. "But it would be ridiculous of me to predict — or even hope — that God is going to intervene to save a single one of us from the H-bomb. If it falls, this particular human experiment may end. But if the H-bomb falls, it will fall on God Himself — just as surely as it will fall on members of this congregation. I am not of the belief that God operates from a seat outside the arena, punishing or rewarding or whatever, untouched by what is happening to His children. He is in the pit with us. He suffers every pain we suffer, dies with each of us when we die, is born when we are born, loves and hopes and fears with every one of us. If the H-bomb and its resulting poison clouds of fallout are going to wipe out all life on this planet, God will suffer with us here, and His Body will be diminished by the exact amount of Him that inhabits the bodies of every one of us. . . ."

Ethyl Snyder, sitting near the front of the church with her daughter Carole, was not following the sermon. She was thinking, instead, of the trip which Howard was planning to that terrible place in Mexico. For weeks now, she had been casting about for some way to avoid going. If Howard had wanted to go to Maine or Florida or some other civilized place, she wouldn't have objected — even though she loathed traveling — but Mexico, with an eight-year-old child! Who could tell what dreadful disease the poor little thing might pick up? Then, too, there was sex. Ethyl had managed to regulate their encounters at home to about once a month, and then she insisted they be decently clothed. Even in the privacy of one's own bedroom, Ethyl said to Howard, there was a standard of morality one must keep. Of course one read, all the time, these pornographic novels in which all sorts of naked squirmings and writhings were played up, just for their popular appeal, but there were so many beautiful things in the world, Ethyl said, that one needn't wallow in the mud unless one chose. Sex was one of the reasons Ethyl did not look forward to vacations. She knew that Howard, despite his acceptance of her rather austere bedroom schedule, always seemed to think that, on vacation, a sharp increase in sex was indicated and acceptable. In the wilds of Mexico, he might be even more demanding than usual. . . .

"The individual," Father Boyer was saying from his pulpit, "the individual, in the final analysis, is the only defense against the H-bomb — or Communism or any other form of dictatorship. We are always talking about the dignity and importance of the individual in this country; and it is certainly true that the individual has more freedom in America than in any other civilized nation in the world. But even here in America, in the last stronghold of democracy, our freedom is gradually eroding away like topsoil off a fertile field. We don't see it go. We don't feel it go. The loss is painless. In fact, in many cases, it is actually pleasant. The Social Security card . . . the vacation with pay . . . the old-age pension: these are all wonderful things in themselves. They make us safer and more comfortable. But what do they do to our inner drive, our daring, and our willingness to step forward into the dark? There is no old-age pension for a rose — and if you hold your Social Security card close enough to your eyes, so you can read the fine print, you hide the stars. Big government . . . big business . . . big unions . . . yes, even big churches . . . all take a bit of individual personal liberty. And it may be that when some of us finally stop and take a look around to see what's happened to our freedom, we'll find we've exchanged it for a silken cocoon of bondage. . . ."

Ethyl Snyder shifted restlessly and looked at her watch. She wished the young minister would stop talking and get on with the service, so that she and Carole could go home. She wouldn't take the short cut that led up the stone steps through the Abbotts' property. By so doing, she would have to pass the McHughs' lower yard where Jack McHugh, on Sunday morning, usually sat in the sun with his shirt off, while decent people were in church getting close to God.

Ethyl glanced around the church at the people who were getting close to God, and she had to admit, looking at them realistically, that a lot of them might as well be sitting in their yards taking a sunbath. Of course Mrs. Dana wasn't there. She was probably in bed with an ice-pack on her head — if she'd got all the vomit scrubbed off her. Ethyl had heard about Mrs. Dana's grand finale at the Carey party, and it was just about the only bright spot of the afternoon. Even that fat hog Herman Stegmeyer had been more socially successful than Ethyl and Howard. She'd seen him talking to Dave Ross, vice president in charge of sales for the company, and with Virginia, his Pittsburgh social-register wife, who, most people said, reminded them so much of the wife of General Douglas MacArthur that they might be twins. Ethyl had read in the newspapers that Virginia Ross had shot a lion or a rhinoceros or something on a safari she and her husband had taken to Africa. Ethyl didn't doubt it, looking at Virginia Ross, smiling and chattering with Herman

Stegmeyer. Virginia Ross, behind all that bright charm, probably was capable of any sort of rudeness or violence, depending upon whom she was addressing. Ethyl had her own ideas of what the Rosses were saying to Herman Stegmeyer, and it wasn't anything to do with Herman's charming personality or social poise. It had to do with money. Herman was a banker and could lend people money, so the Rosses paid attention to him. The Rosses were very rich — but one day they just might need a loan, and when that day came, Herman would be a good man to know — even though he starved his family and ignored the church when it came around for legitimate contributions. Ethyl had been on the Every-Member-Canvass drive last year and she'd been shocked and angered by Herman Stegmeyer's fifty-dollar contribution. Poor little Mrs. Saunders, who had that idiot son and took in washing, had given ten dollars — probably all she had in the world — whereas Herman probably had a million or more stashed away. Well, Herman might think he was getting away with it, but he wasn't. In the afterlife, he'd get what was coming to him — hell-fire!

If hell was yawning in front of Herman Stegmeyer, he gave no indication of it on this bright Sunday morning. He sat beside his family in their familiar pew, his paunch hanging down between his thighs like a taut wineskin, his eyes staring benevolently at the pulpit, his pink clean-shaven dewlaps sagging rosily over his old-fashioned boiled collar and his bald spot shining through the fringe of white hair. He wore a dark suit, despite the heat, white stiff shirt with pleated front, high shoes, polished to a high gloss, and a black knitted tie. The tip of a white handkerchief thrust up from his breast pocket and a heavy gold chain spanned his taut belly. There was no college fraternity pin on the chain. Herman Stegmeyer had come to the presidency of the Carey Furnace First National Bank over the long slow road. He had started when he was in high school, sweeping floors and polishing brass, dumping waste paper and taking care of the appearance of Mr. Leon Elliott's car. Mr. Elliott was the founder of the bank. Like all good bankers, he was a shrewd and careful man with a penny — and a good judge of character

— and he saw that there was a valuable potential of solid Pennsylvania Dutch industry behind the cherubic face and baby-blue eyes of young Herman Stegmeyer. Mr. Leon Elliott, however, had not got where he was in the bank by pampering the help or spoiling them with flattery. He had very little to say to young Herman except "helpful criticism," as he called it, but when the boy finished high school, Mr. Elliott offered him a job as general boy-of-all-work, full time. Herman accepted gladly. He was not afraid of work, and he had his eye on one of those paying-receiving positions behind the brass gratings. Four years after joining the bank, he was occupying one of them, and Mr. Elliott's judgment had been wholly vindicated. Herman's books were always balanced to the penny, his memory for depositors' names was unfailing, his meaty smile was as permanently fixed as the brass plate with his name on it beside his barred window.

Herman was ambitious, however, and when personal income taxes became more and more complicated, and certain depositors complained about the difficulties they were having filling out their forms, Herman Stegmeyer saw a chance to make some extra income. He studied income-tax problems until he became an authority, and one day when Mrs. Slaugenhaupt, a rich widow of a steel company executive, and Pennsylvania Dutch herself, confided in young Herman that she was having a hard time with her taxes, Herman volunteered to help. Herman cleared it with Mr. Elliott, of course, in the president's office in the bank. Mr. Leon Elliott pursed his lips and tapped them gently with his fingertips, a habit of his when about to deliver an ultimatum of some sort, and explained that while he would be happy to have Herman earn a little extra cash in his spare time, there was just one thing; if this income-tax sideline ever interfered, in any way, with Herman's work at the bank, it would have to be abandoned at once. The young man assured his boss that this would never happen, and, indeed, it never had.

As things had turned out, Herman abandoned the tax sideline the very next year for something more lucrative. He married Vivian Elliott, Mr. Leon Elliott's only daughter, under rather unusal circumstances. Vivian had fallen in love with a young man from Pittsburgh, an engineering student at Carnegie Tech named Dick McDonnell. Unfortunately, the young couple had not waited to take their marriage vows before going ahead, but had gone ahead, using contraceptives. Dick had every intention of marrying Vivian, and would have married her, if he hadn't been killed in an auto wreck on the Butler Turnpike, which had recently been turned into a three-lane highway. Dick hadn't been driving. A college chum with whom he was riding had pulled into the middle lane to pass and met another car head on. Nobody in either car had survived. The wreck and another accident, taken together, twisted Vivian's life beyond repair. One time, out of the dozens they had been together, Dick had broken a rubber. He had not told her about it. But that one time happened to be the right time — or the wrong time — and a few days after Dick's death, Vivian Elliott began feeling very ill in the mornings, nauseated and dizzy, on top of her great sorrow.

"I have always observed you to be a young man of the utmost reserve and prudence," Mr. Leon Elliott said to young Herman Stegmeyer in the inner office at the bank, shortly after the untimely death. "You know how to keep your mouth shut," Mr. Elliott said, departing from his usual pompous customer verbiage to make a point he felt vital. "What I am about to say to you now must never get beyond this office. Do you understand that?"

Herman Stegmeyer said he understood.

"Would you like to be head of this bank some day?"

Herman Stegmeyer's blue eyes flickered, but his respectful smile did not waver. "Yes, sir," he said. "I would like that very much."

Then Mr. Leon Elliott told Herman Stegmeyer what had transpired between his foolish young daughter and the deceased Richard McDonnell, and went on to outline the plan he had for repairing the disaster. Herman listened carefully until his boss was through. Then he said, "But Vivian — will she do it?"

Mr. Leon Elliott's eyes were quite cold, and his mouth was gathered like the mouth of a purse when the strings have been pulled taut. "Vivian will do it," he said.

"All right, Mr. Elliott," young Herman said. "If Vivian will do it — I will do it."

"One more thing," Leon Elliott said. "Only three people know about this baby. Myself, my daughter — and you. Neither Vivian nor I will ever tell anybody. If it becomes public knowledge, I will know who is responsible. It will be you, Herman. And if that happens, the damage will be done and I will have no further reason to afford you any preferential treatment whatsoever." Again Mr. Elliott lapsed into bluntness to make his point. "In other words, Herman, if you let this thing out, you will never become president of this bank. In fact, you won't even be working for this bank."

"Yes, sir," Herman said, "I fully understand."

"You will treat the child in every way as if it were your own," Mr. Elliott concluded. "I am sure you and Vivian will have a prosperous life together. It may even be happy and loving. For both your sakes, I hope it is."

"Yes, sir," young Herman said again. "I hope so too, sir."

In the pulpit of the church, Father Boyer had finished his sermon, and the offertory anthem was beginning. Herman Stegmeyer roused himself and reached into his pocket for the small envelope in which he gave his weekly check (a record for income-tax purposes thus being available). The organ was swelling and old Mr. Bashline was coming down the aisle with his carved wooden collection plate. Herman Stegmeyer wasn't thinking of the collection. He was thinking of the roast chicken which Vivian was holding in the oven at home. He was thinking that he would eat both the drumsticks himself, first — he was very partial to drumsticks — and then have a nice helping of breast. . . .

Near the rear of the church, Ellie Saunders sat on the edge of her pew with her contribution to the collection in her hand — a twenty-five-cent piece and two dimes and a nickel. She was not thinking of the collection. She was thinking of the Holy Communion which would come soon. She placed the coins in Mr. Bashline's plate, saw him depart with it up the aisle, saw Father Boyer accept it and turn with his back to the congregation and offer it, holding it aloft, to God Himself on the altar. Something warm and wonderful was happening in Ellie Saunders's body. Her throat had become tight and she could feel tears prickling behind her eyes. Father Boyer began to pray for the whole state of Christ's church, and Ellie Saunders slid to her knees in the pew, listening, feeling herself grow light and full of hope and peace as the minister's thin voice spoke in the quiet church, moving through the prayers to the ancient supplication of humble access.

"We do not presume to come to this thy Table, O merciful Lord, trusting in our own righteousness, but in thy manifold and great mercies. We are not worthy so much as to gather up the crumbs under thy Table. . . ."

Ellie Saunders followed the prayer with her moving lips, not making a sound, but the words were bright and wonderful in her mind, the feeling of peace and love was very close and strong. She did not feel her left knee, now, which ached like a tooth when she knelt to scrub a floor. The years somehow seemed to have been rolled back, and Ellie Saunders was a young girl again, kneeling in the presence of her God, with life and hope all bright before her.

". . . Grant us therefore, gracious Lord, so to eat the flesh of thy dear Son Jesus Christ, and to drink his blood, that our sinful bodies may be made clean by his body, and our souls washed through his most precious blood, and that we may evermore dwell in him, and he in us. Amen."

Ellie Saunders remained kneeling when the prayer ended. She would not go up with the first group to take Holy Communion. She would wait until the last, would savor it, would prolong it—for these were the finest minutes of the week for Ellie Saunders. Without them each Sunday, she did not know how she could have gone on.

On this particular Sunday morning in August, the Arthur Whiteheads were having a leisurely breakfast on the patio off the dining room of their home. The place was on the mountain below the John Carey mansion. It had once been a stable, an elegant cut-stone building erected by John Carey Sr. at a time when a rich man's stable could be a mansion in itself. Modernized with electricity, plumbing, and central heating, and decorated under the tasteful guidance of Mary Whitehead, whose hobby was antiques, the former stable had become one of the more charming homes in the area. It had the further distinction of being higher than any other house in town save John Carey's mansion itself.

"More toast?" Mary Whitehead asked her husband.

"I'd like some, Mary. But I have to watch my waistline."

"Watch your what?"

"Now, now," Arthur Whitehead said. "That's no way to win friends and influence people."

"Why should I try to win or influence you?" Mary Whitehead said. "You left me flat at the party yesterday — and never showed up again until it was time to take me home."

"Oh, fiddlesticks. You and Eve were looking at flowers, and I was up in John's room. You know that —"

"I was only teasing," Mary Whitehead said. "We should have gone to church."

"Why?"

"That young Boyer gives some good sermons — or so I'm told."

"I'm sure he gives good sermons," Pop Whitehead said, "but he doesn't spend fourteen hours a day carrying two hundred and forty pounds through hospital corridors. He has no wife or children to fuss at him. He has an entire week — when he isn't out looking after his flock — to prepare that hour's talk on Sunday. It ought to be good."

Mary laughed. "Now you know that doesn't follow. Many ministers in the United States have pretty much the same chance to get up a sermon, and you know very well that most of the things that are spoken from the pulpit these days go right in one ear of the congregation and out the other — and largely for one reason: there isn't a sharp or original thought in the lot of them."

"What would you have me do about it, dear?"

"Nothing, except one of these days somebody is going to blow us all up, and it kind of worries me. Not personally, so much. I'm fifty-eight, and I've had a good life. But I'd hate to see us kill ourselves just when we've got all this atomic power that's supposed to stamp out poverty and disease and maybe even send us out to the stars. It's like — remember that old movie, *All Quiet on the Western Front?* The war had about an hour to run, as I recall, and Lew Ayres put his hand out to try to catch a butterfly on the top of the trench — and a German sniper shot him dead. Remember?"

"I remember," Dr. Whitehead said. "But I don't think anybody is going to kill us with an H-bomb as we reach for a butterfly. I think we're going to make it. God's put too much effort into us to let us go down the drain at this point."

"Anyhow," Mary Whitehead said, "I'm glad of one thing: I'm glad John's feeling better."

"It might have been the scotch talking," Pop said. "But I don't think so."

"He works too hard. He'll be keeling over with a coronary one of these days."

"No, it isn't hard work that kills them off."

"What does kill them off?"

"Frustration, according to the latest theory. The buttoned-down men in the buttoned-down collars, chasing commas that don't have to be chased — while the H-bomb hangs over their heads. It's like a sheep ranch — all the good little sheep trotting along obediently behind all the other good little sheep, headed for retirement in a warm climate at age sixty-five."

Mary Whitehead smiled slightly. "Maybe it seems like a sheep ranch to you, Arthur, but not to me. Would you call John Carey a sheep? Or Dave Ross? Or even that ambitious young Carpenter? I wouldn't."

"What would you call them?"

"I'd call them tough businessmen — rugged individualists — but if we're being fanciful and comparing them to animals, I suppose I'd call them lions. John Carey, certainly. John even looks like a lion. And he can act like one when he's aroused, as you well know. I wouldn't call the valley a sheep ranch. I guess I'd call it a lion pit."

"Well, to be honest," Pop Whitehead said, "it's both. A handful of lions, a big flock of sheep. But I'm not worried, the way some people seem to be, about this so-called decline of individualism. If you read writers like Reisman and Fromm and Whyte, you begin to think the United States is ready for the ash heap. I don't believe it for a minute. I have a hunch that human beings follow some kind of upward spiral over the long run. It takes some frightening dips and corkscrew turns from time to time, but if you look at it every fifty or a hundred years, you find the dips have leveled off and turned back upward and the corkscrews have straightened out. I know this sounds like a bunch of Chamber of Commerce sweet-talk, but I really believe it's scientifically a fact. Sure we go through periods when everybody is herding indoors out of the rain, waiting for the security cards to be processed, but these are just phases, like the phases kids go through growing up. If you look at some kids around twelve years old, and take all the things they do and say seriously, you'd think they were utter morons and idiots. Give them five more years and they've turned into something else — a different kind of idiot, maybe — but in ten or twelve years, if you stick with them, and give them a boost when it'll help, and pick them up off their muddy faces when they get slapped down — or if the circumstances indicate, let them damned well lie in the mud until they pick themselves up — eventually you find you have a fairly decent human being." He stopped. "Want to know something?"

"What?"

"I love you."

She looked down, as she often did when he told her, unexpectedly, that he loved her. She was a big fair-skinned woman with snow-white hair, a winsome soft mouth, warm brown eyes under haughty brows. She had been, he knew, very much responsible for the success they now both had. When he had started out in Carey Furnace — it seemed like a thousand years ago, so much had happened — he had been fresh from internship, and healing people was the only thing in his mind. Keeping books, sending and collecting bills, keeping his office and waiting room spotless — even painting the outside of the house in which the office and their living quarters were then located — had been handled, together with the myriad of daily details a young doctor could not foresee, and could not handle alone, by his strong big-bodied lovely young wife. She had been supervising nurse in Allegheny General, where he'd interned — a quiet, somewhat solemn girl who did a steady, meticulous job, and whom, at one time or another, most of the unattached doctors, and dozens of men patients, tried to date. Mary Von Holdenburg had not gone out often. Dr. Whitehead had taken her to dinner. He had driven her into Pittsburgh the next night to hear a music recital. On the way home they had stopped in a side road for about an hour. It was in that side road that he asked her to marry him, and she accepted. A week later they were married. It was, Dr. Whitehead knew, the finest and luckiest thing that had happened to him in his life.

"Did you talk to Jake yesterday?" Mary Whitehead now asked her husband.

"Briefly. He was drinking — and having a big religious argument with that young Episcopal minister."

"How is his novel coming?"

"He didn't say."

"Do you think he'll ever really finish it?"

"I don't know. I hope so, for Fran's sake, if nothing else. I hope he finishes it and sends it out — and finds out, once and for all, if he can really write — or if he's just wasting time." He took a piece of toast from the covered container and buttered it. The butter was runny in the heat. He looked at the grape marmalade — resisted it — started to put the toast into his mouth without it — then weakened, and spread the toast thickly with the sweet purple syrup.

His wife shook her head and said, "Dearest, you'll be as fat as Herman Stegmeyer if you don't stop eating so much."

"God forbid!" He popped the toast into his mouth and chewed it with relish. "Had a little chat with Herman yesterday. He was eating canapés like peanuts. Maybe I'll get that way before I'm through. I'm not going to throw any stones at Herm — just in case."

"Poor Vivian," Mary Whitehead said.

"What do you mean, poor Vivian?"

"Herman treats her like a housekeeper," Mary Whitehead said.

"You know, my dear, I may be wrong, but I can't feel too sorry for Vivian Stegmeyer. I know Herm treats her badly, but I have a hunch she likes it. There are some people in this world who enjoy punishment, and I think Vivian Stegmeyer is one of them. I think she fancies herself as a sort of martyr — and the more punishment Herman heaps on her, the better martyr she becomes."

"That's nonsense," Mary Whitehead said. "You men all stick together. Nobody likes to be put upon — particularly in public."

"Now, take Louise," Arthur Whitehead said. "Louise is a different thing. She's a lovely girl under those terrible clothes, with that cute dimple in her chin, but she's never going to get a chance to prove it, I guess."

"She'd be fine if Herman would just send her to a charm school."

"Charm schools cost money — and Louise is working at the steel company, I understand. Some kind of library job. Herman isn't going to pay when he can receive!"

"He's worth over a million now," Mary Whitehead said. "He can't be interested in Louise's little pay check?"

"The more you've got," Arthur Whitehead said, chuckling, "the more you want." He finished his toast and wiped his fingers on a napkin. "Mary, I have to go to the hospital at one to make my rounds. I think I'll lie down in the hammock and catch a wink."

"Can I bring you a drink of water when I come back for the dishes?"

"No, thanks. Wake me up at twelve, if I don't wake up myself. I'd like to take a shower and clean up before I leave for the hospital."

He walked through the blaze of sunlight on the lawn and lay down in the hammock which stretched between two old locust trees at the edge of the woods. For several moments he watched his wife clearing away the dishes, then shut his eyes and delivered himself to the lazy hum of summer. From the valley below came the steady drone of the mills, louder and more continuous than when he had been a kid doctor, fresh out of med school, trying to get started in a strange town with a new wife. He hadn't known John Carey at all then, except to see him fly by in one of his cars, racing to a meeting, or to catch a train.

After the death of Carey Senior, young John Carey had moved fast. He had begun, in the first six months, to expand, to diversify, to change from a horizontal operation which bought all its raw materials and transformed them into a single-tonnage product to a vertical giant which owned its own ore deposits in Chile and Cuba and the Mesabi Range of Minnesota, its own coal mines in West Virginia, had plants strategically located, coast to coast, and sales offices in major cities of the United States and foreign countries, and whose stock ran into the millions.

Back in those days of mushroom growth, young John Carey Jr. had, of necessity, to work at the top. There wasn't enough time to investigate or supervise the details within the Carey Furnace plant. Some of these details sorely needed attention. There were no outside unions, and working conditions were often bad; men went deaf, routinely, in the chipping bays of the billet mill, where the daylong scream of steel chisels gouging out slivers of impurities from steel logs was so loud that a human mouth, pressed close to a human ear, could not shout loud enough to make itself understood. Men got their hands or feet caught, periodically, in unguarded machines, or keeled over from leaking gases, or developed lung trouble in the shakeout room of the steel foundry where the dust was unusally thick. John Carey Jr. did not concern himself with these abuses. He assumed that they were being handled as well as possible by Dr. Hamilton Coombes, who had been running plant medicine under his father. Dr. Coombes was a tall pale-faced man with cold eyes who belonged to the old school of industrial medicine: never pamper a worker, if you do he'll take advantage every time, will soldier on the job, report himself sick or injured without reason, and cause no end of trouble. Coombes knew about the noise level in the chipping bays and the black fog in the shakeout room, but he did not mention these things to his young boss. His record of accident treatments was phenomenally low and his clinic in the plant was spic and span — and deserted. No injured workman would go to see Dr. Coombes if he could possibly avoid it.

Young Dr. Whitehead had never heard of the shakeout room before Mike Wojicki came to him with a hacking cough and a black coating inside his nose.

"Where do you work?" Dr. Whitehead asked.

"Shakeout room at de steel."

"What's that?"

"Place where dey knock de sand outa de castings."

"Pretty dusty in there, from the look of your nose."

Mike Wojicki grinned. "You kidding, Doc? Damn place like night alla time wid de dust."

"Don't they have an evacuation fan?"

"What's dat, Doc?"

"Don't they pull the dust out of the place somehow — so you won't have to breathe it?"

Mike laughed, but the laughing made him cough, and when he stopped coughing he said, in a hoarse voice, "Pull dust? Na. Dey don't pull no dust."

Dr. Whitehead did not own an X-ray machine at the time, so he suggested that Mike Wojicki go to the clinic in the plant, where they did have one, and have some pictures made of his lungs. "Look, Doc," Mike said. "You no got a machine, you send me some place — but not de plant, eh?"

"Why not the plant?"

"Not de plant, Doc. Dey too busy."

"But that's what they're for, Mike. They're paid to help you people."

"Help!" Mike Wojicki said. "Jesus Christ, Doc, help! You go dere sometime, talk some guys. You find out how dey help. Dat sumbitch Coomb' he cut you up with his little knife for see you jerk. I gotta get X-ray in plant, I not get X-ray no place."

Dr. Whitehead arranged to have the lung pictures taken in the old Carey Furnace hospital (John Carey Memorial had not been built at the time), and they showed that Mike Wojicki's lungs were filled with the fibrous tissue which comes from breathing dust for a long time. The name for the disease was silicosis.

Dr. Whitehead called Dr. Hamilton Coombes on the phone and started to explain Wojicki's symptoms, but before he could finish, the voice of the steel plant physician cut him short. "What did you say your name was?" Coombes snapped. "Whitehouse?"

"Whitehead. Dr. Arthur Whitehead."

"You must be new in town. I've never heard of you."

"I've been practicing here about six months."

"Where did you practice before you came here?"

"I didn't. I was interning."

"I see," Coombes's voice said coldly. "Well, I'm going to give you a little advice, Whitehead. I've been running plant medicine here at Carey Furnace for the past fifteen years — without any help from young interns — and I intend to run it for a long time to come. Don't bother me again, please!" And he hung up.

Arthur Whitehead had been born on Pittsburgh's North Side, a tough section in a tough industrial city. He had fought his street fights, and he had shined shoes in the Jenkins Arcade, after his dad died, to help at home, and later he had driven tractor-trailer trucks in the summer, to help pay his way through college. Now, when he put the phone down, he sat a moment, looking at his medical diploma hanging on the wall of his little office. That framed piece of paper meant a great deal to him. He'd worked hard all his life, up to now, to see it there. This Dr. Coombes was undoubtedly backed by the steel company. A word from Coombes in the wrong places could make it very difficult, perhaps impossible, for Dr. Whitehead to stay in Carey Furnace and exercise the skills that diploma authorized him to exercise.

Dr. Whitehead stood up, put on his coat, and left the office. He had no car at the time, so he walked the twelve blocks to the main office of the steel company. He went up the steps and into the front entrance and told the police guard at the desk who he was, and said he wanted to go out into the plant and take a look at the shakeout room of the steel foundry.

"I'm sorry, Doctor, but we can't let anyone out in the plant without a pass."

"All right — how do I get a pass?"

"Who are you going to see out there? I'll call him up and he can come in and vouch for you."

"I'm not going out to see any person," Dr. Whitehead said. "I just want to look at the shakeout room."

"Then I'm afraid you'll have to wait for our next Open House tour."

"When is that?"

"I'm not sure. Not until fall, I believe."

"I can't wait until fall," Dr. Whitehead said. "Who should I see now, to arrange for a pass?"

The police guard, by this time, was getting impatient with this persistent young man. He smiled thinly. "I guess you could see John Carey. He owns the place."

"All right, I will. Call Mr. Carey. Tell him I'm on my way up."

"Hey, now, wait a minute. I don't know what your game is, but we ain't interested in playing games with wise guys. People don't call Mr. Carey and go up, just like that. They have to make an appointment and wait — and maybe he sees them and maybe he don't. Now take my advice, Doc, go on home, and forget the whole thing."

Dr. Whitehead said no more. He walked across the street to a pay phone, called the company, and asked to speak to Mr. John Carey. In a moment, a woman's voice, remote and formal, said, "Mr. Carey's office."

"This is Dr. Arthur Whitehead. I want to speak to Mr. Carey, please."

"Is Mr. Carey expecting this call?"

"No. He's not expecting this call. But it's important. Tell him that people are dying from silicosis from the dust out in his plant — and Dr. Arthur Whitehead is here to talk to him."

"Oh, you should take that up with Dr. Coombes. He's our plant physician."

"I've already taken it up with Dr. Coombes," Dr. Whitehead said. "He told me to mind my own business. I came over to your lobby and your policeman told me to go home and forget it. So now I'm trying to reach John Carey himself — unless he's got God or Jesus or somebody up there with him and can't be bothered."

Dr. Whitehead heard the woman take a quick breath. "Just a moment, Dr. Whitehead," the secretary's voice said. "Hold the phone. . . ."

Several minutes passed. Then a man's voice, husky, soft, said, "All right, Whitehead. This is John Carey. What's this I hear about my workmen dying of silicosis?"

Dr. Whitehead told him, quickly, about Mike Wojicki and the X-ray. John Carey's voice said, "Where are you now?"

"I'm across the street from your main office, in a pay booth."

"I'll meet you in the lobby in three minutes."

"Yes, sir," Dr. Whitehead said. "I'll be there!"

The shakeout room was worse than Dr. Whitehead had imagined. The dust inside the room was so dense that neither he nor John Carey could make out exactly what was being done inside. There was a clanging of metal in the murk, and, from time to time, men who looked as if they had been dipped in lamp-black walked out of the dust clouds to get a drink of water before returning to their work. John Carey looked through the doorway for a while and then was led by the shakeout-room foreman into the clouds of black dust, with Dr. Whitehead close behind him.

They groped through piles of used foundry sand to a central location where a huge steel casting was suspended from the ceiling by a crane-hoist, and men with shovels and pneumatic hammers were prodding it, causing black rivers of dust to shoot downward into the dust clouds, as pockets of foundry sand were dislodged inside the casting and ran free. When the two men returned to the outdoor sunlight, Dr. Whitehead looked at the president of the company, and despite the serious circumstances of the inspection, he had to grin. John Carey's face was sweated, and he'd rubbed it with his fingers, leaving heavy daubs of black dust. He looked like a man preparing for a role in a minstrel show.

"I'm afraid you have a little dust on you, Mr. Carey," Dr. Whitehead said.

Unexpectedly, John Carey chuckled. "I'm afraid you have too, Doctor. You look like Santa Claus after he got stuck in a sooty chimney."

And then the humor passed. "I don't want to discuss this now," John Carey said. "I'll speak to Dr. Coombes and let you know." John Carey turned to the shakeout-room foreman. "Close this operation down until further notice. Now. Pull the men out and send them home."

"Yes, sir, Mr. Carey!" the foreman said.

John Carey and Dr. Whitehead walked together back toward the office. "That man you're treating, what's his name again?"

"Mike Wojicki."

"Whatever is necessary to cure him, do it—and send the bill to me."

"I'm afraid he may be past cure, Mr. Carey, but I'll try."

"How do you know he's past cure?"

"I looked at his X-rays."

"You say you told Dr. Coombes all this?"

"Yes, sir. As much of it as I could."

"What do you mean?"

"Dr. Coombes didn't let me finish. He hung up."

"I see," John Carey said. "Well, thanks for coming over. You'll hear from me when I've decided what to do."

Three days passed before Dr. Whitehead heard. He was sitting in his office when the phone rang. "Dr. Whitehead?" a husky voice asked.

"This is Dr. Whitehead."

"John Carey talking," the husky voice said. "I've been doing a checkup over here. Talked to quite a few people up and down the line." He paused. "Well, it looks as if we need a new plant physician.

I have plenty of choices, of course, all fine men — but I was wondering about you. Would you be interested?"

"In heading up plant medicine?"

"Yes."

He took a deep breath. He wanted it, of course. It was a break such as a young doctor might hope for, but not really expect, once in a lifetime. It would assure his reputation in town if he handled it well, and this he was sure he could do. It would assure his whole future. His every inclination was to shout yes! But he did not. He said, "Mr. Carey, I know what this can mean to me. I want it. I want it very much. But I feel I must tell you that I have no training at all in the administrative side of industrial medicine. I'm a practicing physician. That's all. I will say this. I think I can handle it. I'll do my best if you hire me. But I don't want to sail under false colors."

John Carey's voice said, drily, "We've had too much administration over here — and not enough practicing of medicine. I think you can handle it, or I wouldn't be offering you this job. I'm not hiring you out of sentiment, Doctor — not wholly, at any rate — partly, I guess, because I liked the way you got to me about that man who has silicosis. But I've checked you out, and I feel that we can at least give it a try. It seems you were a good shoe-shine boy, and a good truck driver, and I hear you married the best-looking and hardest-working nurse in Allegheny General. So I'm offering you the chance, at any rate, and if you don't make good, I can always fire you."

"Yes, sir," Arthur Whitehead said, in a somewhat breathless voice. "You can always do that."

"All right, then it's settled. How soon can you get over here and take charge?"

"How soon do you want me?"

"Tomorrow morning."

"I'll be there tomorrow morning," Dr. Whitehead said. "And thank you, very much."

"Never mind the thanks," John Carey's voice said. "Just deliver the goods."

Lying in the hammock now, so many years later, Dr. Whitehead thought with affection of the many things which had happened since then, of the slow growth of the relationship with John Carey, from plant physician to personal physician, to friend, to head of the Carey Furnace Memorial Hospital; and of the remodeled house — which he had insisted on paying for at a good price — on the mountain below John Carey's. The heat and the soft hum of the summer morning lulled him. Gradually, Dr. Whitehead slipped from the far-gone world of his memory, peacefully, into a world of dreams. The mills droned in the valley. Overhead an airplane muttered along the hazy sky. Inside the house, Mary was humming as she straightened up the kitchen, but her husband did not hear her. He slept in the hammock, relaxed and at peace, wrapped in the August heat.

Out in Hunter's Valley, Ken Carpenter was sitting in a pair of shorts and a T-shirt, in his bare feet, answering business mail with a Dictaphone on the screened porch of his house. One of his strictest operating rules had to do with communications. He answered his mail on the day it arrived, if humanly possible, and insisted that all the people in his department do likewise. Actually, he preferred not to write. He preferred to work by telephone when he could. It was faster, and you could achieve a personal touch, and, corporation taxes being what they were, you were silly if you didn't spend your money on tax-deductible expenses — particularly a good-will builder like the phone. As a result, Carey Furnace pipe enjoyed a fine reputation for service among jobbers and warehousemen. "If Carpenter's got it," they said in the field, "you'll get it in a hurry. If he ain't got it, he'll tell you. No snow jobs out of that guy."

Ken knew what the trade was looking for. He had spent five years in the Ohio district office, in Cleveland, calling on jobbers, contractors, and plumbers. He hadn't adopted the approach often used by young college men who were out looking casually at the working stiffs before going back to the leather-backed chair in the main office. He subscribed to the old truism: you ain't learning nothing when you're talking. He listened and evaluated, keeping what he thought would work, and throwing out what he thought wouldn't work.

There were two kinds of salesmen: the boy who hit the high spots, visited the top men only, bought them big steak dinners, a case of whisky at Christmas, and buttered them up in every way he could; and the boy who did all these things — *and* hit the sub-bosses, the sub-sub-bosses and the rank-and-filers as well. Buying steak dinners for the big wheel and bottles of Chanel 5 for his secretary was very necessary — but it was easy. Covering the rank-and-filers wasn't. You had to drive all over the territory, stand up on cold concrete floors in drafty warehouses until your legs ached, sit in offices so full of cigar smoke you could scarcely make out the girlie calendars, train yourself to understand the kind of pidgin English some of the foreign plumbers' helpers used, and above all, remember names — a man's own name sounded sweeter to him than any other word in the language — and try, continuously through it all, to listen. Listening was where most of them failed. Most of them wanted to talk. Ken Carpenter liked to talk too. But during those five years in Cleveland, he consciously disciplined himself to listen, evaluate, and file for future reference. It was this rough-and-tumble training, as much as his engineering background at Lehigh, that had resulted in his rapid rise later, when he returned to the padded chair in Carey Furnace.

It was near the end of his third year in the Cleveland office that he met and began to date a little dark-haired, dark-eyed girl named Deborah Copeland, a secretary for one of the jobbing houses he was calling on. Debbie Copeland was everything Ken knew he wanted and needed in a wife — she was the sort of woman who could move up with him, no matter how high he rose. She was gay and she had a wry sense of humor that could send him into extravagant laughter, and when she kissed him he was sure. He fell in love with her, and six weeks after their first date they were married and he took her to New Orleans, where she'd always wanted to go, for the Mardi Gras, and the most glorious two weeks of his life. They then settled down temporarily in a house in Shaker Heights until Ken should finish in Cleveland and be called home to Carey Furnace. He had high hopes that he might be taken in as assistant to Mr. Vance Prescott, manager of the pipe department, who had suffered a minor heart attack and was under orders to go slow. Ken's record in Ohio had been outstanding. He had a letter from Mr. Prescott which all but promised him the assistant's job. Debbie was the only person with whom he opened up freely in regard to his ambitions, which, even then, were very high for one so young. Debbie listened with her pretty little head cocked to one side, her eyes bright. "I'm with you, honey," she said. "I won't be coy. I like money. We'll have a marvelous life together, darling."

He knew Debbie liked money, and what it could buy, and his only regret, in those days, was that he couldn't give her all the things she wanted. He was still a junior salesman, and his money wasn't coming in as fast as it was with some of their better-established friends.

Looking back on it later, Ken realized that this was where the trouble had begun. Specifically, it had begun when they met Dick and Sandy Remick at a cocktail party. Dick Remick was forty-two or so, and quite rich, having recently inherited his father's real-estate business, and Sandy was a plain woman about his own age who didn't have much to say. Dick made up for his wife's reticence, however. He was a fast and persuasive talker, and, as it later developed when they began seeing the Remicks regularly, a heavy spender. Ken Carpenter did not suspect Debbie of having an interest in Dick Remick, even after he came home from a swing around the state and found her with a mink stole which he certainly hadn't bought her. She said it was a birthday present from her aunt, in Seattle, and showed Ken the sweet little note her aunt had sent with the stole. Ken knew that Debbie had a wealthy aunt in Seattle with whom she corresponded at intervals, and the little hand-written note seemed loving and genuine. Furthermore, the stole looked beautiful on Debbie, and he told her so.

"Aunt Peg's a doll," Debbie had said. "She's just the sweetest old thing in the whole world." And she had snuggled up close to Ken in the front seat of their three-year-old Buick coach.

And then, one Tuesday afternoon in the spring of the second year of their marriage (Ken's last year in Cleveland), he returned from a sales junket a couple of days early, due to a canceled appointment, and found a white Cadillac convertible with a black top parked on the street — not in front of his own house — a block down — but seeing it, he felt a sudden loss of breath and a sick emptiness in his stomach. Either the Cadillac belonged to Dick Remick or it was one exactly like Dick's. Ken walked up the front steps to his house, his heart beating fast, hoping to find Dick standing in the living room maybe delivering something to Debbie, about to leave. But the front door was locked and, looking in, Ken saw that the living room was empty. He found his key, opened the door quietly, stepped inside and stood listening. For a moment he heard nothing. Then there was a sound which affected him like a hot wire touched lightly on his solar plexus. It came from the stairwell upstairs — a giggling laugh, followed by Debbie's voice: "Dick — Dick, for heaven's sake — please —" The rest was lost in a deeper, man's laugh.

Ken Carpenter bent and took off his shoes. In his stockinged feet he crossed the living room silently on the thick rug and tiptoed up the stairs, making so little sound that his heartbeats were loud in his ears. On the landing outside his and Debbie's bedroom he paused and listened. His mouth was quite dry and his knees were quivering and the hallway looked unnaturally bright. Then, with hideous clearness, he heard the sounds coming from inside the bedroom: a steady rhythmic squeak of the bedsprings coupled with a liquid slapping, and then, Debbie's soft moaning. In his mind's eye he saw her on the bed: her face an agony mask of passion, eyes squinted shut, mouth open, full breasts arching upward against the heavy body of her lover. Ken jumped across the hallway and seized the doorknob and wrenched at it. The door was locked.

"Debbie!" he said. "Open up! It's Ken."

Inside, there was utter silence. Then quick footsteps on the carpet, the rustle of clothes, a chair falling over and a window opening. He could have run down then, and caught Dick Remick coming off the low porch roof in his pants and shirt, lurching, terrified, across the lawn toward his car. But somehow, in this moment, he had no will power to do anything. He merely stood and waited, his breath coming in slow, distorted gasps, until he heard the roar of the departing Cadillac's engine, and then he roused himself and said, "Open up, Deb. If you don't, I'm going to kick the door down."

The door opened and his wife stood before him, dead white in her negligee, her mouth and chin pinkly smeared with her own lipstick and pink welts on her neck and shoulders. Ken knew what had made those welts. Debbie liked what she called a kiss-bite. She'd showed Ken how to do it, when they were first married. It was done with the lips, sucking fiercely, without sinking the teeth. It raised blood to the surface, but it did not break the skin.

He moved in past her, not speaking. The bed was turned fully back. They had been lying on the sheet, without covers over them. She was crying now, and begging him not to hurt her, and telling him how sorry she was. He found Dick Remick's coat and wallet on the floor where he had dropped them in his frantic flight. It was the classic comic situation of the men's magazines: the cuckolded husband, the luscious seminude wife, the departed bed companion — a picture you chuckled at in the magazine. He took the wallet out and read Remick's name on the driver's license, to be sure, absolutely sure, who it had been; and then, still not speaking to his wife, he went downstairs and found the commando knife he'd brought home from Europe as a souvenir. It had a serrated steel hand-guard and a long triangular icepick blade. It had been designed for killing quickly, from behind and by surprise. He took it in his right hand and walked down the street to the corner, turned right and covered the five blocks to Dick Remick's house. He went to the front door and knocked with his left hand, holding the commando knife in his right, and Sandy Remick answered. He said, "I'd like to see Dick, please."

She looked at the knife and then at Ken. "He's not here."

"Where is he?"

"He's not here; come in and look if you like." When she spoke, her voice was tired and full of sorrow, not fear. "I should have warned you, Ken. I wanted to, but I thought you knew what you were doing. I thought you knew what kind of a guy my husband is."

Ken looked back at the street, and then at the driveway. The white Cadillac was nowhere to be seen. Sandy was telling the truth. It made sense that Dick would not run home in the condition he'd been in — certainly not when he must expect Ken Carpenter to follow him.

"Ken," Sandy Remick said, "could I please give you a bit of advice? I couldn't care less if you killed my husband. He's had it coming for most of his life. The thing is — if you do, you'll mess up your own life. If the jury doesn't send you to the chair, they could very well put you in prison for a long time — and even if they don't do anything, you'll be all over the front pages of the papers from coast to coast, and your career will be ruined. I know how you feel. I know because I felt that way myself once." She put out her hand, suddenly, and touched his chest. "Ken, don't do it. Don't let the son-of-a-bitch mess you up. He's not worth it."

Debbie was gone when he returned to the house. He did not see her again until the divorce proceedings came into court. She did not contest. She did not ask for alimony. Actually, she wrote Ken a letter begging to come back, saying that she loved him, that what had happened had been due to drunkenness and would not happen again. Ken did not answer the letter, even though, knowing Debbie, he was certain she was speaking what was for her, at this moment, the truth. She did love him. She did think she'd be faithful. And she probably would be, too — until the next big temptation came along.

He was in complete control in the courtroom. To look at him, you would think he was there for a minor traffic violation instead of the blighting of the most precious thing in his life. He had loved and trusted Debbie. He had planned to spend the rest of his life with her. If Debbie Copeland — gay, sweet, sensitive little Debbie — was a tramp, then all women must be tramps. He was able to smile at her, even, at the settlement. The smile was a personal test he had set for himself. From now on he intended to treat women like tender useful machines, not like human beings. He would sleep with them, speak lines to them — but never again would he love them or give them a chance to hurt him.

In Enid's case he had operated in this manner. He had not said that he loved her. He had said that she was very beautiful, which she was; he had said they could go far together, in Carey Furnace, which they could; he had said he wanted to marry her, which he did — but for different reasons than she imagined. He had never spoken of loving her, either before or after their marriage. There was one thing about his life with Debbie which nobody knew, or ever would know. They would not know that Ken Carpenter, when he returned to his house in Shaker Heights with the knife in his hand, after talking to Sandy Remick, and finding his wife gone, had gone down to the cellar and sat on the steps and cried the way he hadn't cried since he was a baby.

A few months after the divorce, he was called back to Carey Furnace to be Vance Prescott's special assistant. There had been a certain amount of publicity connected with the divorce, but while it had been played up in the Cleveland papers, only one short item had appeared in the Carey Furnace *Gazette*. Ken Carpenter had not suffered by it: the fault had not been his. And his record in his work had certainly been outstanding, which was what counted. It was no secret that Ken was Vance Prescott's favorite, and that Vance was grooming him to take over the department when the older man retired in about six years.

But, as it turned out, Ken did not have to wait those six years. One afternoon in June, Vance Prescott sunk a four-foot putt on the eighth green of the Hunter's Valley Golf Club, reached down, scooped up his ball, and turned to his companion, Elwood Price, the company comptroller. Vance started to say something. Elwood Price never found out what it was. Prescott's face suddenly distorted and a hoarse sound came from his lips and he sank down on the putting green. Price sent the caddie racing to the clubhouse to summon a doctor, while he tried to make Vance Prescott comfortable. Prescott, however, was as comfortable as anyone could make him. He was dead.

There was considerable discussion about who should be appointed as Vance Prescott's successor. The assistant sales manager for pipe, T. O. Fischer, was nearing retirement age himself, and when the job was offered to him by Dave Ross, he said he would take it if Dave insisted, but frankly, he was tired, and if he did take it, there would have to be another reorganization in a year or so anyhow. He suggested Carpenter.

"I've thought of him," Ross said. "But he's young."

"He's young," T. O. Fischer said, "but he did a fine job in Cleveland and he's got his feet on the ground. I know Vance had great confidence in him."

"You wouldn't object, T.O.?"

"If I was five years younger, I'd object violently. But now — no, I wouldn't object."

"You'd give him your full support?"

"Yes, I would."

"Well, maybe we'll try him. If he doesn't work out —"

"If he doesn't work out," T. O. Fischer said, "I'll take it, Dave, and give it the best I've got."

There were many people who predicted that it wouldn't work out — that young Carpenter couldn't stand the pressure and that he would fold up in six months or less.

They couldn't have been more wrong. Ken Carpenter was not afraid of responsibility. He welcomed it. He had never been an Organization Man. He had no intention of playing everything close to the vest, keeping his nose clean, running hither and thither for advice in making decisions. He was young and he knew he was bound to make mistakes. But, like the turtle in the cartoon he'd seen in some plumbing warehouse, he "had to stick his neck out to see where the hell he was going." After Debbie, he had the recklessness which sometimes comes to a man who loses the most precious thing in his life: anything else he may lose is not very important, by comparison.

Shortly after taking over, Ken Carpenter made his most vital and unpleasant move: he fired the dead wood in the department—or, where firing was impossible, he moved them into jobs where they would be a minimum hindrance to his program. Then, when the department was smarting and jittering from this major surgery, he called together the salesmen he had left.

"I'm not interested in field reports," he said. "I don't want to read them. I want sales. I don't give a damn how you do it. I don't care if you get drunk every night and lay a different dame in every town. I don't care if you do business by phone from your hotel beds or bang down doors all over the state. What I'm interested in is this: *How much pipe do you sell?"*

He tapped the phone on the desk beside him. "This is where I'll judge you guys. By how often it rings—and by what those jobbers out there order. If you guys produce sales, you're in with Flynn. If you don't, you'll be looking for another job."

He stopped and grinned at them. "I'm not a good Joe where pipe sales are concerned. I'm the biggest son-of-a-bitch any of you guys ever saw. Which is quite a statement, because I haven't had as much practice as some of the old-timers around here." (Guarded smiles from the salesmen.) "But one thing nobody can say of me: Carpenter pinches pennies. Everybody in this room has heard the old saying that you have to spend money to make money. I go with that. I'll never question phone expenses—so long as your sales match up. I won't question entertainment, unless somebody goes ape and tries to keep a mistress in a penthouse. I do want to remind all of you, however, that I'm fresh from the plumbing circuit myself. I know what I had to spend. I don't have to use a microscope on your swindle sheets. I can look at the total and see at a glance if you're screwing the company. I mean a royal screwing—not the usual standup job we all pull, and which I don't object to." (Somewhat broader smiles from the salesmen.) "I've given you the bad news—so now

I'll give you what may be good news. I'm inaugurating a bonus system. It was used to build a great steel company by one of the greatest steel salesman who ever lived — Charley Schwab of Bethlehem. Charley believed in the profit motive, and so do I. The hell with this cradle-to-grave security. I don't want security hounds — I want tigers. So here's my philosophy in a nutshell. The more you sell the more you make."

Ken Carpenter grinned. "How about that?" They were smiling enthusiastically. Suddenly, they broke into spontaneous clapping.

"Okay, men," Ken Carpenter said. "Let's get off our dead asses and go!"

The first year he took over, Ken Carpenter increased the gross sales of Carey Furnace Pipe by eighteen per cent — so much of an increase that the board of directors authorized an enlargement of production lines in the Harrisburg plant, and increased activity in seamless casing for the oil-field market.

Now, in his screened porch in Hunter's Valley, Ken Carpenter looked out across the heat-hazed valley. Cars were beginning to pass along the highway. Church must be over. He wondered, idly, where some of the gay people of yesterday's party were now.

He'd moved around a lot, when he finally joined the party. He'd touched most of the bases except John Carey — Mr. Carey was in his room by the time Ken arrived. He made conversation with this group and that one: a short passage (mostly he'd listened) from Hardwick Benson, in the comptroller's office, about the United Steelworkers of America and how they were ruining the dollar by inflating wages; a garbled and embarrassing muddle with poor Addie Dana on modern art (Addie, dead drunk, said modern art was a crock of s-h-i-t, spelling it out, for delicacy); twenty or so personal contacts with people who could be useful to him politically around the company, among them Ben Oliver, in the treasurer's office. Ken Carpenter spent about half an hour with Oliver, discussing the tax situation, which was Ben's specialty, in the course of which he fetched Ben a drink from Kelly's bar, produced and lit a cigarette for him, and confirmed the rumor he had heard about Ben's being dissatisfied with his job. Ben hadn't said much on the subject, just enough to let Carpenter know he wasn't happy, and that indirectly. But it was all Ken needed to move to the next position in his plan for Ben: namely, setting up a date to talk to him — "to lean on you for a word of advice, old boy, if you can spare me a minute" was how Ken put it — in Ken's office at the plant. The things he had to say to Ben would have to be said cold sober, and with great care. Ben was a little pale-faced man with a prim manner and dead-fish eyes, but he was very sharp indeed along certain lines. Ken would have to move carefully with Ben Oliver, and move in such a manner that he never committed himself at all — unless Ben Oliver committed himself first. . . .

Now, on the screened verandah, Ken Carpenter thought of the one really spectacular thing which had happened to him at the party — the picture he'd taken with the Polaroid-Land camera in the pines above the Carey mansion. Paul Dana was probably wondering who had been behind that flashbulb last night — wondering hard, and worrying, through a horrible hangover. Dottie O'Brien, from what he'd heard of her, wouldn't be worrying much, if at all. She and her late husband, if the reports Ken had heard were even close to accurate, hadn't been averse to publicity, or even to actual onlookers, at their sexual goings on. Ken had heard from alleged eyewitnesses about lights left purposely burning behind the shaggy boxwoods that shielded the front windows of the O'Briens' house in River View Terrace — and about the prolonged seduction, on the living room sofa, of Dottie O'Brien by her husband, in full view of anyone who cared to cross the lawn and peer through the branches of the box. There was a word in the sex specialists' lingo to cover people like that — people who got more thrill out of it when they were being watched.

No, Dottie wouldn't be worried about a flash picture — even though she couldn't know for sure that her own face did not appear on the film. Her face was hidden. Only her short curly hair showed, far from the camera, at the edge of Dana's jacket. In the foreground, however, her full-spread thighs and the flesh between them was caught with diamond sharpness by the lens, and Dana's face, raised, looking into the camera, was detailed as a studio portrait. . . .

Ken Carpenter was correct in his surmise that Dottie O'Brien was not worrying about the happenings of the night. She was not even hung over. Dottie never had liked liquor particularly, even when she was a young debutante and gin parties were the rage. She'd been Dottie Unangst, daughter of a well-to-do lumber dealer in town — a roly-poly baby, a plump, horribly freckled little girl who so much resembled a little golden-red pig that the children nicknamed her Porky, and who was a tomboy who could climb a tree, skip a stone on a pond, or jump from the top of a barn into a haymow as well and bravely as most boys. Porky Unangst was known as a "piggy little tomboy" in those days by people who disapproved of her, and as a "cute little bundle of energy" by those who liked her. The latter group was far in the majority, for she was a child with a sunny disposition, not inclined to mope or pout, and who took her many bumps and abrasions without a great deal of yelling and complaining.

When Porky Unangst got to high school, her freckled roly-poly shape took on womanly curves. Her father, who was a practical man, foresaw that his daughter might be the target of amorous youths bent on seduction, and he took her aside and explained the dangers of pregnancy and venereal disease. Porky listened attentively, not in fear or worry, but with interest, because she had already had intercourse with four different boys in such likely places as the woods, the haymow of the barn of a friend of the family, and twice in the toolshed of her own house with the eighteen-year-old boy who cut the lawn. She had never felt guilty about sex the way other people seemed to. Why feel guilty about something so very enjoyable? You might as well feel guilty about eating a juicy steak! Sex had never given her anything but fun. She had never gotten pregnant nor contracted any disease, and, as she grew older, she was able to be more selective in her choice of sexual companions. She chose only the best, those she considered to be the best, and when she was eighteen, she went to a doctor in Pittsburgh and had herself fitted with a diaphragm, from which time she never worried further about pregnancy. Her high school and college life was probably as active socially as is possible within a twenty-four-hour day or a seven-day week.

She married Tommy O'Brien while she was a senior at Mount Holyoke and he was a senior at Yale. They came back and set up housekeeping in the place in River View Terrace and, until his death in his Mercedes, ten years later, lived a life of unrestrained sensual enjoyment: winters in Nassau or Spain or Hawaii (Tommy had an inheritance of almost a million dollars from his father), summers in Wyoming on a dude ranch, fishing in Canada, or in the social whirl in Carey Furnace itself — golf, riding, swimming, dancing, drinking, parties.

The parties, at least some of the more spectacular ones, might have been compared to Roman orgies. It was in the days before wife-trading got into the headlines, but trade wives they certainly did — whole parties of them. It did not take place immediately, of course. There had been a period of time, and quite a lengthy one, in which the couples merely chatted and drank and danced and conducted themselves the way married couples in more conservative circumstances normally do. But eventually there was a stolen kiss when the lights were low and the dancing was in progress, closer pressing of chest and breasts, a deeper probing of the knees between skirted thighs, which, over a period of time, was not enough. Bob Searles and his wife Susan had known Tommy and Dottie O'Brien (the nickname of Porky had been dropped except when somebody was very drunk and used it inadvertently from the habit of childhood) since they were kids. Bob was a thoughtful, studious-looking man who wore dark-rimmed glasses. Sue was tall and well built, with a small tight bob, full, somewhat loose lips and creases under her eyes from late hours and too much drinking, but she was a good mother when morning came, and Bob had a very successful legal practice in town (he handled all of Tommy O'Brien's work, for one thing).

Tommy O'Brien, apparently, had been wanting Sue Searles for a long time, and one night when they ran out of highball mix and Tommy drove into town, he asked Sue if she wanted to go for the ride. She said she did. They left and did not return for two hours. No questions were asked at the time, but when the party was over, both Bob and Dottie asked their respective spouses what had happened during that two-hour trip for soda which was ten or fifteen minutes away. Sue said they'd had a flat tire. Tommy said the same. But Dottie Unangst was not to be taken in by any such stories without investigating. She went out the next morning, while Tommy was still asleep, and looked at the tires. The four tires which the car had come with were still on it — and the spare, brand-new, still reposed inside the trunk. Dottie lost no time in mentioning this to Tommy. He was hung over at the time, and too weak to think clearly, and in half an hour she had his confession. He and Sue had gone to the ruins of the old Welles mansion, off the Butler Road, and driven in under the wild tangle of abandoned lilac bushes, beside the crumbling swimming pool, and done a little necking. A little necking, Dottie had said — you and Sue have done more than a little necking, right on the dance floor in our house. It must have been more than that. It had been more than that, and before she was through, Dottie had it all. Tommy had got Sue in the back seat and screwed her good was what it amounted to. He admitted it. He even admitted, when he woke up a little and his head began to ache, and he began to get sick of answering questions, that it had been good. In fact, it had been very good. Dottie's eyes had tightened at the corners.

"I wonder what Bob's like," she said.

He looked at her. "Why don't you find out?"

"Well, honey," she said softly, "I think I may just do that."

That was how the wife-trading between the O'Briens and the Searleses had begun. The next time there had been a party, Dottie had asked Bob if he cared to join her in going for highball mix. Tommy had not looked at her when she left. He had made no objection. And Sue had not looked at Bob.

On the way out of the drive, Dottie started to tell Bob Searles about Sue and Tommy, but Bob stopped her. He knew all about it, he said — even the place they'd gone — the old Welles mansion.

Dottie looked across the car in the dashlights and grinned at him. "Would you care to take a little drive?" she said. "Before we pick up the soda?"

"I'd like to take a little drive," Bob Searles said. "Where would you suggest?"

"Well, I was thinking about the old Welles mansion."

"That's funny," Bob said. "I was thinking of the same place."

They were gone an hour and a half, and, from Dottie's point of view, it was very satisfactory. Bob Searles was nervous and excited, as might be expected, and he was very fast the first time. But after they'd smoked a cigarette and talked and looked at the glow from the slag dump on the low clouds, Bob had himself more in hand. The second time it was very good indeed — so good that Dottie cried out and clutched at him in a way she hadn't done with her husband for a long time.

When they got back to the party there was no sign of Sue and Tommy. But after Dottie had looked around the yard and found the Searleses' car still in place and nobody lying under any bushes, she had gone to the bedroom door. It was locked. She paused and listened. She could hear nothing. She went away, and about twenty minutes later, Sue appeared from upstairs looking tousled, well satisfied and drunk, saying she had been in the bathroom. Dottie knew Sue hadn't been in the bathroom, because she had looked in there trying to find her. Tommy never came down at all. When she went up to the now unlocked bedroom, he was in bed under the covers, apparently asleep. The place reeked of *My Sin,* a perfume Dottie did not use, and which Sue was wearing that night. In the morning, when Dottie looked at the bed, she found lipstick on the sheet, down about the middle of the bed. It was an odd place. She had expected to find it around the pillow at the head of the bed, and she asked Tommy about it.

"Look," he said, "are we going to run an inquisition every morning after a party? How the hell would I know how the lipstick got in my bed, down there on the sheet or wherever you said it was?"

"It's not wherever I said it was," Dottie said. "It's where it is. Now. You want to come up and look at it?"

"All right," he said. "Where were you and Bob?"

"At the Welles estate," Dottie told him sweetly. "Parked under the lilacs."

"Then you can't kick, can you?"

"Who said I was kicking, darling? Bob is magnificent, really. A little quick on the trigger — but wonderful staying power."

"I'm so happy for you," Tommy said.

"Sue surprises me a little," Dottie said. "I didn't realize she was so resourceful."

"Oh, Sue is very resourceful indeed."

"How about you, dear? Are you resourceful too?"

"What do you mean?"

"Well, sauce for the goose is sauce for the gander, isn't it?"

"I don't follow you."

"Well, Sue obviously did you a special favor. I was wondering if you rendered the same honors to her."

"What honors?"

"Oh, God," Dottie said, laughing. "Do I have to draw you a diagram?"

"Well," Tommy said, "if you want to know the truth we rendered each other the same special favor at the same time."

"Thank you, dear," Dottie said. "It won't be necessary to spell it out for me. I think I grasp the implications. I suppose I'm right in assuming that if Sue did it with you, she probably does it with Bob too."

"I'm sure she does," Tommy said. "Why not do some research with Bob?"

"That's the second time you've suggested research with Bob," Dottie said. "I took your advice the first time, and I think I'll take it again. This special favor, mutually offered and received, might be a lot of fun."

"It might," Tommy said. "Do we have any Empirin tablets, dear?"

"I'm sure we do, dear," Dottie said. "You'll find them in the bathroom."

"Would you get them for me?" he said. "I mean, we're still friends, aren't we?"

"Oh, of course," Dottie said. "We're the best friends in the world. Tommy and Sue, Bob and Dottie, or Tommy and Dottie and Bob and Sue — like interchangeable parts in the same screwing machine, you might say."

"Please, dear," Tommy said. "The tablets, will you?"

"Oh, definitely," Dottie said. "Coming right up, friend."

The pattern was established, and it progressed onward. Extramarital play, like dope, operates under the law of diminishing returns. Innovations — like a dope addict's increase in his fix — are needed to keep the titillation level high. This time it was Dottie who provided the innovation. One evening when the four of them were sitting in the living room drinking stingers and listening to the hi-fi, she said, "I just had a great idea."

"What was that?" Bob Searles said.

"Let's go to bed."

"You mean you're kicking us out?" Bob said. "Darling, it's only eleven."

"I'm not kicking you out," Dottie said, laughing. "I'm not talking about sleeping. We have twin beds in our room." She paused. "If we tried real hard, I'm sure all four of us could make do with those beds real fine. And if we couldn't, the floor has a nice thick carpet and a nice thick rugmat under it."

Nobody spoke for a few seconds. Then Tommy said, "Dottie, you're a genius. Sue, what do you think?"

"It's new," Sue said. "It's different." She looked at Bob. He wasn't looking at her. He was looking at Dottie O'Brien. Sue laughed. "I guess we don't have to ask old Glassy Eye what he thinks," she said. "I guess we better get up to the bedroom before my darling husband has his way with my darling little redheaded friend — right here in the living room!"

It had been, Dottie thought, indeed new and different. They had left a lamp burning on the dresser, a low-wattage lamp with a pink shade. They had brought their drinks with them. There had been a little confusion about undressing until Sue came up with the idea of playing strip poker — for real, right down to the skin — instead of just to the bra and panties and the undershorts, the way it was mostly played. Finally they had arrived at the natural state, all of them very drunk, and the new experience had proved to be the best thing they'd dreamed up yet. Dottie had been particularly interested in Sue. Sue, it developed, was a talker. She said some rare and wonderful things to Tommy in the dim pink light on the white rug of the O'Brien bedroom. Not bad, Dottie had thought at the time, not bad at all — she would have to remember some of those things and use them herself . . . but she hadn't. In the morning she hadn't remembered anything but a pink haze in which bodies twisted and turned at an odd perspective, and the pounding hangover had discouraged her from further efforts of memory.

But even the new and the different had finally lost its excitement for the O'Briens and the Searleses. By the time Tommy had killed himself in his Mercedes, the foursome had diverted to other partners in the group. Cliff Lambert and Stevie, his Texas wife, had been the next couple to play with the O'Briens. Frank and Sandra Stuckey moved into the game with the Searleses. Nobody got murdered, but two marriages broke up as a result of the parties at the O'Brien house. Nothing got into the newspapers, but the gossip around town was rich and detailed. When Tommy O'Brien smashed himself to a pulp on the highway, people said he had got just about what was coming to him. You couldn't expect much else from the kind of deal that fast rich crowd went in for. Like a mass of worms, somebody said, all writhing around in the same can. And this, at the end, had been a pretty good thumbnail description of the O'Brien house about three in the morning, after a hard-drinking party.

So, sitting up in bed now, in August, in her house overlooking the valley, Dottie O'Brien had no particular worries about the photograph which somebody had taken of her and Paul Dana, vice president in charge of public relations for the steel company. And last night, at least, Dana hadn't worried much either. He'd been too drunk and too eager, and after his first shock and rage were gone, he hadn't lost his nerve and run for home — not Dana. He was a tough and satisfactory man, and Dottie was looking forward to seeing him again, and often. . . .

Monday

MONDAY morning came upon Carey Furnace, Pennsylvania, with the same reluctant weariness with which it came to the other working towns in the United States. The quiet pressing heat that had characterized all mornings for over a month was present. The sun slid up from behind the horizon and flared on the valley, lonely and crimson like the sun of doomsday after a paralyzing atomic attack. Coming through the east window of Howard Snyder's attic bedroom, the sun laid a shaggy pathway of bloody light on the rug; it illuminated the straw inside Hubie's kennel, causing the animal to wiggle peevishly into a dark corner; it painted rich crimson bars from the cracks between the venetian blinds on the wall of the bedroom which Jake Abbott shared with Frances, his wife.

For the past several minutes, Jake had been trying, without success, to shut out the zany palaver which was taking place, across the room, between his wife and his young son. Frances was playing a game known in the family as "eenie weenie pider." The game had evolved from a poem in which an eenie weenie pider had "wun up a water pout," and then "awong had come a wain and washed a pider out." Fran, when she played the game with Hank, reduced herself to the role of a baby. She professed terror of floating feathers, flapping window curtains, or small harmless animals, crying out, in a tiny voice, "Oooo! I'm scared! I'm afwaid!" When on her feet, she would run about with her two hands held under her chin, wrists flopping, eyes staring, stiff-legged, like a doll. When lying down, the game took unpredictable turns. Now Jake could hear Hank's voice saying, disgustedly, "Ah, come *on,* Mummy! Cut the comedy, will yah, and get up!"

Jake heard Fran's voice simper. "Ants is stronger than *you* are! Could pull an elephant with just their little fingies. That's what ants kin do, pull big bugs, big as elephants to them with just their teeny weeny little fingies."

"Oh, boy!" Hank's voice said.

"I wanta be a bee," Fran simpered. " 'Cause bees got more *legs* than *we* got. And they got great big wonderful *eyes!*"

"Mummy!" Hank yelled, driven beyond endurance. "Will you please stop acting like a moron and get up!"

"An' bees kin fly," Fran simpered. "They don't need no planes 'cause they don't have no Russians gonna bomb them." And then, irrelevantly, "Only reason we got a house is 'cause we ain't got no *fur.*"

Hank made a strangled sound and Jake sat up in bed in time to see the boy leaving the room hurriedly, making a cranking motion beside his ear with his clenched fist.

Jake looked across at his wife. She had closed her eyes and was pretending to be asleep. He loved her now, in all ways, far more than when he had married her; and yet, at that time, he had thought he loved her completely. Then she had been an eager and passionate mistress who burned the toast, let the milk sour on the back steps, and threw away socks without darning them, even though Jake was broke. She had never darned a sock in the years of their marriage, but she had done just about everything else. She could, for example, snatch night-crawlers from their gluey tunnels in the lawn by flashlight when Hank was behind in his worm deliveries to the fishing dock above town. She could shorten the hem of a dress in twenty minutes before a party if Nancy suddenly developed a traumatic reluctance to appear with the last two inches "hanging way down around my ankles." She could console a shattered husband when he received a manila envelope containing a rejected manuscript in the mail and opened it to find it crinkled so badly it would have to be retyped. She was a demon in the lost-and-found department, whether it be one stray sock, the car keys, last year's income-tax carbons, or a plane ticket on the morning the plane was due to leave. And yet, with all, she was still a glamour girl when she put on her party clothes, still passionate (and much, much more adept), and still faithful to Jake's stern admonitions not to wear a girdle. With the hips Fran had, Jake always said, a girdle was a crime against organized fanny-watchers. Not that he approved of others watching Frances's fanny — but he liked to watch it himself, and he did not propose to have it yanked out of shape by a bunch of silly elastic threads.

Jake sat up in bed. He said, "Fran, honey . . ."

She did not reply, although he knew she had heard him. Then he got out of bed and made his way to the bathroom, hoping to reach it before Hank or Nancy pre-empted it. He was too late. The door was shut, and when he tried it, it was locked, which meant that Nancy was inside, going through her interminable primping. He said, "Jesus," softly, under his breath — but not softly enough, apparently, since a sigh of the sixteen-year-old martyr, exposed to all the indignities and crudenesses of a barbarian father, was heard from behind the door. He sucked in his breath, and, sternly keeping his early-morning inclination to irritability in check, he said, reasonably, "It's Daddy, honey. Hurry it up, if you can. I've got a big day ahead, and I'm running late. . . ."

Inside the bathroom, Nancy gave no reply. She was thinking of Lady Pamela Brett-Shaw, the beautiful Englishwoman who was the heroine of *The Secret of Marston Moor,* which Nancy was reading. Lady Pamela was not forced to race through her early-morning toilet, or listen to baby talk from a frivolous mother, or suffer the uncouth rampaging of an insensitive little beast of a brother. Nancy gripped her hands tightly over the wash basin and glared at her face in the mirror, her lips compressed. Then she spoke sweetly, controlling herself, "All right, Daddy. I'll hurry."

Twenty minutes later, the Abbott family was seated at the breakfast table in the kitchen. Henry was wearing shorts only, his skin brown as a native pearl diver's. Nancy was wearing a becoming frock, white with vertical pink stripes. Jake was wearing what he called his news-gathering uniform — summer-weight blue suit, white button-down collar, dark red bow tie which fastened to the collar by steel clips, a white handkerchief in his suit-coat pocket, dark red socks and black shoes. Fran wore a skirt and cotton pullover which showed off her full figure. Jake, eating eggs and bacon, said, with his mouth full, "Mighty attractive body you're wearing that cloth on this morning, Mrs. A."

Nancy's nose wrinkled. "Oh, Daddy — please!"

"What's the matter, Nance?"

"Don't mind Daddy, honey," Fran said to her daughter. "He doesn't mean anything."

"Of course I mean something," Jake said. "If I have a wife with a pretty figure, I like to tell her about it."

"Nancy wants you to be dignified," Fran said. "Please — it means a lot to her."

"All right," Jake said, grinning. "I'll have to be dignified this morning, later on, so I may as well start now."

"I don't want any bacon," Henry said. "It smells bad."

"Henry!"

"Okay, okay," Henry said. "But not much. Just a slice."

Fran placed two strips of bacon on her son's plate and smiled at her husband. "News Letter today, dear?"

"Approvals," he said, "on new items. I've really got some gassers lined up this month. You may be glad to know that the inspection department of the billet mill has racked up two million man-hours without a fatal accident, and the State Safety Council has authorized them to hang a plaque to that effect in Mr. Dobelmeyer's office. I have Mr. Dobelmeyer's very own hand-written account of the exciting record, in ten closely spaced pages, including the names of all his family and immediate relatives."

"How can you run ten pages on Mr. Dobelmeyer, Daddy?" Hank said. "The whole letter is only four pages, ain't it?"

"Obviously I can't, son. I'm cutting it to one line. Want to hear another hot flash, Fran?"

"Not particularly," Fran said. "I suppose you have to go to that awful picnic."

"Kindly do not speak of Mr. George Hurd's annual orgy of togetherness as 'that awful picnic,'" Jake said. "Not in public, at least, not if you wish a husband — whose employment in the Carey Furnace Steel Company depends directly on this same George Hurd — to enjoy steady work."

"I suppose Eleanor Keck will be there," Frances said.

Jake grinned. "The annual department picnic would not be complete without La Belle Keck. Last summer she —"

Nancy rose abruptly, and hurried from the room.

"Now what was *that* about?" Jake said, bewildered.

"She thought you were going to tell that horrible story about the poison ivy," Frances said.

"What poison ivy?" Henry asked with sudden interest.

"Nothing, dear," Frances said. "It wouldn't interest you."

"It would too," Henry said. "Aw gee, that's lousy — get a person all interested and then clam up —"

"It's really nothing, Hank," Jake said. "Miss Keck is one of the stenographers at the office and last summer she fell in a poison-ivy patch — and she was very sick with it, and that's all."

"Why did Nancy run away then? If that's all there was?"

"Darling," Frances said, "Nancy is going through a phase. We have to be very careful what we say in front of her — you too, Hen dear."

"Oh, nuts," Henry said. "This place is getting loony."

"Want more coffee, dear?" Frances said, smiling at her husband.

He looked at his watch. "Half a cup. Maybe I can get it down before Jack beeps."

But as it happened, he didn't. Jack McHugh's shave-and-haircut on the horn signaled he was now waiting on the upper driveway, even before Frances could lift the coffee pot. Jake rose. "That's it, baby. Got to run. See you tonight."

"All right, darling. Have a good day."

He kissed his wife and hurried out of the kitchen, brief case in hand.

Eleanor Keck, who worked as a typist in George Hurd's department, was awakened in the small bedroom she shared with her sister Miriam by the sound of Benny running. Benny was a hamster. All day long he slept in his nest of cedar shavings. At night he woke up and began to run in his wire exercise wheel. It made a thin whirring noise and some nights it almost drove Eleanor to distraction. Miriam, who was eight years old, also had other pets. She had a rather lethargic goldfish named Google Eye and a toad named Baldy. Baldy's full name was Everett R. Bibinger (which happened also to be the name of the bald-headed principal of the grade school which Miriam attended). Everett R. Bibinger was reputed to have a brutal sadistic nature, and Miriam had named the toad after him to get even. In truth, Miriam was very fond of Baldy the toad, and went to considerable lengths to keep him fully supplied with fat flies and spiders and other delicacies. Miriam loved all creatures, big and small, and they had a very hard time with her when Eleanor's father — on Sundays when he was sober enough — drove them around through the country. Every time Miriam saw a cow or a horse in a field she would start yelling for her daddy to stop the car so she could get out and coax the animal over to the fence to pet it. All animals seemed to like Miriam as much as she liked them, which wasn't really surprising. When you liked a person, Eleanor knew, they usually liked you too.

Now she sat up in bed, groggy from the eighty-degree heat, and looked at her little sister, who was crouched with her back to Eleanor's bed, peering at Benny running in his cage. "Mir, honey," Eleanor said, "what time is it?"

The younger girl started. "Oh, gee, you scared me, Ellie. I dunno. Mom's up getting breakfast. I been hearing her out in the kitchen."

"Is Daddy up?"

"He didn't come in last night," Miriam said, poking a sunflower seed through the bars of Benny's cage. "I guess he was loaded again."

"Oh Mir — you shouldn't talk like that!"

"Why not?" Miriam said matter-of-factly. "He gets loaded nearly every night, don't he? Hey, Benny, *eat* it, cantcha? Don't go stuffing it in your pouch, stupid!"

Eleanor smiled and put her feet over the side of the bed. The bureau was so close her knees almost touched it. A doll in a pink party dress, which one of Eleanor's boy friends had won at the dart concession at the Butler Fair, stood on the bureau. Beside the doll was her senior yearbook from Carey Furnace High School. There were a number of pictures of Eleanor in the book: one showing her jumping up in the air holding a megaphone, when she was in the cheerleaders; one showing her in the leading role of *Time Out for Ginger;* and quite a few group shots.

Eleanor had been very popular and happy in high school. She had been voted the prettiest girl in the senior class, and the best dancer. There wasn't a boy in the school who hadn't been, at one time or another, a little in love with Eleanor Keck. She was small and dark-haired, with a soft shapely figure, and she learned early to open her lips a little when she kissed and to trail the tips of her fingers over the back of the boy's neck. Eleanor didn't mind kissing on the first date, if she liked the boy, and she fell in love at regular intervals. Puppy love, the old folks called it, and laughed at it as silly. Well, the old folks didn't know a thing. Puppy love was the sweetest, nicest, most exciting kind of love in the world. It made you want to cry and laugh at the same time. Sometimes it was so piercing sweet you could hardly stand it: like the afternoon Jimmy Thompson ran wide around right end, dodged two tacklers, and scatted down the sideline for the winning touchdown against Butler High. Jimmy and Eleanor had been going together at the time, and after Jimmy touched the ball down over the goal, he'd straightened and looked over at the cheering section, and waved to Eleanor. Just to her. And all the cheerleaders had seen it and known Jimmy was dedicating that touchdown to his best girl. Eleanor had been so proud and happy she'd almost wept.

Things had changed now that she was working for the steel company. She was still the prettiest girl around, but the men were different. They wanted one thing from her, most of them, and she could tell by looking at them what it was. She realized that a girl couldn't be simple and sweet all the time and believe everything anyone told her. A girl had to look out for herself. Nobody else was going to do it for her.

Eleanor Keck was, however, in love. She was in love with Don Francisco, who wrote copy, smoked a pipe, had big dark eyes and long eyelashes, who never went through a door ahead of a woman, who tipped his hat the way old-fashioned gentlemen did when he passed you on the street — and who was engaged (at least, that's what everybody said) to Ruthie Delaney. Eleanor Keck did not know Ruthie Delaney personally, because Ruthie had gone to a private school, but she did not like her. There was no reason except the best reason of all: Ruthie was going to get Don Francisco, and Eleanor Keck got a little weak in the knees every time Don placed a piece of copy on her desk to type. Lately, she had begun to take just a little hope. The annual picnic was coming up, and Don had asked her if she would like to take a canoe ride with him. She had said she would, even though she had been suspicious at the time (gentleman or no gentleman) that Don Francisco was just like all the rest of them. He was going to try to get as much as he could from Eleanor Keck — and still keep Ruthie Delaney for the big deal.

Well, if he thought that way, he'd just have another think coming. . . .

"Ellie," Miriam said now, suddenly, "do you believe in God?"

Eleanor looked at her sister, startled. "What's that?"

"Do you believe in God, Ellie?"

"Why, of course I believe in God," Eleanor said. "Everybody believes in God."

"I don't," Miriam said.

"Now, don't you talk that way, you hear? It's terrible and —"

"Well, I don't," Miriam said. "Mom told me it's in the Bible that if you believe in God — really believe in Him — and keep praying long enough, you could move a mountain if you wanted to." Eleanor, watching her sister, saw her eyes narrow. "Well, I don't want to move an old mountain, Ellie. All I want is for Daddy to stop drinking. So I've been praying, every night now for nearly a month, and I've been *believing,* honest I have —"

"Honey," Eleanor said softly. "Listen, honey —"

"And it's a lie!" Miriam suddenly cried out. "It's just a rotten stinkin' lie. God can't move any mountains! He can't even stop my own Daddy from going into a bar! So I don't believe in Him any more, and I never will!"

The door to the room opened and a harassed-looking woman, her face red from the August heat and the stove, called in, "Eggs are ready, girls! You better hurry, Ellie, or you'll be late for your job."

"Coming right away, Mom, as soon as I'm dressed."

"All right — make it snappy!"

"We will, Mom," Miriam said. "We'll be right there."

The door closed. Eleanor got quickly out of bed in her nightgown and started for the door on her way to the bathroom. But she stopped beside her little sister. Impulsively, she put her arm around her and hugged her tight. Then she hurried out to the bathroom.

Mrs. Herman Stegmeyer sat in her kitchen on Grandview Avenue, watching her husband eat his breakfast. On his plate were half a dozen fried eggs and three quarters of a pound of fried bacon. He was maneuvering one of the eggs onto a piece of butter-drenched toast with a silver table knife, holding the toast next to the plate and easing the egg over onto it, being careful not to break the yolk. This completed, he dusted the yolk heavily with pepper and salt, and took the toast up in his pudgy right hand. Vivian Stegmeyer wanted to turn away, or shut her eyes, but she did not. She watched him lay six strips of bacon on the open sandwich with his left hand, then lift it toward his wide-open mouth.

None of the details were spared her. The pink gums, the gleaming false teeth, the dark wet opening of his throat, as he bit juicily into the eggs, bacon, butter, and toast, a little of the yolk spurting out on his thick red lips, and began to move his jaws heavily. He ate slowly, with noisy relish, and she saw his tongue go out, from time to time, to lick his lips, and then he stopped chewing and put his fingers into his mouth, sucking the butter which had dripped onto them from the toast. He was not looking at his wife. He was reading the morning paper. Without looking up from the paper, he picked up his coffee cup, drained it, set it down, and said. "Vivian — more coffee, please."

She went to the stove without speaking and got the pot and poured his cup nearly full. She carried it back and set it beside him. He did not look up or thank her. He said, "Some write-up they got here on the Carey party."

She did not reply. He creamed his coffee heavily, spooned sugar into it, and stirred it. Something, bacon probably, was stuck in his teeth. He made a loud but ineffectual sucking sound, then removed a toothpick from the bowl on the table and began probing for the bit of food. Finally, he managed to dislodge it. He said, "Well, they got our names spelled right on the guest list. That's something." He went on reading. His wife sat silently, and he looked up presently. "What's the matter?" he said. "Are you ill?"

"No, Herman. I'm all right."

He stared at her, his pink jowls moving rhythmically, then picked up a second piece of toast and slid an egg onto it. He bit into this

piece as before, and said, through his chewing, "Where's Louise?"
"She's gone. She got up early."
"Why?"
"They're having an advertising picnic on Thursday, and she's been asked to help with the preparations."
"What preparations could Louise help with?"
"I don't know. Something at Mr. Hurd's camp on Black River. She didn't know herself. She was asked to go up tomorrow and supervise the work, something like that. She wanted to get up early and get it all organized."
Suddenly he belched. He made no effort to reduce the sound of the gas rushing up from his stomach. Instead, he tried to induce a continuance, failed, and looked suddenly at his wife, making no more reference to the picnic, and rapped out: "Watch the lights, will you, Vivian! I don't know if it was you or Louise, but somebody left them burning in the cellar all night. I just happened to go down there before breakfast and caught it — or they'd probably have burned all day. I'm not interested in helping the Pennsylvania Power and Light Company declare extra dividends, dear."
She nodded.
"And pick those blackberries out by the garage. There must be a quart there, at least — a little bit dried up by the heat, but still worth picking."
She nodded again.
"I won't be home for lunch. I'm eating at the hotel."
"All right."
"What are you planning for supper?"
"I don't know. I haven't thought about it yet."
"I think we might have chicken breasts," he said. "The usual servings."
"All right."
"My God, Vivian! 'All right. All right.' Is that all you can say?" He stared at her a moment.
She made no reply. She sat and thought about Jesus Christ and how He had suffered on the cross and how anybody who turned to

Him could be comforted. She knew that Jesus was watching, right now, and had been watching her all her life, and she knew that He had a sweet and sorrowful smile on His face, and that His hands were waiting at all moments of the day and night to touch His children with a cooling, reassuring touch when they were frightened or confused or in any sort of trouble. During her life with Herman, there was one Friend who had never forsaken her and never would forsake her, and she knew this even though He never spoke to her or appeared before her or gave any sign. If you had faith, you did not need a sign, and Vivian had faith. There were times when she felt guilty because she felt good, almost exultant, when her personal lot grew harder. She, too, was bearing a cross. She was not climbing Calvary, and no nails would pierce her hands nor a spear her side, but she was bearing a cross and the thought of it made her eyes moist, and a great hot ache spread from her mouth down into her throat. She was trudging the same sort of path Our Lord had trod, and, like Him, one day she would be with God in paradise. Thy Will be done, on earth as it is in Heaven.

"Vivian," Herman said sharply. "Are you sick?"

"What?"

"You look like a sick cow," Herman said.

"I'm not sick," Vivian said.

"Communing with Our Lord, eh? That it?"

May God have mercy on him, she thought.

"You shouldn't talk that way," she said.

Herman gave her a bored look. "Oh, you're loony," he said.

He took his eyes away from her and looked at his plate, where only two eggs yet remained. He was out of toast. He picked up his fork. Vivian closed her eyes. Ten more minutes. That was all. Then he'd be gone. Ten more minutes. The sounds of his chewing and swallowing were again audible in the quiet kitchen. . . .

Paul Dana, vice president in charge of public relations for the Carey Furnace Steel Company, had slept badly since the night of the party when someone had taken a flash photograph of him and

Dottie O'Brien in the pines above the Carey house. Who the photographer might be, Dana had no idea, but he was reasonably sure it was a blackmailer, and expected that he would be contacted by phone at any time. He had been too intoxicated that night, and too engrossed in what he was doing, to react quickly after the flash. His eyes had been temporarily blinded so that he had no way of knowing whether the photographer had been a man or a woman. Whoever it was, Dana thought grimly, had him dead to rights. If that picture was in the hands of an unscrupulous person, Dana's career and his marriage were both ruined beyond repair.

Dana had not worried too much the night it had happened. He had been too drunk and too confused, and — he might as well face it — too hot. He had been unable to give chase to the intruder and, surprisingly enough, Dottie O'Brien hadn't seemed particularly upset. In fact, she'd even giggled a little and acted as if the whole thing were a lark. The fat was in the fire, she'd said, so there wasn't much use in worrying. If Paul wanted to, they could go over to her house on River View Terrace and complete what they had so happily begun. Dana, drunk and excited, had agreed. They left the party, leaving Adelaide to drive home alone in Dana's car, and had covered the back roads in Dottie's car to her house. There they had gone into the kitchen and had three very strong scotch-on-the-rocks, gone upstairs and taken a shower together, and gone into the bedroom. They should have gone there in the first place, Paul Dana said, when they were lying together on the smooth sheets in the dark. It was much better than pine needles.

"You're just a little country boy, Paul," Dottie had chuckled. "Anybody can have fun in the bedroom. The real kicks come when you have a chance of being caught."

"Shut up," Paul gasped, the conversation coming at a time when he was involved elsewhere. "Just shut up and lie still now. . . ."

Dottie had shut up, but she had not lain still. It had been a most exciting night — but the morning after had been quite another matter. Dana had gotten home just before dawn with a fiercely aching head, the guilt feelings which always came to him after a night of heavy drinking, and the worry that the alcohol and the sex had pushed out of his mind during the hours of darkness now bore down upon him. He'd have two choices, very probably: pay off the blackmailer; or refuse to pay him and be exposed and lose his job and his wife. Of course he also had a third choice that he sometimes read about in the tabloids. He could pretend to go along with the blackmailer, and then, if and when he was sure the man or woman had no accomplices, he could kill him or her. This, Paul Dana had no intention of doing. He had plenty of money, and he had been bored with his wife (and even with his job) for a long time. He was a tough, realistic man. He could dish it out, but when the time came, as it sometimes did, he could also take it. He resolved that he would tell the blackmailer to go to hell and then brace himself for the worst. When it came, he would simply liquidate his holdings, give his wife (for whom he felt responsible, even though he didn't love her) enough money to live on comfortably, and take off for Europe or South America. It would be messy and embarrassing, but it would be short — and ten days after it was over the local gossip would turn to something newer.

But no blackmail phone call came — not on Sunday at least — and now, at his desk on Monday morning, Paul Dana was beginning to hope faintly that a miracle had happened — that the photographer had somehow bitched up the picture and there was no real evidence at all. Dana did not really believe this, but it was a positive approach, and he was a man who believed in taking the positive approach whenever possible.

Just before lunchtime he left the office and went across the street and put in a call from a pay booth. When a familiar woman's voice answered, he said, "Hello, sweetheart. It's Paul."

"Oh . . . Paul . . . I was just thinking about you. Anything happen yet?"

"Not a thing."

"Maybe they're giving us time to worry a little," Dottie O'Brien said.

"Maybe," Paul said. He paused. "Dottie . . ."

"Yes?"

"I was wondering—if you were doing anything around four o'clock . . ."

He heard her giggle. "Why, yes," she said. "As it happens, I do have some plans. I'm going to take a nice bath and go up to the bedroom and relax. . . ."

"With the downstairs door unlocked?"

Dottie laughed outright. "Of course, silly," she said. "Of course with the downstairs door unlocked. What did you expect?"

When Jake Abbott reached his office in the advertising department of the steel company, he found Doug Schroeder, the assistant art director, waiting for him. Schroeder was a thin-faced, hawk-nosed man with the ability to find the vulnerable point of any person he disliked—and then suddenly dig into it, like a sadistic doctor needlessly probing a wound. Jake never had liked him. He had heard him and seen him in action too often. Sometimes he was genuinely funny, but more often his humor depended on inflicting real distress on his victims. Max Roth, in the photographic department, had a large nose, and Doug Schroeder referred to it as a Durante Special, and speculated on how many nickels it might hold if stuffed full. Nellie Laubach, in the stenographers' bullpen, had an apologetic, bewildered manner of speaking and acting which was Doug Schroeder's meat. He could mimic Nellie so well, most people couldn't help laughing, even though they knew they shouldn't, and a lot of them said Doug had missed his calling. He should be doing imitations of Lionel Barrymore or Jimmy Cagney on television. Be this as it might, Schroeder was a conscientious and competent layout man who did not spare any effort to produce the effect he envisioned. However, once Doug had completed a layout, it was very difficult to get him to change it, even when the sales people or the metallurgists (who must be satisfied downstairs) did not like it.

Now, as Jake Abbott saw that Doug had a layout in his hand, he felt the usual twinge of apprehension for the argument he suspected was coming. But he made an effort to be casual, until he was sure, "Hi, Doug — hot enough for you?"

"I'm about to melt, Jake. No hope in sight, either, according to the radio." Schoeder opened the layout and spread it on Jake's desk. It was a stylistic drawing of some pipe, prepared for insertion in the *Plumbing and Heating Trade Journal.* "Jake, I want your frank opinion on this layout. Is it good — or is it bad?"

"Look, Doug — Don Francisco's told me about this flap already, and it isn't a question of good or bad. It's a question, or so Don tells me, of not being able to get it approved in pipe sales. Ken Carpenter just doesn't like it, according to Don."

"You know what I think of Don, Jake? I think he's a young kid who can't talk up for our layouts. I think he just goes down there to the sales department and puts the layout on the desk, and whatever the guy says, Francisco says yes, sir, we'll do that, sir. And I don't think that's the kind of copy-contact man we should have around here."

"Look, Doug, I'm carrying two jobs now — copy chief and the News Letter. Al Bishop's going to hire a new copy chief, as you know. But until he does, I'm so damned rushed I can't see straight. To be honest about this layout, it's stylized to the point where it's not exactly clear what's being shown. Here, Carpenter writes on the layout: 'New drawing — not sure what this is.' Carpenter just wants detail, Doug. It's dead simple. A little detail —"

"Detail," Doug Schroeder interrupted. "This is the contact man's job, Jake — to explain these little details to the man. Not just sit there and say yes sir, no sir!"

Jake felt his control slip a little. "Maybe Don didn't get in to see Carpenter, Doug. Maybe he had to leave this with Eileen O'Conner and come back for it later. Carpenter's a busy guy. I used to contact him myself at one time."

"Oh, come on, Jake. Let's not try to pass the buck to Carpenter. Let's put it where it belongs, with Francisco. The kid's a dreamboat all right — a regular stenographers' delight — and I'm told Eleanor Keck is burning a small candle in his honor on her desk, morning and night, and the guy's too dumb to take advantage of it. But one thing I can really tell you, Jake. Francisco doesn't belong in the copy department. He belongs in the mail room!"

"All right, Doug," Jake said. "But don't tell it to me. I'm not in a position to put Don in the mail room, even if —"

A knock on the door stopped him. Jake took a breath, welcoming the interruption, and said, "Come in, come in!"

The door opened and Louise Stegmeyer peered in uncertainly through her glasses. She wore a gray skirt with many pleats which made her waist seem enormous, and her hair was a billowing mess. "Oh — it's you, Mr. Schroeder. I thought it was Mr. McHugh. . . ." She started to shut the door.

"Come in, Louise," Jake said. "Come in. Is there anything I can do?"

"No, thanks. I was just looking for Mr. McHugh."

"Unless I am badly mistaken," Doug Schroeder said, "Mr. McHugh will now be taking his usual coffee break. The early one, that is. Eight to nine-thirty — as opposed to the later one, ten to eleven-thirty. At which time he begins to prepare for his lunch break which comes at ten minutes to twelve."

"Don't mind Doug," Jake said to the girl. "He's on his ear this morning. Can I give Jack a message if I see him?"

"Oh, would you? It's about the picnic. . . ."

"What do they want McHugh to do? Doug Schroeder said. "Bake a cake?"

Louise smiled embarrassedly. "I don't know," she said. "I think it's about the games —"

"Old Jack is good at games," Doug Schroeder said. "They're working on the right fella. Paper-shuffling, double-talking, apple-polishing. You name it — old Jack can play it."

Louise stepped backward, her face flushed. "Well, thank you," she said, to the room in general. "Thank you very much," and shut the door.

Doug Schroeder said, "Brother . . . I've seen snappier outfits on scarecrows."

Jake Abbott felt an urge to stand up and hit Doug Schroeder. He closed the layout and handed it to the art director. "If you want my advice," he said, "you'll do this over. Use a photograph if you want to. We've got hundreds of good pipe photos in the files. I'm sure Carpenter would buy a photograph."

"Photograph, eh? All I need to be an art director is a Brownie camera and a pot of glue, eh?" Schroeder picked up the layout and went to the door. He opened it, then paused. "Jake, boy," he said softly, almost sweetly, "I've got a word to cover you geniuses in the copy department. Chickenshit!" He stepped through the door and closed it gently after him.

Eileen O'Conner, Ken Carpenter's secretary, had deferred twelve phone calls since the office had opened an hour and a half ago. She had done it on her boss's orders. He had Ben Oliver, of the treasury department, with him, and he did not want to be disturbed. Which was very unusual, Eileen thought, since her boss normally took phone calls even during a meeting. He did not hang on and gab, but he took them, and if there was a decision to be made, he'd make it, and hang up. But Ben Oliver — what in the world could Mr. Carpenter find important in him? Eileen had heard about him from Kitty O'Neill, a stenographer in the treasury department, who lived four doors from Eileen on the top of the hill. Ben Oliver was, according to Kitty, a "horrible little human adding machine," not nice at all, like Mr. Donovan or Mr. Detweiler.

On her desk, Eileen's phone rang again and she picked it up. A woman's voice, assured, husky, low, said, "This is Margaret Fiori. Put Mr. Carpenter on, please."

Eileen felt her nerves tighten. "Oh, Mrs. Fiori, I'm dreadfully sorry, but he's in conference, and I have strict orders not to disturb him."

"My dear, I'm completely familiar with the conference routine, and it doesn't apply to me. Now just ring his phone, or push one of your little buttons, or whatever you do, and let me speak to the man a moment."

"Oh dear," Eileen said. "I shouldn't, Mrs. Fiori. I really —"

"Come, now," the husky voice snapped, and Eileen felt the storm lying behind it. "Come, girl. Don't keep me hanging here!"

"All right, Mrs. Fiori."

With doubt and apprehension, Eileen pushed the button which caused a buzzer to sound in Mr. Carpenter's office. His voice came back to her at once, curt and irritated. "Eileen, I told you not to disturb —"

"It's Mrs. Fiori," Eileen gasped. "On number three. She insisted —"

The voice changed. "Oh, all right, Eileen. I'll take it."

In the high-back leather chair with the brass studding, Ken Carpenter smiled across the phone at Ben Oliver, holding his hand over the receiver. "Excuse me, Ben. Emergency." He winked, uncovered the phone, and spoke, "Hello, Margaret. Well, this is a pleasure."

"You tell your girl," Maggie Fiori's husky voice said, "you tell the loyal little dear not to go into a tailspin when I call up — just put me on."

"I'll tell her that."

"Kenny —"

"Yes?"

"I hope I'm not breaking into anything important."

"When you call, that could never be the case."

"Is sweetie pants out there listening on the extension?"

"Definitely not."

"I can speak freely?"

"Within reason."

"Well, Enid's going to Sewickly tomorrow, to see a girl friend or something, and she'll be gone for two or three days. Bert's immobile, as you know. I was wondering — could you come over tomorrow night? I planned to let the servants off, and —" She left it there, hanging.

"I don't see why not," he said.

"Good. I could serve us a little dinner, after Bert's sedative, if you like, and we could listen to music."

"That would be fine. What time?"

"Well, might as well wait until it gets dark, I guess. Say ten or a little after."

"Fine," he said.

"Good. I'll be expecting you. Goodbye."

"Goodbye," Ken said, and hung up.

He smiled at Ben Oliver. "Sorry, Ben. Now then, I'll wrap up my harangue. I know you've got things to attend to." He picked up the subject he'd been outlining to Oliver for the past hour and a half, to wit, the New Carey Furnace Supply Company, which was being considered as a means of distributing Carey Furnace seamless tubing to the oil fields of Texas and Oklahoma. The project had been proposed by Ken himself, after a trip he had taken through the oil fields two years ago, but only recently had the board of directors authorized a tentative go-ahead. Seamless tubing was a big new product of the Ohio mill of Carey Furnace Steel. The tonnage was increasing, and Ken was pressing for a more efficient method of distribution than through established jobbers, as was the usual method with ordinary plumbing supplies. He advocated establishing a string of company-owned outlets — outlets he could control himself, personally, from this desk. But it was a touchy matter, going into competition with the company's own middlemen. To pull it off effectively, one of two things had to be done: buy out control of the existing outlets, and keep personnel on Carey Furnace's payroll — or build new warehouse facilities in key locations and staff them with such skilled oil-well supply people as might be hired quickly. Ken Carpenter was in favor of the first method — taking over existing suppliers — if this could be done without being held up for exorbitant purchase fees on the part of greedy or reluctant sellers. The move would be a very big one, amounting to many millions of dollars, and was more or less an open secret in the trade, which was why Ken could afford to outline it to Ben Oliver. He had nearly finished that outline when Maggie Fiori called.

Now, after finishing the conversation, there was a natural break in which Ken could put his proposition. He said, "We've done a lot of preliminary feeling out, among the people in the trade. By that, I mean we've contacted all of the jobbers we'd like to buy out, and gotten a fairly firm idea of their reaction. With the exception of Kaness Tool and Supply, in Waco, they are all pretty much in line with what we're willing to pay. If Kaness holds out, it won't matter much — to us. It will to him, of course, before he's through, and for that reason I think he'll come into line with the rest."

Ken stopped. "Now then, Ben, to get to the reason I asked you to drop over. I've gone into this deal so thoroughly I *think* I know what I'm doing — but there's always the danger, when a man is that close to a problem, that he misses some small but critical point which can ruin the whole deal. We're talking about an investment of close to fifty million dollars. I know your department will review this thing anyhow, before the board hands down its decision, so I wanted to come direct to you, to — well, to ask your advice on the soundness of the whole plan, before I let it leave my desk."

Ben Oliver sat silently, drumming on the arm of his chair with his fingers. "I can understand your wanting to set up a sound plan," he said presently, in his colorless voice. "But I'm sure you must realize that what you're doing — what you're asking me to do, actually — is hardly conventional procedure."

"I'm well aware of that," Ken Carpenter said. "And I'll be frank. I hesitated to ask you, for that very reason. And if you'd rather not comment in any way, I'll certainly understand." He sighed and sank back in the leather chair. "In that case, Ben, I guess I'll just have to try and see Mr. Detweiler."

Ben Oliver smiled thinly. "I'm afraid you won't be able to do that — unless you're prepared to go to Scotland."

"Oh, that so? Then I suppose I'll have to go through his assistant — George Donovan."

For a moment, Ben Oliver was able to keep his feelings submerged. Carpenter could see him react, his fingers whiten, slightly, on the chair arm, his pale fishlike eyes narrow, then widen, the pupils dilating and the prim nostrils flaring slightly. Ken held his breath. It was now, he knew, or it was never. . . .

Ben Oliver fought with the feelings of injustice and outrage that had been gathering in his heart and mind for years: items large and small that had been accumulating inside him like a growing pressure of steam in a boiler. He knew he should hold them in — now, in this office — just as he had held them in everywhere else, had been the good little company man, through his long and industrious career in the treasury department. But — why should he? What had prudence and loyalty gotten him in the past? Nothing. Not a goddamned thing.

He said, tightly, "You can see George Donovan if you like, Mr. Carpenter, but I can tell you right now, you'll be wasting your time. You might as well wait until Black Angus Detweiler returns from Scotland — if he ever does — and then, frankly, I doubt if you'll get anywhere. The whole thing will get referred to Donovan, who may, or may not, refer it to me. . . ."

Ken Carpenter smiled gently. "But I thought Mr. Donovan was executive assistant to Mr. Detweiler."

"That's his title."

"You sound as if you didn't feel it meant a great deal."

"Do I?"

Ken Carpenter waited. He could see that there was a struggle of some kind going on inside Ben Oliver's head. Ben's fingers were moving slightly, in his palms, his usually pale face was flushed.

"I understand," Ken Carpenter said gently. "I don't blame you for being loyal to George, even though you might have some personal reservations. I guess he's a good boss, no matter what his other failings might be."

Ben Oliver flinched as if he'd been struck. "Good boss," he said, in a low voice. "Are you trying to kid me? Listen, do you want to know how George Donovan spends a typical day? Would you really like to know?"

"If you feel you can tell me," Ken Carpenter said, "I'd like to know how George spends his day."

"I shouldn't tell you," Ben Oliver said, his face quite red now, and his voice shrill. "It could get me fired bright and early tomorrow;

but you know something? I don't care. I'm fed up. So I'll tell you how George Donovan spends a typical day. He sits on his fat can from nine in the morning until five in the afternoon — time out for lunch — and do you know what he reads? Financial reports? Financial reports my aunt Nellie! He reads comic books! Li'l Abner. He's really nuts about Li'l Abner. Likes to see the half-naked hillbilly babes running in the underbrush. And he likes baseball. Has a radio in his office, and when the season begins he shuts the door and listens to the ball games in the afternoon. He has one more thing he does. He sleeps. The son-of-a-bitch has a couch in his anteroom and when J.P isn't around — which is just about all the time — old George Donovan sleeps. You may not believe this, but it's God's truth!"

Ben Oliver took a deep breath. He could feel his heart pounding, and the room seemed to be brighter, clearer, as if by his words he was somehow cleansing his body of impurities, sharpening all his senses. Now that he was started, it was easy — in fact, it was imperative — that he get rid of all the fury and frustration which had gathered inside him, like an enormous pus sac. He laughed, dry and harsh. "Let me fix our operation in your mind, Mr. Carpenter — in case you've been working under an illusion. Mr. J. P. Detweiler, treasurer, so-called, of Carey Furnace Steel Company, is in the Black Angus cattle business. George P. Donovan, executive assistant to the great cattle man, reads comic books and sleeps. Ben Oliver, who has no title that anybody ever heard of, gets out the work. And by getting out the work, I don't mean answering the mail and the telephone. I mean all the work — the budget, the tax problem, the planning, the supervising of our staff of accountants and actuaries — the whole ball of wax. And do you know how much the said Ben Oliver is paid? Have you any idea?"

Ken Carpenter shook his head, and was silent.

"Well, I'll tell you," Ben Oliver said, and his voice shook with anger. "I get fifteen thousand a year. I happen to know — because I help with the farm books too — that J. P. Detweiler pays Frank Hewitt ten thousand just for diddling around with those cows, and gives him a house, rent free, plus a lot of knock-downs. I'm sure Hewitt makes out on the farm purchases — which, I may add, are considerable. Now Frank Hewitt never went through the eighth grade. And yet, when you figure it out, he's probably making just about as much take-home pay — maybe more — than I am. Okay. I probably should have kept this all to myself. Now all you have to do to get me fired is go tell fat-ass Donovan, and I'm through."

Ken Carpenter picked up an embossed leather box full of cigarettes and held it out across the desk. Ben Oliver hesitated — then took one. His fingers shook slightly as he flicked the lighter and held it to the cigarette.

"Ben," Ken Carpenter said. "I had no idea this situation existed. Fifteen thousand a year, did you say?"

"Yeah, that's what I said. With the dollar down to forty cents in purchasing power, that comes to six thousand in real value in today's inflation. Hell, I was making almost that much eight years ago, when I was getting started around here!"

"I guess you're right, Ben," Ken Carpenter said, reflectively. "The inflation has really cut real buying power." He stared at his visitor, biting his lips, and then seemed to make up his mind. "Ben, are you open to a proposition?"

"What?"

"I've been doing some fast thinking in the past few minutes and I've got an idea to toss in your lap, if you're interested."

"Go ahead," Ben Oliver said. "Toss it."

"Don't answer me now," Ken Carpenter said. "Give yourself time to cool down. But the fact is this: I'm going to need a good financial coordinator for this supply thing, when and if it shapes up. A guy with pretty much your background and abilities, Ben. I hadn't given much thought to the salary. But I wouldn't think of anything less than thirty thousand, to start." He smiled. "That's exactly double what you're making now, Ben. This venture can stand or fall on its tax structure — its financial plumbing — and, most of all, on its financial functioning. There'll be a hell of a lot of tough paperwork here, and I think it's your meat, Ben. Go back and think it over. If you want thirty thousand a year for a new job, and a new chance — let me know."

Ben Oliver rubbed his chin with his left hand. His flush had deepened, and there was a hot glassy stare in his eyes. He took an awkward puff from his cagarette, coughed slightly, and said, "I thank you for the offer, Mr. Carpenter, but I doubt if the company would authorize my transfer, under the circumstances, or if J.P. would let me go —"

"Let's put it this way then," Ken Carpenter said. "You've just said you were ready to quit anyhow. So trying couldn't hurt you much, even if we failed. If I can get the transfer authorized, would you take the job?"

Ben Oliver took a deep drag on his cigarette, exhaled in a thin funnel, upward, into a shaft of sunlight from the window. Then he met Ken Carpenter's eyes. "If you can get me transferred," Ben Oliver said flatly, "I'll come to work for you this afternoon, right after lunch!"

"Good! I'm glad to hear that. Now — there's just one thing."

"Yes?"

"This conversation we've just had is off the record. The way I'm going to have to move on this transfer will be greatly expedited if I can move suddenly, with the element of surprise. I'm sure you'll understand that."

"Off the record," Ben Oliver said, and stood up. "Thank you very much, Mr. Carpenter."

"Don't thank me, Ben. This is a business deal. I wouldn't be after you if I didn't think you're the best man for the job." He rose and shook his visitor's hand. "One thing I can promise you — you won't be bothered by comic books in this office." He grinned. "Now go back to the treasury and take it easy. I'll be back to you officially — with your new job, I hope — very soon!"

John Carey was staying in the company suite of the Richelieu Hotel, in midtown Manhattan. He had flown over from Carey Furnace on the previous evening. The air had been rough with thunderheads coming over the mountains, and he had not felt well when he reached the hotel. He had had a scotch, a light supper, and gone to his room, undressed and lain down on the bed. Across the street a neon sign winked on and off, casting pinkish flares of light on the ceiling of John Carey's suite, and he lay and watched the glow come and go, like luminous breathing. He felt better after having eaten, and the scotch had relaxed him somewhat. He thought of picking up the phone and calling his son, but did not do it. John Jr. would probably be out with some of his cronies, or maybe listening to his record machine, if he did reach him, and it would be a strain, as it always was, to keep any kind of a conversation going. John Carey did not know much about the kind of music his son liked, and the boy (he still thought of him as the boy, even though he was nearly thirty) would not be interested in the market situation for steel in South America.

He sighed, without realizing it. If young John had been different — Well, he hadn't. He was an expert in woofers, tweeters, coaxial speakers, and compression horns. . . .

John Carey lay on his back on the bed looking up at the soft crimson breathing of the neon reflection on the ceiling. He felt relaxed but vaguely uncomfortable, without knowing the seat of the discomfort. He closed his eyes, inviting drowsiness, but it did not come. He had Seconal in his bag, but he did not get up to get it. He had come, he realized, to a sorrowful place in life: he no longer cared. He did not care, really, what happened at the meeting tomorrow, whether they settled the South American problems well or badly, whether he got home to Carey Furnace in the evening or the following day, whether he saw his boy or not, whether he ate sirloin steak or a ham sandwich, whether he and Eva went to Paris and Rome or sat on the lawn looking at the steel plant in the smog. Perhaps he would care again, at some later point in his life, when his body chemistry changed or circumstances drove a bright splinter of fear or joy or curiosity into his quiescent flesh; or the threat of nuclear war surged forward, as it seemed to do at more or less regular intervals, and he could awake for a moment in horror and hope, and care what happened to the human race, at least.

But now, lying on his bed in the middle of New York City, he could not care — no, not even about the nuclear war. He felt like a passenger in a gray ship, becalmed in a gray ocean with no wind, where only time existed in a motionless world. Maybe it was the heat, the hot spell. Maybe it was his physical condition. Maybe he had just passed the point of no return, was old, really old. He tried to think of something which, if offered to him now, he would accept with some spark of eagerness — an ambassadorship, Secretary of Defense for the United States of America, a fresh and lovely girl deeply in love with him, a certified check for a billion dollars tax free, a best-selling biography of his life; but these were five-and-ten gewgaws. No, at this moment he was not even interested in being young again himself, with his life bright and empty ahead, waiting to be filled by finer deeds and richer experiences than before.

It will pass, he thought. *Everything passes. Everything passes in time. . . .* Then he opened his eyes and made the first determined effort he had made since entering the room. He got out of bed and opened his bag and found the Seconal. Half an hour later, he was asleep.

Father William Boyer, after his Sunday sermon, had stood at the door of the church, shaking his parishioners by the hand and accepting their standard polite comments on his sermon, which he was always reasonably sure most of them had not listened to carefully, if at all. He had smiled and murmured and bowed his head in giving his own standard polite replies to his flock until he had come to Mrs. Vivian Stegmeyer, and had been surprised to see that she had tears in her eyes. "Oh, Father," she had said in a low voice. "Oh, tell me you didn't mean what you said . . . about God . . . about God dying with us, like one of us, in an H-bomb war. . . ."

He took her hand and felt the fingers trembling, and he was at a loss for words. She looked at him, doubtful, troubled and old, with her eyes glistening and pleading, and he was gripped by a sudden terrible urge to run from the church, ripping his surplice from his neck as he ran, but he smiled gently and said, "My opinions or ideas of God aren't necessarily infallible, Mrs. Stegmeyer. They are only the way I think myself, and you have every right to think the absolute opposite — and you have every right to feel that your belief is just as true as mine."

"Oh, thank you," Vivian Stegmeyer whispered. "I knew — I knew in my heart you didn't mean it — I knew it was only your way of making us listen. Thank you, Father. . . ." And she had passed on, following her pink and well-fed husband out of the church, and he had shaken more hands, automatically, but his mind had not heard what his well-meaning flock was saying.

They did not come for truth. Nobody came to anybody for truth, or if they did, it happened so seldom as to be a phenomenon like an eclipse of the sun. He knew that Vivian Stegmeyer was unhappy, had been unhappy for a very long time, but he had not, seeing tears in her eyes, felt pity. Instead he had felt like running away from what he saw, not because of sympathy but because he had suddenly hated Mrs. Stegmeyer and all of the other people who did not have the strength to accept truth and reality, and made you, by their weakness and their wet, unwanted supplications, turn yourself into a reluctant comforter when it was not comfort they needed, but a good hard slap across the face. But he knew that was wrong too. Vivian Stegmeyer might be a martyr, might enjoy it because it was all she had to enjoy, but a slap across the face would not help her, not now. Perhaps in the beginning, when whatever it was that had turned her into a pathetic vegetable had begun — but not now. Now a hard slap would only confirm her martyrhood.

No, the fault did not lie with Vivian Stegmeyer or in any of the parishioners. It lay in William Boyer. He should never have been a minister. He should have been an ambulance driver, perhaps, or a steeple jack, or a faro dealer — but certainly not a minister. A minister dealt in dreams, mainly set in rose glades or in the shades of death, and William Boyer, whatever else he was, was not a dreamer. That night, in his room at the rectory, he got out a pint bottle of Schenley's Reserve, locked the door and drank most of it, then lay down and went to sleep on the couch with his clothes on. When he awoke in the morning he had a bad hangover but he felt purged — felt better, mentally at least, than he had felt for a long time.

John Carey, thanks to the Seconal, slept soundly through the night. When the desk clerk woke him by phone he got out of bed at once and went into the bathroom and examined his face in the mirror over the washbowl. His head felt woolly from the sleeping drug, but otherwise there was no ill effect. His face was still good: not too pouchy under the eyes, the dewlaps under his chin small and taut, the gray hair, in contrast to his darkly tanned face, giving him a look of health and virility. He smiled at the dark face in the mirror, gratified by the white teeth, his own. He felt a lift of spirit. "A plate of bacon and eggs," he said to the brown face in the mirror, "a double order of ice-cold tomato juice, and two hot cups of coffee, and you'll be up to anything, my boy."

He shaved, and went to the bowl and urinated. He was about to flush the bowl when he noted the clear water was clouded dark yellow, almost brown. He paused, then he flushed the bowl. It was kidneys; nothing to worry about — he'd had it before.

He ate a good breakfast in the hotel coffee shop, reading the morning paper as he ate his toast. A new satellite of some kind had been launched by the Air Force; a woman had been killed by her husband, apparently with a screwdriver; and the dry spell was causing great hardship in the Middle West. He had two cups of coffee and part of a cigar. But the cigar didn't taste good and he put it out and signed his check. He spoke a few words with his waiter in the Richilieu Coffee Shop, an old man, who always waited on him if on duty. Then he went to his room again, feeling the need to go to the bathroom, but not being able to urinate when he got there. He put some papers which he would need at the meeting into his brief case and went downstairs and out to the street.

It was a short cab ride from the Richelieu to the Carey Furnace Building on Park Avenue. John Carey paid the cabbie, gave him a quarter tip, and walked across the sidewalk into the brightly lit lobby. Luke Monahan, who'd been elevator starter in the Carey Furnace Building for fifteen years, smiled widely and bobbed his head up and down, excited and nervous, as always, in the presence of the big boss. "Good mornin', Mr. Carey, sir," Luke said in his Irish brogue, pressing and holding the call button — the signal that somebody very important was waiting.

"Good morning, Luke," John Carey said. "You're looking fine. How's the family?"

"They're jist foin, Mr. Carey, thank you for askin'. How's Mrs. Carey, sir?"

"Just fine, Luke."

An elevator arrived at the lobby level, and Luke stepped aside, placing his left hand on the door as an extra precaution against its closing prematurely. "Here's your car, Mr. Carey. Hope you have a good day, sir!"

"Thank you, Luke."

Luke Monahan leaned close to the curly-headed young man who was operating the elevator and said softly, "Jimmy, it's Mr. Carey himself, lad. No stoppin' for buzzers or the like of that. Take Mr. Carey straight to his floor." Luke looked at John Carey. "Which floor would you be wantin', sir?"

"Fourteen, thanks, Luke."

"Fourteen, Jimmy," Luke Monahan said, and let the door slide shut. The elevator started with a slight jerk, and something seemed to tear, very slightly, inside John Carey's body, low down, on the right side. As the elevator passed the third floor, he felt the pain begin, deep in, as if chunks of broken glass, secretly embedded there, were suddenly being forced violently through his flesh. He sucked in his breath and leaned back against the wall of the car, closing his eyes briefly against the pain. When he opened them, he saw the elevator boy looking at him with an alarmed expression.

"Are you all right, sir?"

"Yes," he said shortly.

The elevator rose smoothly, then slowed for the fourteenth floor, went a little past, and stopped abruptly. John Carey felt the pain surge down through his groin, into his testicles, into the nerves of his inner thigh, like a douche of acid. He gritted his teeth. The boy was jiggling the controls nervously, trying to level the car exactly with the floor. John Carey said softly, "Jesus Christ . . ."

"Sir?"

"Nothing," John Carey said tightly, holding his breath. "Just open the door. Never mind the minor adjustments."

"Oh, yes, sir."

The door opened and he let go of the wall of the elevator which he had been using as a support, and staggered, in spite of himself, as he stepped out of the elevator. From behind him, the boy spoke anxiously, "Mr. Carey — you sure you're all right, sir? Should I get some help?"

He turned and shook his head, keeping his lips tight against the pain. It was leaving him now, slowly, as if an attacking animal, having bloodied its talons, were reluctantly releasing its prey. He took a deep breath and straightened his body experimentally. The pain was draining away, leaving a warm steady pressure in his side. His heart was pounding and there was a sour chemical taste in his mouth. But he managed a smile for the elevator boy. "All over now, son. Stitch in my side. Had 'em ever since I was a kid."

"Oh, I'm glad it's not serious, sir."

"You can go now," John Carey said. "I'm perfectly all right."

When the elevator had gone, he stood with his shoulders against the wall, breathing deeply, getting himself in hand. He did not know what it had been: a heart attack, perhaps? No, not a heart attack. He remembered vaguely, from reading, that with a heart attack it was your arm that pained. He had felt no pain in his arm. Anyhow, his breathing was easier, and the pain in the groin had subsided. Then, suddenly, he realized what it must be. Gallstones. Of course. You got violent pain, suddenly, with gallstones, or maybe it was kidney stones — some kind of stones, anyhow — when they left the gall bladder or the kidney and got into the tubes, trying to get out of the body. When you passed one, you had this awful pain. He'd heard people talk about it. Well . . .

Now that his breathing was easier, the knowledge that he had a meeting set up in Stanley Sucek's office took possession of his mind. They would be in there now, waiting for him. It wouldn't do not to appear, if he could make it — particularly since Luke Monahan knew he was in the building. He let go of the wall and took a step. His legs were strong enough. He did not stagger. He was coming out of it nicely, whatever it had been. The thing to do now was to go to this meeting — keep moving — and maybe the whole thing would pass without a trace.

When John Carey stepped into the conference room a minute later, Stanley Sucek rose to greet him: youthful-looking, curly-headed, smiling. There was plenty of iron under that boyish exterior. Stanley could wear several hats with equal ease: diplomat, salesman, trouble shooter — and hatchet wielder, if it became necessary. There was a touch of gray at his temples, and John Carey, observing it, was able to make a small witticism. "Well, Stan — you're looking fit, boy. The whisky people been around yet for the man-of-distinction endorsement?"

Stanley Sucek grinned. "Last week, Mr. Carey — they came last week. But I don't come cheap, sir, We've been haggling over terms." He turned to the other men who had been sitting around the conference table. John Carey knew then all well. He smiled at them and sat down. "You want to run the meeting, Mr. Carey?" Stanley Sucek said.

"Nope, Stan. You run it. I'll stick my oar in when I feel like it."

He did not miss the brief look of pleasure in his export manager's eyes. Stan was a protégé of John Carey's. He'd spotted him in a district sales offices, recognized his potential, and given him a chance to prove himself. And Stanley had certainly come through. "Thank you, sir," Stanley Sucek said now. "I'll get the show right on the road, then, since we've got plenty of ground to cover."

The meeting began. It was like hundreds of other meetings John

Carey had attended, and now, with a dull ache still in his side, he found himself following with difficulty until Stanley Sucek asked Pete Estrada, the company's South American trouble shooter, if there was really a dangerous Communist movement in Latin America as a whole.

Estrada shrugged. "The Communists are everywhere, Stan. Poor people always seem to listen to them."

"Don't they know what happened in Hungary?"

"They don't care what happened in Hungary. They only care what happens in their own village."

"But don't they see through this crap?"

Estrada smiled. "Look, Stan — to them it's not crap. The Commie agent stops in front of some miserable shack and gets into a conversation with the owner. Presently he points across the road at a nice parcel of land — asks the guy if he'd like to have it. Well, if you were the guy, what would you say?"

"I'd want to know what the strings were."

"Oh, come on, Stan. Most of those poor peasants feel they couldn't be any worse off than they are right now. They couldn't care less about strings. Of course they change their minds later, when they find they're hooked on a collective farm deal — like in Red China. They start bitching about it in the local meeting, and then the manure hits the fan. The Commie agent tells them to shut up or get kicked out of the collective farm — the local anthill — which is a polite way of saying shut up or starve."

"A commune," Stanley Sucek said, "that's just a bunch of collective farms — a bigger anthill? Right?"

"It's a bunch of collective farms — and a bunch of collective industries. Your little man, by now, is a versatile cog. You can slip him into a tomato patch — or into a factory while the tomatoes are ripening — and keep him working all the time. It's a miserable way to live — but it's a tough system to beat."

John Carey learned back in his chair. He felt weak and sick. He personally regarded Communism as a kind of infection which had attacked the freedom of the human race. It would have to run its course, like any disease. Time alone would tell if the patient would survive or die.

He was relieved when, just before lunch, the meeting broke up. He had had no more severe pain, but he was very tired and wanted to get back to his hotel and lie down. Perhaps if he had a nap he'd feel good again, and it would not be necessary to mention his attack in the elevator to Pop Whitehead. . . .

Things did not work out that way. After lunch, he lay down in his hotel room and fell asleep. He did not know how long he slept, but he was awakened by a deep, aching sensation in his groin, tolerable, but alarming. He sat up and looked at his watch. It was after four o'clock. There was no choice now. He picked up the phone beside his bed and placed a call for Dr. Arthur Whitehead in Carey Furnace. There was a wait, and when he heard the familiar voice on the line, he said, "Hello, Pop. Hope I didn't break into an operation or anything. This is John."

"No, you didn't, John. I was just wandering out in the ward, nothing important. What is it?"

"I don't know. Nothing, I hope. I had a pain this morning — pretty severe — in my right side. It went away in a few minutes. But it's back now, in the groin. Not as bad as this morning, but no picnic. I was wondering if you could take a look at me this evening when I come in on the plane."

"Certainly can," Pop Whitehead said. "Which plane will you be on? I'll meet it."

"Oh, don't take the trouble. I'll get a cab."

"It's no trouble. I'll be glad to get some air. We've been having a hundred and two here today. Which flight will you be on?"

"It'll be the American flight — I don't know the number. But it's due in Carey Furnace a few minutes after eight."

"I'll be waiting," Pop Whitehead said. "Take it easy till I see you."

"I'll do that, Pop."

"Goodbye, John."

"Goodbye, Pop."

He hung up. He did not think — or he tried not to think —

about the cause of his pain. Gallstones, or kidney stones, they couldn't possibly affect the groin — or could they? For the first time in years, John Carey felt like having a drink to relax his nerves. . . . *Now settle down, boy,* he thought, *Just settle down. Don't start yelling before you're hurt. . . .*

While John Carey was phoning from New York, Ken Carpenter was leaving his office at the steel company in Carey Furnace to drive over the mountain to his home in Hunter's Valley. On his way, he stopped at Dutch Huber's Linger Awhile. He was ahead of the five-o'clockers who came in for one or two drinks on their way home. Except for a farmer having a beer, he was alone with Dutch. He petted Skipper briefly and ordered a Coke.

"Hot enough for you, Mr. Carpenter?" Dutch said.

Ken grinned. "When are you going to break down and admit you need air conditioning, Dutch?"

"Oh, these hot spells don't come very often."

"Just every summer."

"Maybe next summer I'll have something put in," Dutch said. "It's not much use doing anything now. By the time I let the contract, the cold weather's here."

"Dutch?"

"Yes, Mr. Carpenter?"

"I don't know if you heard me talking to Frank Hewitt in here the other day — about buying a calf?"

"Yeah, I heard a little of it."

"Well, I thought it was pretty nice of Frank, helping me like that — and I'd like to show my appreciation. You happen to know if Frank drinks whisky? All I've ever seen him take is beer."

Dutch grinned. "Oh, Frank drinks a little whisky at times."

"He partial to any brand in particular?"

"Yeah, he's kind of partial to Old Grand-dad."

"You have any Old Grand-dad in stock?"

"I do."

"Give me a couple of bottles, please."

"Sure, Mr. Carpenter. Want 'em wrapped?"

"Yes, you might as well, I guess."

He paid for the whisky and the Coke, bought Skipper some corn curls, and went back out to his car. A few minutes later he parked in the driveway outside Frank Hewitt's office at Four Oaks. A heavy man with a red face who was working on a manure pile nearby stopped using his fork and approached the car. "Help you, Mister?"

"Yes — is Frank Hewitt around?"

"You Mr. Carpenter, ain't you?"

"Yes, I am."

"Well, Frank's not here right this minute. He's out in the field. But he told me if you come lookin' for him, tell you to go in the office and make yourself to home. He'll be back in about fifteen or twenty minutes."

"All right," Ken Carpenter said. "Thanks. I guess I'll wait a few minutes anyhow, as long as I'm here."

"You should be able to see Frank comin' through the office window," the man said. "He'll be down in the pasture that borders the crick."

"Well, thanks," Carpenter said. "I'll keep watch."

The man left and went back to his work, and Carpenter went into the office and shut the door behind him. He looked through the window. Far away, across the shimmering heat of the meadows, he could see a lone man kneeling, doing something to the fence by Old Mine Creek. The man was doubtless Frank Hewitt. Even if he jumped up this instant, and returned to his office on the run, it would take him maybe ten minutes to get here. Obviously, he was not going to do that. Ken Carpenter would probably have almost a half-hour alone in the office before Hewitt arrived. He stood very still, listening. He could hear no sound. He went to the door, opened it a crack, and peered out. The man with the pitchfork was back at work.

Without further delay, Ken Carpenter crossed to the filing cabinet, opened it, and began to go quickly, but with sharp-eyed concentration, through Frank Hewitt's files. For close to three minutes he sorted and peered, glancing out of the window periodically. Presently he saw the tiny figure leave the fence and begin plodding back through the fields. He did not have a great deal more time. Perhaps he would not find what he was after this trip — it might take another, or many. And then he flipped a folder and came upon a tab, written in ink, on the face of the next folder: *J. P. Detweiler, Personal Correspondence.* He lifted the file out, opened it, and began to go through it, his heart beating quickly. . . .

The twin-engined Convair 340 of American Airlines banked in the early darkness, wallowing in the buoyant air rising from the fairways of the Hunter's Valley Golf Course, still hot after the cloudless August day. The engines lost their solid roar and fell to a mutter, and bright sparks of carbon flicked from the exhaust stacks past the window where John Carey sat. He heard the remote grinding of internal machinery and felt a thump as the wheels came down, and then, looking to the left past the circular blur of the port propellor, he saw the bonfire glow of the steel plant. The plane straightened out and began to sink rapidly into the pit of darkness on the riverbank. His ears felt the change in pressure as the plane lost altitude; he caught a glimpse of orange beads rising out of the dark, felt the wheels brush the runway, and saw the orange lights suck past like flying tracer bullets, then slow as the plane's engines roared explosively in reverse pitch. On the public address system, the stewardess asked that the passengers remain seated for their own comfort and safety until the plane had reached a full stop in front of the terminal, and she came down the aisle and stopped beside John Carey's seat. "I hope we didn't shake you up too much coming over the mountains, Mr. Carey."

"No, it was fine."

She smiled at him, showing her pretty teeth. "Come fly with us again soon, won't you, sir?"

"I'll try to do that," John Carey said.

When the plane stopped he got up, moving carefully, and walked out and down the stairway into the warm floodlit night. Pop Whitehead was waiting at the gate, a big-bellied man in white slacks and a white short-sleeved shirt, his round Santa Claus face glistening with sweat under the greenish lights. "Take your bag, John?"

"No, thanks. I can handle it."

"Any other baggage?"

"No, this is it."

"All right. I've got the Chevy over in the lot."

John Carey followed his friend to a 1951 Chevy coupe which Pop insisted on driving (it had a hand shift, plenty of room for his feet, and didn't take half an hour to wedge into a parking space), and when they got in, Pop said, "We can go right to the hospital, John — or I can take you home first, if you'd like to speak to Eve and drop your bag."

"Let's just go to the hospital."

"All right."

They pulled out of the lot and Pop turned onto the highway leading up the hill. John Carey did not speak. Now that he was nearing the actual examination, he could feel his body gathering itself for whatever shock it might have to meet. Pop parked in his private parking place behind the hospital and they went in through the ambulance entrance and directly up to his office, a large white room with a desk, and several hospital-type easy chairs — leather-upholstered, but functional and antiseptic-looking. Adjoining the office was an examination room with a metal table and special lights.

"All right, John," Pop said. "Step in the next room and take off your clothes and we'll see what's what."

"All of them?"

"You can leave the shorts on."

With John Carey in his shorts, Pop turned on a strong lamp. He had put on a white smock and donned a circular illuminator — a mirror with a hole in it, like a beacon on his forehead — making him look formidable and alien. John Carey realized his heart was beating heavily.

"Still got that pain, John?"

"No — it seems to be gone."

"Where was it?"

"Here — in my right side — just about there — deep in."

"Any other symptoms you recall offhand?"

"No. Oh, yes, wait a minute — this morning, in New York, when I went to the bathroom, the urine was dark — almost brown."

"I see. Well, lie down on the examining table now — no, on your back first."

He crawled onto the narrow table and lay, looking up at the shadowy ceiling outside the bright circle the lamp threw on it, and felt Pop's fingers gently exploring the surface of his abdomen, moving methodically about, first touching gently, then a little harder, and there was no pain, or if there was, it might be just from the pressure itself. The fingers moved to his right side, below the rib cage, and he felt his body gather in tense hope that this area, where the pain had been, would not be painful now. The fingers massaged gently, then more deeply, and John Carey felt an odd fullness and a pressure, but still no great pain. The fingers went to the groin, touched, pressed, and he winced.

"Hurts there, eh?"

"Yes."

"A lot?"

"Well, it hurts."

The fingers moved across to the left groin, pressed, and John Carey said, "Yes, there too — but not so much."

"Lift your arms above your head and clasp your hands."

On the table, John Carey did it, felt the doctor's fingers probing into his armpits.

"Yeah," he said, tightly. "There too, Pop. But not bad. Just tender, is all."

"All right, John, now turn over on your stomach."

He turned over, his head sideways, cradled in his arms, so he could see Pop's white smock next to his face, freshly starched and smelling of ironing, and Pop's fingers moved across his back, hesitated, and stopped. "This mole on your back — have you noticed it?"

"I've had it all my life."

"Has it bothered you lately?"

"No, not that I know of. How do you mean?"

"Well, pain — blood specks on the sheets in the morning?"

"Not that I remember. Oh, Eve said a couple of weeks ago that I ought to have it taken off. Just for looks. I forgot it until now."

"How big was it then?"

"I don't know. Not big. Like a match-head maybe. Why?"

"Nothing. It's bigger than a match-head now. John, as long as I've got you here, I'm going to take this thing off. We'll run it through the lab."

He felt the terror, then, like an electric current, ripple through his body. He did not speak for a moment. He was aware of his chest, rising and falling, of the sweat on his face, of the fact that his hands were gripping the steel legs of the table very tightly.

Pop was talking again. "I'll load up a couple of needles, John, and numb it for you and we'll lift it off. Just relax now. I'll go and wash up and alert the lab. We might as well let them look tonight, and have it over."

John Carey did not speak. He lay still, breathing deeply, through the jabs of the anesthetic needle, through the waiting period while the Novocain took effect and Pop phoned the laboratory to prepare for a tissue analysis, through the soft wet pressure of the scalpel, and the quick trickles of blood down his rib cage, quickly sponged away, through the final application of a gauze pad, taped firmly over the excision.

"Well," Pop said, "that's it, John. You can dress now."

John Carey sat up. He felt very strong and full of nervous energy, very alive: it must be the adrenalin pouring into his bloodstream from fear. He said, "You're looking for cancer, of course."

"Yes."

"How long will the test take to run?"

"We'll do a frozen section," Pop said. "I'm going down myself, and supervise it. I should say we'd know in twenty minutes to half an hour."

"I see."

"Would you like me to have the kitchen send you up a cup of coffee or anything?"

"No, thanks, Pop."

"All right. I'll take the specimen down now. Don't worry until you have to, John. I should be back here inside of half an hour."

Dr. Whitehead left the office and went down two floors to the technician's laboratory, where he had alerted his best technician, young Al Rosen, to be ready and waiting. Al had the equipment set up. Pop placed the suspected neoplasm on the preparation table. He said, "Al, I want the results of this test to be kept between you and me — absolutely. Whether it's positive or negative. You understand that?"

Al Rosen looked quickly up. "Yes, sir!"

"The patient is John Carey."

He saw Al's face twitch slightly. "Yes, Dr. Whitehead," Al said. "I understand."

"All right," Pop said. "Let's get at it."

He was standing outside the laboratory now, in the dim end of the corridor where a high window opened to the west, faintly nauseated, his wrists and knees feeling empty and flabby, the sweat on his face like a film of grease. There was a thin, piercing singing of some insect in the maple tree outside. All through the frozen-section examination, working beside Al Rosen in the bright laboratory, Dr. Whitehead had tried to reject the evidence John Carey had given him in conversation: the debilitation, the dark urine, the sudden pain. But then, as he had gotten to his own examination of a few moments ago, rejection of evidence was no longer possible. He had seen the dark mole. He had felt the unnaturally enlarged lymph glands, painful to the touch, in the groin and the armpits — dangerous signs of metastasis. And then he had touched and explored, in detail, the massive liver involvement, big as a gourd under his probing fingers — the classic involvement mentioned in all the textbooks. Dr. Whitehead had known that his friend John Carey had malignant melanoma, that the disease had spread — that even radical surgery would be hopeless. He had known this even before Al Rosen showed him the slide of the frozen section, his young face pale and tight, and said, "It's — it's positive, Doctor. I'm sorry . . ."

Now Pop Whitehead stood by the window looking out into the starry night. John was doomed. Mercifully, it would be soon. Melanoma was the fastest and most deadly killer of them all. And then, suddenly, Pop Whitehead realized that his cheeks were wet, and that he must have been crying for a long time.

Tuesday

ARCHIE SAUNDERS, on this Tuesday morning, was walking on a rail on his way to work. He felt good for a change. It was just as hot as ever, but the itchy pain was gone from his head and he felt carefree, even rich. He had clipped Mrs. Abbott's privet hedge after finishing at the River Avenue Market yesterday and she had let him listen to her play the piano, which he loved very much, particularly that loud thundery piece which made him think of a freight train roaring through the valley, and she had given him three dollars, which was as much as he could make in a whole day working for Mr. Brothers. Mrs. Abbott was a very nice lady. She always had a cold Coke or an orange pop in the icebox waiting for him, and sometimes a nice piece of cake or a cookie, and she wasn't always badgering him with questions about how was his dear mother, and they'd been missing him in Sunday school lately. Mrs. Abbott just handed him the clippers and showed him where she wanted the hedge cut, and smiled and said, "All right, Archie, my husband backed out — it's up to you."

"Mrs. Abbott?"

"Yes, Archie?"

"Would you — play that piece?"

"You mean the Rachmaninoff concerto?"

"The big one like a train coming."

She smiled. "Archie — I love you. You're the only person I know who asks me to play, and I'm sure really wants me to play. You go ahead and start clipping. I'll open the window and play the Rachmaninoff for you — and a couple of encores for good measure."

Archie had been to the movies. He knew that when a piano player stopped after a big piece, everybody clapped, and so when Mrs. Abbott finished playing he put down his shears quickly, out in the yard, and clapped, looking in through the screen to see if she heard. And she heard all right. She would turn, at the sound of his clapping, and bow at him through the screen, without getting up from the bench.

Three dollars. Boy! And cake and music. After that red-faced pot-bellied big-assed shitheel, Mr. Brothers!

Of course there were a few drawbacks to working at the Abbotts. There was the little brown dog next door that yapped at him all the time, like sudden sharp pains in his ears, and made his head ache. That little dog better watch out. One of these days, when Archie was clipping the hedge, he might have a chance to slip over and see the dog for a second or so, when nobody was looking. He thought how surprised the dog would be when he looked around and found he had no tail. Those hedge clippers would cut through a heavy sapling branch easily enough, and they could snip a dog's tail off even easier.

Archie, walking on the rail on the track above his house, thinking about the look of surprise on the little brown dog's face when he looked around and found he had no tail, lost his balance and teetered wildly, and then had to step off. It was ten minutes before eight, which gave him plenty of time to reach the River Avenue Market and get into his apron before work began. But still he mustn't loiter. He mustn't be late this morning, or any other morning, or Mr. Brothers would fire him. The last time he'd been late, Mr. Brothers had said: "I'm telling you something, kid. You're not working here because you are a good worker — or because anybody in the store likes you. We're trying to help your poor mother, and if it wasn't for her —"

Archie's attention, at this point, had wavered to a red-slatted truck which was pulling into the unloading area outside, and Mr. Brothers suddenly grabbed him by the shirt and jerked him around and thrust his big red face in close. "Some day you'll catch me wrong, you little shit, and I'll — Even your mother and her sad condition won't help you!" He let go of Archie's shirt and shoved him away. "G'wan, get outa here before I lose my temper and wrap you around a desk!"

Archie got back on the rail and walked carefully, teetering, in the hot morning. A train was coming. He could tell, because he could feel a faint tickling in his feet. He stepped down from the rail and looked expectantly at the upper curve. He liked to see a train go by even better in the daytime than at night. It sucked up dust and old chewing-gum wrappers and whirled the horseweeds like a high wind, and if the engineer saw him waving, he might wave back. It was very exciting. Archie stopped beside the siding that led into the rear of the Carey Furnace freight station to watch the train go by. Presently the train rounded the upper curve and bore down on him and he stood on tiptoe, ready to wave. The onrushing diesel towered above him like a building, he fluttered his hand, saw the engineer reply, in his high window, with a small careless motion, and the train exploded past and Archie yelled for joy, forgetting everything in the power and fury of the train.

When he reached the River Avenue Market the front doors were open and Mr. Brothers was standing there looking out. He looked at Archie, and then at his watch, and Archie had a sudden urge to turn and run. He was late again. The train had made him late. But it was too late to run. Mr. Brothers was beckoning to him. "It was the train, Mr. Brothers," he said, walking quickly, trying to smile. "It was blocking me from getting over the track. Gee, I gotta run fast now, and get into my uniform."

"I was on the loading platform," Mr. Brothers said in his ugly voice, the one he used when he was mad. "I saw you. You were on this side of the tracks. The train wasn't blocking you."

He saw Mr. Brothers's red fingers tighten into a fist. He tensed himself to dodge back and run. But the big-bellied man did not strike him. The fingers unclenched and Archie knew it was all right. "Hurry up," Mr. Brothers muttered at him. "Get the hell in there. Hurry up. . . ."

Louise Stegmeyer was growing nervous as she sat at her desk in the library of the steel company. She had got there early, as Mr. Hurd had asked her to do, prepared to take Nellie Laubach and Norman Kraft up to Mr. Hurd's camp on Black River, to start with the picnic preparations. But after she punched in at the time clock and went to look for Nellie, she was told that Mr. Bishop had called Nellie in to take dictation. Now almost an hour had passed and Nellie was still in with Mr. Bishop. Louise was torn between knocking on the door and incurring Mr. Bishop's wrath at the interruption, or maybe waiting half the morning for Nellie to come out (Mr. Bishop had been known to dictate for most of a morning on one letter, when he was searching for just the right words).

To complicate matters, the library, which had been more or less deserted, suddenly had a rush of business. Howard Snyder was over in the stacks looking for some engineering information having to do with a handbook he was trying to finish up before going on vacation. Doug Schroeder, of the art department, was sitting at one of the tables doing research on a layout. Jack McHugh was fooling around the late-magazine rack, leafing through a *Life* magazine, and old Dan Foy had come in with some of his latest camp photos.

Dan was the projectionist for the department. He kept the film and tape libraries, and showed the many company motion pictures illustrating the manufacture of various Carey Furnace products to jobber conventions, churches, schools, and the like. Dan was a camera bug. Every Sunday, in summer, he took pictures of his camp up on the Allegheny River, developed, enlarged, and hand-tinted his masterpieces on company time, and then began his grand tour of the office to show off the results. Dan was a stumpy troglodyte of a man with a hoarse voice and a smelly cigar invariably clamped in his yellow teeth. He was, in truth, a nuisance, but one that the employees of the department had learned to accept when he appeared to show his pictures. The best technique was to give the old boy what he was looking for: extravagant praise — tell him the hand-tinted photos were great, the camp was certainly a paradise on earth, and how were the grandchildren? If you had the patience to follow this routine, you need endure the cigar smoke and the old duffer's small talk for maybe as little as two or three minutes.

Dan had showed the current pictures to Louise, who had exclaimed over them, and was turning to go over to Jack McHugh when he spied Doug Schroeder sitting at the reading table. Louise saw the old man hesitate (even in Dan's uncomplicated brain, some dim warning must have sounded at the sight of the intent hawk profile of the art director, concentrating on his research). But Louise Stegmeyer had just looked at the pictures, and her praise was still in old Dan's ears, and, tempted by more praise to come (if you could get it from Doug, you had really scored!), he crossed the room, puffing his cigar, and dropped the latest masterpiece on the page of the magazine Schroeder was reading. It was not the most diplomatic thing to do with anybody — much less with a man of Schroeder's reputation — so perhaps old Dan rated what he got. Schroeder twisted almost violently in his chair, just as Dan blew a cloud of cigar smoke at him and said, with smug assurance, "Well, Doug, what do you think of that one?"

For an instant Louise half expected the art director to strike the old man. Schroeder's face tightened in a look of anger — and then, for some reason, smoothed out. He picked up the colored photo and held it carefully, upside down, studying it. "Not bad," he said judiciously, pursing his lips and cocking his head in the manner of the engrossed critic. "In fact, pretty good."

"Hey, wait!" Dan said, grabbing at the photo. "You got it upside down!"

Doug Schroeder held the photograph out of Dan's reach, still upside down. "It's got wonderful composition," he said. "And the color — breath-taking. Simply breath-taking!"

"Hey," Dan yelled, reaching over the table trying to grab the photograph. "You must be nuts! You got it upside down! Lemme have —"

Doug Schroeder leaned away, keeping the photo out of the old man's grasp, and then, with a flick of his wrist, sailed it away across the table onto the floor by the stacks. Dan stood and looked at the picture, lying ten feet away, and then at Schroeder. "Hey," he said stupidly. "Hey — what you tryin' to pull?"

Doug Schroeder brought the old man off to perfection. He let his face go slack, slumped in his seat, and his voice was mumbly and full of angered bewilderment. "Hey," Doug Schroeder mimicked. "Hey — what you tryin' to pull?"

Dan Foy stared uncertainly. Doug Schroeder suddenly stopped his comedy, and his mouth grew harsh. "Listen, Dan," he said. "Go pick up that silly picture and go back down to the projection room where you belong! You're annoying people who want to work!"

Dan opened his mouth, like an aged fish, then closed it. He shuffled over, stooped, and retrieved the picture, not looking at it now, not even bothering to dust it off, and started for the door of the library. Louise noticed Jack McHugh had put the copy of *Life* back in the rack and as the old man was about to pass him, on the way out, Jack turned as if he hadn't noticed any of the byplay and said, "Well, if it ain't old Dan? How you doing, Dan?"

"All right," Dan mumbled.

"What you got there, son? Pictures of that paradise on the Allegheny, otherwise known as Foy's Folly?"

"Aw, hell, Jack," Dan Foy said in a low voice. "Lemme past."

"Oh, no," Jack McHugh said. "Gimme a look-see." He took the

photograph from Dan Foy's hand and looked at it carefully and briefly. "Hey, you goofed, buddy. You got young Danny's noggin in this picture, right?"

Dan Foy looked up. A slight gleam had returned to his eyes. "Yeah, that's little Danny. The little bugger jumped up just as I was snappin' the picture."

Jack McHugh said, "You got a nickel on you, Dan?"

"Sure, I guess so —"

"Then you can buy me a cup of coffee," Jack McHugh said. "You ain't bought a cup of coffee since Hector was a pup. You are the tightest old guy in this department."

Dan Foy's old eyes glowed with the light of battle. "Ain't bought — hey, listen, Jack McHugh! I bought the coffee the last time you and I was down, and don't you say I didn't! Tightest guy in the department, hey?" Dan paused. "I'm onto you, Jack McHugh. You think you can kid me into buying! Well, we'll flip for it, see!"

"Okay, okay," Jack McHugh said. "We'll flip for it. But let's blow this firetrap before Louise over there reports us to the management. We'll flip down at the cafeteria."

Shortly after the two men had left, Doug Schroeder rose and came over to Louise Stegmeyer's desk. "Like to take out this thing," he said, putting a magazine down. "Think I'll be able to concentrate better in my office than in this art gallery."

Louise made a notation of the magazine, and stamped it. Schroeder said, "Some cornball, that McHugh."

Louise looked up.

"I said old Jack McHugh is a cornball — big sweet blob type — protector of the old and infirm, that stuff."

Louise looked at him.

Doug Schroeder's eyes narrowed slightly. "Or maybe you don't agree, Miss Stegmeyer. Maybe you think Old Dan's art work is for the ages. Maybe I'm offending your finer sensibilities with my coarse carping."

Louise felt her face getting hot, and she dropped her eyes. "I don't know," she said. "I guess it's all he's got."

"You're a sweet girl," Doug Schroeder said. "You're a dear sweet girl, Louise, and if some nasty person comes around and tries to tell you there's no Santy Claus, you just send them in to old Doug. Old Doug will slap them on the wrist for you. Hard. Real real hard."

Louise took a quick deep breath. "I know you're making fun of me, Mr. Schroeder," she said. "I know Mr. Foy's pictures aren't very good." Her face was flushed now. She lifted her eyes and looked at him directly. "But if Mr. McHugh is a cornball, I guess I like cornballs better than —"

"Yes, Louise — you like cornballs better than what?"

Howard Snyder had finished in the stacks and come out with a book and was standing behind Doug Schroeder. Now he made a sound in his throat, and Doug Schroeder, who had not realized he was there, turned and looked at him. A smile gathered around his lips. "Oh," he said, "it's you, Marco Polo. I thought you'd be out roaming around the hills of Pakistan or Tibet or some place this fine morning. Tell me — do you like cornballs too, Mr. Snyder?"

"I like Jack McHugh," Howard Snyder said in a low voice. "He's a friend of mine."

"Well, that's fine," Doug Schroeder said. "Howie, old man, I'm sure you'll be very happy around here, if you like cornballs. This joint is jumping with them."

Neither Howard Snyder nor Louise Stegmeyer spoke. Schroeder glanced from one to the other, shook his head, and said, "Miss Stegmeyer, check my magazine yet?"

"It's all ready," Louise said.

"Good," Doug Schroeder said. "I'll take it and leave. The sweetness and light around here is beginning to make me a little nauseated."

He picked up the magazine, stepped past Howard Snyder, and started for the door. As he neared the door, it opened, and Nellie Laubach came in hurriedly. Doug Schroeder turned, looked at Nellie, and said, "Well — it looks as if you've got enough to hold a meeting of the association." Then he went out.

Nellie Laubach looked uncertainly at the door and then at Louise Stegmeyer. "What was that about?"

"Nothing," Louise said. "Just a sample of Mr. Schroeder's sense of humor. Nellie, I've been waiting all morning. Are you ready to go?"

"It wasn't my fault," Nellie said. "Mr. Bishop kept me in there dictating. You know how he is when —"

"I know," Louise cut in. "Look, Nellie, we're running very late. Suppose you check with Norman Kraft. See if he's ready, while I take care of Mr. Snyder."

"All right, Louise. I'll go right now and check with Norman. And if he's ready I should bring him back with me?"

"Yes, why don't you? It'll save time."

When Nellie Laubach left, Howard Snyder put his books on the desk. His heart was beating heavily, as it always did when he got into an argument, and his knees felt trembly and his mouth was very dry. He felt weak and inadequate. He had been standing there in the stacks and had seen the whole incident from the time Dan Foy had dropped the snapshot on Doug Schroeder's magazine. When Doug had started to needle Louise, Howard had come out with the idea of getting into the argument and taking her side — had even gotten so far as to clear his throat — but when Doug had turned to him, suddenly, with that crack about Marco Polo, he'd gone tight inside, unable to do anything but mumble that he was a friend of Jack McHugh's. He was a washout when the heat went on, and it didn't matter much who put it on — Doug Schroeder, his own wife, or some little stenographer in the bullpen. When anybody showed teeth, Howard Snyder came apart. Now he did not look at Louise Stegmeyer's eyes. He looked at the books he was holding. He said, "I'd like to take out these three, please."

He saw her hands take the books. "Certainly, Mr. Snyder," she said, and her voice was not contemptuous of him, as it might have been after his weak performance. It was friendly. He looked at her. She was smiling.

"Mr. Snyder . . ."

"Yes?"

"Could I say something out of the line of business?"

"Why, yes — of course."

"I was awfully glad to hear you stick up for Mr. McHugh."

"Well — thanks —"

Their eyes met, and held, for an instant, and Howard Snyder felt his nervous system pinch tight. Then she was stamping the books and he was picking them up, his heart thudding, and he was standing in front of her desk wanting to say something more, but unable to think of anything. Then he was turning away, but not quite. He stopped. "Goodbye," he said, feeling infinitely silly and schoolboyish. You didn't say goodbye to a librarian when you took out a book. But Louise Stegmeyer didn't act as if he was silly. She said, "Goodbye, Mr. Snyder," as if she liked him. He went out into the hall, carrying his books. And he was not thinking of Tehuantepec, Mexico, or the silky scream of a jet transport, high in the sky. He was thinking of how Louise Stegmeyer's eyes had looked in the instant when they'd met his, and his heart was brushing quickly in his ears, like wire brushes on a snare drum.

Mr. Frank Brothers, manager of the River Avenue Market, was engaged in a duty which suited him perfectly: he was helping Mrs. Ethyl Snyder pick out some special groceries for a surprise party she was going to give for her husband, Howard. Normally Mr. Brothers did not concern himself with waiting on customers. He was the manager. Waiting on customers was for the cheap help. But always, when he had a chance, he made it a point to wait on Ethyl Snyder. He had had his eye on Mrs. Snyder for nearly two years now, since she had started buying at the River Avenue Market. Mrs. Snyder's breasts were what principally intrigued Frank Brothers. He was, as he admitted in male company, a tit man. And if you were a tit man, Ethyl Snyder was certainly your doll. Now, in the store, Brothers brought down a bottle from one of the higher shelves. "Capers, Mrs. Snyder? These are imported — very choice — and I'm sure —"

"No, thank you," Ethyl Snyder said, smiling automatically, showing her lovely white teeth, seeing Frank Brothers, not as a person at all, but as a sort of store fixture, a red-faced automaton who went about pulling cans and boxes off shelves for her convenience. She did not dream what was going on inside Mr. Brothers's head. Had she known, she would have hurried from the store instantly and never returned.

The truth was, Mr. Brothers had been mentally undressing Mrs. Snyder for the past half-hour. He had started, naturally enough, with her breasts and had gone down the belly with the fine womanly bulge to it, to the full hips and the deep soft promise between the thighs. Mrs. Snyder's legs were a bit thin for Mr. Brothers's taste, from ankle to knee, but above that, she was fine. The thighs swelled out and she would no doubt wrap them around you, Mr. Brothers thought, after she got in a state. She would go in for a lot of panting and gasping, Mr. Brothers thought, and maybe she'd bite his ears a little, or cry. The crying, he thought, would be more likely. Ethyl Snyder looked like the crying type, under the proper stimulation, in the proper setting. He knew how she would look when she cried: her nose would get red and her face would get blotchy and her lovely blue eyes would get a little bloodshot. The vision intrigued him — it was more exciting than the vision of pink schoolteacher perfection she now exhibited. It was the vision of the passionate, tearful victim in the battle of the sexes, as much as the vision of the swollen nipples of the heavy breasts, and the spasmodic gripping of thin red-nailed fingers in the flesh of his back, that excited Mr. Brothers. Yes, he thought, happily lustful in the August heat amid the rich smells from the meat and fruit counters, Ethyl Snyder was certainly his dish of tea. Hotter than a firecracker — want it every night — and tied to that sad little character who smoked a pipe and never opened his yap. The poor dope. He wasn't good enough for a sweet, passionate nymphomaniac like Ethyl — chances were he couldn't begin to satisfy her.

Frank Brothers had seen Howard Snyder on a number of occasions when driving past the Snyder place on a Sunday afternoon, hoping that he might accidentally on purpose find Howard gone on some business trip and his wife pottering in the yard. But Howard never seemed to go on business trips. Howard was usually out in the yard fooling around with sandpaper on some hunk of junk his wife must have bought at a sale. The dope. Fooling with furnitute when he could be inside fooling with her. But then, maybe Ethyl made him do it, in return for her favors. If that was the case, the guy got his money's worth. If Frank Brothers could fool with tits like that he would refinish pisspots — pisspots by the dozens. . . .

"Avocados," Mrs. Snyder was saying. "I want three of your best avocados, and some fresh shrimp. Howard especially likes shrimp."

With an effort, Frank Brothers wrenched himself back from his happy imaginings and became the attentive merchant. "We have some fine fresh-frozen shrimp," he said. "Your husband's birthday, perhaps?"

"Oh no — something special."

"I see."

Ethyl Snyder glanced at the wide sweaty face and she had a slight feeling of violation. It was all right to be helpful and solicitous, but this inquiry into the purpose of the food, this was going a bit far. He was getting forward, and it had better be stopped, right now. She said, chilly and curt, "The shrimp will be all. Two pounds. Now I must hurry. I've a great many things to do today." And turning her back, she wheeled her wire buggy of special foods quickly toward the fish counter, leaving Mr. Brothers behind.

John Carey had slept very poorly. The night had been heavy and hot, and the needle which Pop had given him — the pain in his right side was steady now — had let him doze, but he did not feel rested. He had forced Pop to tell him the truth. Pop had been weeping when he spoke, and John Carey had never seen him weep before in all the years he had known him. The only hope, Pop had said, would have been the Pack operation — a massive radical excision of all the lymph nodes in the groins, the armpits — which Pop said he would definitely have undertaken if the liver had not been involved. Radical lymph-node surgery would be useless without taking the liver too — and the liver, of course, was not dispensable. There was no point in taking any part of a cancer if you could not get it all. The miracle was, Pop had finally admitted, that the liver involvement had not already made John Carey violently ill.

As he had forced Pop to tell him the truth — and been grateful for the truth, even through his terrible fear — John Carey had, in characteristic fashion, been planning his attack on the problem. Time was now obviously short. It might, indeed, be numbered in days. If he could just keep the whole thing secret from everybody — even his wife — until the necessary steps had been taken, at least he could leave everything in a neat, tightly tied package.

Well, he had fooled Eva last night after Pop had dropped him in the driveway. He had laughed and joked and sat in the kitchen with the morphine working inside him, while Eva broiled steaks, and all the time in the bright kitchen he had seemed to be inside an iron box, with just a slit to look through, and everything and everybody else was outside in a bright, incredibly precious world he could no longer inhabit. Eva had remarked that he looked tired; and he had blamed it on the heat again, and then he had kissed her and gone up to bed and undressed.

But he had not at once lain in the bed. It was natural, he supposed, when you knew you must soon be shut away from sight and sound and feeling forever, to want to avail yourself of every impression, even pain, until the end. He sat down in a chair by the window and stared out at the night sky. The town lights made a murky glow over the valley, but to the west, above the Allegheny hills, the sky was velvet-black with hot, isolated stars burning sharp and clear, and, high overhead, he saw the Milky Way, drifts of smudged light which looked like pale smoke, a system so incredibly vast that a man could not hope to encompass its entirety in a normal lifetime, even moving at the speed of light. Was the blackness endless? Were these drifts of stars operating by blind chance, and when he died and went into the dark would it be as if he had never been at all? He thought so. He had never believed, really, in a personal God who observed the sparrow's fall; he had never had any respect for the foxhole religion: no God with his wits about him, and a rudimentary sense of justice, would be taken in by the frightened deathbed conversion of any human being who had been selfish and cruel and without pity for a lifetime and who, when faced with the pit of darkness, wished to wipe the slate clean, be forgiven, and enter the same kingdom through the same door as the fellow who had put up with meanness and had shared the things he really wanted and had muddled through as best he could when plucked savagely by the taloned fingers of circumstance. John Carey was not afraid of punishment visited upon him by a God who was piqued because he had not gone to church regularly, not given lip service to the conventional religion, and not done all of the many other things which most ministers advocated as a passport to heaven. The God he believed in — and he did hope, though not with great conviction, that this God might be a personal one, who, watching John Carey personally, might, at some later time, resurrect him and place him back in this pitiless, compassionate, wonderful, horrible, dull, exciting human condition — this God would certainly not be a nitpicker. He would be a power — cool, never-changing, as Spinoza said, always operating within the rigid eternal framework of His own inexorable laws. The great miracle, according to Spinoza, was simply the fact that no miracles were possible, ever. Which, considered, was the only thing which made mankind's practical existence possible. If steamships rose capriciously and flew through the air, and men could walk on water, the chaos and uncertainty would be such that no plans, no progress could ever be made.

John Carey was not afraid to die, and he was not afraid of his God. He had done the best he could, most of the time, and he was prepared to accept whatever judgment might befall. He was, however, lonely. There was no comfort, not even self-pity, inside the iron box. There was only the vision of the outside — still bright — and never more precious, now that it would soon be gone. . . .

Now, in the early morning, John Carey sat up in bed and swung his legs over the edge. He was dizzy from the drugs Pop had given him. He put his weight on his feet carefully and stood up. His left foot felt normal, but his right foot felt queer — a little numb, as if he had lain on it wrong in the night. He sat down on the bed and bent and squeezed his right foot with his fingers. It was cool and the big toe and second toe felt wooden. Feeling did not begin until the third toe. He flexed his fingers. They were all right. No numbness. It was just his right foot — two toes on his right foot — this morning. . . .

He straightened and sat a moment, and the solution which had been in his mind — tentative, waiting, on call — ever since he realized he was going to die, took solid, firm shape. He had read somewhere — Somerset Maugham had said it, he thought — that one of man's great advantages over the animals was man's choice of the moment of his death. There were times when life was no longer useful or desirable to a human being, or to those around him. Why should God punish anyone for vacating his body under such conditions? God had given man free will for everything else. He could hardly deny him its use in this particular area.

John Carey went into the bathroom, shaved, and bathed, then came back and dressed in a light business suit, white shirt, bow tie, and summer-weight brown shoes. He had decided to act today, while he was still able. Walking to and from the bathroom, his right foot had tended to drag slightly. Tomorrow, or the day after, he might not be able to leave his bed. He went to his dresser and opened the right-hand top drawer where he had kept a thirty-eight police revolver, fully loaded, since an anonymous letter threatening his life had been received some years ago. He stared at the gun, dull blue and evil-looking behind the stacks of folded handkerchiefs, and a superstitious fear, mixed with a vain senseless hope, held him in check. Perhaps a miracle would happen, and the cancer would somehow go away. He had read of such things occurring. No — that was impossible. The cancer had spread. He was living on borrowed time right now. If he waited, he might no longer have the power to decide. He might be paralyzed, blind, in agony — and helpless.

He lifted the revolver into his brief case, and left the room, moving quietly. Outside his wife's bedroom he paused. This was his last and greatest decision. Should he go in and tell her, and say goodbye — or should he go quietly, leaving a note? He had always, somehow, had a contempt for people who did things and left notes telling about it. And yet, from Eva's standpoint, mightn't a note be the easiest and best? He could not go in and tell her, of course, that he intended to kill himself. He could only tell her that he had the disease, and that he was going to the office now, for the last time, very probably, to hold a final board meeting. She would, as a result, worry from the instant he told her — all through the morning, until the news of his suicide had time to reach her. For what? For nothing. By this afternoon he would be dead. Let Eva sleep. . . .

"John, is that you?"

He stiffened at the sound of her voice from behind her bedroom door. He hesitated, then said, in a normal tone, "Yes, dear."

"My clock has stopped — what time is it?"

"A little after six."

"Why are you up so early?"

"I have some urgent things to do at the office."

"Oh, I see — well, aren't you coming in and kiss me?"

He stepped forward and opened the door, holding his brief case with the gun in it. His wife was sitting up in bed, tousled and flushed from the hot night, smiling at him. He placed the brief case on the floor near the door. He crossed the room, and his right foot did not drag at all, and bent down. Their eyes met. She pulled her face back suddenly and stared at him. "John — what is it?"

"What's what?"

"Something's wrong," she said. "I don't know how I know — but I know. Something's awful, John. Oh, please — tell me!"

He sat down on the edge of the bed. He put his arm around her and held her tightly. "Don't be sorry," he said. "There's no use being sorry about anything — you know what we used to say: if you can't change it, forget it?"

He could feel the swift beat of her heart against the side of his chest. He took a deep breath. "Pop says it's going to be very quick. I've got a cancer — and it's gone past the operative stage — Now Eve, Eve, damn it — don't cry — you hear me!" And then, inside him, he felt the pain coming, very fast and very big, as if somebody had fetched a hot iron from a forge and held it close to his side and then touched him with it . . . and then jammed it savagely into him. He caught his lower lip under his teeth and bit down, then released his lip and breathed in sharply. "Get Pop, Eve," he said. "Quick . . ."

Louise Stegmeyer was driving Nellie Laubach and little Norman Kraft, who kept the photo files, toward George Hurd's camp on Black River. It was a fourteen-mile trip — up to Lundyville, across the bridge, then back over the hill to the woods road leading to the camp. The stretch up Black River itself — three miles — was one of the most scenic in western Pennsylvania. Until a few years ago, the road had been a pair of stony ruts, used only by oil-pumpers — a tunnel through solid walls of wild grape, rhododendron, and mountain laurel. The coming of the steel company men had changed all that. Bulldozers had straightened out the bends in the haphazard track and wiped out the fern and laurel and grape; stone and gravel had filled in the mudholes; and dynamite and clamshell buckets and chain saws had ripped down sections of the virgin jungle and let in the sky. There was a colony now: George Hurd, who had blazed the trail; Mark Hunter from the blast furnace division; Elliott Fleming from accounting; and the land had been bought for several miles beyond the last camp. And recently, it had become fashionable to have a dock in the river.

George Hurd's dock could be seen thrusting out into the dark, foam-flecked eddy water in front of his camp when Louise drove the Chevy around the final bend and turned in at the sign which said *Shady Glen Cottage, George A. Hurd.* A truck loaded with beer was standing in the sun in a clearing which Mr. Hurd would use as a parking lot for the picnic cars. Louise stopped the car and they all got out. The driver of the truck was sitting on the running board, picking his teeth, when she approached.

"Sorry we're late," Louise said nervously. She had never really been in charge of anything before, and the responsibility, coupled with the jitters she still had from the run-in with Schroeder, made her feel a little weak in the knees.

"That's okay, lady," the driver said. "I'm paid by the hour."

Louise made herself look at the man. He was darkly tanned, had black curly hair, a well-muscled chest, and a roguish eye. He wore heavy work shoes, khaki pants, and an undershirt. At this moment he reached into the cab of the truck and brought out a cigar, then fished in his pants pocket for a match. Louise felt a thrill of panic. Mr. Hurd had told her there was to be absolutely no smoking at the camp because of the danger of fire in the dry woods. The driver had a packet of matches out now and was about to light up.

She took a convulsive breath. "Oh, driver — I'm sorry — but Mr. Hurd, the owner of this camp, asked me particularly not to smoke while I was here." She swallowed. "Or — or anybody else — on account of forest fires. . . ."

The man did not strike his match. He looked at her with sudden combativeness, opened his mouth as if to bellow some terrible obscenity, then shut it and peered more closely at her with his hot-looking eyes. Louise was not wearing her pleated skirt and her frilly Martha Washington blouse which, at the office, completely camouflaged her figure. She had put on a plain skirt and a short-sleeved pullover, and as the driver looked at her she felt her face grow warm.

He said, "I don't know who this guy Hurd is, and I don't give a rip, but if you're telling me on your own, Miss, I guess I hafta be a good boy and do what the pretty lady says." He winked, took the cigar out of his mouth, and made a great ceremony about putting it back in the cab.

Louise was rigid inside. Never in her life had anybody looked at her with such uninhibited appreciation of her physical appearance, or called her a pretty lady, and for a moment, she thought the truck driver was making fun of her. But only for an instant did she think this. He wasn't making fun. He was looking at her the way she'd seen men looking at the semiclothed color posters of Italian movie stars in front of the theatre in Carey Furnace. It was crude, and horrible, and frightening — and she realized, with a guilty pang, that she loved it. She said, "We've got a spring in back somewhere, I think. I'm not sure where. But we want the beer put in it."

"All this beer in one little spring?" the driver said. "You know how much beer I got on the truck? Fifty cases. You ain't got no spring big enough to hold fifty cases, have you, gorgeous?"

Louise ignored the familiarity. A strange and wonderful transformation was going on inside of her. The rigid tension was melting away, and in its place was coming a strange thrill — the thrill of power a well-built female has over the interested male. She spoke in a friendly but businesslike way. "I'm sure I don't know. I guess I'd better go back and have a look."

"You need any help looking," the driver said, "just call on little Ralph, here. Little Ralph will be happy to help you look for the spring — or anything else."

Louise smiled. "I won't need your help, thank you, Ralph. You just stay here. I'll be right back."

The spring was in a ravine on the far side of the camp, a large concrete basin fed by a cold jet of water from a pipe embedded in the hillside. The basin was big enough to hold the beer, but she saw that there was no way for the truck to back in to unload. She returned to the truck on the other side of the cabin. "I'm sorry," she said. "I'm afraid you'll have to unload here and carry the cases around to the spring. There's no way to drive in."

"Lady, I can unload the truck for you. But I ain't supposed to carry stuff all over your property. That's up to you."

Louise glanced at Nellie Laubach, fussing in the kitchen, and little Norman Kraft, staggering ineffectually under a medium-sized watermelon. She looked at the driver. "I've got to get the beer in the spring, if it's going to be cold enough to drink when the picnic starts. There's just the three of us and we've got a million things to do."

"You cryin' on my shoulder, gorgeous?"

Louise Stegmeyer, in her twenty-six years, had never had any opportunity to develop feminine wiles. She had always felt herself too big and ungainly to be trying the little tricks which were so transparent, but which seemed to work so magically when some small dainty girl tried them. She had always been the Good Sport, the Willing Volunteer, the Silent Accepter of Life as it Had to Be. But now, on this most unusual morning, she surprised herself. She did not meekly give up and tell the man she'd get the beer into the spring herself, somehow. She looked at him and grinned the first coquettish grin of her life — her eyes partly closed, looking down, her mouth open a little (it was something that must be built into girls, like the homing instinct into pigeons), and said, "Ralph, if I have to cry on your shoulder to get this beer in the spring, I'll sure do it."

He looked at her — and suddenly he began to laugh. Not a mean laugh, but a delighted laugh, an appreciative laugh. "By God," he said, "it ain't allowed. The union got some kind of rule against it — movin' stuff around after it's off the truck. That's for the hod carriers or somebody, I think. But the hell — pardon me — the heck with the hod carriers. Where's this spring of yours, baby?"

"Back here," Louise said. "I'll show you. . . ."

Now, half an hour later, the beer was in the spring, the rolls were neatly packed in the kitchen, the watermelons were stacked and secured in the shade on the picnic tables, and Louise Stegmeyer was getting a proposition. She was standing out by the truck, signing for the beer, and Ralph, the curly-headed driver, was saying, "Miss — you work at the Steel, I guess?"

"Yes, I do."

"Which department?"

"Advertising."

"What do you do there — pose for the illustrations?"

She smiled. "Well, thank you, kind sir. No, I'm only the librarian."

He looked at her, shyly now, surprisingly enough. "My name is Ralph Smith. I just wanted to say . . . what I mean is . . . it's been a great pleasure working with you, Miss —"

"Stegmeyer. Louise Stegmeyer."

"Louise. That's a pretty name." The driver, who'd been so aggressive at the start, now seemed almost as nervous as Louise had been at the start. He glanced down at his sweaty clothes. "I don't look like this when I get dressed up — Louise . . . I got a new Ford convertible, and — well, I was wonderin' if I could take you for a drive some night?"

She looked at her hands. She did not feel big or ungainly now. She felt happy and sure of herself. She said, "Oh thank you, Ralph. It's kind of sudden. Could I think about it a little?"

"Sure, you think about it," he said. "But think about it real soon — because I'm gonna call you up real soon. Well — 'bye now."

"Goodbye, Ralph," Louise said. "Thanks — thanks very much. . . ."

The public address system was being installed in the big living room of the camp when George Hurd arrived. Nellie Laubach saw the black Cadillac turn up through the trees and ran, panicky and breathless, to Louise, who was trying to show the electricians how she thought the hookup to the gasoline generator should be made.

"Louise — oh, dear! It's Mr. Hurd! He's here! What'll I *do?*"

Louise felt a stab of nerves, but she said, "Go in the kitchen. Start polishing the sink or something. I'll handle it."

"Oh, thanks — thanks, Louise!"

George Hurd had parked his car and he waved a friendly greeting when Louise stepped outside. This was the time of the annual picnic, George Hurd's time to unbend, to show his employees that he was a regular fellow, after all. He called out, "You're Miss Stegmeyer, aren't you?"

"Yes, Mr. Hurd."

"The beer truck passed me, coming out — so I guess he unloaded — but I don't see it anywhere."

"He put the beer in the spring, Mr. Hurd."

"He did? Well, *that's* something new. We've been holding these parties out here ever since I built — and this is the first time any driver ever put any beer in the spring. We've always had to do it ourselves. What did you do, Miss Stegmeyer, wave a magic wand?"

She smiled. "Oh, no, sir. He was just a very nice man." Again she surprised herself. She did not simper or giggle or twist her dress nervously. She felt light-headed and a little dizzy, but she could feel confidence welling up inside her from some hidden source she had not known she possessed. "I'm glad you've come, Mr. Hurd. I was wondering if you could give us directions on what to do now."

"The way it looks to me, young lady, you've just about finished all the important things." He cocked his head on one side, and looked at her. "Say, I just had an idea. I wonder if you'd like a short guided tour of the place. I'm — well, I guess I'm kind of proud of things, and if you'd like to see the layout, I'd be glad to show you."

"Oh, I'd love it!"

George Hurd smiled at Louise. "Mrs. Hurd thought all this was silly," he said. "She was against building way out here. We'd never use it, she said. Nobody would come to see us. We'd sell out — at a loss — in a year. Well, just look up the line, Miss Stegmeyer. Three camps already. And three docks. In another couple of years the camps will be around the bend. I guess we've started a colony all right."

"Does Mrs. Hurd like it now?"

He chuckled. "She won't admit it. You know women. If old Andy Mellon rose from his grave and built a mansion right next door, Mrs. Hurd would still have reservations, I bet. But, to answer your question, she likes it. Sure she does."

They walked across the woods road, down a winding path to the dock. The river was a tawny brown sheet, flecked with suds of foam from the rapids above. The big stones across the river were bone-white in the sun, and the hillside rose almost vertically, a dark dry wall rising to meet the bright blue of the sky. There was a dead tree on the crest of the hill, silvery and gnarled, with a bird sitting motionless on one of the limbs. George Hurd pointed at the bird. "Want me to make him fly?"

"Could you?"

Suddenly he yelled, a shockingly loud sound in the silence. It took a second or so for the sound to reach the bird. It seemed to be going to ignore the shout. And then, ponderously, almost lazily, the bird's wings flapped, and it rose and wheeled over the ridge line and was gone.

George Hurd looked at Louise Stegmeyer. "Did you see that? Did you see him fly? I made him fly, Louise — just like I said I could do!"

She felt a thrill.

Louise. Mr. George Hurd, head of the department, had called her Louise. And not only that. She'd noticed him looking at her as he showed off his place. His eyes had had some trace of the same look that had been in the eyes of Ralph Smith. This day, Louise thought, as she followed Mr. Hurd off the long dock — this day was strange. Very, very strange.

They left the river and walked back to the cottage and Mr. Hurd got into his car. When he had turned it and was driving out, he waved to her and shouted, "Goodbye, Louise — see you at the picnic!"

Nellie Laubach was still polishing the sink when Louise walked into the kitchen. Nellie looked up, nervously, and seeing Louise was alone, she sighed and said, "Oh — is he gone?"

"Yes, he's gone."

"Was it awful?"

"No, it wasn't awful. It was fun."

Nellie Laubach was looking at her curiously — almost fearfully.

"What is it?" Louise said. "Have I got dirt on my face or anything?"

"Oh no — it's not that. But you look — different —"

"Different? How do you mean?"

"I don't know how I mean. I couldn't say. Prettier, I guess. Yes, that's it. Lots prettier than I ever saw you, Louise. Like a bride, or something."

"Thank you, Nellie."

"That's all right. They say Mr. Hurd is different outside the office —"

"Mr. Hurd is an old darling."

Nellie Laubach's sad eyes widened. "My goodness, Louise, you haven't been out there drinking beer with him, have you?"

"No, I haven't. But Nellie, it's an idea. Drinking beer, I mean. We've got fifty cases. They'll never miss a couple of bottles. What do you say?"

"Louise!"

"Oh, come on, Nellie. We've earned it — if you like beer —"

"Well —"

"Fine," Louise said. "Round up Norman and the electricians and meet me at the spring. I'll get an opener. It'll be kind of a little celebration. All right?"

"All right," Nellie Laubach said weakly. "All right, if you say so, Louise. . . ."

In the office he shared with Willie Martin at the steel company, Howard Snyder was, as Willie described it, goofing off. For the past three days he had not really done a greal deal of productive work. The trip to Mexico was too close. How could a man concentrate on the inside diameter of a length of double-galvanized copper-bearing steel pipe when he was actually seeing the distant glitter of the sea? At this moment, Howard was peering at a full-color photograph of a huge jet transport, soaring in a warm blue sky past a snow-capped mountain peak. The ad said this airplane flew six hundred miles an hour, was so free of vibration you could balance a fifty-cent piece on edge in the cabin, and there were free champagne and Rock Cornish game hen served on the nonstop flight from Greater Pittsburgh

Airport straight into Mexico City. Mexico City, he thought. Ancient buildings, drenched in white sunlight; then the winding roads through the purple mountains down to the burning palm-thatched margin of the Pacific. *In that November off Tehuantepec . . . the slopping of the sea grew still one night. . . .*

"Hey, Howie," Willie Martin said. "Come back, Little Sheba!"

Howard Snyder dropped from six hundred miles an hour at thirty thousand feet, out of the blue sky over a mountain peak, to his desk four feet away from Willie Martin's. He turned in his chair. "Huh?"

"Yah," Willie Martin said. "Huh!"

"What's the problem, Willie?"

"No problem, little buddy. I just been tryin' to tell you about this memo of Al Bishop's, and you been off on cloud nine and didn't hear a word I said."

"I'm sorry, Willie. What was it?"

"This memo of Al's says there's gonna be a big parking problem at the picnic on account of the road's so narrow and they need the cleared space for softball, so we got to organize car pools. What I was sayin', Jack McHugh is takin' his car, and I'm ridin' with him — and Jack says to ask you to come too, if you want to."

"That sounds fine."

"Jack wants to start around lunchtime. He's in charge of the games or some damned thing, and he has to be there a little early. We don't work Thursday morning, and you can work it out with Jack when you see him."

"All right."

"This picnic is gonna be a pisscutter," Willie said, twining his fingers behind his neck and leaning back in his swivel chair. "They got bets going in the photo lab that young Don Francisco will wind up laying La Belle Keck before it's over. I'm not saying he won't. He's going with Kevin Delaney's daughter Ruthie — and Ruthie ain't in the same league with Keck no matter how you look at it, but her old man is manager of structural sales, and that means Don's future is in the bag if he marries old Kevin's daughter. I doubt if

Don'll louse up a cozy deal like that for a quick jump — even if he lands in the same pile of pine needles with the best-looking girl in the whole blessed company."

Howard Snyder made no comment. He occasionally had typing done by Eleanor Keck, and he liked her. She usually had a smile, no matter if it was raining or snowing, and while she did make mistakes she was never surly about changing or retyping. He had heard stories about her wildness, but he had seen no proof of it personally, and until he did he wasn't going to add any fuel to Willie's fire.

Willie, however, didn't need fuel. "If I was Don Francisco," Willie was saying, "I wouldn't give a damn if the daughter of the richest man in the outfit was willing to marry me . . . if I could get Ellie Keck, I'd take her. A man doesn't live by bread alone." Willie leered. "Matter of fact," he said, "if Ellie gets good and drunk I may be able to coax her out into the boondocks myself, and cut me a nice fat slice of that wonderful stuff."

Howard Snyder smiled. Willie Martin's accounts of his own sexual prowess, past and future, were a standing joke in the department. When Willie went on a business trip, he invariably returned with a tale of lust and intrigue which was beyond belief. The plot was always the same. Some incredibly lovely girl, sitting at a bar alone, had spotted Willie and found him irresistible; a conversation had been joined; the lovely girl had turned out to have a lavish apartment, stocked with vintage wines and mellow old whiskies, and she had coaxed Willie into coming up for a short nightcap — which, of course, had turned out to be an all-night session. The lovely girl had turned out to be a nymphomaniac, in addition to being rich and lovely, and Willie had had to give it to her eight times before she could get any sleep at all. The universal feeling in the office was that Willie never had been, and never would be, unfaithful to Stephy, his little Polish wife — even if he could persuade anybody to share his lusts, which was doubtful. Now Howard Snyder said, "Willie, if Stephy found out you'd so much as looked sideways at Eleanor Keck, she'd cut your ears off, and you know it."

"Stephy would like hell!" Willie cried. "Stephy knows who wears the pants in this family. She'd just keep her mouth shut and like it! Nobody pushes Willie Martin around — and that includes old man Hurd and Stephy and that son-of-a-bitch that lives across the street from me. I tell you about that prick? No? Well, hell — the guy got on me the other day about my boxer Goliath, barking and keeping him awake. You know what I says to the lug? I says, look, mister, Goliath is just a dog and a dog gotta bark at times, just like you gotta yell at times. And furthermore, I says, I ain't gonna sit out there in Goliath's kennel all night and hold his mouth shut with my hands. You don't like the noise, you should plug your ears."

"You're a tough man," Howard Snyder said. (He had already heard another variation of the Goliath incident from a witness, in which Willie had not said or done anything remotely resembling his truculent story, but he did not mention this.) "I wish you could have been in the library a couple of minutes ago."

"Why?"

"Doug Schroeder was in there sounding off."

"Sounding off?"

"It wasn't much — just about those hand-colored pictures old Dan Foy is always bringing around to show us. He dropped one on a magazine Doug Schroeder was reading, and Doug pretended to be impressed with it, until he got Dan on the hook, and then he threw it on the floor and told Dan off."

"That Schroeder!" Willie Martin said. "Somebody ought to paste that son-of-a-bitch on the kisser, and believe me, if I ever get a decent excuse, it'll be me. Did old Dan fight back?"

"No, he took it. He works for Schroeder — the projection stuff is under the art department. I guess he was scared, and to tell the truth, it was a little silly for him to do what he did. He knows Doug Schroeder. He was more or less asking for it, I guess."

"Old Dan just slunk away, eh?"

"He started to. Jack McHugh was standing beside the magazines and he got Dan into a conversation — took the bitchiness out of it, more or less. They went down for coffee." Howard Snyder stopped. The memory of his own small intrusion into the incident brought back, unpleasantly, his own feeling of inadequacy and defeat. But there was another feeling which he couldn't quite define. The other feeling had to do with Louise Stegmeyer. He kept seeing her eyes — looking into his own — holding just a fraction of a second longer than necessary. The thought made him feel nervous and upset, but good. *I'm nuts,* he thought. *I'm thirty-eight and she's only a kid. And even if she did like me, I wouldn't have the guts to do anything about it.*

For three years Ken Carpenter had been gathering bits and pieces of useful information — forming alliances — and thinking about the operating details of his secret plan. At first he had worked slowly, and with great attention to covering his motives, but as time went on he had seen that much of this caution was not really necessary. His goal was so high that nobody, even if Ken had spoken of it, would have believed he was serious. Who would believe that a young sales manager in a relatively small department of Carey Furnace Steel Company had a working blueprint going, not just to move up to the next slot, or even to board membership, but to take over, suddenly, and in a single concentrated attack, control of the company itself? Nobody, obviously, would believe such a thing. Yet power grabs of this type really did happen. Ken had read about them, in detail, in profiles of Boy Wonders in *Fortune* magazine. You had to be smart, tough, and unscrupulous. And you had to be prepared, fully and overwhelmingly, before you struck. When Ken had been a lieutenant at OCS school in Georgia, he had listened to various lectures on military tactics and strategy, much of which had been obvious, or merely windy platitudes. One lecture, however, had remained permanently in his mind. It had been given by a tank commander who had been brought back from Libya. Just a few days before talking to the young tank-corps officers at the school, this commander had been in actual combat with Rommel's tanks outside Mersa Matruh. He had been burned nearly black by the sun, so that his eyeballs looked unnaturally white, like the eyes of a comic in a minstrel show. He had spoken in a flat, truculent manner.

"If you don't remember one other thing I say today," the combat tanker had said, "remember this. This war is not like an old von Richthofen movie, where we wave godspeed to a brave adversary after he has expended his ammunition in a clean fair fight, and wishes to retire to fight another day. This war is to kill people — to burn them, to smash them to bone splinters and raw meat, or starve them, or any way you can. There is one best way to do this: superior force — applied very suddenly. Not just enough force so you are hopeful of taking the objective. And not just enough force to take the objective easily." The officer had clenched his jaws and spat out the next words, glaring around the room. *"If you can possibly do it, use enough force to pulverize the enemy into dust!* I know they'll caution you about overkilling. Wasteful of manpower and weaponry. Bullshit! Overkill every time, if you possibly can — and then you'll be goddamned sure the bastards are dead!"

Ken Carpenter had been building his plans to take control of the steel company on the philosophy of this far-gone lecture in Georgia. He was amassing enough power, he hoped, to smash his adversaries completely and without their being able to mount a counterattack. But power in a corporation battle was more varied and sophisticated than power on a field of churning tanks. The successful executive had to be ruthless, of course. But he must be smooth, even self-righteous about his ruthlessness. If possible, he must make it appear that his motives, selfish and unfair as they might be, were the very essence of rightness and justice. The successful executive must also be a politician, capable of meeting people at many different levels, and charming them at their own particular level. You wouldn't use a Harvard accent with a rolling-mill foreman, and you wouldn't use four-letter words at a Washington tea party. You couldn't be an indiscriminate Good Joe either, letting bores and fools take up too much of your time. But even bores and fools could be valuable, under certain conditions, so you never antagonized anybody gratuitously. Those Ken Carpenter antagonized, he antagonized on purpose, having carefully weighed the results beforehand. Ken knew where he was going, and he knew how he hoped to get there, and he moved in a chosen direction (sometimes by making necessary and devious detours), leaving corpses or converts in his wake, depending upon the strategy of the battle.

He was equipped with the natural resources of success: a keen mind, a strong body, and the drive to keep working twelve hours a day, seven days a week, as long as was necessary to accomplish whatever task he had set for himself. He had tried, since Debbie Copeland, to perfect his will to do his bidding, regardless of how difficult or onerous the task. He had no interest in drink. He cared little for money, for the luxury or comfort it might bring. He did care for the power money brought with it. Since Debbie Copeland, he had gotten his kicks from conflict. Nothing big ever emerged without conflict — the force that brought forth the counterforce. He had joined the Carey Furnace unit of the National Guard because it was equipped with Patton M-48 tanks, and, very shortly after joining, he was made commander of the unit. Other steel company executives might relax on the golf course, or play bridge or poker, or get a feel from a neighbor's wife on the dance floor when the lights went down, but Major Ken Carpenter (he'd had a peacetime promotion) relaxed in the turret of an M-48. He wangled extra gasoline for his unit, and when they ran short he paid for it himself. He insisted that his tanks — in fact, all the vehicles in the Carey Furnace Guard unit housed at the armory overlooking the plant — be topped off with gasoline, armed, and in perfect running order, ready to go in seconds when the tankers hit the seats. That was how he had done it in combat and that was how he proposed to do it now.

During the summer maneuvers, Major Ken Carpenter's outfit made a name for itself. Even the regular Army people, who usually underrated the performance of the Guard, had learned to respect Carpenter's tankers. "Those silly sons-of-bitches act like they were fighting a real war," one disgruntled regular colonel told his adjutant. "Get that wild-assed Carpenter in here, so I can slow him down before he gets somebody killed."

The regular colonel had had Ken Carpenter in, but he hadn't

slowed him down. The conference had wound up with the regular colonel making certain critical changes in the structure of the operation then going on — at the suggestion of his wild-assed Major Carpenter — and coming out with one of the most brilliant breakthroughs he'd enjoyed in years of these mock war games.

"If you ever get bored selling steel," the colonel had said to Carpenter, later on, before they broke bivouac for the summer, "I think I can wangle you a permanent commission as lieutenant colonel in my outfit. Make you my exec, as a matter of fact."

"Thank you, sir," Major Carpenter had said. "If I ever get sick of selling steel, I may just do that."

Ken Carpenter drove tanks on weekends, when he had nothing better to do, but he did not neglect the steel company, neither its executives nor its rank-and-filers. He had a compartment in his mind where he kept useful assorted information on people: first names, closeted skeletons, thumbscrews, private terrors, and dreams — information which one day he expected to use in the campaign he was planning.

Old Dan Foy, the projectionist in the advertising department, was one of the very minor individuals in Ken Carpenter's catalog of useful people. Dan had shown movies for the pipe department from time to time. Carpenter knew that Dan's hobby was taking pictures of his camp on the river and hand-coloring them to show to his friends, and when he passed Dan in the halls, which wasn't often, he would say, "Hi, there, Dan — how's the camp these days?"

It took five seconds, but it had its result: of all the sales managers in the company, old Dan Foy thought young Ken Carpenter was the best. This afternoon, when Ken called Dan from his office and asked if he could see the film, *The Romance of Pipe,* Dan did not hesitate, even though he had another showing tentatively scheduled. He'd simply cancel it. "Yes, sir, Mr. Carpenter," Dan said briskly. "Happy to show it."

"What's the best time for you Dan?"

"Any time you say, Mr. Carpenter."

"How about three o'clock?"

"That's fine," Dan Foy said. "I'll be set up and ready at three — in the projection room on the twelfth floor."

"Fine, Dan. And thanks."

"That's all right, Mr. Carpenter. It's a pleasure."

Carpenter arrived at three sharp and took a seat in the projection room. Dan Foy turned off the overhead lights and started the documentary at once. Carpenter settled back and watched the color film begin to roll: a preliminary panorama of the steel plant, great raw hills of ore against a blue sky . . . a brief glare of the furnaces . . . a smiling girl in a kitchen, bending down, peering under her sink at the Carey Furnace steel pipe installed there . . . and then the rich, enthusiastic voice of the narrator, explaining that in the making of Carey Furnace pipe, nothing — not the slightest detail — was left to chance. Every detail of production was checked and double-checked by skilled and seasoned experts. . . .

Ken had seen the movie a number of times before. He waited until it had been on for five minutes, then got up and slipped out into the hall and back to the door of the projection booth, which he opened. Dan Foy had not been watching the movie. He was seated in an easy chair he had rigged for himself, smoking a cigar and reading a magazine under a small lamp. He was surprised and flustered to find Carpenter staring at him.

"Oh — something wrong, Mr. Carpenter?"

"No, no, Dan. Everything's fine. But I just remembered I left my brief case on my desk in my office. I need it for some papers I want to check against the last part of this movie. But I don't want to break up the showing. Dan — I was wondering if you'd do me a big favor — slip down and ask Miss O'Conner to give you the brief case for me?"

"Glad to, Mr. Carpenter!"

"Which one of these levers turns off the machine?" Ken asked. "I'll sit and watch back here — and if anything starts to go haywire, I'll shut her down."

Dan Foy pointed to a switch at the base of the projector. "Here's the master, Mr. Carpenter. Just flip it, and everything will stop. I won't be long, though, and I don't think anything will go wrong."

"Take your time," Ken said. "I'll be here when you get back."

When Dan Foy left, Ken Carpenter began, at once, to hunt for the board-room tapes. The booth was crammed with cans of film and various pieces of gear. He knew that the tapes, which were recorded at every meeting of the directors in John Carey's board room on the fourteenth floor, were stored in this room. The tape he wanted had been recorded either in September or October of last year. It concerned a verbal battle between Bill Caldwell, vice president in charge of research and development, and Walter Eberhardt, vice president in charge of production. Ken had heard about the fight through one of his pipelines — Stew Roberts — in Caldwell's department. "It must have been a lulu," Stew had reported, sitting in Ken's den in Hunter's Valley, sipping a highball. "Bill Caldwell came back to the office red as a beet and so mad he could hardly spit. Walt got abusive in the meeting. And when Walt gets abusive, I mean, he really gets abusive! All Walt can think about is tonnage, tonnage, tonnage. And Bill, of course, is after money for research and development."

"Who won the argument?" Ken had asked his informant.

"I don't know who won," Stew had laughed. "But from what I gathered, the poor stockholders lost. Bill said he brought up the argument that the company had a responsibility to the stockholders, and Walt yelled, "Fuck the stockholders! They'll take whatever dividends we give 'em — and like it!"

Ken had chuckled. "You really mean he said it that way?"

"Exactly that way," Stew Roberts had laughed. "Those were his exact words. Quote — Fuck the stockholders — unquote."

Now Ken scanned the open shelves, packed with cans of film, did not find what he was looking for, and moved to the steel filing cabinet next to the projector. Time was passing. Dan was slow — but he would be back in a few minutes. Ken checked the alphabetical tabs on the drawers, opened several without results. Then, under the B's, he found what he was looking for: *Board-Room Tapes*. Dan

Foy had been neat. He had last year's tapes lined up in a row and marked by the months. Ken quickly pried out the September and October tapes, slid the rest back tightly together, and shut the cabinet. Unless somebody was looking for these precise tapes, which he didn't think was likely, the absence of the two spools would never be noticed.

Ken opened the door of the booth and peered into the hall. It was empty. He ducked into the audience-viewing room, where the movie was still unfolding in color on the screen, and put the two spools of tape in the fold of his New York *Times*. Then he hurried back to the booth. He was breathing fast. Gradually the breathing subsided. He was at ease, peering through the slit at the movie screen, when Dan Foy arrived with the brief case.

"Sorry to be so long, Mr. Carpenter," Dan wheezed. "Those elevator guys sure take their time. Have any trouble, sir?"

"None at all, Dan." Ken took the case. "I'll go on back to the front now. Thanks a lot!"

"Happy to do it, Mr. Carpenter," Dan said, glancing at the diminishing thickness of the film on the turning reel. "I hope I got back in time for you to make your notes. We got ten, twelve minutes to go."

"Plenty of time."

"You want a flashlight?"

"No, I can see enough by the light from the screen."

He went back up front and sat down. He took a note pad from his brief case, putting the newspaper with the spools of tape into the case in its stead. Then he turned his attention to the film, holding a pencil, making random notes on his pad, as the last minutes of *The Romance of Pipe* whirled steadily in the darkened room.

In the kitchen of her house on Mountain Avenue, Ethyl Snyder was preparing dinner. She had iced the avocados and was peeling the boiled shrimp, and now that the ordeal was at hand, she had stopped being nervous about it. In fact, she was glad it was coming. It had to come, sooner or later. She didn't intend to go on, year after year, inventing excuses for not going to those ridiculous places Howard was always dreaming of. Might as well get it settled, once and for all. Still, she had to be clever. Howard was a good-natured man, and he would do almost anything if you handled him right, but even Howard had his limits. Nobody could have his ego squashed, regularly, like a bug on the kitchen table, without eventually making some feeble attempt at fighting back. Howard, fortunately, always fought ineffectually, hurting himself more than anyone else. He went and got dead drunk and wound up vomiting all over himself and having a bilious attack. He was messy, but he was very easy to handle at this point. A little warm broth, some loving words, a phone call in his behalf to the company saying he had the summer flu, and in the end, actually, Howard wound up thinking Ethyl had done him a favor — instead of ruining his vacation plans for another year. . . .

Ethyl finished the shrimp, dumped them into a clean bowl, covered them with ice cubes and slices of lime, and put them into the refrigerator. She opened the oven and saw that the chicken was browning nicely, basted it, turned down the temperature, and closed the oven. Things were going well. Now she must prepare Carole for her role in the little drama. She left the kitchen and went into Carole's room. The child was in bed, the blinds were drawn, and the transistor radio was playing. 'Carole," Ethyl called softly. "Carole honey — are you awake?"

The child stirred and sat up, peevish and groggy with sleep and heat. "Oh, Mummy — why did you have to wake me up?"

"How do you feel, dearest?"

"Awful!"

"I'm going to call the doctor, dear."

"Doctor? What for? I'm not sick. I'm just hot."

"You said you felt awful."

"Well, I do. I feel hot and sweaty and awful. I want to get up and take a shower. Right now."

"Carole!"

"What, Mummy?"

"Do you want to go to Mexico and get bitten by scorpions and bedbugs and get an awful tummy ache and have to stay in bed the rest of the summer?"

"Oh, Mummy, you've never been to Mexico. How do you know they've got —"

"Now stop that!" Ethyl said sharply. "You just stop that at once!"

"All right. . . ."

"That's better! That's much better. Now you remember what I told you. When Daddy comes home you are going to be sick — *real sick* — so *Daddy* will think you're sick. I know my girl can do that. I know, because when she does it, Mummy is going to buy her that new dress she liked so much in Foyle's window, the one with the lace cuffs and the pretty silver buttons."

"And the little hat, too, Mummy?"

"Oh, my, such a greedy little pig! Yes, and the little hat, too. But you have to be sick — *really* sick!"

"When can I get the dress and hat?"

"As soon as you're better, honey."

"When will that be?"

Ethyl smiled a little. "I should say you'd be better about next Tuesday morning — the day after we are scheduled to fly to Mexico. Now Mummy's got to run and phone Daddy — about the wonderful dinner she's cooking for him."

Ethyl phoned from the kitchen. When she heard Howard's voice on his extension at the steel company, she spoke softly, gravely, with just a hint of disaster, without making it too obvious. "It's Ethyl, darling. I — I hate to bother you when I know you're busy, but — well, Carole's not feeling too well."

She heard him take a breath. "Not feeling too well," he said. "What's the matter?"

"I'm not sure. She didn't sleep at all well last night, and this morning she just picked at her breakfast like a little bird — wouldn't touch her lunch at all."

"Have you had a doctor?"

"Not yet. I wanted to call Dr. Widdoss, but Carole made such a fuss — you know how she is about doctors — so I put it off."

"Have you taken her temperature?"

"Yes, this morning. It was over a hundred."

"How about now?"

"I think it's come down a little now." She paused. "Really, Howard, you sound more like a lawyer cross-examining a witness than a father who's got a sick girl. I rather expected you'd be concerned, with all this polio going around."

"All right," Howard said. "I'm concerned. What do you want me to do?"

"I thought, on your way home, you might pick up some little gift — just a little thing, to show you were thinking about her."

He did not speak for a moment. Then he said, "All right, Ethyl. I'll bring something."

"Oh, Howard, you're a dear. I've got a wonderful supper planned for you. All your favorite things. Shrimp, avocado, roast chicken." She gave a warm little laugh. "So get yourself prepared. No use starving my big man, just because his little daughter is sick. 'Bye now."

"Goodbye," Howard said.

He was carrying a package when she opened the door for him a little before six o'clock. He held it out to her. It was a doll in a cellophane-topped box. She took the doll with her left hand, and with her right she touched her lips. She whispered, "The poor little thing is sleeping now. She's just worn out. Oh, I'm so worried. The radio, just now, said there are some new cases of polio in Wilkensburgh."

"She's had her Salk vaccine, hasn't she?"

"Of course, but it isn't always effective." She looked at him with her little-girl expression, woeful and yet smiling. "I hoped my big man would be a little more worried about his little daughter."

"Well, if Carole has no temperature, and she's sleeping, I don't see what there is to worry about."

"I didn't say she has no temperature."

"I know you didn't," Howard said. "But she hasn't, has she?"

"I'm not sure. She's terribly weak."

Howard put his straw hat on the table and faced his wife. "All right," he said. "I'm ready — say it."

"Say what, dear?"

"Say we aren't going to Mexico as planned because Carole is sick and we can't leave her — or take her along, either. That's what you're going to say, isn't it?"

Ethyl fretted her lower lip with her teeth. Her eyes were bright and her full bosom was moving heavily. But she still maintained her control. "Well, Howard, you couldn't really expect me to take a sick child into a wild place like that, no doctors, no hospitals, and heaven knows what other kinds of disease floating around."

"They have doctors and hospitals in Mexico."

"But not good ones," Ethyl said. "Half-baked natives with dirty instruments — worse than none at all, really. You know how much I hate to disappoint you, dear, but actually I couldn't —"

"Stop it!" he said suddenly and harshly. "Stop it right there! The record is worn out!"

She started at the sound of his voice, and now it was next to impossible to be calm, but she was. "I'm afraid I don't understand what you are talking about."

"You don't? Then I'll tell you. Carole isn't any sicker than you or I are. This is just one more of your last-minute fadeouts. Like your mother's heart, like your phony sprained ankle. You aren't going to Mexico and you never had the slightest intention of going. So let's stop all this silly business about how much you hate to disappoint me!"

She took a deep breath and met his eyes, and suddenly she felt good — felt justified and full of righteousness and anger. The gloves were off. He'd taken them off first, and now she could hit back as hard as she like. She smiled — her sweet, solicitous smile. Her voice, when she spoke, was the voice of the fourth-grade schoolteacher soothing a fractious but not very bright child. "Oh, now, Howard," she said, "you're just hot. You'll feel better after you've had a nice supper and can lie down for a while."

She saw his quick incredulous look and felt a thin fierce thrill:

she'd put the needle in gently, but it had gone deep. If she'd screamed or wept he could have had his pride, at least. He could have salvaged some of his self-respect. But by treating him like a child, she had robbed him of even that. She had stabbed him deep, where he lived.

He stood a moment, looking at her. Then he picked up his hat, without a word, turned, and walked quickly out of the house. She watched him go. She made no effort to call him back. He would go and get drunk, probably, and come stumbling home in the morning with a blinding headache, expecting broth and sympathy. Well, this time he'd expect in vain, because he wouldn't get any broth or sympathy. Ethyl had made her final stand, and she had won. She smiled. *Well,* she thought, *I can get Carole up now, and we can eat the dinner ourselves. And we'll never have to worry, ever again, about these insane trips. Never, as long as we live. . . .*

Wednesday

JOHN CAREY had called a board meeting for ten o'clock on this Wednesday morning. He had not been able to get to the office on the previous day. He had had a hemorrhage following the attack on Tuesday morning — not serious enough to incapacitate him, but by the time it was over, and Pop Whitehead had him sedated, it was too late to set up this final meeting. Pop had suggested having the board members come to the house today, but John Carey had ruled it out. He had wanted to meet, once more, in the board room where he had made the major decisions of his business career; and he wanted to meet his people fully dressed, sitting at the head of the table, as always.

"I can't be responsible for the consequences," Pop Whitehead had said when John Carey made his wishes known. "It will be a strain. It might be —"

"It might be the end of me?" John Carey said, smiling slightly. "Is that what you mean? Well, hell, Pop — don't tell me you're worried about that?"

Pop had looked at him. Then he had smiled. "Okay, John. I'll give you some pills that will knock the pain, but won't blur you in any serious way. Good luck."

"Thanks, Pop. I won't need to hold a long meeting. I figure I can get through twenty minutes, standing on my hands, if I have to."

Eva had crossed from the doorway then, holding his brief case. She had lifted it, apparently, and the catch had slipped and it had opened, and she was staring down into it, her face white and horrified.

"Put that away for me, will you, dear?" John Carey said.

She looked up, closing the case. "Oh, John — you weren't —"

"I didn't know," he said. "I wasn't sure."

"You were going past my room when I called," she said, her voice ragged and low. "You weren't — not without even saying goodbye —"

"I didn't know," he said. "I wasn't sure which was best."

Pop said, "What is it, John?"

"Nothing," he said. "Nothing, really, Pop. Eve — you put the bag away for me, will you?"

"I will," she said, and started to say something else, and then her face broke up and she turned abruptly, carrying the brief case, and hurried out of the room.

Now, at ten o'clock, John Carey was seated at the head of the long table in the board room, which adjoined his executive offices. He was fortified against pain by Pop's pills. But he was finding it difficult to hear with his right ear, and his right foot had dragged when he went in and took his seat prior to the arrival of his vice presidents. They were assembled now, looking up the table at him, and he knew they had no inkling that anything was wrong.

On his immediate left was Dave Ross, vice president in charge of sales, big, smiling, tanned, wearing a white summer suit; Elwood

Price, the comptroller, was next, tiny, bald, bright-eyed, with his pinch-nose glasses on their black ribbon and his bright-red bow tie and his gray suit; next came Bill Caldwell, research and development, the boy wonder of the company, apple-cheeked, crew-cut, somewhat pudgy from good living, but, at thirty-seven, one of the most brilliant research engineers in American industry. The chair at John Carey's right, the place of honor, was vacant. J. P. Detweiler, the white-maned lion with the face like folded leather, was absent in a distant land, looking at cattle. Paul Dana, vice president in charge of public relations, sat next to the empty chair, tough, dapper, with his little Adolf Hitler mustache and his sunken eyes; and finally, old Walter Eberhardt, in charge of production, was sitting, as was his custom, in his shirt sleeves with a cigar stuck in his thick liver lips, and his beetling brows scowling. Walt did not look like a vice president; he looked like an aging truck driver.

John Carey glanced at the scratch pad on the polished wood beside his hand, then along the table. He felt dizzy from the drugs and remote from these people. He saw them, now, through the narrowing slit in his iron cage. Suddenly, without warning, a feeling of almost intolerable emotion flooded through him. This meeting was it. His last. And these were his boys. They'd been through strikes, depressions, wars, cutthroat competition, miscellaneous disasters, Acts of God. They were tough men. They had had bitter interpersonal battles, some fought right in this room. But against outside aggression they were, and always had been, a solid front. They were like the hot-headed Irish housewife who drove her poor husband out of the kitchen with a mop, and proclaimed his grievous shortcomings to the neighborhood in angry shouts — then instantly changed her tune when faced with the criticism of a stranger. An outsider who attacked one of them attacked them all.

John Carey did not rise to address them. He spoke slowly, because of the ringing in his head, and the weakness, but he did not speak at length. "This is my last board meeting," he said. "I've called you together for one main thing: to appoint my successor. I am not going to be flowery. You all know our company — the way I've run it

— has had only one boss. I've been it. I've listened to you, every one of you, but I've reserved the final decision to myself. I don't know how my successor will do it. That will be up to him. I know that the modern trend is to split up management and run it by committee. Personally, I have never agreed with this concept. I don't think committee rule will ever be as good as the judgment — for better or worse — of one smart, tough man. He'll make mistakes, but he'll get things done, and he'll move — if he's good — in one direction. Now I've been giving this a lot of thought for a long time, and I've picked my man." John Carey turned to his left, and smiled at his vice president in charge of sales. "Dave — you're it. Congratulations, and good luck!"

They stared at him. For a moment there was no sound. Then Dave Ross spoke. "John," he said, and his voice was strained and bewildered. "My God — John —"

"You want it, don't you, Dave?"

"Want it, John? You bet I want it! I'll do my damnedest, right up and down the line, as you well know. But John — why? Why now? You've got ten good years left — maybe lots more!"

"I wish you were right, Dave. Until day before yesterday, in the evening, I thought I had those years too. That was before I went to see Pop about an attack I had in New York. Pop looked me over and made some tests. I've got a year, at the outside, Pop says. Probably much less. I've got cancer. A quick-acting type they call melanoma. It's already spread beyond the point where it can be operated. Now, goddamn it, I don't want a single man of you to say you're sorry. I don't want to hear a word of sympathy. I've said all I have to say — except — the best of luck to every one of you. When you go back to your departments, it's business as usual. Dave, will you take the meeting now? I'm going home and have a drink of whisky."

He rose, helping to lift his body with his hands pressed on the table top, but when he turned to leave the table, his right leg buckled and he would have fallen if Dave Ross, quick as a cat, hadn't twisted in his chair and steadied him. He was erect now, and Dave's hand left his arm, and he stood alone. He looked at them. They were staring at him. Young Bill Caldwell's face was very red, as if he'd been holding his breath. Paul Dana's lips were tightly compressed and his face was pale. Elwood Price's eyes glistened behind his pinch-nose glasses, and as John Carey looked at him he saw the tears well out of his eyes and run down his face, leaving wet crooked lines which caught the light.

Then, suddenly, Walt Eberhardt shoved his chair back and came heavily and awkwardly around the table. Big Walt did a surprising thing. He grabbed John Carey in his arms and hugged him. "John," Walt said loudly, "goddamn it, John! Goddamn it!"

He let go and leaned back, his big truck-driver hands gripping his friend's arms. He was beyond speech. His face worked and his rough tobacco-stained mouth twitched, and then, suddenly, they were all on their feet, close around him, like an elite guard forming a last shield of love and fury around a beloved and desperately beset general. Elwood Price was saying, urgently, "Maybe Pop's wrong, John. Maybe Pop's wrong for once. You should —"

Suddenly he had to get out. He straightened his shoulders and produced, with almost the last of his strength, an old-time grin. "You're a bunch of sentimental bastards," he said, in his boardroom voice, strong and clear. "But I don't hold it against you. I'm a sentimental bastard myself. Now get the hell out of my way while I still have the poop to walk out of here on my own two feet!"

Ken Carpenter got the news a little before lunchtime. Eileen O'Conner appeared, white-faced and staring, in the doorway. "Oh, Mr. Carpenter — I hate to bother you — but — but I just heard Mr. Carey has incurable cancer and he's going to die!"

"What!"

"They just held a special board meeting upstairs. Mr. Carey called it to tell the board about the cancer. He turned over the company to Mr. Ross. As I understand it, Mr. Carey's got less than a year to live."

"Why, that's fantastic. I saw Mr. Carey at the lawn party on Saturday, and he looked fine. Who's spreading this wild rumor?"

"It's not a rumor, the way I was told," Eileen said. "Mr. Carey authorized Mr. Ross to release it to the company — said we'd all have to know sooner or later, and it might as well be now. At least that's what I heard, Mr. Carpenter. But I can tell you one thing, it's all over the building."

"Well, thanks for telling me, Eileen."

"Yes, sir."

For a few moments after his secretary left, Ken Carpenter sat without moving. This rumor, or release, or whatever it was — all over the building — not being denied — might well be true. If it was true, here was the break he'd been waiting for. But he didn't feel the way he might have expected: excited, ready to jump. He felt a little sick at his stomach. His own grandfather had died of cancer. Ken had seen the old gentleman at the end — a tough, proud man who'd never complained or whined — trying to bottle up the fury inside him, and succeeding until the day of his death, when Ken's mother had had to take Ken away from the house so he couldn't hear the howls and the cursing.

But there was no use getting excited about John Carey now, one way or the other, until he was sure. There was one way to find out in a hurry. He looked up John Carey's office number, hesitated — then dialed it, and waited. There was a delay. Then Kay Blount, John Carey's secretary for the past sixteen years, came on the line, and instantly, without asking, he knew the rumor was true. Kay was weeping.

He said, "This is Mr. Carpenter, in pipe sales. I just heard the news and I wanted to tell Mr. Carey how terribly sorry I am."

He heard her sob. Then her voice, naked with sorrow, said, "I'll tell him — if he comes back —" There was a click.

Ken Carpenter hung up the phone. His face was composed now, and calm. He must think clearly, without sentiment. The battle he had been preparing for for so long had taken a critical turn. He was faced with a unique opportunity that would never be presented again. John Carey was going to die, and soon, no matter what Ken Carpenter did. He had laid the groundwork for his campaign. His ammunition was ready. This was war, a war of his own waging, and if he hoped to follow that African tank commander's doctrine he must strike now, with overpowering force, suddenly, and without warning.

Archie Saunders had the hot itchy feeling inside his head when he came to work at the River Avenue Market on Wednesday morning. He got this feeling at intervals, but more often in hot weather. Everything looked slightly bigger than normal, with a bright rim around it, as if there was a light bulb hidden around the corner some place. There was a thin pain behind his eyes, like when he had a head cold, and it all made him very nervous and more sensitive to everything — touch, sound, smell, sight. Sight was the worst. It was as if he had X-ray eyes. When he passed through the chicken yard he could see the parts inside the chickens; not really, of course, but almost really — the parts he took out after his mother killed the chicken with a hatchet: the liver, heart, delicate soft blobs with blood on them, and the big mess of guts that looked like tangled white worms and which squirted doodoo, stinking and liquid black, if you squeezed them in your hands. He could see these things through the chicken feathers; not really, but almost really. And he could imagine what the flies must be seeing, as they crawled nervously on the piles of chicken doodoo, through their bulgy green eyes covered with little windowpanes. It must be funny, being a fly and looking at things through those windowpanes. You must see hundreds of other bugs, or whatever you were looking at — one for each window. It must drive you crazy, trying to figure out which bug was the real one.

Walking past the chicken yard, Archie could imagine the worms under the crusty beak-picked mud of the yard, stinking worms with yellow rings around them, that squirted yellow goo when you stuck a fish hook into them — not the fat night-crawlers you could grab on rich people's lawns at night, particularly after a rain or when there was a heavy dew, lying there glistening in the flashlight beam, sometimes two of them stuck together, playing poontang, so you could grab both at once, and when you did, your fingers got slimed and could feel the soft squirming of the worms, and it made you feel funny — good-funny. It was strange, but when he had this itchy feeling in his head, his mind always seemed to think of worms, chicken guts, and bloody things. . . .

He did not want to work today. He did not feel like listening to Mr. Brothers with his big mouth and his red face, yap-yap-yap-yap, watch yourself, Archie, don't drop that bottle, don't step on the electric mat just to see the door pop open, don't stand outside goggling after you load an order into a car. It was bad enough having to listen to Mr. Yap-Yap Brothers when Archie felt good; but with the itchy pain behind his eyes, and everything bright and splintery-looking, it was worse than usual.

He put on his white apron and white cap with *River Avenue Market* embroidered on it in red thread, and went to Miss Van Sant's counter. Miss Van Sant was a stoop-shouldered and pimply girl and she didn't have anything up front. She disliked Archie, and he knew she had asked Mr. Brothers to shift him to another counter. But she wasn't alone in not wanting him to pack for her. Nobody wanted him packing for them. He was very fast — it wasn't that. He had the stuff in the boxes almost as soon as Miss Van Sant had the purple-numbered tape out of the adding machine. But he wasn't to be trusted. Sometimes he'd be perfect — cans in first, heavy boxes next, lighter stuff carefully on top. But then, when his mind would wander out of the store into the city dump or some place, he would really bungle the job. He would put a plastic bag of marshmallows on the bottom of a carton and pile a sack of potatoes on top of it; or he would force a bag of grapes into a space so small the juice would spurt out of them and soak through the bottom of the box. And somehow the customers would think Miss Van Sant was to blame. Miss Van Sant was running the counter; Miss Van Sant ought to be able to teach poor Archie Saunders, whose mother was trying so hard to get along; Miss Van Sant should be able to get the poor boy to pack his boxes better, after all this time.

But of course Miss Van Sant had no control over Archie's mind when it left the store. She could talk to him until she was blue in the face, and he would listen and agree with everything she said—but once his mind took a jump, that was the end of it. And Mr. Brothers couldn't help Miss Van Sant, or wouldn't. Miss Van Sant had tried to wish Archie off on Mabel Wellman, but Mabel's father was in the same volunteer fire company as Mr. Brothers, so that was useless. Nor would Mr. Brothers put Archie with Ruth Quinn. Ruth was forty-five, but she was plump and liked a beer after work, and the rumor was that if you got four or five beers into Ruth it was no trick at all to get something else into her. Which was disgusting, Miss Van Sant thought. But it sure was enough to keep Mr. Brothers from shifting this little moron to Ruth Quinn's counter.

She said, "Watch yourself today, stupid. Don't mess things up, the way you usually do or I'll brain you."

Archie smiled brightly. Miss Van Sant wouldn't brain anybody. She was just talking to hear herself talk. He could see through her, and he knew she had the same kind of parts in her skinny belly as the chickens had, only bigger and more of them. What would she look like if you took a butcher knife and slit her open? The thought made him giggle.

"Oh," Miss Van Sant said, "you think it's funny."

Archie giggled again.

"You're nuts," Miss Van Sant said. "You ought to be in a nut house instead of running around loose."

In the early part of the morning there was a parade of customers Archie did not know. Then, about ten-thirty, Mrs. Snyder, the one who owned the little brown dog which always barked at Archie when he mowed the Abbotts' yard, came in. Usually Mrs. Snyder was smiling at everybody, looking like a toothpaste ad, and talking in that funny way she had, like a teacher reading a Christmas story to a bunch of little kids; but today Mrs. Snyder looked real mad. She wasn't smiling a bit, and she wasn't saying anything, just standing there unloading her groceries from the wire-mesh buggy to the counter, her big tits bouncing around under her dress like a couple of jelly bags. And when she told Archie where her car was located in the parking lot, she bit her words off as if she had a toothache.

Ethyl Snyder was indeed angry, and she had her reasons. Howard had left home the preceding evening and hadn't returned this morning, as she had expected, hung over and remorseful, trying to patch things up. If he'd come back early, she might have relented and babied him. But now he'd waited too long. When he did come home, as he would certainly do, sooner or later, she would let him stew in his own juice. A few days of the silent treatment, perhaps; no meals, to give him a taste of what it was like to get along without her cooking and companionship . . . And if he still wasn't suitably subdued, there were always more drastic measures which could be taken.

Howard's absence, however, wasn't the only aggravation on this hot day. Hubie, the Pekingese, had somehow gotten a bone stuck in his throat and she had taken him, at great trouble (he fought and jerked and covered her with saliva) to see the veterinary. The vet had taken the bone out, but in the process he had completely ruined the remains of the dog's disposition. Hubie had barked and fussed and tried to bite the vet, and was out in the car barking now. She could hear him, dimly, as she stood inside the store. Ethyl was concerned for the dog because little Carole loved him so much. This shopping trip itself was in Carole's behalf. The child was making a doll's wardrobe, and Ethyl had stopped at the five-and-ten and picked up a list of items her daughter had asked for: needles, thread, cloth, safety pins, buttons. She had had to pass the River Avenue Market on her way home, and since the day was ruined anyhow, she stopped for her weekly supply of staples. She'd been so intent on pleasing Howard yesterday, with all those exotic things, that she'd neglected the more mundane items: soap powder, cereals, eggs, a new mop. Her purchases filled two large boxes, one of which the boy had taken out to the car, and Ethyl was digging in her handbag for her wallet when that red-faced manager appeared and spoke to her.

"Hot enough for you, Mrs. Snyder?"

"Yes, it's hot," she said shortly. "And I'm in a hurry."

The man apparently was too insensitive to realize he wasn't wanted. "It's not the heat," he was saying, "it's the humidity which bothers me. The humidity is worse, I think, down here close to the river."

"No doubt it is," Ethyl said, looking at Miss Van Sant. But Miss Van Sant had a problem of her own. She had let the list from the adding machine slip out of her hand onto the floor, and was bending down, looking for it under the counter. *Oh, God,* Ethyl Snyder thought, listening to the voice of Mr. Brothers. *Shut up . . . shut up, you red-faced fool. . . .* She turned her face deliberately away from him, and stood, waiting for the clumsy girl to find the cash-register tape, so she could pay and get out of this stifling store.

Meanwhile Archie, carrying Mrs. Snyder's box of groceries, found her car in the parking lot, the windows shut, and a small furious ball of brown fur yapping at him hysterically from the back seat. Little Hubie had not been idle in Mrs. Snyder's absence. He had torn open the parcel from the five-and-ten and scattered thread, buttons, and safety pins all over the back seat. Now, looking through the window at the grinning face of Archie Saunders, Hubie's rage rose to a new height. He held all tall two-legged creatures in contempt. He knew they were loonies who would take anything he had to give, and come back at him with a bunch of silly babble. Except, of course, that nasty creature he'd just left, who'd smelled of medicine and held Hubie's mouth open with a hard, unrelenting grip, so he couldn't bite, and had pulled and poked around in his throat, causing no end of pain. He'd tried his best to bite the man, but the man had been too clever. This grinning idiot outside the car now might not be so wary. Hubie stopped barking and watched Archie put the box of groceries down on the cement and open the back door. Craftily, Hubie let the boy put the box into the back seat of the car beside him — and then, when both the boy's arms were inside, shoving the box, making it impossible for him to withdraw quickly, Hubie lunged and sank his small white teeth deep into the boy's left hand.

Archie screamed, not loud, and more out of surprise than fear, and when Hubie opened his jaws to bark, Archie snatched his bitten hand away and slammed the door. Hubie flung himself at the windows, hoping for another chance to bite, but the boy was nowhere to be seen. He must have run away.

Archie had not run. He was crouching low on the cement and the pain in his hand was sharp, but not bothering him really — feeling almost good, in a crazy way. A smile formed on Archie's lips. He circled behind the car, keeping low, moving quickly and without sound, and lifted his head and peered into the back seat. The dog was still facing the other side — the side Archie had just vacated, standing with his paws on the sill, and now it was barking again. Archie took a light grip on the doorhandle with his left hand, balanced on his toes, then jerked the door open and lunged across the seat in the same instant. He had the dog by the back of the neck, shoving it deeply into the upholstery in the corner of the car seat.

The dog was small, and Archie was wiry and strong. The dog was trying to bark, but only a smothered gasping was coming from the upholstery, and Archie held the dog tightly, using both hands. He was going to kill it. It would be easy enough. He would just hold it there for a minute or two, so it couldn't breathe, and it would be dead. He knew this because he had done it to a baby rabbit once, using a pillow. The dog had stopped trying to bark now and was struggling frantically for its life. Archie held tight, grinning, until the struggles weakened and diminished to almost nothing — and then he caught sight of the safety pins lying on the floor where Hubie had spilled them, and a much more exciting plan flashed into his mind. Holding the almost limp animal with his left hand, he picked up a safety pin with his right, opening it dextrously with his thumb and fingers. It was then the work of an instant to pin the dog's silky brown ear to the fabric of the back seat. He thought of releasing the dog now, to see if it would rip its ear, trying to get free, but the idea of adding a few more pins was too inviting. Quickly he forced one pin after another through the dog's ear, into the fabric, and hasped the bloody spike under the safety head.

He had three pins in place when a woman's voice behind him suddenly cried out. "Oh! Oh you little fiend! Stop that! Stop that!"

Archie was back out of the car before Ethyl Snyder could grab him, smiling as he danced out of reach. "He bit me," he said, holding up his hand. "Your dog bit me. So I pinned him to the seat." He giggled. "He won't bite me again. He can't. He's pinned to the seat."

Mr. Brothers suddenly appeared beside Archie in the sunlight, his red face brighter red than usual, his breath coming in gasps from the sprint he'd made when he heard the commotion begin.

"I want this boy locked up!" Ethyl Snyder cried out. "I want him locked up right now! Do you hear?"

"I'll take care of everything," Mr. Brothers panted. "I'll handle it. What happened? Now, what exactly happened?"

"Look in the car!" Ethyl Snyder cried. "Look at what that terrible boy did to my dog. That boy's insane, to do a thing like that, and I want him locked up! Do you hear that, Mr. Manager? Locked up!"

"Yes, ma'am," Mr. Brothers said. "I hear. I'll take care of him, never fear." He looked into the car. The dog was recovering slowly from its nearly fatal smothering, and was tugging weakly with its ear at the confining pins. A small crowd had gathered in the lot and was pushing to look into the car. "He's pinned down all right," Mr. Brothers said. "You want me to release him, Mrs. Snyder?"

"Yes, yes, of course — release him!"

Mr. Brothers leaned into the car and Archie could not see what he was doing, and then suddenly there was a feeble, peevish yip and Mr. Brothers straightened suddenly and hit his head on the door. He staggered a little from the force of the blow, and made a grunting sound, and it was too much for Archie. He couldn't help it — he tittered.

Mr. Brothers swung toward him, his big red fingers nursing the bloody spot on his left wrist where the dog had nipped him, and Archie leaped back, ready to run. But Mr. Brothers did not try to chase him or hit him. He turned, instead, to Mrs. Snyder, and said, "I'm sorry, but I guess you better turn him loose yourself, ma'am. He just bit me too."

The crowd of onlookers tittered.

Ethyl Snyder had had enough. She said, sharply, "Deliver my last purchases to the house, please. They are still inside. I've paid for them." And she got into her car, started it, and drove out of the parking lot. Mr. Brothers spoke to Archie and his voice was surprisingly low and reasonable. "These things happen sometimes in the grocery business," he said. "We have to expect them, son."

Archie looked at Mr. Brothers in amazement. "You ain't going to fire me?"

"No, I'm not going to fire you, Archie. I don't think this was entirely your fault. But I do think we have to have a little talk. Tell you what, why don't we duck into the warehouse, where we can be alone, and talk a minute or so?"

Archie had an uneasy feeling. Something seemed to be telling him not to go into the warehouse with Mr. Brothers. But when he looked at Mr. Brothers, and saw the gentle smile on his face, and saw the blood on Mr. Brothers's wrist, the uneasy feeling went away. Mr. Brothers was on his side. They'd both been bitten by the dog. That made them like friends.

"All right," Archie said. "Let's do it, Mr. Brothers."

They walked across the hot parking lot and climbed the wooden ramp in the rear to the shade of the loading platform. Archie looked at the steel rails as they left the platform and passed the rear of the Carey Furnace freight station to the main line, shining like mirrors in the sun. Heat rose from the crushed gravel and quivered in the air between the rails. Mr. Brothers unlocked and opened the big roller door and Archie smelled sawdust and a mixture of food odors coming from the interior of the warehouse. The door was heavy and hard to move, and Mr. Brothers opened it just enough to let them in. "Go ahead, Archie," he said. "It'll be cooler inside, boy."

It was cooler inside, and a relief from the bright sunshine, and when Mr. Brothers put his weight against the door and rolled it shut, the warehouse was even darker. It was piled high with cardboard cartons bearing nationally advertised brand names of soups, juices, soap flakes, and dozens of other products. The windows were barred against thieves, with steel gratings. Archie's eyes quickly became accustomed to the shadow, and he saw that Mr. Brothers was smiling at him.

Mr. Brothers stepped close, still smiling, and said, "Well, Archie, I guess we can start our little talk now."

Then Mr. Brothers hit him in the face and knocked him down. He scrambled up and tried to jump past the big man toward the door, but a hand grabbed him and hurled him violently backwards and he slammed into a stack of cartons and fell again. Mr. Brothers jumped for him, and Archie saw him through a red mist of pain and terror, smiling, panting, like the monster in a horror movie. Archie tried to scream, but a hand clamped over his mouth, and he bit it, and then a chunk of meat with the bones close to the surface hit the side of his head and he saw a peppery shower of sparks, and the warehouse began to glimmer jaggedly. Mr. Brothers held him up with one hand, and slapped his head with the other — savage, jolting slaps that would not break the skin but that snapped his head this way and that, like blows from a club.

Then Mr. Brothers stopped and let go. Archie sank down on the floor in the sawdust. Mr. Brothers was brushing his pants off, as if nothing had happened. "Get up, boy," he said, panting slightly. "Take off your apron and hand it to me."

Archie rose unsteadily and fumbled with his apron in a whirling mist, feeling as if he might be going to throw up. He had trouble with the apron. Mr. Brothers looked at him, smiling. Finally he got the apron off and handed it to the man.

"All right now," Mr. Brothers said. "Get out. And don't come back. And don't tell anybody about this. Not anybody, not even your mother. Because if you do, I'm going to find out, and I'm going to catch you and beat you again. Only much worse. The next time," Mr. Brothers said, smiling, "I might beat you until I kill you."

Archie nodded. He had never been so frightened. He believed every word the big man was saying. Mr. Brothers would kill him, for sure, if he told anyone. He wouldn't tell. He whispered, "Let me go — please. I won't tell. I won't tell. . . ."

"If you do tell," Mr. Brothers said, "nobody will believe you anyhow. You're a crazy kid and everybody knows it, always dreaming up crazy nonsense. So telling won't help you — and if I hear you tried it, I'll come looking for you. And when I find you, you'll wish you'd never been born."

Archie felt the blood trickling out of his nose and down over his cut mouth. "I won't tell," he whispered. "Honest I won't."

"Ahh," Mr. Brothers said. "Get out of my sight, you little shit! Just looking at you makes me want to kick you!"

Mr. Brothers shoved the heavy door open and Archie squeezed through it, limped painfully across the hot loading platform and down onto the spur track. He did not look back. When he reached the track he began to run. He was suddenly in nightmare fear that Mr. Brothers was only playing with him, that he would grab him and drag him back and beat him some more. He ran along the ties for a hundred yards, and then, out of breath, the pain of his beating making it hard to breathe, he stopped and looked back. Mr. Brothers was not following. The loading platform was empty.

From behind him on the main line, Archie heard the sound of a freight train coming. He turned and looked. It rounded the curve and approached like a bright steel tornado and as it roared past, Archie saw the engineer peering through his front window and then the train was flying by, flailing dust and cinders in his eyes, and he shut them. . . .

It was then that the idea came. It came to his mind, behind his shut lids, with vivid suddenness, the way he thought of his inventions. Archie opened his eyes and looked at the loading platform of the River Avenue Market, a hundred yards away. The warehouse was wood. It stood directly behind the River Avenue Market — directly behind Mr. Brothers's office, to be exact. Archie looked down at the switch itself. It was simple — much simpler than a watch. The switch was shifted by steel rods that moved in a shallow pit under the ties. Archie looked at the lever. It was a counterbalanced weight on the end of a short throw-arm. It was locked in place by a brass padlock. Archie rubbed his face gently with his fingers and brought them down smeared with blood. As he looked at the blood, a hot thin singing began inside his head, like the singing of a locust in a distant tree. And then, for the first time since he'd left the parking lot with Mr. Brothers, Archie Saunders began to smile. . . .

Margaret Fiori heard about John Carey from her daughter Enid, by phone, before Ken Carpenter called. Enid had been told by her friend Sue Moorehead, whose father was in Elwood Price's department, and she had phoned her mother at once. "It's something they call melanoma," Enid said in the drawly voice she'd acquired at boarding school, casually, as if reporting a meeting of the Junior League for Tuesday night. "I guess it's a bad kind of cancer, Mums. I guess the poor man hasn't got very long. I mean, the way Sue talked, I guess he's going to die pretty soon."

Maggie Fiori's fingers tightened on the edge of the telephone stand.

"Mother — are you still on?"

"Yes, I'm still on. Are you sure, Enid? This isn't one of your sick jokes?"

"Mother, really." Enid's drawly voice took on an aggrieved note. "I thought you'd be glad for a little fresh news. I didn't dream you'd take it this way, darling, or I wouldn't have —"

"Oh, shit!" Maggie said suddenly, violently, and snapped the phone down.

She sat beside the phone table, trembling. She wasn't thinking of her vapid daughter. She was thinking of John Carey, the big, strong, shrewd, wonderful guy that nothing could touch; but it had. Cancer. What kind? A bad kind. Melanoma. That was what Enid had said. Melanoma. She'd never heard of it, but just the sound of it was bad. She wasn't crying. You didn't cry for people like John Carey — at least not if you were a person like Maggie Hunter. You got mad for him. You suddenly hated that strange word, that melanoma. Maggie's mouth curled: what kind of a goddamned thing was this, sending this crummy stuff to a man like John Carey? Who in this big mysterious universe decided these things? Who? Whoever it was, he sure seemed to botch it — to botch it real bad, a very great deal of the time. . . .

I'll phone John, she thought. *I'll tell him how mad I am — what a crummy deal they laid on for him. I'll tell him to curse it in its teeth, and the one that sent it, whoever the jerk may be.*

But she knew she couldn't call John Carey and tell him that, or tell him anything else. And then she realized she wasn't as tough as she'd thought, because she wasn't mad now, she was scared and sorry and there wasn't anything she could do, and she was crying.

Beside her, on the stand, the phone rang. She swallowed, shook her head sharply, and picked up the receiver, and her voice was quite clear and strong when she spoke, "Hello — this is Mrs. Fiori speaking."

"Margie — it's Ken. You've heard, I guess?"

"Yes, I've heard. Is it true?"

"Yes, it's true."

"Cancer," she said softly. "Poor John — the poor, poor guy."

"Margie —"

"Yes?"

"I have to talk to you. It's very important. Could I come out to the house?"

"Now?"

"If it's convenient, yes."

"Certainly it's convenient."

"Then I'll jump in my car and be right over."

"Have you had lunch?" she asked.

"No, I'm not very hungry."

"How about some iced coffee and a sandwich?"

"Oh, don't go to any trouble," he said.

"It's no trouble," she said. "The cook can do it."

"All right."

"Kenny —"

"Yes?"

"I — feel bad about John Carey — real bad. Isn't there anything anybody can do? Is it really hopeless?"

"Yes," he said. "From what I hear, it's really hopeless."

"Why couldn't it happen to somebody else — some creep, some bastard?"

"I don't know," he said. "I'm coming now. I'll see you in a few minutes."

She'd changed to a silk print and was sitting on the verandah, but not with iced coffee, with a very dry Martini, when he drove in. She waved to him and he waved back and a moment later he was on the porch beside her. He said, "Under different circumstances, I'd kiss you. You look lovely, Margie."

Never mind the circumstances, she thought, with death crouching dimly in the back of her mind, and then her love for this man suddenly crowding forward and blotting out the nightmare shape. *Never mind anything, darling, you kiss me.* But she said, "I'm having a Martini. I don't know — I can't just sit and think about a thing like John . . . Do you want one?"

"No, thanks . . . No, wait. Yes, I will."

She poured from a shaker. He lifted the cold drink in the flaring glass. She lifted hers. "A toast," she said softly. "To John Carey."

He hesitated. He knew, then, that he could not say what he had come here to say. Not now. Not today. He could say it tomorrow — and he was sure that Margaret would be with him, all the way. But he couldn't say it today. He would have to go ahead with Dave Ross this afternoon. And he would have to bluff. Dave Ross knew — must know — how Maggie Fiori felt about her son-in-law. If Ken told Dave he could deliver Margaret Fiori's Carey Furnace common — all two million three hundred thousand dollars of it — in a proxy fight, Dave would believe him.

He smiled at Margaret Fiori over the glass. "Here's to John Carey," he said.

At a little after three o'clock that afternoon, Ken Carpenter called Dave Ross on his office phone. Dave's secretary, Helene DeWitt, answered the phone, and Ken said, "This is Mr. Carpenter speaking. In pipe sales. I'd like to speak to Mr. Ross, please."

"I'm sorry," Helene DeWitt's voice said (it had a precious, rather English accent). "I'm afraid Mr. Ross is tied up just now. Could I have him call you back?"

"When will he be free?"

"I really couldn't say. Probably not until tomorrow though. Perhaps the next day."

"This is very urgent," Ken Carpenter said. "Could you put Mr. Ross on for just a minute, please?"

"I don't know," Helene DeWitt said doubtfully. "But I'll tell him you're calling, and it's urgent."

"Thank you."

There was a wait. Then Dave Ross's voice said, shortly, "What is this, Carpenter? I'm busy."

"I have to see you right away," Ken Carpenter said. "It's a matter of the most urgent importance."

"Well, what the hell is it? Spit it out. I've got people here and I'm in the middle of something important myself."

"I know you have important things right now, Mr. Ross. I know you've been made chairman of the board, and there are big decisions you have to make right now — this afternoon. But I am sure you can't have anything more important than seeing me." He took a breath. He said, "I'm thinking of starting a proxy battle, Mr. Ross, for control of this company. I think you'll want to see me, as soon as you can get finished with your people."

There was a pause. Then Ross's voice said, "All right, Carpenter. You in your office?"

"Yes, I am."

"Stand by. I'll call you as soon as I can."

"Thank you." He hung up.

He felt tense and very alert. He felt the way he had felt before they jumped off for a tank assault against a Nazi strong point. Fighting Dave Ross and the rest of the men at the top of Carey Furnace was, in a way, like fighting Hitler's elite tiger tankers. The Nazis had been brutal soldiers — but they had also been good. They had done everything coolly, to bring about the maximum calculated destruction, without fanfare or histrionics. The Japanese had come tumbling into the machine guns in an insanely brave wave of screaming humanity — and they had piled up in heaps, and had been stopped. The Italians had had great style, dazzling uniforms, and had conducted themselves smartly — until the pressure hit; and then they had wilted and died. The Nazis — the good ones — had placed their 88's coldly and carefully, had used reconnaissance to its limits and theory of warfare where recon left off, so that when you moved forward in a tank charge to take a strong point — a point the Krauts really meant to hold — you must expect to leave a certain number of burned-out vehicles, filled with smashed and blackened dead men, if you meant to press determinedly for a breakthrough. Until the instant the 88's let loose, the enemy country looked peaceful and quiet in the summer sunlight. Then, simultaneously, the guns began to fire, each one having a target carefully zeroed in its sight before the firing order was given.

Fighting Ross and the rest, Ken Carpenter knew, would be somewhat like that. They would not yell at him or threaten him. They would listen to what he had to say, thinking fast as he talked, planning, even then, exactly how and where to launch the counterattack.

Dave Ross called back in thirty-five minutes. He said, "All right, Carpenter. You can come up here now."

Helene DeWitt looked up from her typewriter as he stepped into Dave Ross's outer office, a hostile, well-perserved corporation secretary in her late forties, and spoke as if it hurt her lips. "Mr. Ross," Helene said, "is expecting you. You can go on in."

Dave Ross had one of the largest and best offices in the company, paneled in walnut, with a sound-proofed ceiling, wall-to-wall carpet, bookcases filled with leather-bound books, expensive dark-red draperies at the windows. There was an adjoining private bathroom, and there were framed photographs on the walls — portraits of some of the great men in American industry and government: Eugene

Grace of Bethlehem Steel, Ben Fairless of U. S. Steel, Senator Stuart Symington, and many others, signed with informal scrawls. On his big clean-topped desk, Ross had pictures of his own family beside the interoffice communication box. He was looking at some papers when Ken Carpenter entered. He finished reading and looked up. His face was slightly red, which could be Sunday's golf sunburn. Otherwise he looked perfectly normal and at ease. Well, why not? He was boss of the company now. His word was law.

"Hello, Mr. Ross," Ken Carpenter said, and smiled, but his lips were stiff, and his legs felt strange when he walked, the way they had felt in Holland when he was crossing an area suspected of being mined. "Thank you for seeing me."

"Let's have it, Carpenter," Dave Ross said, without inflection and without raising his voice. "What's this about a proxy fight?"

Ken Carpenter crossed the thick carpet and put his brief case on the table which stood against the wall, opened it, and looked in. On top of the stack of papers was a manila envelope with a copy of a photograph taken at night, with a Polaroid-Land camera. Ken looked at the envelope, hesitated — and took out a spool of magnetic tape instead. It was not the spool he had taken in Dan Foy's projection booth. It was a copy which he had recorded on his own machine at home.

Dave Ross was big, and he was in condition. The stories about his early violence in strikes indicated to Ken that he might decide to take direct action, seize the evidence on the spot and destroy it, then and there. Ken was many years younger and in good condition, but he was not sure he could have prevented Dave Ross. The big man must weigh two-twenty, and Ken had seen him hit a golf ball. He hit it with a body snap, like a boxer shooting a left hook, and he put it out two hundred and fifty yards with what seemed no effort at all.

"I'd like to play this copy of a tape I have in my possession," Ken Carpenter said. "If you've got a recorder, I could borrow it and save time. If not, I can send down for our own machine."

"We've got one," Ross said. "In the closet behind you."

Ken took the machine out of the closet. It was the same make and model as his own, so he was familiar with its operation. He placed the tape on the machine, plugged it into a wall receptacle, waited a moment for the tubes to warm, and started the playback. The tape hummed emptily for several seconds. Then there was the sound of a door shutting, and a voice — a voice of unmistakable authority — said, "All right gentlemen — I'm calling the meeting to order. . . ."

Ken Carpenter was watching Ross's face when he heard the sound of John Carey's voice, opening last September's board meeting, but the big man gave no sign. He was a famous poker player — as good, in his way, as John Carey himself. Ken had heard many stories of the savage pots — in one of them an entire Caribbean island (a good one, not a deserted sand spit) had changed hands in a single showdown. Ross's poker face was working for him now, as the tape continued. There were several speakers, among them Dave Ross himself, running over a routine discussion about an artesian well the company was thinking of drilling to augment its local plant water supply, and then the part Ken Carpenter was playing for Ross's benefit came on. A rough voice, which Ross must recognize as belonging to Walter Eberhardt, vice president in charge of production, said harshly, "Now, goddamn it, Caldwell, I don't give a hoot about this guided missile crap. Nor this space stuff either. I'm not interested in getting to the moon. I need a new blast furnace to replace Number 3. The lining's wore out, and the furnace is so old it's got to be screwed together by a maintenance crew every morning before breakfast — just to keep it running at all."

A reasoned, controlled voice, belonging to Bill Caldwell, in charge of research and development, said, "Mr. Carey — may I have the floor a minute? I want to say something to Walt."

"Go ahead," John Carey's voice said.

"Now look, Walt," Bill Caldwell's voice said. "I know you need a new blast furnace to replace Number 3. I have no quarrel with that. I know your outlook on tonnage — and I have no quarrel with that, either. We have to build bridges and big buildings and superhighways if we want to keep the mills rolling. But I would like to point out that we are now working in very unusual times. Our wage scale is so high we've just about priced ourselves out of the foreign markets — if they can get delivery elsewhere — and you must know this. For example, I can buy a ton of Swedish carbon steel on the dock at Cleveland, Ohio, for fifty-five dollars a ton less than I can buy a ton of Carey Furnace steel right out in our own mill — without a cent of transportation on it. In other words, the Swedes can ship their steel four or five thousand miles across an ocean and through a complicated inland waterway — and still undersell us by fifty-five dollars a ton.

"Now, Walt, my point is this. We can't seem to stop these strikes and wage hikes. Ever since Franklin Roosevelt gave John L. Lewis Section 7A of the National Recovery Act — stating that employers must bargain with unions of their employees' choosing — the unions have had the whip hand. Lewis called 7A 'Labor's Magna Carta.' I'm not going to rant and rave over whether it was good or bad — but there can be no argument that it has taken wage control largely out of our hands. So we can't hope to reduce the prices of our tonnage items, or any items, with the techniques in use today. And this is exactly my point. There's only one hope, as I see it, and that's to improve our products, and our production techniques — through R and D! Better steels — tougher, more ductile, more heat-resistant. Missile nose cones, for example —"

"Missile nose cones!" Walt Eberhardt's voice bellowed. "There you go again! You're a space cadet, Caldwell! What kind of tonnage can we expect from the nose cones of a couple of hundred or even a couple of thousand of these goddamned missiles? It's just a drop in the bucket. We're not a little specialty lab, for Christ's sake. We're one of the biggest son-of-a-bitching outfits in the world —"

"Wait a minute!" Bill Caldwell's voice shouted. "Let me finish, will you? Will you let me finish, before you start goddamning and son-of-a-bitching? I was using the missiles as just one example. I'm thinking of space ships. No — hold on, Walt — I mean it. Before we get through with this space race we'll be building ships as big as the Empire State building, to go to the planets and back. It's not space-cadet crap. It's a matter of doing it — or letting the Russians do it, and accepting the role of second-class power. And if you don't think a great nation can sink to a second-class power in a quick hurry, take a look around you. Take a look at Great Britain, and Germany, and France. Big Three, they used to be called. No more. The Russians and ourselves — and, in twenty years or less, Red China, will be the Big Three. At least I hope we'll be in the same league with Russia and China. If we bury our heads in old-fashioned production methods, and are afraid to put dough in research, we'll sink back into second or third place."

"Oh bullshit!" Walt Eberhardt yelled. "You've been reading science fiction! I'm interested in a new blast furnace now — not a fifty-story space ship in the twenty-fifth century!"

"If you don't think of anything else," Bill Caldwell said, "think about our stockholders. They've put their money behind us. They expect us to figure out ways and means to beat these inflated wages, without passing all of it on to the public — which, as you know, inflates the whole economy, and brings on another round of wage demands. Our stockholders expect us to be smart enough to meet foreign competition — here at home, and in South America and the NATO countries and everywhere else. Our stockholders expect us to make profits. That's why they bought our stock. And there's only one way to continue to make profits in the long run, in this company or any company — research!"

"Don't talk to me about the stockholders," Walt Eberhardt said then. "Fuck the stockholders! The slobs just sit around and bitch if we don't declare a dividend every five minutes. They don't know a thing about making steel and they couldn't care less. All they do is come to annual meetings and heckle the officers who are trying to meet their demands. If you want my opinion, I think the stockholders are becoming almost as much a pain in the ass as the unions. . . ."

Ken Carpenter bent and switched off the recording machine.

Dave Ross said, "That it? Or do you have more tapes to play?"

"That's it on the tapes."

"All right. What else?"

Ken felt the enormous reserve power of the man across the desk. Dave Ross must fully appreciate how this tape would sound if it were played to a group of stockholders at an annual meeting—particularly if, before the tape was played, the stockholders were skillfully inflamed against the dictatorial conduct of their board of directors. A lesser man than Dave Ross might have begun to bluster at this point, or have attempted diplomacy, or perhaps even begun to try for some deal. Ross did nothing. Ken felt the sweat under his armpits and wet his lips before he spoke. "I've got a few photostats of letters I'd like you to read."

He took out the stats of the letters he had taken from the files in Frank Hewitt's office and placed them in front of Ross. He knew their contents in detail. They were more damning, by far, than the tape — which was a psychological weapon, mainly. They had been written between Mr. John Carey and Mr. J. P. Detweiler and their import was abundantly clear. Mr. Detweiler wanted to resign. Mr. Carey did not want him to. In fact, Mr. Carey was quite specific about how badly he wanted Detweiler to remain in an advisory capacity in the treasurer's office, if nothing else. "I need you — on your own terms —" John Carey wrote. "But I need you."

J. P. Detweiler's own terms (Ken Carpenter had Ben Oliver to prove it) were costing the steel company almost $190,000 a year, when you considered Detweiler's salary, bonuses, stock options, and travel expenses.

"I have proof," Ken Carpenter said, as Dave Ross looked up from the letters, "that J. P. Detweiler has not done a single act of constructive work for this company since March . . . and it's August."

"You do, eh? What proof?"

"I've got his time cards for the year," Ken Carpenter said. "You know Mr. Carey's rule. Everybody punches in and out — even Mr. Carey himself — when he comes to work. And there's a fresh card with the date placed in racks beside the time clocks for every employee, even Mr. Detweiler, every week. I've got all of Mr. Detweiler's cards — and every one of them since March is blank. He hasn't punched in or out since then."

Ross looked at the letters again.

"I have further proof," Ken Carpenter said, "that George Donovan, J. P. Detweiler's second in command, hasn't done any real honest work in years. He reads comic books at his desk, as a matter of fact. Li'l Abner is his favorite."

"And how are you going to prove that?"

"I'm not going to say," Ken Carpenter said. "But I'm not bluffing, Mr. Ross. I can prove it."

Dave Ross continued reading. Presently, having finished, he pushed the letters aside. "What else do you have to show me?"

"Do you feel you need anything more?"

"That depends on your proposition, Carpenter. I assume you have one."

Ken Carpenter spoke slowly, making his voice sound as reasonable and logical — and friendly — as he could. "First, I want to make something very clear, Mr. Ross. I have the highest regard for your personal ability. I'm not trying to be polite. You are certainly aware of your ability as well or better than I could possibly be. So I am going to be frank. I can't do what I'm trying to do, without Dave Ross as chairman of the board of Carey Furnace Steel. . . ."

And now, for the first time, he saw Ross react, very slightly, and went on. "Give me twenty years, Mr. Ross — with the experience in steel that you've had, and I'll be a fair carbon copy of Dave Ross. I'm a smart kid now, and I know it, but I'm not Dave Ross now, and I know that too. I have just one problem. I don't want to wait twenty years — "

"Go on."

"I want four seats on the board," Ken Carpenter said. "I want Dana, Eberhardt, and Detweiler out. And I want you to vote with me on issues I consider vital."

"I suppose you have the men picked to go into these vacant slots."

"No, sir," Ken Carpenter said. "I figured I'd ask your advice on that, sir."

"How much common stock do you control, Carpenter?"

He met the big man's eyes. "I hear you are a very good poker player, Mr. Ross. Do you make a habit of lifting your hole card, in a game of stud, so everybody can see it?"

"You've got Maggie Hunter's."

"Yes, I have," Ken Carpenter said "And I've got some other odds and ends to go with it. In fact, I can say this much. I've got quite a few odds and ends to go with it — and if I use my data right, I think I can pick up a good deal more."

"You're quite a bastard, aren't you, Carpenter — with the old man dying? Can't you wait until he's gone before you start your proxy fight?"

"If you were in my shoes, would you wait?"

Dave Ross looked at him. "I wouldn't be in your shoes, Carpenter. You may not believe this, but I'd walk down River Avenue, right now, if the old man asked me to, and jump in the river. But you wouldn't understand that."

Ken Carpenter felt himself trembling. He said, earnestly, "It isn't as if I was trying to wreck the company, Mr. Ross. Actually, what I'm recommending is just business. J.P.'s long overdue. You must know that yourself. And so is Eberhardt. The time has come when bulls in china shops are out of style in American industry. And as far as Dana goes —" He stopped. "As far as Dana goes, he's a good man, but I happen to have something in my possession which could blow him to bits like a bomb."

"What is that?"

"I'm not going to use it," Ken Carpenter said. "I thought I could, but I can't. But I'm not bluffing, Mr. Ross. Actually I feel that I'm fronting for the stockholders of Carey Furnace Steel Company. This stuff in the folder isn't an evil plot I've cooked up. It's honest information. That's why I can't fail when we get in open session with the stockholders. I may be a bastard, but I'm a bastard who's working for the American dollar in behalf of his backers — and that wins in just about any business I've ever tried to play in."

"That it, Carpenter?"

"That's about it, Mr. Ross."

Dave Ross was now tapping lightly with his pencil on the desk, and Ken Carpenter saw that Ross was smiling. "You make a good case, Carpenter," he said. "I'd be silly not to admit to you that some of these things you say are perfectly true. In fact, I don't mind telling you that I intended making certain of these changes myself, eventually. But now that you've been so obliging and pointed these matters out to me, I don't think I'll wait. I'll just make the changes at once — so that by the time we come to the annual stockholders' meeting, all this seemingly disastrous evidence will be ancient history. You'll have no case at all."

And then Dave Ross stopped smiling. His eyes were hard and contemptuous, and his voice was harsh, but careless, as if he were addressing a minor clerk. "Now then, Carpenter," he said. "Get out of my office. I've got important work to do."

When Ethyl Snyder told Howard, once and for all, that she was not going to Mexico or anywhere else, he went directly to the Steel Room of the Carey House and had one of Kelly's double ryes. Then he had another. And then another. He was not thinking about anything in particular. He was just sitting in the air-conditioned bar, drinking massive jolts of whisky. When the oil paintings of the blast furnaces on the walls began to swim, gently, to the left, Howard got off the bar stool, paid his bill and walked up to the desk and asked for a room with a bath. Ed Hurley was the night desk man. He was a scarecrow of an Irishman with little red veins in his nose and bulgy bloodshot eyes, and he liked Howard Snyder. Ed Hurley drank, himself. He usually saw Howard at times when Howard was drinking hard, and he felt a bond between them. He gave Howard the key. "You got any luggage, Mr. Snyder?"

"What?" Howard said, looking at Ed Hurley swimming gently to the left in the golden haze of the desk lamps. "What's that?"

"I was wondering if you have any suitcase, or bag, or anything?"

"Oh," Howard said. "I gotta have a suitcase, do I?"

"Oh, no — not you, Mr. Snyder. You want me to come up with you and show you the room? The bellboy's off now."

"Oh, no," Howard said. "I'll find it. I'll find it myself."

"You want to leave a call?"

"What?"

"Do you want to leave a time for us to call you in the morning?"

"Oh, yes. Seven. Seven o'clock."

"Seven it is. Good night now, Mr. Snyder."

"Good night," Howard said. "Good night now."

He walked up to his room, which was on the second floor, and let himself in, after considerable fumbling with the key. The window was shut and the room was superheated. He opened the window and turned on the electric fan. Hot air blew around the room. He loosened his tie and lay down for a minute, to get up his strength to undress. He was quite drunk. When he shut his eyes he had the feeling he was turning, slowly, end over end. He opened his eyes and looked through the screen at the smoky orange glow from the mills which hung in the smog over the town.

It was all over. He would not go to Mexico. He must turn the tickets in tomorrow. And he would not be able to take any trips — not even plan them — in the coming summers. Through the churning of the alcohol, he felt the weight and the pointlessness of his life press down upon him like physical pressure, and tears of self-pity burned in his eyes. It was all Ethyl's fault. Ethyl was frigid. Ethyl was dominating. Ethyl was too strong for him. And it wouldn't change and get better. It would get worse. The vista of his life stretched ahead of him, in his drunken brain, like a dimly lit tunnel filled with the shapes of bolts and nuts and tables of the breaking strengths of wire rope, and the sink at home, full of unwashed dishes, and Carole in a new dress, and Ethyl smiling, and the little dog barking, and no bright circle in the distance, anywhere, denoting any exit. Why go on, he thought; why make any effort to do anything, ever? He was whipped. He was alive, but he might as well be dead. He shut his eyes, and almost immediately he fell asleep. . . .

The ringing of the telephone beside the bed wakened him and he opened his eyes to the light which was like bright splinters jagging his eyes, and fumbled the receiver off the hook.

"Seven o'clock sir!" a girl's voice sang out at the other end of the wire.

"Thanks," he mumbled. "Thanks a lot."

He got the phone back in its cradle and fell back on the bed, and noticed he was still in his clothes. His head ached fiercely. Each time his heart beat it felt as if a small spurt of liquid fire was pumping up through the base of his neck, and he was nauseated. Lying on the bed, he salivated. His stomach lurched. He rolled off the bed and stumbled toward the bathroom, but he did not reach the toilet in time. He vomited propulsively across the tile floor, and then fell on his knees in front of the bowl and his body was racked with spasms of retching; sour burning liquid, mixed with chunks of curd, came out of his mouth and nose, and he gagged and choked and lay weakly against the fouled porcelain bowl, his head still aching with a blinding violence, accentuated by the retching.

He knew what it was, of course. He was having one of his bilious attacks. They went on, sometimes, for hours — vomiting until his stomach was empty, and then the dry heaves (he had once broken a blood vessel in his throat and vomited blood), until he could bring up a few ounces of bitter bile, and then, at once, the attack would be over. He sat helplessly on the floor for some time. Slowly and painfully, he managed to remove his clothes. Finally he turned on the water in the bathtub and lay down in it, but there was no abatement of the nausea or the savage throbbing in his head. Presently he got out of the bathtub, without drying himself, and went back and lay down, wet, on the hot and rumpled bed. He shivered, not from cold, but from the nausea and pain, and tried to close his eyes and get to sleep. It was no good. He felt the nausea coming fast, lurched off the bed and into the bathroom. And this time he stayed there, sitting on the floor next to the toilet bowl. It was past noon when the bile finally came, and he lay back, cleansed and weak, knowing the attack was over.

He got to the Diffenbaugh Travel Bureau, on the town square, at three o'clock in the afternoon. Old Tom Diffenbaugh was behind the counter. He said, "Oh — it's you, Mr. Snyder," as if he had been expecting this visit.

"Yes, it's me," Howard said. "I'm sorry, but I'm going to have to turn in my plane tickets to Mexico."

Mr. Diffenbaugh did not smile. He said, "I can't refund your money right now, Mr. Snyder. We'll have to wait until tomorrow, I'm afraid. I'm short of cash."

"Tomorrow will be all right," Howard Snyder said.

Tom Diffenbaugh looked at him without the usual friendly travel-agency smile. "Mr. Snyder — we — I mean, I hate to have to say this — but we don't like to cancel reservations any oftener than we have to. It gives us a bad name with the airlines and the rest of the carriers, if you know what I mean. It isn't my province to ask you why, of course, but this is the third time you've made elaborate summer plans with us and canceled at the last minute." Tom Diffenbaugh paused. "It isn't that I don't want your business, Mr. Snyder — please don't misunderstand me — but —"

"I understand you," Howard Snyder said. "And don't worry about it. I won't be making any more reservations here."

"Now, it isn't necessary to get mad," Tom Diffenbaugh said. "I didn't mean that you should —"

"I'm not mad," Howard Snyder said. "It has nothing to do with what you said just now. I won't be making any reservations with you, or anybody, that's all. Could you send the money to the steel company, tomorrow, or do you want me to come by and pick it up?"

"Either way you wish, Mr. Snyder."

"Oh, I forgot," Howard said. "We're having a department picnic tomorrow, and nobody will be at the office. I'll come in and pick it up."

"All right," Tom Diffenbaugh said. "Don't come before nine-thirty. I don't have my supply of cash from the bank until then. By the way, are they going to close the company tomorrow?"

Howard Snyder stared at him. "Close the company? Oh, no — just the advertising department. We're having our picnic. The rest of the company isn't affected."

"I didn't mean because of the picnic," Tom Diffenbaugh said. "I meant on account of Mr. Carey."

"Mr. Carey?" Howard said, bewildered.

"Didn't you hear?"

"No. I just got — I just got into town."

"He's supposed to have cancer — incurable cancer. The news just broke this morning. He's only got a couple of weeks to live, the way it was told to me."

"Cancer," Howard Snyder said.

"Yes," Tom Diffenbaugh said. "It sure is a hell of a thing. The last time I saw Mr. Carey he looked as if he'd live to be a hundred. I guess you just never know. Maybe you haven't got any more time than it takes to walk down to the corner and get hit by a truck. It makes a man think."

"Cancer," Howard Snyder said. "Mr. Carey has cancer?"

Tom Diffenbaugh looked at him. *This poor guy isn't quite bright,* he thought. *Maybe he's better off not going to Mexico after all.*

In his room at home, after dark on that Wednesday night, Ken Carpenter was looking at a photograph, and he was, he knew, at a crucial fork in the pathway he had been following all his life toward what he hoped would be great success in American industry. This afternoon he had been dealt a body blow, and it had been his own fault. To rush into Dave Ross's office and lay all his cards on the table now stood revealed for what it had been, an incredibly naïve blunder. He had been looking at it so hard from one point of view — the idea of striking, with overwhelming power, when the opposition was confused and ill prepared — that he had not seen the simple countermove which he had presented to Dave Ross. He had been like a kid, actually, flying at an adult with his hands flailing impotently.

But he still had one ace, which he hadn't used because of natural reluctance, and also because (to be honest) he hadn't felt he needed it: the picture he had taken of Dottie O'Brien and Paul Dana in the pines the night of the Carey party. Now he looked at it carefully under the table lamp. It was dynamite, all right, if he cared to use it. Normal sex was bad enough — but this was worse. This was something the papers couldn't print — something that would have to be shown in private, to certain people, who could then pass the word to the others. Ken Carpenter had done a good job of photography that night. He had crept softly through the darkness, stopping from time to time to listen — and then he had heard the cracking of twigs and the rustling sound of clothing being pushed up or loosened, and finally, the unmistakable sounds of love. He had crept closer until, in the dim shadows, he could see the two bodies locked on the forest floor; he had aimed the camera with great care, placed his finger on the shutter release and hissed, softly but sharply. . . .

Dana's face had jerked up from between Dottie O'Brien's widespread thighs, and in that instant, Ken had pressed the button and bathed the couple in a blinding flash of light. He had turned instantly and run, not afraid of pursuit, because he had, on this occasion, literally caught Paul Dana with his pants down.

He looked at the flash photo again. Dottie O'Brien, lying under Dana, was not recognizable. Only her short curly hair showed at the edge of his jacket. But her full and open thighs were quite clear: the camera had caught the bright glint of her garter fasteners, the soft sag of flesh over the confining upper edge of the silk stockings, even the scuff marks in her sport pumps. Paul Dana's face, a mixture of outrage, lust and drunken dismay, staring straight into the camera above the open thighs, was so ludicrous it was impossible not to smile when you looked at it. It must have been a shock, Ken thought — it must really have been a shock for the poor guy, thinking they were alone, to suddenly have his portrait taken. The picture would eliminate Dana instantly, of course, and it might do much more. Stockholders in big companies were not noted for their tolerance of company officers who were caught in strange sex practices. Here on the table in front of him, Ken Carpenter had the big smear which might touch off a successful proxy fight based on the need for a clean new management. It was not nearly as strong as his first case. But it was potent, if handled right, and with Margaret Fiori's stock behind him he might still be able to take control of the company.

He put his hand into his brief case and brought out the photostat he'd taken to Dave Ross's office and not used. It was muddy. It did not have the detail of the original — but the identity of one of the principals was abundantly clear. These two pictures represented the only tangible evidence he had against Paul Dana. He hesitated. . . .

Then he carefully laid the two pictures together, one on top of the other, and tore them methodically into tiny, unrecognizable scraps. . . .

He had thrown the scraps into the waste basket and was rising to leave the room when his phone rang. He picked it up. "Yes?" he said. "Carpenter here."

"Ah, good," a voice said. "I've been trying to get you a long time, Mr. Carpenter. This is Frank Hewitt. I got your heifer and she's a little beauty. I was wondering if you wanted to come over and take a look."

For a moment Ken Carpenter was at a loss. So many things had happened so rapidly that he had forgotten about the heifer. Its whole purpose had been to give him an excuse to get into Frank Hewitt's office and into his files — which he had already done. He had no use for the heifer now. He grinned, suddenly, into the phone. He felt good — better than he had felt since before Debbie Copeland had failed him in Cleveland, Ohio. He said, "Why not, Frank? I haven't a blessed thing to do — and I'll be over there in ten minutes and take a look at that little beauty you've got for me!"

Thursday

LOUISE STEGMEYER roused from sleep on Thursday morning with her usual reluctance to meet another day. She lay with her eyes shut, resisting the awakening process, and then, from somewhere deep in her brain, the events at Mr. Hurd's cottage broke free and rippled upward like a quicksilver cloud of bubbles from the bottom of a pool.

She opened her eyes and stared at the ceiling. Deliberately, she let the wonderful things that had happened move luxuriously through her mind. A man had leered at her, and there had been absolutely no doubt that he meant it. Suppose he *was* the driver of a beer truck — he was a very nice one! Mr. George Hurd, the big boss of the department, had called her by her first name and praised her work at the camp. Howard Snyder, shy and reserved as he was, had tried to come to her rescue in the argument with Doug Schroeder. And Nellie Laubach and Norman Kraft had taken her orders without a murmur. . . .

From outside the bedroom window, there came the sound of a car's engine being started. Louise sat up and peered out in time to see her father back out of the driveway, and felt instant relief. With him gone, she could take a bath and run as much water as she liked and lie in the tub for an hour. This was the day of the department picnic and she did not need to go to work. She got out of bed in her nightgown and had started for the bathroom when the phone rang downstairs. She paused in the open doorway of the bedroom and listened.

"Hello," Vivian Stegmeyer's voice said. "Who? Oh — Nellie Laubach. . . . Yes, she's here, but she's still asleep —"

"I'm up, Mummy!" Louise called at once. "Tell Nellie I'll be right down."

She slipped into a dressing gown and hurried to the phone. "Hello, Nellie. This is Louise."

"Louise — oh, my goodness, I don't know what to do! Mr. Hurd just phoned — phoned *me,* Louise — and he wants me to be a hostess at the picnic today. Me — a hostess. I'm so nervous I don't know what to do."

"Now, calm down, Nellie. What will your duties be — did Mr. Hurd say?"

"Walk around and see if everybody is having a good time, and if they aren't, go up and talk to them and ask them if they'd like a hot dog or to play horseshoes or something. That's why I'm calling you, Louise. Mr. Hurd wants you to be a hostess too. He said he tried to get you but there was somebody on your party line. I know you'll be great as a hostess, Louise — but golly! I'm the kind of person that *needs a hostess to help them!*"

Louise smiled a little. "When does Mr. Hurd want us?"

"One o'clock sharp. We don't have to do anything about the food. Just the people. Could you pick me up in your car, Louise?"

"Certainly, Nellie. I'll be at your house about twelve-fifteen. That should give us plenty of time."

"Oh, thank you, Louise. Thank you very much. Goodbye."

Louise Stegmeyer hung up. Her lips were dry. As Nellie had been talking, Louise had been looking at herself in the mirror which hung in the living room. As usual, her hair billowed out in a dowdy mass and the remains of her pale lipstick (Herman Stegmeyer objected strongly to bright shades) looked sickly in the shadows. Her heart, which had beat so high with the memories of yesterday, had quieted. *I'm a mess,* she thought miserably. *I'm just a hopeless mess. What happened at the camp was an accident . . . it must have been. . . .*

She rose and walked into the kitchen, where her mother was standing by the stove in a house dress and apron. When the older woman smiled her mouth drew down at the corners. The kitchen was full of the rich smells of frying eggs and bacon and coffee. Herman Stegmeyer had just foraged there.

"What did Nellie want, dear?" Mrs. Stegmeyer asked.

"Mr. Hurd wants her and me to be hostesses at the picnic this afternoon."

"Well, that's nice, isn't it?"

Louise did not reply. She crossed the kitchen and sat down at the table.

"What's the matter, honey?" Mrs. Stegmeyer said. "Don't you want to be a hostess?"

Louise looked up. "Mother, do you remember Matilda Miller — the woman who has the beauty shop? She came to the house one night a couple of years ago to ask Daddy for a loan from his bank."

"Matilda Miller? Why, yes, I remember her."

"Do you remember she looked at me and said I was pretty — said Daddy ought to buy me some nice clothes and send me over to her shop so she could make me into a glamour girl?"

"Yes, Matilda did say that."

"Well, Daddy wouldn't send me. When Matilda left the house he said she was just trying to flatter me so he'd give her the loan. He said I wasn't a glamour girl and never could be one, and I'd better forget all that foolishness."

Mrs. Stegmeyer nodded.

"Mother, was that the truth — what Daddy said?"

Mrs. Stegmeyer was silent. She was looking at her daughter curiously, almost with alarm. "Honey, what are you trying to say?"

"Well, Tuesday, when I was out at Mr. Hurd's camp, I was wearing a skirt and pullover, and the man who drove the beer truck — he wasn't much, maybe, but he certainly wasn't trying to get a loan — he asked me for a date and called me gorgeous. And then Mr. Hurd showed me his camp and looked at me — well, the same way the truck driver did, and he called me Louise. Even Nellie — even Nellie said I looked pretty —"

"You do look pretty, dear. You always have."

"Daddy doesn't think so."

A shadow crossed Vivian Stegmeyer's face and her lips compressed slightly. Louise saw the change.

"Mother — what is it?"

"Nothing — nothing, dear."

Louise was silent for a moment. Her heart was beating heavily. She wet her lips and spoke. "Mother — I've heard that Matilda is just wonderful. A lot of the rich wives of steel company executives go to her instead of to Pittsburgh. I was wondering — I mean, if I'm going to be a hostess — I was wondering if I could risk going to Matilda? Right this morning, I mean, and have her fix me up as pretty as she can?"

Mrs. Stegmeyer did not speak. Her bosom was rising and falling and there was a pink flush in her usually pale cheeks.

"Mother, what is it? Is something the matter?"

"Nothing, dear," Vivian Stegmeyer said in a low voice. "I was just thinking about Matilda Miller. At the time I thought you should have gone to her. I didn't think she was flattering you at all. But I couldn't speak up then. You were still dependent on your — on Herman Stegmeyer." The older woman's voice had grown stronger and there was a brightness in her eyes that Louise had never seen before. "Well, you aren't dependent on him now. You have a job. You can keep yourself if you have to. That's true, isn't it? You can keep yourself now, can't you, Louise?"

Louise stared at her mother in surprise. "Why, yes, Mother, of course I can."

Vivian Stegmeyer lifted her hands, then, and fumbled at the throat of her dress. She unbuttoned it and drew out a gold locket which she wore on a chain. Louise had never seen her mother without the locket. She had asked about it many times when she was small, but her mother had never told her what was in it, and Louise had not asked her for years. It was just one of those strange affectations people had, a good-luck charm, perhaps — something her mother, by a quirk of mind, felt she needed around her neck. Vivian Stegmeyer unhooked the chain and placed the locket gently on the table in front of Louise. She moved her fingers to a spot near the top, pressed, and the locket flew open. There was a young man's picture in it. He had wide-set eyes, his hair was parted in the middle, barroom style, and he was grinning, showing strong white teeth. The jaw had a dimple in it, and was slightly outthrust, as if this young man was happy to see the world out in front of him and was impatient to run forth to meet it.

Louise looked at the photograph with surprise and bewilderment. She looked up at her mother. Her mother's eyes were filled with tears.

"Mother! What is it?"

"Look at his chin," Vivian Stegmeyer said, her voice almost harsh. "Take a good look at it — then go look into the kitchen mirror, and when you come back I'll tell you everything. It's time now. It's exactly time."

At nine o'clock sharp, Louise Stegmeyer was sitting in Matilda Miller's beauty shop. There had been a short discussion. Louise had told Matilda about the picnic, about being a hostess, about wanting to look nice — and then, as she began to warm up, about all the exciting things that had happened to her. One thing only she withheld — the most important news of her life — the fact that she was not Herman Stegmeyer's daughter. Matilda listened, and when Louise was through, she said, "Honey, leave it up to me. Whatever we do will be an improvement, if you don't mind my saying so. We aren't starting on the ground floor. We're starting in the basement."

Louise smiled with stiff lips. She was frightened.

"You're a lucky kid in one way," Matilda said. "You've been going around in a burlap bag all your life, and nobody knows what's under it. I'm not saying Matilda will get you a proposal of marriage this very afternoon — but I'll bet my last cent it won't be long. You've got what a grown man wants, and Matilda is now going to show them how lovely it all is." Matilda laughed her gravelly laugh. "Just take a tip from an old campaigner and keep your guard up. It's easy to get carried away sometimes, particularly when you haven't been used to having the big louts grabbing at you."

Matilda worked quickly with her scissors, stepping back from the chair from moment to moment to size up the proportions of what she was trying to do. She had decided on a pageboy bob, very simple and close to the head, a sheath of clean-brushed hair that would fall to the neck like a helmet — a shining helmet, because Matilda had decided to shoot the works. Not just cut the hair — tint it. She was going to give Louise's mousy hair a new brown rinse which would brush up into a nice little glow, which, as she told Louise, "would cost you fifty bucks in any self-respecting New York salon."

Louise did not speak. She was tense. She had thought it over and decided that if Matilda went too far, if she made her look ridiculous or cheap, she would not go to the picnic at all. She would beg off and go home and try to repair the damage before appearing in public anywhere. But, scared and nervous as she was, one thought glowed like sunshine in the back of Louise Stegmeyer's mind. No matter what Matilda did to her hair — even if she cut it off at the roots — she couldn't change the wonderful news Louise had just received this morning: *Louise was not fat Herman's daughter; not a single drop of Stegmeyer blood flowed in her veins. . . .*

"I'm going to shape the eyebrows," Matilda said, and smiled at Louise's instinctive tensing in the chair. "Now, don't worry, honey. Just a little devilish uptilt at the outer corners. You have enough excess to shape 'em without it looking faked."

"Oh, Matilda — I — I won't look like some dance-hall floozy, will I?"

"You're scared stiff, is all," Matilda said. "I know. Well, stop worrying. Let me do the worrying."

"All right."

"That's my doll."

Louise stopped talking, but she did not stop worrying. Matilda finished cutting the hair, went for the brown rinse, took up the scissors upon returning, made some minor snips, then took Louise to a shampoo booth. As Louise passed a mirror, she caught sight of her hair and almost screamed in dismay. She looked — oh, God! — she looked horrible. She clenched her fingers in her palms and sat down, fighting back the tears, and submitted to the brown rinse. Too late, now, to turn back: she was ruined. It was going to be worse than she had imagined in her most fearful dreams. The self-confidence of yesterday was gone. She lacked the strength now to do anything, even to ask Matilda to stop — to try to restore the safe anonymity of yesterday to her poor head.

She did not look in the mirror when the rinse was complete. She sat, frozen, while Matilda set the pageboy with metal curlers, curling the hair under at the base of the neck, and making bangs that came down on her forehead. The setting did not take very long, and then Matilda said, "All right now, honey. The dryer."

She glanced at her wrist watch. It was ten-thirty. She did not ask how long she would be under the dryer. It didn't matter now, really, if she was there all day. She wasn't going anywhere but home, to call Nellie and tell her to find another way of getting out to the picnic. Poor Nellie. She'd be scared to death on her own, but it couldn't be helped. Louise sat still while Matilda's assistant put the cotton band across her forehead to protect the skin from being marked by the drying net, and then she took her place under the metal dome and felt warm air flowing strongly around her head. "If it gets too hot for you," the girl said, "just let me know, and I'll turn it down."

"All right."

She was under the dryer for forty minutes. Then the girl came and took her back to Matilda. Matilda checked, found the hair dry enough for her liking, took out the metal curlers and began brushing.

It seemed to Louise that Matilda took a very long time in the brushing. Probably she saw how terrible the hair looked and was trying to put off the moment when she'd have to show her client what a mess she'd made of her. After she had brushed Louise's hair, Matilda made up her face with lipstick and mascara. Louise could not see what she looked like. She felt sick at her stomach, and her head had begun to ache. If the woman would only hurry, get it over with, give her a chance to pay and get away. That was what she wanted now — a chance to run from this shop, to get to her own room, lock the door, and lie down on the bed and weep. Suddenly, Matilda said "All right, Miss Stegmeyer — I guess that's the best I can do for you. Want to take a look?"

Louise nodded miserably.

"All right, here you are — the new Miss Louise Stegmeyer!"

Matilda held a large mirror up in front of her. She looked into it. For an instant she couldn't take hold of the sight with her mind. The girl who looked out at her was so different from Louise Stegmeyer that Louise did not recognize her for an instant. Then her nerves contracted fiercely, and her spine ached like a tooth. The girl in the mirror had a subtle, arrogant arch to her eyebrows. Her lips were a vivid red shade and had a different shape — like the mouths of the young glamour stars in the movies. What Matilda had done did not alter the fact that one of Louise's teeth had grown crookedly in one side of her mouth (Herman had not believed in wasting money on fancy orthodontists); it did not change the fact that her nose was just a little too thick; it did not take the strained look from her eyes. But those things were minor, were lost in the total effect. It was her hair — looking at her hair — which made Louise Stegmeyer's eyes fill with tears. Her hair was beautiful: a sleek, glowing sheath that made her face seem thinner, her eyes bigger, her head regal and proud.

"Okay, honey," Matilda said, "what's the verdict?"

Louise could not speak. Her throat was too cramped and tight, and hot tears welled out of her eyes and ran down her cheeks.

"Oh, my God," Matilda laughed, understanding. "It can't be that bad — that you've got to cry about it!"

"Oh, it's not bad!" Louise cried out. "It's not bad at all, Matilda. It's wonderful . . . just wonderful!"

"Yeah," Matilda said, "it ain't too bad, really. Now we haven't got much time. You'll need a new dress and some new shoes to go with it. Do you have any money?"

"I have the money for you — twenty-five dollars."

Matilda hesitated. She cocked her head to one side, observing her handiwork and finding it good. She grinned. "Well," she said, "I got you started — I can hardly leave you until you're finished. I'll lend you the money for the rest. All right, let's get over to Foyle's Town and Country Shop. I hope they haven't sold that sharkskin number I have in mind."

"Oh, Matilda — you'll come with me?"

"I surely wouldn't let you go alone."

Fifteen minutes later, Louise was standing on the thick white rug in Foyle's Town and Country Shop in spike-heeled pumps, fifteen-denier nylons, and a white dress that did nothing but show off her smooth shoulders and swelling hips and her bright new pageboy bob.

"Stand straight!" Matilda said sharply. "For God's sake, what are you trying to hide?" Matilda chuckled. "I don't know," she said, looking solemnly at the salesgirl. "Maybe I ought to go along on this party. If they're as wild as some of these company picnics I've heard about, maybe our little girl here will need a bodyguard at that . . . ."

Howard Snyder had waited until dark to come home on the day of his bilious attack. Ethyl and Carole were not there. He went upstairs, took a bath, shaved, and laid out clothes for the next day. He was feeling weak from his bout of drinking, but his head was clear and the ache was gone. He put on his pajamas, lit a cigarette, and lay down on the bed in the warm darkness. He could hear the Abbotts' radio going, down the hill, and the voices of some neighborhood kids playing on a lawn across Mountain Avenue. He lay there for quite a while before Ethyl drove in. He felt his stomach tighten up. He got out of bed, put on his bathrobe and slippers and went downstairs just as they came in.

Ethyl saw him, and he saw her face tighten. She said, "If you're sick from a hangover, don't come whining to me and Carole. Go to a hospital."

"I'm not sick," he said. "I just wanted to say —"

"I'm not interested in what you want to say," Ethyl said sharply. "All I ask of you is to let us alone!"

He stood there looking at them across the room. Carole had moved close to her mother's side and was glaring at him. He did not know what Ethyl had told the child; but obviously, whatever it had been, it hadn't been calculated to make her feel closer to her father.

"All right," he said. "If that's how it is, I'm going to bed."

"That's exactly how it is," Ethyl snapped. "And another thing, Howard, consideration is a two-way street, in case you hadn't realized it. You stormed out of here last night and stayed out all night and all day, without bothering to tell us where you'd gone. You had no consideration at all for either of us. So you can't expect us to have any for you. From now on, for one thing, I'd suggest you get your breakfast at the diner, on your way to work, the way a lot of other husbands do."

"Carole seems to be a lot better," Howard said.

"She isn't well — not at all! It was just so hot I took her out for a ride to cool her off."

"I see. Well, good night."

Ethyl glared at him. "Good *night!* For heaven's sake, go to bed and let us alone!"

He turned, without saying anything more, and went up to the attic. He took off the robe and lay down. Suddenly he wasn't sorry for himself any more — and he didn't blame Ethyl any more. Ethyl couldn't have pushed him around the way she'd done if he'd been a man instead of a wishy-washy little fellow who was willing to appease, no matter what it cost, to obtain peace.

Appeasement, he saw now, operated in much the same manner between individual people as between nations. The underlying factor in any sort of appeasement was human nature. If one side was willing to give in, the other side was naturally, by the law of human nature, going to demand more and more. He couldn't put the blame for his disappointments on his wife. He must — if he was honest — take a good part of it on himself. If he hadn't been so weak, Ethyl would not now be so strong. His life might stretch away in a dark tunnel, as it had done last night in his drunken vision on the hotel bed, but at least he could eliminate one thing — would eliminate one thing: self-pity. He lay back on the pillow and relaxed his legs and arms. *The hell with it,* he thought. *The utter complete hell with it.* . . . And somehow, he did not know why, this thought gave him a reckless kind of peace. A man on the bottom of the tank had no place to sink. He was as far down as he was going to get. . . .

Willie Martin came out of his house on Grandview Avenue in a bright yellow sports shirt, shiny blue slacks, new sneakers, and a dark green sunshade with a webbing headband. Stephanie Martin, trim and cute in slacks and a cotton pullover, her head wrapped in a turban, Polish-style (she had just washed her hair) stood in the doorway of Willie's neat little house, smiling and waving at Willie as he got into Jack McHugh's Buick sedan beside Howard Snyder, who had moved over in the middle to give him room.

"Bye-bye, baby!" Willie yelled. "Don't expect me home until you see me! This is my day to howl." (Willie then gave a drawn-out wolf howl which caused Goliath, the boxer, to rouse in his house and peer out suspiciously with his black and wrinkled mug.)

Stephanie did not seem the least upset by her husband's cavalier statement. She merely smiled, waved once more, and stepped back into the house. She knew she had nothing to fear from Willie, for the very good reason that she had given it to him twice — once last evening, and again in the morning, before they got up. Stephy and Willie had a most satisfactory love life from all standpoints. Stephy liked to be on top. She liked to play the man. And Willie like to be on the bottom. He liked to play the woman. Stephy was not a lesbian — the idea made her sick — and Willie was certainly not a fairy, in any sense of the word. It just happened that they liked to do it in this manner — with, at times, a few frills. Stephy hadn't done it last night or this morning, but every now and then she tied Willie to the bed, stark naked, and whipped him lightly. It made him jerk and throb like a bull at breeding time. Willie, like many small men, was magnificently endowed. "I may not have Charles Atlas here in bed with me," Stephy would sometimes whisper into her husband's ear when she was on top, "but I wouldn't trade what you got for Charles Atlas and all his pupils rolled into one."

The light whipping was special. After one of those sessions (if Stephy was particularly hot she might bite Willie's ear and bring blood), they would lie like the dead for an hour or so, after Stephy untied him, and then get up and she'd cook him a steak. He'd eat the steak and give the bone to Goliath.

Now, as she watched Willie drive away, Stephy felt happy and relaxed. Willie was a good guy. He really was. She loved him more than anything in the world, and he loved her — and that damned Goliath. . . .

In the car, Willie was saying to Howard Snyder, "Yep, I got her trained. Old Stephy knows who's boss."

"She sure does," Jack McHugh said, and winked at Howard in the mirror — a wink which Willie Martin also caught.

"Now, just what the hell was that for?" Willie shouted. "That goddamn wink, McHugh!"

"Wink, Willie?" Jack McHugh said, aggrieved. "I don't know what you're talking about."

"The hell you don't!" Willie yelled. "You think Stephy runs me, eh?"

"Heaven forbid, Willie!"

"Well, she don't, goddamn it. I'm the goddamn boss. Me. Get that through your thick head — see!"

"Sure, Willie," Jack smiled. "I beg your pardon, Willie, for Christ's sake. You're the boss. You're the goddamn boss, boy!"

Willie sulked while they drove through town. But when they passed the Carey Furnace dump on the way upriver to the Lundyville bridge, his natural good humor, and his almost instant forgetting of any slights which happened to him, washed away his temper. He looked at the wilted trees and the tinder-dry weeds. "Some heat, hey," Willie said. "I hope to God nobody throws a butt in the woods up by Mr. Hurd's shack — or, Dad, we'll all be swimming in the river to keep ourselves from being barbecued."

"They had one in the hills up above Oil City — toward Tionesta," Jack McHugh said. "I heard about it on the radio. I don't know how many thousands of acres it burned before it hit the Allegheny and went out."

"It'll rain someday," Willie said. "Maybe not this summer. Maybe not next summer. But someday. Jeeze, I was surprised they didn't cancel the picnic, with Mr. Carey in that kind of shape."

"Mr. Carey passed the word himself," Jack McHugh said. "Business as usual, he said. Good old boy, Mr. Carey."

"You bet," Willie Martin said. "Usually I don't give these rich bastards much, but old man Carey is a square guy. At least from my seat in the bleachers. Maybe he beats his wife and screws the stockholders — but I ain't seen it. Cancer — Jesus — cancer. . . ."

They crossed the bridge at Lundyville, climbed the hill, and doubled back through the Lundy estate and down to Black River.

Other cars had come ahead of them and the trees and grass beside the road were coated with dust, and a faint dust haze still hung in the air. At least after they came down the hill to the river it was cooler, in the shaded road between the laurel. A large number of cars were already parked — pulled off on both sides of the road into the brush and weeds. Jack McHugh pulled off the road too, behind the last one in the line, and stopped.

"Well, boys, from now on we'll have to hoof it, I guess."

Sounds of gaiety came to them as they walked along the woods road and up the private drive to the Hurd cottage. There were cars parked in a place reserved for those helping with the preparations, but the major portion of the clearing was open. Norman Kraft was putting down some bases, in preparation for the softball contest, but the horseshoe pitchers were already at it. They could hear the clink of the shoes, a slow beat of recorded jazz music from inside the cottage, and the rise and fall of talk, punctuated at times by a feminine scream or a masculine roar of laughter. Howard Snyder saw Al Bishop in a white short-sleeved shirt, neat gray slacks, and gray suède shoes, standing with a highball in his hand, talking to Charlie Bender, who also held a highball. Al was speaking solemnly and Charlie was listening attentively, like a well-behaved dog waiting for a bone. Out in the glare of sunshine, which looked brighter than normal because of the contrasting shade, Jake Abbott was lying in a canvas chair with his shirt off, getting sun on his chest. His eyes were shut and there was a drink in his hand, which, as Howard watched, he lifted and drank from, eyes still shut.

"It looks as if the fun and games have gotten started without me," Jack McHugh said.

John Hendershot and Max Roth, of the photographic department, were sitting under nearby trees in hot-looking suits, ill at ease, drinking beer out of bottles. Just then young Don Francisco came out of the rear of the lodge, where the men's dressing room was, in a pair of dark blue bathing trunks and dark blue sneakers, looking like a young Italian film star with his good tan, his sculptured muscles, his thick blue-black hair, and his long eyelashes. He was joined immediately by Eleanor Keck. Eleanor was wearing a skimpy white bathing suit out of which her bronze body thrust and swelled provocatively, and when she smiled up at Don Francisco her teeth flashed white against her dark skin. They took the path down toward the dock, where swimming was already in progress.

"I'd give a year's salary," Willie Martin whispered into Howard Snyder's ear, "for just one night with that little bitch." Then Willie's whisper stopped, he took a quick breath and let out a sudden wolf whistle, followed by a shout, "Hey, Jack — Howie — look what just stepped out of the back door there!"

Howard Snyder looked in the direction Willie was pointing and saw a tall buxom girl in a tight-fitting white dress, a smooth, glowing pageboy bob, white shoes with heels too high for a picnic, and a vivid red mouth.

"It's Louise," Willie yelled. "It's our own little Louise, you guys! Holy cats, Jack, lookit her! Hey Louise! Hey, good-looking! What happened? You run out to Hollywood last night and get glamorized? My gawd, fellas, ain't she a dream?"

Louise Stegmeyer came toward them, teetering a little on her high heels, peering a little near-sightedly without her glasses, and her face was pink with nervousness and excitement. "Oh — hello, Willie, Jack, Mr. Snyder. I'm — I'm supposed to be a hostess here — at least that's what Mr. Hurd said. Is there anything I can do for you boys?"

"There certainly is, honeybunch," Willie Martin said. "You can just pucker up and give this boy a great big kiss, Miss Marilyn Monroe!"

"Oh, Willie — please —"

"Where'd you get that hairdo? It's a darb. Where'd you get it? Where?"

"Do you like it?"

"I love it. I could run through it in my bare feet. Honest, it makes you a lot like Marilyn in that last picture of hers."

"Matilda Miller gave it to me. This morning."

"Matilda, hey? Well, I'll tell you what I'm gonna do. I'm gonna get my little Stephy by the arm the minute I get home and twist it good, and tell her to get her a — to get over to Matilda's the first thing in the morning and get a hairdo just like yours, Louise."

"It's pretty," Jack McHugh said. "Willie's right, Louise. You do look mighty cute."

"Thanks, Jack. Thank you very much. Do any of you boys want a cold beer?"

"I'd like an Old Taylor on the rocks," Jack said. "Any chance of that?"

"Those you'll have to get at the bar inside," Louise said. "There's a gentleman in there who knows how to pour."

"Don't tell me it's old Kelly?"

"Nobody else," Louise said. "It was Mr. Hurd's idea. No party is really complete without Kelly behind the bar, is what he said."

"Mr. Hurd is right," Jack McHugh said. "So — reluctantly I say farewell to you, my good friends, and wend my way into the smoky depths of yonder bar."

"I'm with you, Jack," Willie Martin said. "See you later, Marilyn. And don't forget that kiss, you hear?"

Howard Snyder found himself standing alone with Louise Stegmeyer, and realized that he was nervous. It was because he was remembering the optical clinch they'd had — a fleeting and minor one, to be sure, but maybe she'd not forgotten it. No, that was silly. She probably hadn't even noticed it. She'd just looked at him, the way she'd look at anybody who was standing at her desk with a book. He said, formally, "Nice day for a picnic, don't you think?"

"Yes, it is. Hot, though."

"Yes, it's hot," Howard said. The strained feeling did not leave him. He could not think of anything else to say.

"I guess you and your family are pretty excited," Louise said.

"Excited?" He looked at her in bewilderment. "What about?"

"Why, your trip. The trip you're taking to Mexico."

Howard looked down at his hands. There was no use bringing up the fact that he wasn't going — not here, not now. He said nothing.

"If I were going to Mexico," Louise was saying, "I'd be so excited I doubt if I'd sleep for a week before the plane took off."

"You like Mexico?"

"Gee, I don't know if I would or not. But I'd love to go there and see."

"I think I would like that beer," Howard said, "if you could show me how to get it."

"I'll not show you how to get it. I'll get it for you myself. Come on."

He followed her across the pine-needle litter in the yard, and it was now impossible for him not to notice how good her figure was in the white sharkskin dress. She was a big girl, but she was shapely. Very shapely. And the high heels might not be just right for a picnic, but they certainly were just right for showing off her smooth, silky-looking legs. Louise went into the kitchen, which smelled of frying hamburgers and beer. It was dark inside after the glare of sunshine, and when his eyes grew accustomed to the light he saw that one wall was lined with galvanized GI cans full of ice water in which brown beer bottles were sunk invitingly, their labels coming unglued in the water.

"Have you any preference, Mr. Snyder? We have Budweiser, Schlitz, Miller's High Life, Iron City —

"Miller's," he said. "If you can find one. Otherwise, anything that's within reach."

"One Miller's High Life coming up," Louise Stegmeyer said, sounding happy and sure of herself.

She uncapped the bottle and handed it to him, bubbling foam. She was smiling. He tipped the bottle and drank deeply, the beer ice-cold and yet warm in his stomach. He wiped the suds off his mouth. "Thank you, ma'am," he said. "That's good beer — from a very charming hostess." The compliment sounded bald and lame to him, but he had never been able to give compliments easily, the way Willie and Jack could.

"Thank you, kind sir," Louise said. "We aim to please."

Howard Snyder did not see Doug Schroeder come in from the yard. He was standing with his back to the door and he did not know Doug was in the room until he spoke, in a loud kidding voice. "Well, bless my soul," Doug said. "Look what we got here! If it ain't little Lulu. What happened to you, little Lulu? This isn't a costume ball by any chance, is it? Nobody told me. I thought it was just a little old company picnic." Doug Schroeder's eyes moved slowly from Louise Stegmeyer's hair to her shoes, and stopped, and he said, "Those heels — my gracious, am I seeing things? You aren't by any chance practicing up for Cinderella, are you, Steggie?"

Howard Snyder had been watching Louise Stegmeyer's face and he saw, with the suddenness of a light snapping out, the joy and pride drain out of it, leaving it helpless and scared: scared the way Howard knew a shy person could be scared when caught trying to break out of the shyness, caught and held up to ridicule and not having any defense, feeling suddenly helpless and ridiculous. Howard Snyder had never been an athletic man. In his adult life he had never struck a blow in anger; he had, in fact, shrunk from harsh words and altercations if at all possible. But now, without thinking what he was doing or why, he stepped in front of Louise Stegmeyer and faced Doug Schroeder and said, his voice trembling and thin, like a little kid's: "Why don't you keep your mouth shut? Louise isn't bothering you. Why can't you go away and let her alone?"

Schroeder's eyes lit with the sudden happiness of a man used to rough-and-tumble verbal battles, about to join in the conflict with a man who was obviously not up to it; in fact, in Howard Snyder's case, a proven milk-toast. He smiled at Howard, and spoke in a friendly tone. "Well, now, what's this, little man? Don't tell me that our little catalogue writer is carrying the torch for Lulubelle Stegmeyer here? I don't think Mrs. Snyder would approve of that. I don't think she'd approve at all."

"I'm not carrying a torch," Howard said, fighting to keep his voice from shaking, but not succeeding. "I'm just saying — I'm saying —"

"Well," Doug Schroeder said, "don't have a nervous fit, for goodness' sake. What *are* you just saying?"

"I'm saying Louise looks fine today. And if she wants to wear high-heeled shoes, that's her business, not yours. I think she looks just great."

"Well, now, that's sweet," Doug Schroeder said. "That's just as sweet and touching as it can be." He turned and smiled at the faces which were now pressed to the screen outside. "I didn't happen to see your white horse tied outside, Howie, when I came in. Maybe I missed it. I didn't see your armor, either. Must be a bit warm in this weather, though — the armor, that is."

From the doorway somebody laughed, and a nervous chuckle ran through the crowd which had gathered. Doug Schroeder moved across the kitchen and stood close in front of Howard Snyder, and said, "Don't worry, little man. I won't tell on you and Lulu-belle. . . ." He laughed shortly, his mouth twisting. "Your guilty secret is safe with me, Howie my boy."

With all his might, Howard swung his right fist at Doug Schroeder's face. It was a clumsy blow, awkwardly delivered, but it came with such surprise that Schroeder could not avoid it. It snapped his head around and staggered him, and Howard was on him, pounding with both fists. Howard felt Doug shove him away. He felt Doug hit him in the face — a glancing blow — then again, solid, like a two-by-four shoved against his mouth; felt the floor slam into his back . . . and then, oddly, there was no longer any pain or any fear. He was scrambling to his feet, sobbing, his breath coming in gasps, but moving faster than he had dreamed he could move. Doug Schroeder hit him again, another glancing blow, not enough to knock him down; and then, perhaps by luck, Howard hit Doug Schroeder solidly with his right hand and Doug staggered against a GI can and fell down.

Then the room was full of people pulling them apart, and he could hear Doug Schroeder yelling to let him go, let him get at this little jerk and finish him off — through the glimmerings in his head, he could see that it was only old Max Roth holding Doug — Doug could pull away from Max easily if he wanted to. And then a surprising thing happened. Howard Snyder realized that he *wanted* to fight some more. He tore himself loose from whoever was holding him and lunged across the floor; and Doug Schroeder, suddenly, put his hands over his face and yelled for somebody to get this madman away from him.

Somebody had Howard's arms now, pinned behind him, and it was Jack McHugh. Jack's voice said in his ear, "Howie — come on now — take it easy! Mr. Hurd's here! Mr. Hurd, boy — now settle down. . . ."

Howard Snyder looked over his shoulder at Jack McHugh. He could feel his mouth bleeding inside, and feel the blood trickling out through his teeth and down his chin onto his white shirt. He turned from Jack McHugh and looked across at Schroeder. With his bloody mouth, Howard Snyder smiled.

Mr. George Hurd had pushed into the kitchen, his face grim and angry. He said, "That'll be enough of this now, both of you. We're supposed to be having a party here, not a prize fight. Snyder, I hear you struck first. I think you'd better leave the party. I'll deal with you later."

"All right, Mr. Hurd," Howard Snyder said. "I'll leave — but I'll have to walk. I didn't bring my own car."

"Never mind that, Snyder. We'll send you in the pickup truck."

"All right, sir," Howard Snyder said. "I'm ready whenever the pickup is."

Then Louise Stegmeyer spoke. "That won't be necessary, Mr. Hurd," Louise said. "I've got my car here. I'll drive Mr. Snyder to town."

Frances Abbott had heard about John Carey from her mother the day before the picnic. Mary Whitehead had known about the melanoma since Monday evening, when Pop had come home and told her, but she had waited to tell even Frances until John Carey himself had authorized its release at the board meeting. Then she had called Frances. Mary Whitehead was not a demonstrative woman. She met personal sorrows and fears with a stoical calm which those who did not know her well mistook for coldness. Mary

Whitehead was not cold: she was a realist. She had been a trained nurse, and she knew that nothing was changed by outbursts of sentiment. On the phone, talking to her daughter, her voice was quite calm, almost matter-of-fact. "I don't know if you've heard yet, honey," Mary Whitehead said. "About John Carey?"

"No, Mother. What?"

"Daddy took a lesion off his back, Monday night. It was malignant melanoma — already metastasized in the armpits and groin. The liver was as big as a large gourd, Daddy said. It's inoperable. Daddy took a biopsy and ran a frozen section, but it was just to make absolutely sure. He knew, he said, before he even finished his examination."

"Oh, Mother. Oh — Uncle John. Is Daddy *sure?*"

"I'm afraid he is."

"How long does Uncle John have?"

"Daddy says a year at the outside, but he hopes it won't drag out that long — for John's sake. He thinks there'll be a lot of pain any day now — any hour, in fact. He may have to cut some nerves if it drags out."

"Mother, is there anything in the world either I or Jake can do for Uncle John?"

"Honey, there's nothing anybody can do."

"Is there anything we can do for Aunt Eva?"

"No, I guess not. She'll be with John as much as possible from now on. He's appointed Dave Ross to head up the company, and he's got all his personal affairs in order — has had them in order, Daddy says, for a long time. Not because he was thinking he'd die; it was just the way he ran things."

"Oh, Mother, this is awful. . . . Mother, I'm sorry, but I'm crying. . . ."

"I know, honey. But there's nothing you can do. If something comes up, I'll call you."

"All right, Mother. Goodbye."

"Goodbye, honey," Mary Whitehead said in her quiet, calm voice.

After she hung up, Frances Abbott sat beside the phone looking out of the window into the sun-dried yard. She felt the tears on her cheeks. John Carey was going to die. The husky-voiced rock of a man who'd held her on his knee when she was so young that all she could recall were his eyes, bright blue through the blur of time, and the bigness and gentleness of his hands. Uncle John, she'd called him then, and he had not been a remote and awe-inspiring giant of industry to little Frances. He'd been her second daddy — and now, suddenly, he was going to die. . . .

Frances had never given much thought to her own death. It had seemed like some far-distant place, where people went till you forgot their faces — but not a place she was concerned with personally. Even when she told Jake he didn't have forever, she was merely speaking words. Now she knew it was true: you didn't have forever. You had this moment, maybe not even the next — and you had better use each one with skill and love and attention, for it would never pass your way again. . . .

The phone call had come yesterday. Frances had slept badly. Now, she was alone in the house and Jake was at the picnic. She thought about John Carey as she looked out into the yard. Summer lay bright on the trees. But behind that brightness, always waiting, was an invisible film, and that film was death. In the space of a heartbeat those summer trees could turn black as midnight. There was no time to lose.

She rose and walked out of the house then, and down to the workshop where Jake did his writing. The door was unlocked. The room was hot and smelled of stale cigarette smoke and Jake's body odor, and there was a wasp buzzing angrily at the window screen. Nailed to the wall over the typewriter was a crude map of Tomoka River, Florida, where she and Jake had been stationed during the war. Frances moved close and peered at the map, which Jake obviously had drawn himself. As she stood there, she had an odd feeling that the war was still back in Tomoka River even now, waiting — that if she should return, everything would be as it had been: the big blue-black Hellcat fighters drumming over the palmettos on their way out to sea to practice gunnery . . . the beach, deserted because of gasoline rationing and the absence of tourists, strewn with sand dollars and seaweed and the purplish bladders of the Portuguese men-o'-war . . . the spikes of the palmetto fans, jet-black against the orchid-pink of a Tomoka River sunset. The war was still there for her, and it must be still there for Jake. It was what he said he felt, what he was trying to capture on paper.

She looked on his desk. The novel was not there. She opened the top drawer and found a neat stack of white paper with the top sheet labeled *Hold — Important.* She lifted the sheet, her heart pounding, sure that underneath it would be the title page of the novel. Instead she read: *Item: Softball standing, Open-hearth Division, Harrisburg Plant, July. Item: New mold-coring system developed by Foundry Division, Carey Furnace Plant. Item: A case of bourbon will be given for a slogan which best portrays . . .*

She stopped reading. This was Jake's job, the work that paid their heat, light, food, clothing, transportation, amusement: the softball standings of the Open-hearth Division of the Harrisburg Plant, a case of bourbon for the best slogan . . . with Communism on the march, riots in Africa and Asia, hydrogen bombs waiting and ready in their revetments, and missiles to shoot down missiles high on the defense agenda. What armor did they have? Would Americans go marching to Armageddon with their Social Security cards drawn and their old-age pension plans at the ready? Was this beehive civilization, peopled by Status-seekers, Organization Men, Image-makers, and Other-directed robots milling about in a Lonely Crowd, going to die with a bang or with a whimper? Would the first ICBM perhaps catch them presenting their case of bourbon or playing softball?

Frances closed the drawer.

Across the room stood Jake's rickety filing cabinet. She crossed and knelt in front of it, opening the bottom drawer first. An old woollen sweater of Jake's which she'd been missing for months was stuffed into the drawer. She pulled it out. It had concealed a fifth of Old Taylor, which, when she lifted it, had two inches of brown liquid in the bottom. Beneath it was a magazine with a nearly nude girl on the cover, lying on her side, with one buxom leg drawn up to where her breasts bulged out of her low-cut blouse, smiling with heavy-lidded eyes and an open wet mouth. Frances suddenly felt a little sick. She put the whisky bottle back and stuffed the sweater on top of it and closed the drawer. What was Jake doing out here when he was supposed to be writing — titillating himself with whisky and girlie magazines? She felt a coldness, a premonition of disaster.

She opened the second drawer. It was stuffed with bills and receipts. In the third drawer she found a thick sheaf of yellow pages, dirty and dog-eared from much fingering, and lifted it out. On the dirty top sheet she read: *A Feather on the Wind: A novel by John M. Abbott* (Jake's given name was John: he had been nicknamed Jake because of a part he'd taken in a play in his early school days). Her heart was beating heavily. She knew she held Jake's future — at least his future as a would-be writer — in her hands. This sheaf of yellow paper, on which Jake had written the best that was in him in this, his forty-first year of life, had to be, at least, promising. It had to have some kind of valid spark, some hope that eventual recasting and polishing would make it live and hold the interest of people — or Jake was kidding himself. A man did not start, at forty-one, to be a writer. At forty-one, a man must have a hard core of developed talent, of sensitive experience, of mature ability in expression, or it was hopeless. Fran held the heavy dirty manuscript in her hands and saw that they were trembling. Then she turned and sat down in Jake's typing chair and began to read, from the beginning, the original manuscript of *A Feather on the Wind*. . . .

Gradually the pattern of light and shadow shifted inside the workshop as the sun moved overhead and sank low in the west. The wasp which had been buzzing on the screen was still, his wings folded, like a tiny brown envelope on the window sill. Occasionally a car went by on Grandview Avenue, its tires making a sound like strips of adhesive being torn off skin. The only sounds in the room were Frances's breathing and the rustle of paper as she handled the pages. The sun was going down and the room was turning dim with shadow when Frances stopped and laid aside the first batch of manuscript — about two hundred pages. Her mouth was dry and her eyes felt as if she had been staring into a strong light. She closed them and sat quite still. For the past hour she had not been in Carey Furnace at all. She had been in Tomoka River, Florida, in wartime. The feeling Jake had created of Tomoka River in those dog-eared pages of typing was still so strong that Frances half expected to hear palmetto fans rattle drily, out in the gathering twilight, as the night wind of the Florida east coast began to blow. But there were no palmetto fans and no wind and she was not in Florida. She was in Carey Furnace, Pennsylvania, and up in the house she heard one of the children cry out peevishly. She rose and began to collect the manuscript and to replace it in the drawer. . . .

And then, suddenly, she felt weak all over — so weak she had to sit down again, by the typewriter. It was going to be all right. It was going to be all right, after all. *Jake,* she thought. *Oh Jake, my very very dearest, I'm so glad. . . .*

During the long, hot afternoon, Archie Saunders had grown steadily more tense. He had lain in the high grass near the switch which shunted freight off the main line to the River Avenue Market warehouse, studying the working of the semaphore signals a quarter of a mile up the track. That semaphore guarded the switch. When its brightly painted arm stood straight up and the light was green, the trains tore through without slackening speed. But as soon as the engine passed the signal, the arm came down level and the light went red. One thing was very clear to Archie. If he hoped to bring a fast freight off the main line and drive it through the rear of the River Avenue Market — and smash Mr. Brothers to a bloody jelly, he must have that arm sticking straight up, and the light must be green. Otherwise the engineer would stop his train and Archie's plan would be spoiled. . . .

The switch itself was childishly simple when compared to even the works of an alarm clock; and Archie could take an alarm clock apart in his sleep. The switch was merely a steel rod working under the rails. To shift the switch points, and throw a train off the main line into the siding, all Archie needed to do was unlock the big brass padlock and throw the lever. The lever was heavy. It was counterbalanced to make the throw easier. Archie had seen old man Lewis, conductor on a local train, change the switch many times. Old man Lewis was seventy years old, and just a wisp of a man. If he could do it, Archie, who was wiry and strong, could do it too. . . .

Getting the brass lock open bothered him not at all. He had a dozen locks of the same type at home and he had made a skeleton key which worked on them all. He had tried this key in the brass lock on the switch, stooping down casually as if to tie his shoe, in case anybody was watching, and it had fitted. The lock had fallen open under his fingers with no effort at all.

But then he had met the obstacle. He had pulled the lock free and grabbed the counterbalanced arm and actually thrown the switch — to make sure he could do it — and a frightening thing had happened. Up there, a quarter of a mile away, the guardian of the switch had reacted. The semaphore arm had begun to drop toward the horizontal and the light had turned red. Quickly, his heart thudding with fear, Archie had shoved the arm back to its original position, and returned the switch points to their main-line setting. When he did this, the semaphore arm up the tracks, obediently went back to the vertical and the light went back to green. Archie had quickly relocked the arm and fled to the safety of the weeds, where he had crouched, panting, looking out furtively to see if he had been observed. Nothing moved in the quiet afternoon heat. He was alone. He was safe. . . .

Archie sat in the hot sun, hidden by the weeds, thinking. There must be some way to do this without giving the engineer warning. He stared at the switch. He looked up the track to the semaphore towers. And suddenly it came to him. It was quite simple. All he needed to do to send the train off the main track into the River Avenue Market at the end of the short spur was to exercise a little timing. He would unlock the switch and lie in the weeds, hidden from sight. He would let the train pass the signal tower — so the engineer could no longer see the warning lights. He would let the train roar down almost to the switch, to a point where the engineer, even if he saw Archie, would not have time to apply his brakes. Then Archie would leap out of the weeds, throw the switch, and race up the bank to safety. The train would crash wide open into the back of the River Avenue Market.

Archie's thin face broke into a happy smile. It would work. It certainly would. He could use it any time he saw fit, and no power on earth could stop him. He rubbed his chin, and winced. His face still ached from the beating Mr. Brothers had given him. His smile vanished, and his eyes grew bright and he began to breathe through his mouth. A loop of spittle brimmed, unnoticed, over his full girl's lips and fell on the ground. He would wait for the Super — the seventy-mile-an-hour double-header from Buffalo that came through town just at dusk with more than a mile of loaded hopper cars. The Super arrived at ten minutes after eight. Today was Thursday. Mr. Brothers would be in the store — would probably be in his office at the rear, working on his records — when the two monster diesels came crashing in upon him. . . .

Tonight, Archie thought, shivering slightly with excitement. *I'll do it tonight.*

Ethyl Snyder was sitting in the living room of her house on Mountain Avenue, thinking about her husband driving to the company picnic with Jack McHugh. She had not discovered this from anything Howard had said. Howard had gotten up early and eaten his breakfast and left before she and Carole had gotten up. Ethyl had learned about the ride from Trixie McHugh, whom she had chanced to pass in the driveway. Trixie and Ethyl were always painfully polite to each other when they met, making some perfunctory comment, and passing along. This time Trixie's comment had been that she hoped Jack and Howard reached the party safely over those awful back roads. Ethyl's comment had been that she was sure they would, and wasn't it hot? And Trixie's parting civility had been that yes indeed, it certainly was hot.

Now Ethyl was thinking of what Trixie had said about the back roads. It wouldn't be the roads which would cause Jack McHugh to crack up a car, she thought. It would be booze. These annual parties were the most drunken affairs of the entire year — and Jack McHugh would undoubtedly be loaded to the gills. But he wouldn't go over the side of a mountain. Oh, no, not Jack. He bore a charmed life. He might wobble around a bit, but he'd never really lose control and get himself killed. And then, with a slight shock, Ethyl realized that she was having a feeling of loss — of a wonderful chance lost — when she thought of McHugh and Howard wobbling, near the brink, and not going over. Underlying that feeling of a lost chance was a hope — unbidden, vague, involuntary. Howard carried heavy insurance. If — if it did happen — just she and Carole — it would be so peaceful and so comfortable — just she and Carole. . . .

In the kitchen, the phone began to ring. Ethyl rose and walked through the adjoining doorway and picked it up. "Hello. This is Mrs. Snyder speaking."

"Oh, Mrs. Snyder. This is Mrs. Thatcher — Thatcher's Green Barn. I know how you're always on the lookout for an especially fine piece, particularly if it's at bargain prices. Well, I've got one. A beautiful secretary, and I thought I'd give you first look."

"A secretary? Is it in good condition?"

"The wood is perfect, but I must admit the owners had horrible taste. They painted it an awful mustard yellow and decorated it with holly leaves and berries — dreadful, I know — but, well, I know how much Mr. Snyder enjoys refinishing antiques. . . ." Mrs. Thatcher chuckled. "If he likes refinishing antiques, he's going to have a fine time with this one."

"How much are you asking?"

"Well, I'd thought of a hundred and fifty. . . ."

"A hundred and fifty! Why, Mrs. Thatcher — I can get a secretary, authentic Wallace Nutting reproduction, already finished, at the Copper Kettle, for that money!"

"For you, Mrs. Snyder, I might consider coming down a little. Why don't you come over and see it, anyhow?"

"It's too hot, right now, to move."

"How about in the evening, then? I keep the shop open until nine."

"I'll think about it, Mrs. Thatcher. I may come over."

"You'll be missing a real bargain if you don't," Mrs. Thatcher said. "I'll be looking for you, my dear. Goodbye."

"Goodbye, Mrs. Thatcher," Ethyl Snyder said, and hung up. Well, she thought, standing in the kitchen, why not? They wouldn't be going to Mexico, so they'd have some spare cash to play with — and Mrs. Thatcher had said the piece was messed up pretty badly with paint. Probably vitrified, if Ethyl knew anything about Mrs. Thatcher. That meant getting it off would be a miserable job, even after loosening the stuff with paint remover. Ethyl smiled slightly. Maybe she ought to get this secretary — if she could get Mrs. Thatcher down to a hundred — just to give Howard some exercise. He'd need exercise after this party, and after his temper tantrum, to sweat all that alcohol out of his system.

Eva Carey had been trying for two days to reach her son John. She had tried his New York apartment and had received no answer, and finally had called Stanley Sucek in the New York office and asked him to trace the boy if possible. Stanley had heard about the cancer. He was a very sensitive man, and he loved John Carey in the same way that he loved his own father. He had said that of course, he would go personally, as soon as he hung up the phone, and try to locate John Carey Jr. Then he had said to Eva Carey that he had tried, in his work with the company, to pattern himself as nearly after John Carey, her husband, as he could. He said, "You know something, Eve — an example is a thing you can't put a price tag on. It's more potent than anything in the world — at least, anything I know of. John's monument isn't the mills. It's people like — well, like myself, who got a look at him in action. You understand me, don't you, Eve?"

"Yes," Eva Carey said. "I do understand you, Stanley."

"I'll go look for the boy now," Stanley Sucek said. "I'll be back to you at the very earliest moment I can."

Stanley had called back in forty minutes to say that John Carey III had gone on a motor trip. To Maine, apparently, or perhaps to Vermont. The superintendent of the apartment house was not sure which. And he was not sure when John Carey III was expected to return. It was either two weeks or two months, as he recalled. He had no itinerary, no forwarding address, nothing.

"I put a note in John's bedroom," Stanley said. "The superintendent let me in — and I left word with the man himself to tell John to contact you immediately upon his return. Now, Eve, there's one way we might get him. We might start broadcasting over the radio and on the TV —"

"No," Eva Carey said. "No, Stanley, we won't do that."

"I'm sorry," Stanley Sucek said. "I just want to say one thing more. If I can do anything for you or John — I mean, anything — I'm here, Eve."

"I know that," Eva Carey said. "Goodbye — and thanks."

"Goodbye, Eve — and give my very, very best to John."

"I will, Stanley. I will."

She sat by the phone after putting it down, her fists clenched, her eyes shut. All day long it had been building up inside her — this red mist in her head. With an effort, she opened her eyes and breathed deeply. The young minister, Father Boyer, was in the living room waiting to see her. She did not want to see him, but she was going to, just for a minute. He meant well. He was kind. You couldn't just let go and come apart, even if you felt, inside, as if even one more minute, one more second, would be too much to stand.

She rose and walked through the doorway and young Father

Boyer rose and came to meet her, his face grave, his hands out toward her. He took her hands in his. "It's terrible," he said softly. "It's terrible, Mrs. Carey. There is nothing I can say, except that God —"

"God?" she said, and suddenly the red mist swirled tightly into solid fire inside her head. "Don't talk to me of God! Not one word! Not one word!" She threw back her head and stared up at the ceiling, as if God might be clinging there, like a huge bat, watching her. "Come out," she said softly. "Come out wherever you are. Show yourself. Just show yourself. Let somebody get at you for a change — instead of you always getting at us. . . ."

"Mrs. Carey," Father Boyer said gently. "That won't help any —"

She was still looking at the ceiling. Her lips were twisted in a bitter smile. "Oh, I know it won't," she said, speaking conversationally now. "I'm fully aware that it won't. He won't come out. Not big old lover boy. He'll stay back — and send his son — and have his fun and games, with the nails and the spears and the black tumors that won't stop because nobody knows how to make them stop but him, and he's too busy having fun and listening to the screaming, and posing as a big lover boy, to give us any hint."

And then, suddenly, Eva Carey put her hands up and covered her face and wept. . . .

Neither Howard Snyder nor Louise Stegmeyer spoke again in the kitchen of the Hurd cottage. Nobody spoke to them. The ring of faces was shocked and staring. The only sound came from the river, where people who had not yet heard of the fist fight were shouting and splashing happily. Mr. Hurd stood aside, his face composed but grim, to let them out of the door, and the crowd outside parted to let them pass. When they reached Louise's car, Howard went around and held the door for her. His head ached violently and he could taste blood in his mouth, but he felt invincible, somehow, and the sun was like green neon among the ferns and the sky was savage as blue fire through the treetops. He walked to his own side of the car and looked back at the cottage. They were standing there, all of them, looking at him, quiet. He smiled, and his cut mouth pinched with pain. He got into the car, still smiling.

"Do I have room to back?" Louise said.

He twisted. "Come on — straight back. I'll tell you when to stop."

He directed her. She backed into the clear, cut the wheels, and the car moved down through the lane onto the river road. He looked at her, beside him, driving the car, looking ahead through the windshield, and it was with difficulty that he restrained himself from sweeping her against him and kissing her on the mouth. An odd transformation had taken place in Howard Snyder in the past hour. He was thirty-eight years old, husband, father, provider, finisher of antique furniture, faithful employee, waiter for his twenty-five-year watch, his pension, and his old age. An hour ago he had been all these things — but now it was all changed. He had broken out. He was bloody and unafraid and free. And, looking at Louise Stegmeyer, driving beside him, he realized something else. He was in love — suddenly, violently, and probably hopelessly, in love.

"Louise."

"Yes?"

"Why did you offer to drive me in?"

"You hit Doug Schroeder —" She hesitated. "And I saw Mr. Hurd's face. I —"

"What about Hurd's face?"

"He was very angry. I think he is going to fire you — and I couldn't let you ride in on the truck, by yourself."

"Now maybe he'll fire you, too," Howard said.

"I don't care. I'm leaving town anyhow."

"You are?" Howard said. "Why?"

"I don't have to stay any longer," Louise said. "My mother told me something this morning. My whole life is changed now. I can't tell you why, but it is. Only I'm sorry about you, Mr. Snyder — just when you're ready to go on your vacation to Mexico."

"I'm not going," he said. "I turned the tickets in yesterday."

"What!"

"I'm not going. The plans are changed."

"Oh, I'm sorry. I know you were counting on it."

"Louise — do you have to go home, or any place, in the next hour?"

She glanced sideways at him. The car was nearing the mouth of the Black River. The trees were opening up and they could see the gap over the Allegheny and the sky in the west was yellow with smoke from the mills. She said, "No — no, I don't. . . ."

"Could we stop somewhere — maybe I could buy you a beer or something — and talk?"

"What about?"

"Don't laugh at me," Howard Snyder said in a low voice. "I don't think I could stand it if you laughed. But I love you, Louise. I love you more than I've ever loved anything or anybody as long as I've lived. That's what I want to talk about."

He stopped, and did not look at her. She said, "But — but you're married and you have a family."

"I know. That's why I want to stop. I want to tell you about me and about my family. There are things that happen in a family, even in a town like Carey Furnace, where everybody knows everybody else's business — things you'd never dream of. . . ."

In spite of herself, Louise smiled slightly. He was certainly right about that! Until this morning, Louise hadn't had the slightest inkling of the secret her own mother had carried around inside a gold locket for twenty-six years.

"There's a nice place out on the Butler Turnpike," he said. "Frank Danaher's Blue Mountain Inn." He hesitated. "But if this whole thing is just because you're sorry for me . . . because I hit Doug Schroeder . . . because you don't know how to get rid of me without hurting my feelings . . . if those are the reasons, I'd just as soon you dropped me off in town, and drove off and we never saw each other again."

She did not look at him. The car was in second gear, climbing the hill toward the Lundy estate, and it was necessary for her to pay strict attention to her driving. Her voice, however, was clear enough. "We'll go to Frank Danaher's Blue Mountain Inn," she said, "on the Butler Turnpike."

It was twelve minutes before 8 P.M., Eastern Standard Time. Ethyl Snyder had finished the supper dishes and was preparing to drive across the river to Mrs. Thatcher's antique shop to look at the secretary with the yellow paint and the holly decorations. The phone had been ringing every so often during the afternoon, as people called her up to ask if she had heard about Mr. Carey and his cancer. The first call, when she hadn't yet heard, had been interesting, but now the subject bored her. Mr. Carey was a great man, certainly, but he hadn't been very hospitable when she met him going through the reception line at his party on Saturday. He'd pressed her hand and smiled and spoken to her and then looked on to the next person, as if they were parts on one of his assembly lines instead of people coming to his house for a social occasion. It was too bad, his having cancer. She was sorry for him, but after all, there wasn't anything she could do about it, personally, so there wasn't any use in getting upset. The last call — Marie Richards — she'd cut short: "Oh, yes, Marie. I've heard about John Carey. From six separate people, to be exact. I think it's awful, but right now I have to run. I've got a date to look at some furniture. I'll call you back tomorrow, maybe. 'Bye."

"Mummy," Carole called from her bedroom. "Oh, Mummy."

"Yes, sweetheart?"

"Will you stop at the drugstore and get me some comic books?"

"Now, honey, you know how Mummy feels about comic books."

"Not the bad ones, Mummy. The nice ones. *You* pick them out."

"All right, honey."

The sun was setting as she drove down town. She stopped at O'Toole's drugstore on Fourth Avenue to get the comic books, and by the time she stepped out on the sidewalk dusk had fallen. The sky was still bright in the west but the street lights had begun to come on. Up the river, in the distance, she heard the sound of a freight train, rushing like a storm through the hills. She glanced at her wrist watch. It was after eight. That meant that long double-header with all those cars was coming. If she hurried she could get across the tracks by the River Avenue Market, and go on over the bridge, and not have to wait for the train. She got into her car, started the engine, and sped down the street. But the light on the corner of River Avenue was against her. By the time it had turned green, and she made a right-hand turn toward the railroad tracks, the red blinkers had begun to flash and the crossing bars were down. Ethyl pulled up behind several cars ahead of her which were also held up by the coming train. She was parked in front of the River Avenue Market. She looked through the window and saw Mr. Brothers, red-faced and sweating, doing something to a counter display near the front of the store. She looked away quickly, lest he chance to glance out and see her watching him. She could hear the freight train plainly now, coming into the outskirts of Carey Furnace, moving very fast, thundering through the quiet twilight.

In the library of his home on the mountain, John Carey sat near an open casement window looking down at the town and the mills in the gathering dusk. Street lights had begun to come on in firefly rows. The big red neon sign over the Valley Furniture Mart had begun to glow with its huge illuminated thermometer dial, which even at this distance, could be seen to read above ninety. Down the street the Allegheny Theatre, its old-fashioned marquee a winking mass of white, was still holding on, grimly, despite television. The night was clear except for the mill smoke. John Carey could see Venus, the evening star, bright in the yellow haze against the coming on of night. Across from him sat his wife and his two friends Pop and Mary Whitehead. John had been in heavy pain when Pop had arrived, but the hypo had dimmed it to a dull warmth in his lower abdomen. There was, however, a faint odor in his nostrils. It came from the lesion on his back. The lesion had begun to weep, under the bandage, and the perspiration in his armpits, too, had a faint, different odor — a horrible foul odor — the odor of the disease — the odor of death. He said, "Pop, I wonder if you've got a cigar?"

"Sure, John. Want one?"

"Yes."

Pop fished a cigar out of his inner pocket and handed it to him. He bit off the tip, put it into his mouth, and Pop held his lighter. In a moment he drew in the heavy rich smoke and blew it out, effectively blanketing the faint smell of death. "Thanks, Pop."

Pop said something, but John Carey did not hear it well enough to understand it. The hearing in his right ear, in the past day, had diminished greatly. There was a steady humming sound in that ear. And there was very little feeling — or strength — in his right hand. The right side of his body, apparently, was becoming paralyzed. In another day or so he might not be able to walk, possibly not even able to get out of bed. Pop said something else, which he couldn't catch, and he said, "I'm sorry, Pop — I don't hear you."

"I was saying it hadn't got much cooler," Pop Whitehead said, raising his voice, "even though the sun's gone down."

"No," John Carey said. "I guess it hasn't."

"It was a hundred and three in the sun, outside the hospital this afternoon," Pop said, keeping his voice loud. "I guess that's some sort of record."

"I imagine it is," John Carey said. "Any hope of rain?"

"The radio says not," Pop Whitehead said. "It's this way clear across the nation. They've declared an emergency in Kansas."

"Oh, I hadn't heard that."

"Yes," Pop said loudly. "This is one of the worst spells we've ever had — the longest, certainly, that I've ever seen myself."

Pop Whitehead avoided looking at Eva Carey. He did not want to see her eyes as he made this inane conversation about the weather with the man who was his best friend. Pop wanted to pick up the lamp which stood beside him on the table and smash it against the stone fireplace. He sat still on the sofa, smiling at John Carey, and down in the valley, the sound of an approaching freight train became audible. He grasped at the sound. It was a subject of conversation, like the weather. He said, "There's a freight coming, John."

"What?"

"There's a freight coming. It must be that big fast one, from the sound it's making. You know, the one that goes through wide open with two engines pulling."

"Oh," John Carey said. "A freight. I see."

He turned slightly in his chair and looked out over the lawn, tawny in the afterglow, at the swiftly darkening town. The streets had become canyons of multicolored light, and the river was a dark well of shadow, and from the north on the upper curve above Lundyville, he saw the headlight of the freight rush around the curve, a blazing eye that lit the river shacks and the right-of-way as it hurled itself over the Mill Street culvert, passed the city dump, and hooted hoarsely for the River Avenue crossing.

"He's really moving," John Carey said, leaning forward, watching the train. "He's — oh — oh God —"

The train had almost reached the River Avenue crossing when it swerved sharply to the right, into the spur track, without slackening its speed, shot past the back of the Carey Furnace freight station, and John Carey saw, in frozen horror, the glare of its headlight on the loading ramp of the River Avenue Market warehouse for a heartbeat, just before the hundred-car coal train crashed into it, at seventy miles an hour, without the engineer having time to touch the brakes. There was no immediate sound. From this height and distance, the train was like a toy. The diesel engines, both of them still under power, went through the flimsy warehouse and store, tore over the automobiles waiting for the crossing outside, and crashed into the base of No. 4 blast furnace across the street. The loaded hopper cars followed, piling up in a tumbling avalanche, flipping end over end, disintegrating, spewing their coal in puffs of black dust. An explosion of fire under the blast furnace lit the valley and the hills like the glare of a huge bomb, with a terrible acid brightness, and then the sound arrived on top of the mountain, a savage, grinding, impacting roar of steel on steel and steel on concrete, and the deeper, more powerful sound as the blast furnace was ripped open and its hundreds of tons of white-hot iron gushed forth, exploding as they hit the cold iron and moist coal of the three-story jackstraw pile of wrecked cars.

John Carey saw the second breakout — from No. 3 furnace — start with a sun-bright trickle of molten iron from a cracked hearth, which widened quickly into an incandescent river; and then, horribly, nightmarishly, the second furnace exploded and the town was lit with a giant steady bonfire glare, and the sound came thundering through the windows, heavy and terrible, going on and on and on. . . .

John Carey staggered to his feet. He stood a moment, getting his balance, then, with the help of the furniture, began moving toward the door. Instantly Eva was beside him. "John! John, what is it?"

He was standing beside the door, his hand steadying his body. She could see his face looking at her — every detail of his face, mouth, jaws, eyes, the tilt of his head, slightly back. He said, "I'm going down, Eve. There may be something I can do. I'm going."

"Oh, John — no! It's too awful — too big. There's nothing —"

She stopped. He was smiling: she understood. She put her arms around him and kissed him on the mouth. She held him against her with all her might, and then she stepped back; and now, she too, was smiling. "Hurry," she said. "Hurry, my darling. Hurry. . . ."

Archie Saunders was running up through the lower alley of Little Italy, toward the city dump. He was badly frightened. He had done everything as he had planned. He had crouched in the weeds beside the unlocked switch until the double-header had roared past the green-lit semaphore and was almost upon him; then he had risen to his knees, lifted the short throw-bar and turned the switch points into the siding; then he had whirled and scrambled up the bank through the tall grass into the alley, and the crash had come before he could even turn and look. When he had turned to look, a monstrous wind and a blinding flash of light had knocked him down, and then the whole world was filled with fire and fury. For a moment he didn't understand. Then, suddenly, he knew. It was the blast furnaces. It had to be the blast furnaces. He'd never even thought about them. He'd merely intended killing Mr. Brothers and maybe Miss Van Sant and a few like that. Nothing more. But now the whole world was burning, and it would go hard with Archie Saunders if anybody found out who'd thrown that switch. They mustn't find out. He knew how he could outwit them. He could run and hide in his private place in the horseweeds. Nobody could find him there. And if they couldn't find him, how could they blame him? Once he reached the horseweeds he'd be quite safe.

He ran swiftly down the firelit alley, dodging past people who had come out of their houses, shouting and screaming the way Italians always did when they were excited, and presently he was past the buildings, out of town, and the dump was ahead of him and he could see the tops of the horseweeds, faintly tinged with the light of the fire. He plunged into the weeds and sank down, his breath coming in hoarse gasps.

Presently his breathing quieted a little and he looked back at the town. All of it seemed to be on fire now. *The whole town,* he thought. *The whole town is going to burn and everybody in it.* A smile plucked at his lips. Boy, this was something. This was really something. He hadn't planned it this way, but it was working out pretty terrific. The whole town burning. The steel company too. Maybe the whole world. In the thickest of the horseweeds, sitting on the dry ground, Archie Saunders began to titter in the flickering shadows. . . .

Frances Abbott was sleeping in her bedroom at eight o'clock. She had eaten nothing for supper. She had been too excited, waiting for Jake to come home, so that she could tell him what she thought about his novel. That it was good; that in places it was as good as anything she had ever read. That he had it — he could write. When she had come up from the shack, the evening sun, coming through the trees behind the McHughs' house, had never seemed more golden, or the air sweeter and nicer to breathe. Fran had taken a nip or two of Jake's bourbon, to celebrate. The kids were inside the house watching TV, and she asked them if she could get them anything, and they said no, they'd rather eat ice-cream sandwiches, of which there was a fresh supply in the freezer, and drink Coke. Normally Frances would have argued with them, but this evening she was glad to let them have their way. She didn't want anything to spoil the feeling of relief, mixed with triumph, and love, and gratitude, and all the other emotions which piled on top of each other as she finished reading in the fading light below. So she had three shots of bourbon, on the rocks, got a pleasant buzz, presently felt sleepy and lay down on the bed in the lower bedroom and went to sleep.

A scream, close beside her in the room, brought her sitting straight up, screaming a little herself in her confusion and fright, peering wildly around, trying to collect her thoughts.

"Mummy! Mummy!" Henry's voice was crying out beside her. "Something blew up! Twice! Like bombs! Is it the Russians, Mummy? *Is it the Russians, Mummy?*"

She floundered out of bed and to the window, and her heart seemed to constrict in her breast. There was a bloody sort of light in the yard, like a dark twilight, but the buildings between her and the steel company were outlined, knife-sharp, against a fierce glare that seemed to fill the whole sky, and now she could hear the rumble of the explosions. She turned. "Where's Nancy?"

"Here, Mummy," Nancy's voice said, thin and tight. "I'm right here, Mummy."

"Are you all right?"

"Yes. Is it — the Russians, Mummy?"

"I don't know," Frances said. "I don't know yet. Don't go out, either of you. And don't look at the sky. If a bomb falls — if you look at it — it can blind you. . . ."

Jake, she thought. *Oh, Jake, where are you? On Black River? Oh please, God, let him be still on Black River . . . safe. . . .*

Howard Snyder and Louise Stegmeyer had reached Frank Danaher's Blue Mountain Inn, fifteen miles west of Carey Furnace on the

Butler Turnpike, late in the afternoon. They had sat in a booth and ordered beers, and they had been stiff and formal, and now that Howard had a chance to talk, he couldn't say what he wanted to say, and Louise, apparently, couldn't help him. They drank the beers that came. The beer did not make them drunk, but it gave them something to do with their hands, and relaxed their nervousness, and presently they got started talking about travel. It turned out that Louise Stegmeyer, too, had always wanted to travel.

"Once when I was a kid in high school," Louise said, "I saw a movie with Errol Flynn, made in Australia. It showed these rolling hills covered with light-colored grass, and the trees were funny, kind of gnarled and crooked, and I wanted to go there and see it."

"Was it the trees you wanted to see," Howard said, smiling, "or was it Errol?"

"Both."

They laughed. The ice was broken. She said, "Tell me — why aren't you going to Mexico as you had planned?"

"Do you really want me to tell you?"

"Of course."

"I'm afraid I'm going to sound like the typical misunderstood husband, if I do."

"Well, suppose you do sound like the typical misunderstood husband," she said, the beer humming gently in her head. "I'll listen anyhow."

"All right," he said. "I'll tell you. But stop me if I get boring. Once I get started, I might not be able to stop."

It was now getting dusk at the Blue Mountain Inn. Below them, on the sunken dance floor, the orchestra had begun to play. They had had dinner. It was time for them to go — but they did not go. Down on the floor a song began which had been popular back in 1950 or '51, when Dorothy Collins had sung it on the Lucky Strike Hit Parade. It was called "Sin." The floor, which was small, began to fill with dancers. Presently a young man stood up on the orchestra platform, holding a mute over his cornet, and took a solo chorus. He built smoothly to a climax, cut, and a rose spotlight turned on the band's vocalist, a pretty girl in a glittering evening gown, who had the microphone in front of her. She drew the microphone gently toward her and began to sing in a whispering, intimate voice — full of hurt and yearning, like the cry of a lonely child in the night. Howard felt his throat tighten. "Louise — would you care to dance?"

"I — I don't dance well. . . ."

"Neither do I. But let's try."

"Do you really want to?"

"Yes."

"All right, I'll try, then."

In the press of the crowd on the tiny dance floor, it was impossible to move about. They were forced to stay in one spot and hold each other. It was not necessary to know how to dance. Howard felt her body, young and strong and soft, against his own. He smelled the faint fresh soap which she had used and felt her hair tickle his cheek. He was very nervous. The muscles of one of his legs were cramping with the strain of trying to do everything precisely, and he was sweating profusely. It was not very romantic — the body — when it was frightened and tense. The girl singer's voice took the lyric of the song a second time, crying softly, alone and lost in the crowded room. . . . *Is it a sin . . . to love you so . . . even though I know you are leaving. . . .*

"Louise," he whispered, close to her ear.

"Yes, Howard?"

"I love you. It's wrong, but I can't help it. I love you so much —"

There was a sudden commotion at the front door of the inn. A voice, loud and excited, carrying above the music, shouted, "Look! Look at the sky! A fire! A great big fire! Look. . . ."

Howard turned to the windows on the east wall and caught his breath. The eastern sky, toward Carey Furnace, was vivid luminous pink, like some eerie, nighttime dawn. The whole range of mountains was outlined by the glow. It would take more than a single building, or even a block of buildings, to make a fire like that, Howard Snyder knew. It would take molten steel. The plant itself must be burning. He held Louise Stegmeyer tightly, saw the pink light of the distant fire reflected in her eyes as she stared out at it. He said, "It's the plant. It's very big. We have to get back, right away!"

John Carey did not get farther than Maple Avenue in his car. The streets were a mass of fire hoses, jammed traffic, and people, some dazed, their faces slack in the bloody glow of the now monstrous fire, some frantic with fear or worry for loved ones, screaming or running, or being held by friends or neighbors or relatives. The fire itself made a sucking sound. The sound was soft yet very big. It was a background of all the other puny sounds, man-made sounds — the sirens, the screams, and the crash of axes. Contained in the sucking sound of the fire was a rushing sound, like a high wind through dry brush, and a deep, horrible purring that seemed to come from nowhere and everywhere, filling the ears with a cottony pressure. The heat grew more intense as John Carey, who had abandoned his car, lurched rapidly, using telephone poles and parked cars as supports in his downhill movement, toward the corner of First Street and River Avenue. Paint was blistering on the exposed walls of frame houses, and already the stores across First Street had begun to burn spontaneously, like pine knots kindling in the glow of embers.

John Carey's right leg was dragging badly. He fell repeatedly, but rose at once, dragging his almost useless leg, fending off people who got in his way, driving toward the corner he had decided to reach. He saw no policemen. All the town police were on the job, but their efforts were lost in the expanding disaster. There were not even enough men to handle the approaches to the fire. John Carey got to the corner of First and River, and the heat was now so savage that he had to stay in the shadow of Knapp's drugstore, out of the direct glare. The store had been left exactly as it had been when the train struck. There were half-finished sodas on the fountain counter, magazines strewn from the display rack, and the lights, somehow, still burned.

Behind him, John Carey could hear somebody shouting, hoarsely, angrily, ordering him back. He paid no attention. He had to get across the savage heat of the intersection, to the high brick wall which ran along First Street. It would be very hot behind the wall — but cool enough, if he hurried, for him to make it to the Miller Avenue gate. The blowing engines, which were still on — he could hear air shrieking from the broken mains — were about two hundred feet inside the Miller Avenue gate. John Carey planned to get to those engines and shut them off. The tenders must have panicked — or perhaps they were dead. With the engines hurling a hurricane of high-pressure air into the blazing debris, there was no hope of saving the last two furnaces in the line. The miracle was that these two had not already broken out. He had to stop those engines, down in their pits, blindly running, blindly pumping air, like oversized bellows playing over hot coals. He put his face around the corner of the drugstore and the heat struck it like a fist, and he recoiled with a strangled cry.

He held his face a moment. Then he looked into the drugstore. Near the door was a specialty counter. On it were bathing supplies, sunglasses, terry-cloth robes. It took a minute or so for him to soak one of those robes under the tap behind the fountain, wrap it around his head, with a gap for his eyes, like a mummy, and step back into the street. It was bright as high noon out here now, and the air was full of choking chemical smoke. There was no more time to deliberate: he must get across that intersection now, if he hoped to get across at all.

He took a deep breath and left the protection of the building. He was halfway across the street, hobbling quickly, holding the steaming terry cloth tight to his head, when the No. 2 blast furnace broke out with a thunderous roar. White-hot iron, under pressure, squirted levelly across the cast-house floor, cut through thin girders like an oxy torch, splattered and gurgled down the vertical I-beams which held the floor, and spread in a molten tidewash across the tracks to the brick retaining wall beside River Avenue. The wall held the molten tide for a moment. Then a section of the wall sagged and collapsed before the glaring torrent.

John Carey made no attempt to run. He stood in the middle of the intersection, facing the molten iron. It hissed on the streetcar rails, and washed over his feet. His body stood a heartbeat, erect, looming dark and small against the chaos and the glare, and then burst spontaneously into flame and fell, and the iron swept on, and there was nothing, not even a mound or a ripple, in the blazing sheet of flowing iron.

In the dusk of Thursday evening, Ken Carpenter and Margaret Fiori were sitting in his car on a back road in Hunter's Valley. He had told her about his showdown with Dave Ross — what he had tried to do, and how neatly Ross had handled him, waiting, silently, letting his young attacker show all his weapons, assessing his strength, evaluating the strategy, and then, when he was sure, swiftly clubbing him down.

"I don't blame Ross," Ken Carpenter said. "In fact, I admire him. He did this the way I'd have done it myself — if I were twenty years smarter, and somebody like me tried to do something like I just tried."

"What do you plan to do now?" Margaret said.

"Do now? Why there's nothing I can do now, except resign before I'm fired, and get out of town."

"What about Enid?"

"I haven't told Enid yet. I don't know how she'll take it. If she wants to come with me, she can come."

"I don't know," Margaret said. "I don't know what Enid will do."

"I had one ace in the hole," Ken said. "I had a picture I might have used — but I tore it up."

"A picture? A picture of what?"

"Paul Dana and his little friend Dottie O'Brien."

"Oh — what kind of picture was it?"

He told her. She was silent a moment. Then she said, "I'm glad you tore it up."

He did not speak.

"When you move, do you know where you'll go?"

"No," he said. "I haven't made any plans."

"Will I see you — from time to time?"

"Do you want to?"

"Yes," she said. "I want to very much. But I know you don't love me. You never loved me. You were interested in using my stock for this thing you were trying to pull." Her voice was not angry. It was low and dull and full of sorrow and loss and humiliation.

Instinctively he reached across the seat and touched her. "I said I loved you, Margie. At the time I said it, I guess you're right, I didn't mean it. I was trying to get your stock votes, like you say. But right now, when it's over, and your stock votes don't mean a thing to me, I can tell you something and mean it. I love you, Margie. I didn't know it — but I do."

She made a strangled sound and pulled away, and he said, "No, wait a minute. I don't mean I love you like a lover, even though we've slept together. Even though, God knows, it was good. It was very good, sleeping with you, Margie, and you never need think I did it as a duty. I liked it — I'd like it again, to be quite frank, but I know you'll never give it. But when I said just now that I loved you, I meant I love a fighter, a heads-up fighter who doesn't settle for junk. You've never settled for junk, Margie, except once, and then you were too proud to go back — and I respect you for that, too. I know I sound like a goddamned Boy Scout master or missionary or something, and I don't expect you to believe what I'm saying. I'm just saying it because you've been wonderful to me, and if you ever need me for anything, ever, Margie, just put out your hand. I may be in China — but I'll be with you, as fast as jet power can bring me."

"Oh, Ken — oh, Kenny — oh, God, my darling. . . ."

He held her against him, tightly, and kissed her mouth, feeling her body jerk awkwardly like a little kid as she cried against his throat. In the valley on the other side of the mountain, there was the distant rumble of a train. He heard it change its pitch as it came around the curve in the valley above the town, and the opposite hills reflected its roar in a different way. He heard it hoot with its air horn for the River Avenue crossing. He saw the light shortly thereafter — a sudden heavy flash, like lightning, only soundless; and then, bending and looking out of the car window, over the trees and the mountain rim, he saw the growing glare in the sky, and finally the sound reached them, a heavy continuing thunder that went on horribly and steadily in the dusk.

Margaret pulled away. "Ken! What was that?"

"I don't know," he said. "I don't know, but I'm going to find out." He reached down, flicked the ignition, pressed the starter, and the car's engine roared.

"What are you going to do, Ken?"

"I'm going to drop you at your house, and then I'm going to town. I'm in charge of the Guard. I think we'll be needed — are needed, right now."

"Oh, don't drop me, please! Let me go with you!"

As he backed around in the narrow lane, he heard the explosion of the second blast furnace, rolling like thunder through the hills, and a brighter flare surged up into the sky. He flipped his lights to bright, put the car in drive, and shot out of the lane onto the narrow blacktop road.

"Turn on the radio, Margie. Get WCAR."

He drove fast, not taking his eyes off the curving road that rushed at them from behind the hedges in the dark. They had come to a fairly remote part of the valley and were about three miles from the main highway which joined Pittsburgh and Carey Furnace. Long before they reached it, they could see the stream of headlights moving toward the spreading glow — tiny rushing flares of light, thrill-seekers, probably, for the most part, but doubtless many people who had friends or relatives in the town and were rushing to try to reach them.

The local radio station was broadcasting the news of the disaster when Margaret turned it on. The announcer's voice was hurried and excited, and his speech tumbled out without organization or planning, his news catch-as-catch-can, based on the confused reports he must now be getting. But there was a hard core of practicality in the broadcast. "Attention, all residents of Carey Furnace," the announcer was saying. "All residents of Carey Furnace with homes or business establishments on the hillside above the plant are advised to evacuate immediately. The fire has jumped First Street. The fire chief has advised me he cannot control it. Two blast furnaces have exploded already, and more are expected to go at any moment. . . ."

Ken braked hard for the intersection on the main highway, wheeled out in front of oncoming headlights, stamped his gas-feed to the floor, and accelerated toward the town on the main highway. He had always been a hard driver, and now he passed car after car as he tore up the back side of the mountain toward the ever-brightening eastern sky. Margaret was braced on her side of the seat, but she was making no sound.

"The cause of the disaster," the radio announcer was saying, "at least as nearly as we can find out, was a derailment of some kind. A freight seems to have jumped the track and crashed into one of the blast furnaces. This is what we've heard. We have no confirmation as yet. Oh — a bulletin. The mayor has just ordered all firemen, rescue-squad members, auxiliary police, and National Guardsmen to report at once to their units. I say again — all firemen, rescue-squad members, auxiliary police and National Guardsmen report to your units at once, if you have not already done so!"

Ken Carpenter was stopped by a roadblock halfway up the mountain. He got out of his car and hurried to the man with a flashlight who was bossing the block.

"I'm Carpenter," Ken said. "I'm CO of the local Guard unit. I want to get to the armory at once. Will you put me through, please?"

"Where are you? You driving?"

"Back behind those other cars."

"Okay, Carpenter. Come on! We'll clear you through."

Ken turned and shoved roughly through the swelling crowd, back to his car. "Margie, you'll have to get out now."

"I want to go with you, Ken."

"You can't. I'm headed for the armory. We may have to roll the outfit, I don't know. I'm sorry — no time to argue. Quick, honey! Out!"

She looked at him, smiled a little, and said, "All right. I'm obeying, Major! Good luck!"

She got out as he got in. Ahead of him a whistle shrilled, and he began to move through the crowd, blowing his horn, actually pushing people out of the way with his bumper. He heard angry yells and mutters in the dark, and then he was past the barricade, with no traffic, building up speed again.

The armory was on top of the hill in a large lot, just before the residential section of town began. When he drove into the access road he saw that his men had already been arriving ahead of him, in cars or on foot. The city power had failed — at least as far as the armory was concerned — but the emergency generator was on and the day room blazed with lights as he left his car and ran quickly through it into the main drill hall. Captain Al Lineberger, his adjutant, with the help of First Sergeant Dave Hickey, was issuing field gear: steel helmets to the security squads, forty-five-caliber automatics, walkie-talkie radios. Across the big room, Carpenter could see his tankers getting into battle dress; the drivers, gunners, loaders, and commanders, crouching in front of their lockers, pulling on their heavy shoes, yanking out their white crash helmets which housed their radio earphones.

Outside, through the big open doors, in the glare of the emergency flood lights, stood the rows of tanks — sixteen Patton M-48 heavies, their guns locked in trail, over the engine louvers, mechanics already swarming over them, opening hatches, preparing to leap off. Everything was orderly. Nobody was pushing the panic button. But all of them were moving fast, and moving according to a plan — the plan Ken Carpenter had organized for them, and they had practiced on shotgun alerts, over and over. Now, as in any emergency, the troops were reacting no better or no worse than their training. Here, on this Thursday evening in Carey Furnace, in August, they were reacting very well indeed.

Carpenter moved quickly across to Captain Lineberger. Lineberger turned, recognized him, and saluted. "Emergency plan implemented, sir," Lineberger said formally. "All officers and men alerted. Coming nicely up to strength, sir."

"Very good, Lineberger," Carpenter said. "I'm going in and suit up. Man the tanks, in case we have to roll. I'll be right with it."

As he ran across the floor he heard Lineberger's voice coming over the public address system they used on the drill field, which his adjutant had activated, according to the emergency plan. "Major Carpenter has arrived," Lineberger's voice said, deliberately and without excitement. "He is suiting up now. He has ordered us to assume combat configuration." Lineberger paused, and then his voice cracked like a pistol as he barked, "Tankers — man your tanks! On the double!"

Harold C. Mills, mayor of Carey Furnace, had been watching his favorite TV Western, which had only just begun when the windows of his home near the Carey Furnace Hospital on Main Street lit up suddenly with a fearful glare, and within seconds the house jolted heavily with the shock wave of an explosion. Harold C. Mills was a small, compact, silent man, and a very efficient one, which was why he was now in his sixth term as city mayor. His first thought was that the town was under Russian attack, and that the flash came from a miss with an H-bomb. He did not panic. He had given some thought to just this situation, and had decided what he would do if it arose. Now he did it. He went to the phone, dialed the number of Herbert Johnson, the man he had appointed as local director of Civil Defense.

In any disaster or attack, the CD director was the pivot around which the safety of the community would turn. He had to be good. He had, in fact, to be the very best man the mayor knew of — politics and partisanship aside — and Herb Johnson was exactly this. He was a big, slow-spoken man, with a shock of hair he parted on the side, a relaxed manner, and almost unlimited energy and drive. He operated a real-estate office and an insurance business, owned the controlling interest in the Simmons Coal and Lumber Company, and had been asked to run for state public office many times, but had turned it down, being far too busy on his own. Herb Johnson was cool, capable, tough, and Harold C. Mills knew it; and now, as he dialed Johnson's number, he was glad of the thought which had gone into his appointment. He finished dialing and listened. He got a busy signal. Johnson was probably calling somebody himself.

Mills did not sit by the phone and wait to try again. He rose at once and went outside the house. The sky was now as bright as day over the valley. The fire lit the hospital down the street, glinting off the windows, and Mills could see the flames themselves, rising in huge lazy billows through the smoke, like terrible churning clouds. The yard was bright. His neighbors were out. There were shouts and screams, and cars racing crazily past through the firelight toward the hospital. Driving, Mills saw at once, would be hazardous if not impossible. City Hall was only four blocks away, straight down Main Street, in the same building as the police station. Without hesitation, Mills left the yard and began hurrying along the street toward his office. According to the emergency plan, he would meet Herb Johnson there, and any decisions which might have to be made could be made on the spot and implemented at once.

Johnson was in the office, sitting beside the short-wave radio, when Mills arrived, panting from his haste, eyes smarting from the smoke, and sat down in a chair to recover his breath. A voice which Mayor Mills recognized as belonging to Mike Keegan, the fire chief, was coming over the loudspeaker. "We can't hold it on the north, Herb. It's halfway through Little Italy now, and the thing's beginning to shape into a fire storm. I'm up near the dump, and I can feel the suction — not strong, but definitely suction. She'll take Little Italy and the dump for sure, and unless I'm badly mistaken she'll be way the hell and gone up toward Lundyville in another half-hour. You put in calls for help?"

Herb Johnson had a microphone in his hand. "This is Herb, Mike. Yeah, I've sent the word out. Everybody within a hundred miles is rolling — or at least will be rolling in another couple of minutes. We're pulling them from Greater Pittsburgh, Latrobe, Kittanning, Butler, Apollo, Vandergrift — the whole works. The state police are coming in from all over. What do you figure on doing now, Mike?"

"We'll have to backfire, Herb. I don't want to start it too close to town, but I figure it's our only hope. There's a big stand of weeds in the dump — it'll make a quick natural spot to put the torch — but it'll burn into the back end of the Italian section if we do."

"The Italian section'll go anyhow, won't it?"

"Sure as hell will."

"Torch the weeds then, Mike — right now."

"Okay, Herb. Mike Keegan out!"

The steel plant was now completely buried in thick smoke through which tongues of flame, higher than the fifteen-story office building, rose and twisted brightly. Inside the plant, where chemicals and gases burned, there were unexpected pyrotechnics as tanks and holders blew up, or cracked and spewed their contents into the fire storm. Half of Little Italy was solid fire. There was no wind, but in a way this helped the vast suction which the fire was exerting upon the oxygen in the valley, pulling it in as a hurricane sucks power out of the sea, and force-drafting it upward into the giant funnel of flame. Sparks rose skyward and fell on rooftops, which ignited in their turn, and people raced frantically for safety, leaving everything they possessed behind them.

Archie Saunders, crouching in the horseweeds in the city dump, watched the growing fury of the fire with excitement and fear. He was looking toward the plant, and he did not, at first, notice the backfire which Mike Keegan's men had started at the other end of the dump, behind him. He heard it before he saw it — a fearsome, crackling sound — and turned to see the fire racing through the horseweeds toward him from the direction of Lundyville. For an instant he was frozen with surprise and shock. Then he rose and ran swiftly through his tunnels toward the only sanctuary he now had, the green slime of Honeysuckle Pond.

He reached the slime ahead of the racing fire and flung himself into it, face down, trying to burrow in the muck which the pond had become in the prolonged drought. There was about two inches of water and perhaps a foot of liquid mud. He got nearly under the water and mud by the time the sheets of flame of the burning weeds roared over his head. He screamed and tried to burrow deeper. His back began to cook as the heat grew greater and the water in his shirt turned to steam, and then his wet hair, dried out by the heat, suddenly burst into flame. He screamed and plunged his head under the mud and water, but he could not hold it there. He raised it, took a great gasping breath of superheated air, and fell back, unconscious. The fire seethed steadily over his prostrate body. The clothing burned off his back. His back roasted, and turned shiny black as it charred. Then the flames were gone. The dump was burned out, black, a wide fire lane between Little Italy and the homes and woodland to the north. Mike Keegan's backfire had been a success.

Howard Snyder and Louise Stegmeyer were stopped by a roadblock on Route 81 above Carey Furnace. The roadside was solid with cars: people who had been out pleasure-driving, transient traffic, and others who had rushed out of their houses and jumped into their cars and headed for the glare in the sky to see the excitement. Only emergency traffic was getting through: fire trucks, ambulances, wrecking cars from outlying rescue units. Pennsylvania state police were handling this particular roadblock. Howard pulled off the road as far as he could, to avoid being banged by subsequent rescue traffic. He turned to Louise. "This is the end of the line," he said.

"Now what?" she said.

"Can you walk the rest of it?"

"Sure I can!"

"Well, let's go, then!"

They locked the car quickly, left it, and started through the throng of jostling curious people who lined the roadside. There were sounds of weeping, and somewhere a woman was screaming, over and over, something about her children whom she had left alone down there in the valley, and now must reach and save. The smell of smoke was heavy, and the full moon of August was dull brown behind the moving smoke clouds; presently, as the smoke thickened, the moon was lost altogether, as it might have been behind a rain cloud. They could see, from time to time, sudden upward surges of flame, as a new source of combustion was found and claimed by the fire.

Howard held Louise's hand tightly. She had not panicked and she was keeping up with him well. He wanted to get home, to see if Carole and Ethyl were there, to help them if possible. He did not know, as yet, what had happened. Wild rumors were racing through the mob. The Russians had attacked; somebody had put an atomic time-bomb under a blast furnace; a gasoline supply truck had been hit, trying to cross the railroad, by a freight train. One thing was certain: a fire of this magnitude, however it had started, must now be centered in the mill itself — which meant that Howard's house on the hillside, and Louise's as well, should be at least a mile from the center of the flames, and so, presumably, still untouched.

They had several delays, once by a rope stretched completely across the highway and roadside ditches, manned by Civil Defense personnel, who were turning back all foot-travelers. Howard saw the block while they were still some distance away, and drew Louise through a hedge into the fields. Even the fields were now full of people, standing in the unnatural light, staring fascinatedly at the sky. They ran through the stubble of a wheatfield, climbed a barbed-wire fence, ducked down a lane past a farmer's house, and got back onto the roadside beyond the block. Fire trucks roared past them, from time to time, sirens moaning, red lights flashing. The air was full of dust as well as smoke as they came to the outskirts of town. Louise fell, once, and tore her stocking. Howard bent beside her. "You hurt?"

"No, I'm fine. Look — up ahead — there's the Esso station at the corner of Mountain Avenue. We're close to your house."

"Can you run?"

"Yes, if you don't go too fast."

"If I do, say so."

When they reached Mountain Avenue, they got their first unobstructed view of the fire, and stared at it with awe and terror. It was terrible — worse than terrible — it was a solid ocean of fire, covering their whole field of vision. Then they moved again, rubber-legged, gasping, their eyes smarting from the smoke, and reached the yard of Howard's house.

"You go in," Louise panted. "I'll stay —"

"No, no. Come on!" He grasped her hand tightly and drew her with him onto the porch. The front door was shut. He pulled it open and called through the screen into the dark house. "Ethyl! Ethyl! It's Howard!"

The darkness was silent for a moment. Then, from the upper landing, a child's voice screamed, "Daddy! Daddy! Oh, Daddy!"

Then the screen door burst open and his daughter rushed into his arms, sobbing. He held her against him, stroking her, trying to calm his own exhausted gasping. "It's all right," he said hoarsely. "It's all right, sweetheart. Don't be afraid now. . . ."

The child pulled away. "Where's Mummy? Where's Mummy, Daddy?" Then in the semi-darkness she saw Louise and ran to her. "Mummy, Mummy, Mummy . . ."

Louise put her arms around the child. She did not speak at once. She merely held her against her, waiting for the hysterical sobbing to abate, and Howard saw her hand, moving gently and steadily, stroking the child's hair. Out in the yard the light grew brighter and the smoke thicker. The fire was not coming under control, apparently, but growing worse.

At a quarter to ten, Mike Keegan, the fire chief, radioed Herb Johnson to tell him that all four of the blast furnaces had exploded and the fire on the hillside above the plant was completely out of control.

"We've run out of water from the hydrants," Mike's exhausted voice came over the speaker. "Not that it matters. Water's no good to us now. It looks — it looks as if the whole goddamn town's going to go. If we could backfire —"

"What do you mean, Mike?"

"Our backfire did the job north of town, when we burned the dump. We got her stopped on that side. But right in the middle of town we can't do that, Herb. So we'll just have to start evacking the whole mess, everything — even the hospital. The hospital'll go, sure as hell, when the fire comes up the hill past the cemetery."

"Backfiring is the only way you figure it could be stopped?"

"I don't figure, Herb. I know. But we can't put the torch to people's homes — even if we know the fire'll take 'em in an hour or so anyway. Not under the law, Herb. Not unless —"

"Unless what?"

"Well, Herb — you could call the governor, in Harrisburg, if you wanted to, and have him declare martial law. I hate that. Martial law's a bitch — it's almost worse than anything — but if we're gonna operate at all, it's that or nothing now —"

"If you had the go-ahead to backfire," Herb Johnson said into his microphone, "where would you start?"

"Why, there's only one place we'd have a chance," Mike Keegan said. "We'd have to start at Main Street and burn the whole hillside. Main's double lane, with the grass island in the middle. It's a natural firebreak in itself. If we put the torch to everything east of Main, and let her burn down to meet the stuff coming up, we might do it."

Herb Johnson sat a moment. He looked across his desk at Harold Mills, who had been listening. Putting his hand over the microphone, he said, "Harold, how about it? Should I call the governor?"

Harold Mills nodded. Herb Johnson uncovered the mike. "Okay, Mike," he said shortly. "Stand by. I'm going after the governor right now!"

"Herb!"

"Yes?"

"When you get the governor, tell him to get on the radio and issue a goddamn proclamation. There'll be a hell of a lot of possible opposition to this thing, and I want everybody that can get the word to get it. And one more thing. I'll need the Guard now, if we're gonna backfire. I'll want those tanks to move down the middle of Main and smash all the trees and shrubs and stuff flat, so we can reduce the possibility of the backfire itself jumping the street. And tell them to bring flame-throwers. I know they got 'em. Carpenter requisitioned them for some special exercise he was running last summer. We're set up to put out fires. Not to start 'em —"

"Right, Mike," Herb Johnson said. "I'll get on it right away."

Major Carpenter was sitting in his command jeep at the armory, monitoring the conversation going on between the Civil Defense director and the fire chief on his two-way radio. Now he triggered the transmitter and spoke, "This is Guard Commander — calling the fire chief. This is Carpenter, Mike. Come in, please."

In a moment, Mike Keegan's voice came in over the jeep radio. "Hello, Carpenter. This is Mike. Go ahead."

"I'm up here at the armory. I've got sixteen tanks, fueled and manned, ready to roll. I've got three security squads. I hadn't issued flame-throwers, but I will now — and I'll put them in the hands of my security boys, who'll be riding on the decks of the tanks." He paused. "Mike —"

"Yes, Carpenter?"

"We can start this operation on Johnson's orders, under the law, as I understand it. If we have any difficulty reaching the governor, I'd suggest Herb be contacted —"

The jeep radio crackled, and the voice of Harold Mills broke in. "Hello, Carpenter. This is Mills, the mayor, speaking. Johnson is on the phone right now, trying to get the governor. But I heard what you said, and it's right. If we can't get the governor, Herb'll be right back to you, I'm sure. Issue those flame-throwers, load your boys on the tanks, and get down here as quick as you can move!"

"Okay, Mayor Mills," Ken Carpenter said. "I'm starting the deployment now."

Beside Ken Carpenter, between him and his driver in the command jeep, there was a power megaphone. It was not an item normally issued on the Table of Organization and Equipment. Like the flame-throwers, it was a special item procurable on the Table of Allowances, not on the TO and E. He had drawn four of them two years ago, when he had been running some extensive exercises on the fifty-acre practice field the battalion used in training. He had anticipated the need for it, and had brought one with him to the jeep. Now he lifted it, switched on the power, and brought it to his lips, turning toward the open doors of the armory. When he spoke, his voice roared out over the area.

"This is Major Carpenter. All tank commanders, attention. We will probably shortly go down Main Street, under the orders of the Civil Defense director, and start a backfire to save the rest of town. Smash all trees and shrubs in the central grass island, in preparation for setting fire to all houses on the east side of the street with flame-throwers. I say again: the east side of the street — the side nearest the plant. This will be done by flame-throwers. Sergeant Hickey — issue flame-throwers to men of the security squads as soon as possible. Men of the security squads, take battle stations on the rear decks of the tanks as soon as you are equipped with flame-throwers. Two men to each tank. All right — hit it, men!"

He lowered the megaphone. Already he could see men running through the armory toward the weapons locker where the flame-throwers were kept. Then a big man, Sergeant Hickey, sprinted out of the armory across the lighted area to the jeep. "Major, we've got the throwers, but they're empty — and they take napalm — and we ain't got no napalm."

"Can you use regular gasoline instead of napalm, Sergeant?"

"I don't know, sir. We can try."

"Load one and give a quick test!"

"Roger, sir!"

Out across the hardstand, the tank generators began to start up like strings of firecrackers, supplying the power to get the big 850-horsepower main engines going. One by one, the big tank engines cut in, until the yard roared with solid sullen fury, in which no power megaphone could possibly be heard. Ken Carpenter felt the hair on his neck prickle. This was like it had been in Holland, against the Nazis; this was like combat; he was tense, rigid in his seat, waiting for whatever order might come. Sergeant Hickey was outside now, with a pair of heavy cylinders strapped to his back, fiddling with a hose and nozzle. Hickey did something with the hose and a long tongue of fire, soft and bright, licked forty feet from his hand, held steady — and winked out. Carpenter saw Hickey crouch while one of the security squad men pulled the flame-thrower off his back, then turn and disappear into the armory to fuel the rest. Straight gasoline, apparently, was going to work.

The radio hummed in his helmet earphones, and Herb Johnson's voice said, "Major Carpenter — are you there? This is Johnson again."

"Go ahead, Johnson."

"I got the governor. He'd heard of the emergency, and was expecting a call. He's going on the air as soon as he can, to designate this a disaster area, and to proclaim martial law. But he's given his go-ahead, as of right now, to do whatever we have to do to save the town. Whatever Mike wants, and you can give him, Major. Let's go!"

"I've got that, Johnson," Ken Carpenter said. "Mike — what are your orders?"

"Start backfiring at the corner of Cemetery Street and Main Street, next to the hospital," Mike Keegan said. "That's the most important spot right now . . . and keep going right down until you hit the square."

"Start backfiring at the corner of Cemetery and Main," Ken Carpenter said. "And go on down to the square, on the east side of the street. That right?"

"That's right," Mike Keegan said. "And hurry. We may be too late, even now!"

The fight between Doug Schroeder and Howard Snyder had taken the carefree enjoyment out of the party for most people there. After Louise and Howard drove away, George Hurd made a short speech in which he asked all of them to go back and enjoy themselves as if nothing had happened. Most of them could not, of course. The fight — and the sudden teaming of Louise with Howard Snyder — was far headier excitement than beer and horseshoe games. Gossip, of course, got going even before Louise's car had disappeared behind the trees. There was speculation that she and Howard had been carrying on a secret love affair — a story which, within the hour, had hardened into a full case history of clandestine lust. There was speculation as to whether or not Howard or Louise, or both, would be fired, and the betting was about two to one that they would be.

Doug Schroeder, in the meantime, had apparently been absolved of blame, for George Hurd, personally, was seen to uncap a beer and hand it to him. But for once the company line, as laid down by the boss, did not touch off a general reaction in which the rest of them suddenly followed his lead and became friendly with Schroeder. With one exception — Al Lanphier, who worked directly under Schroeder and more or less had to be friendly — they let Schroeder alone. Gossiping about Louise and Howard Snyder was one thing — that was only human under the circumstances — but buddying up to Schroeder was something that even little Norman Kraft refused to do. When Schroeder paused beside him in the kitchen, where they both were getting fresh beers, and said something about the air being clearer in here now than it had been a little while ago, Norman did not reply. He picked out his beer as if Doug Schroeder wasn't within a mile of him, uncapped it, and walked off. Which was the wildest kind of revolt, in the case of Norman Kraft, as Nellie Laubach, who'd seen the whole thing, knew full well. Norman's example had so thrilled and impressed Nellie that when Doug Schroeder came past for a hot dog, she hadn't spoken to him either. Let him start something. Nellie was only a stenographer, but she was sensitive, under her shyness and her seeming muddle-headedness. She'd been aware, for a long time, that Doug had been imitating her mannerisms, and always before she had taken it lying down. But let him say something now against Louise Stegmeyer, and Nellie would give him a piece of her mind. She was almost sorry that Doug did not mention either Louise or Howard, but just took his hot dog and walked out of the kitchen, without saying anything at all.

The only people who were not upset by the fight and its aftermath were Don Francisco and Eleanor Keck. Don and Eleanor had taken off in one of Mr. Hurd's canoes for an exploring trip upriver. They had paddled about a mile, to the end of the eddy water, and then had dragged the canoe through a rapid, which was gurgling impotently in the low water of the drought, and reached another eddy, this one six miles long. They were headed for a place called Blue Rock, a remote spot which had once been accessible by a road coming down the hill from the direction of Lundyville, until erosion had made the road impassable, and the jungle had moved in and choked it shut. Now Blue Rock was almost as isolated as the moon, except for a lone fisherman once or twice a year. Eleanor had heard of it, but had never seen it, and Don was now taking her there for a look.

Don sat in the rear of the canoe and paddled, and Eleanor lay on an inflated air mattress on the floor, in her bathing suit, taking a sunbath. Looking at her continuously, as he inevitably must do, during a full hour of paddling, Don Francisco's vision of his fiancée, the daughter of Mr. Delaney in structural sales, had dimmed considerably. He had had three beers and three shots of whisky, and he wanted to find some lonely spot and do a little exciting necking. He had not planned to try to go any further than that. But looking at the ripe golden flesh swelling from the brief white bathing trunks and bra, the idea of kissing only had gone by the board. Don Francisco leaned forward as he paddled, so that if Eleanor sat up suddenly, and looked at him, she would not see how his bathing suit stuck out in front.

"Don," Eleanor said, "are we getting close?"

"Close to what?" he said, coming back with a jerk from where he had been.

"Close to Blue Rock, silly! Where else?"

"Oh — Blue Rock. Yes. It's only about a mile further."

She sat up and turned around and looked forward, giving him a look at her smooth soft back. He crouched over further in his paddling. "On the left there," he said, "kind of embedded in the trees, in kind of layers — see it?"

"Those things that look like big loaves of bread, piled on top of each other?"

"That's right."

She turned toward him, inscrutable behind her dark glasses. "Oh, I wish I'd brought my suntan lotion."

He grinned. "You don't need suntan lotion. You've got enough tan so the sun won't bother you."

He paddled onward. The river flowed by the canoe, coffee-brown, mysterious, flecked with foam, and the hills were monstrous walls shutting in the silent valley. Overhead an airplane, probably coming out of Greater Pittsburgh Airport, droned across the blue sky, white and ghostly, for some reason, instead of black. On the floor of the canoe lay Don's sneakers and Eleanor's sneakers and her compact, shining gold in the sun.

"The trees will start to change next month," Eleanor Keck said.

"Yes, I guess they will."

"I love to look at autumn trees, don't you?"

"You bet," he said. "It's nice now though, don't you think?"

"Oh, I don't know," Eleanor said. "For me, it's too quiet. It's spooky, sort of, with nobody around."

"I'm glad nobody's around."

She leaned over and trailed her hands in the water. "Oh, it's warm — I bet it's as warm as human blood."

"Do you want to go swimming?"

"All right, when we get there. I can see a big tree of some kind now, where we can put the canoe." She laughed a little gay laugh. "We should have brought some sandwiches. We could have had a picnic."

He hurried his paddling. The three beers and the three whisky-and-sodas had filled his bladder and he was anxious to get into the water, where he could relieve himself. Presently the canoe moved in out of the sunlight to the shade of the mountain and then into the deeper shade under the swamp-willow trees that lined the bank, and grated aground. He got out at once in hip-deep water and pushed the canoe up on a limestone ledge between two willow trees.

"Last one in's a goofball!" he yelled, and turning, he plunged shallowly out into deeper water, beginning instantly, and with untold relief, to urinate through his trunks. He floated, relieving himself, while she followed. She had had some beer too, and he assumed she might be going to do the same thing. When she let down her feet and stood on the bottom in water up to her neck, he was pretty sure she was.

Then they began to swim. The water was warm and there was no current, and both of them were expert swimmers.

"Want to race across to the other bank?" he said.

"All right — but you have to give me a head start."

"All right. Start — and when you think you've got enough of a lead, yell."

He wanted to suggest that they take off their suits, but he did not dare. He wished he'd had the foresight to bring along a bottle. If they had a few more drinks, both of them, maybe he'd have had the courage to suggest nude swimming. He watched her start swimming away from him. Presently she called to him to start. He struck out across the river in an easy six-beat crawl, his body flat, his feet fluttering expertly and powerfully, getting his breath in the little air space caused by his head moving through the water and leaving a wake behind his nose when he turned to gulp air through his mouth. He was an expert swimmer, in good condition, in fact, he had been an outstanding football player in college, and he could have beaten her with ease. But he held back until the end, and then sprinted and caught her in the shallows and grabbed her. She fought him off, laughing and splashing. "I win — I win, don't I, Don?"

"On one condition," he said. "You have to kiss the loser!"

He tried to pull her face to his, but she twisted away, laughing, and he felt her breasts against his bare chest, soft and full through her bathing suit, and bent and kissed her neck and her throat, his mouth tight and hard on the wet skin. She fought him a moment, then he felt her shiver, and then he was kissing her on the mouth and her lips were opening and she was turned toward him and he was holding her full length, standing up in the shallows. She broke away, gasping. "My God, Don — honestly —"

"I'm sorry."

"Who do you think you are — Tarzan?"

He grinned. "Sure. Why not? It's a great place for it."

She had to smile at him, and looking at his powerful body, tanned by the sun, glittering with water, she thought he would have made a Tarzan good enough for any movie screen. She had a sudden loosening feeling all over her body, a feeling that had been gathering inside her with every foot they had paddled upward into the silent wilderness. She was no longer little Ellie Keck, stenographer in George Hurd's department at the steel company. She was a woman, a free and happy woman, alone in the jungle with the man she wanted for a mate. If they only had this afternoon, just the hours between now and sundown, it would be enough: it would be enough no matter what happened to her after that.

But when he tried to take her in his arms again she ducked away, belly-flopped in the shallow water and began swimming back toward the canoe on the other side of the river.

When they climbed out on the bank they were both quiet. Eleanor did not look at him. Her heart was beating very fast and there was a chemical taste in her mouth and the nipples of her breasts felt sensitive under the tight wet cloth of her bathing-suit bra. *We'd better go back,* she thought. *If I'm going to hold off this time, we'd better go back right away.* But she said nothing.

Don said, "Ellie . . ."

"Uh-huh?"

"Come here."

"No — no, Don, please . . ."

"I love you."

"No, you don't. You love Ruthie Delaney."

"I don't love Ruth Delaney. I love you."

"Then why are you engaged to her?"

"I'm not — really."

"You gave her a ring, didn't you?"

"No, I never gave her any ring. All this engaged stuff — it's just something the Delaneys are saying, have been saying."

She looked at him. His eyes looked very black in the shadow of his brows in the late sun, and his mouth was compressed as if he were angry. "Oh, Don — I want to believe you — but —"

"Do you love me, Ellie?"

"I — I don't know —"

He bent and flipped the rubber mattress out of the canoe into the coarse river grass. He took her by the shoulders. He was scowling at her, his brows drawn down, his eyes glittering, and his fingers bit into her shoulders.

"Don — please — you're hurting me . . ."

He crouched toward the rubber mat, pulling her down with him. She resisted a moment, then lost her balance under the pressure of his arms, and would have fallen if he had not caught her and held her in his arms, like a baby. Holding her, half crouching, half sitting, he kissed her throat, her chin, her cheek. Resolutely, she held her mouth away from his. Then, in a small easy gesture, he turned her around in his arms and deposited her on the rubber air mattress. . . .

"Don — you stop that!"

He bent away from her, grinning. "Scared?"

"Sure I'm scared — you big baboon!"

But, when she had the chance, she did not scramble to her feet and run for the canoe. She lay there, trembling inside, knowing that it was going to happen, knowing that she wanted it to happen, now, now, now. . . .

He bent then, suddenly, and put his mouth over hers. She kept her lips closed. She felt his tongue probe hard between them, against her teeth, and she opened her mouth fully and let his tongue come in, and her hands went around his neck and held him tightly. He pulled her farther down on the mattress until they were side by side, and tried to get her on her back. She pushed him away, still kissing him, then twisted her mouth away and said, "No Don — no, please . . ."

He laughed, or tried to: it came out hoarse, almost a gasp. But he did not rush now. He lay beside her and presently she let him kiss her again, but when he tried to undo the bra of her bathing suit, she held his hand with hers. He stopped and kissed her deeply. He could feel her move against him then, very slightly, her hips pushing and undulating a little against his own. He put down his hand and touched her bra, and she put her hand on his, but when he pulled harder she did not match it with resistance, and then she said, "Oh — oh, you're hurting . . . wait a minute, please . . ."

She sat up, raised her arm and twisted it behind her back, and suddenly she brought the bra away. When he put his hand back a thrill like an electric current prickled through him. Her breasts were out, warm and full, and when he gently explored them with his fingertips and touched the swollen nipples, she shuddered and gave a small jerking tremor. He bent his head quickly and took the nipple of her left breast in his mouth and he touched it with his tongue and now she began moaning and her hand thrust under the top of his bathing trunks, pushing them back, touching him. With his right hand he shoved his trunks down over his hips and she held him fully, in her palm. He pulled at her bathing trunks but they would not come off.

"Oh darling," she said hoarsely. "Oh, wait —"

She lifted her hips and took her hands away from him and pushed downward. The wet trunks slid down onto her thighs and he grabbed them with his right hand and pulled them down over her knees and legs. Then she was on her back, with her thighs wide open, and he was on top of her, going into her, and she was clutching his back, pulling him deeper and harder. He felt it coming, in a blinding, racking flood that knotted his legs and tore the breath out of him and he thrust his hands under her buttocks and yanked her to him, his eyes squeezed shut, every muscle in his body rigid as steel. . . .

Later they lay side by side with their bathing suits on, smoking cigarettes. They were quiet now, and thoughtful. Now that it was over, Eleanor was already beginning to be tortured by fear and regret. She'd been easy, after all. Not only that. She'd been reckless. Don hadn't taken any precautions. She knew he hadn't. It had been too quick. So she'd wound up doing everything a girl who wanted a man to marry her should not do: she'd given in on the first date, and maybe even gotten pregnant in the bargain. It was a remote chance — girls didn't often get pregnant with one slip — but this was the dangerous time of the month for her, a week after the curse. She lay, feeling sick and scared and awful, looking up at the evening sky.

"Ellie . . ."

"Uh-huh?"

"That — what we just did — that was the nicest thing that ever happened to me in my life."

She said nothing.

"Ellie — did you hear me?"

"Yes, I heard."

He sat up and bent over her and she looked up into his eyes. He rubbed his lips with his teeth. Then he said, "Ellie — would you think I'd lost my mind, would you think I was nuts — if I asked you to marry me, right now, right tonight?"

There was a sudden wild incredulous leaping in her heart, and as she looked at his head against the sky it blurred and she could not see him clearly any more. She felt his hands on her shoulders, very gentle now, and his voice, close, "Ellie — don't cry . . . don't cry, my darling . . . I love you . . ."

She winked her eyes fast, and rubbed them with her knuckles as she sat up. She had never felt more wonderful, never again would feel more wonderful, than at this moment. She grinned at him. "I love you, too, darling. Yes, I'll marry you. Of course I will. Any place, any time. And we'll have a grand life. We'll have the grandest life of anybody. I know it. Kiss me, now, darling, and then we'd better get back, while we can still see to paddle. . . ."

They replaced the air mattress in the canoe and paddled back to the rapids, slapping frantically at mosquitoes, and were wading beside the canoe, walking it through the shallows, when the sky beyond the mountains suddenly grew very bright. Eleanor said, "Look, Don — it's like a fire over there — see it?"

"It's the town," he said, looking at the bright sky, "or it's the mill. Come on, let's get in this thing and see if we can't sneak through paddling!"

They were moving down the lower portion of the rapids, using the paddle to push on the bottom to guide the canoe, when the sound of the explosions reached them, like the rumble of heavy thunder, and they saw the sky grow more fiercely bright with every passing moment. "Oh God," Eleanor Keck cried out. "Something awful's happening, Don! Hurry — hurry. . . ."

Willie Martin had left the party early, with a car that was going in. He had eaten and drunk too much, and while he was not sick, he was tired and stuffed and ready to go home and go to bed. Jack McHugh had to stay until the end to collect the athletic gear in his car, for return to the recreation department of the steel company, which had issued it for use at the picnic. Jake Abbott had stayed because he was writing the picnic up for the News Letter, and while he would be able to devote only a few lines to it, he knew how sensitive Mr. Hurd was about this coverage. If Jake left early, Hurd would notice it, and be hurt. The picnic was his baby. The reporter, at least, was expected to stay to the bitter end.

By eight o'clock the party had pretty well broken up and the parking lot and the roadside were empty of all but a few cars. Mr. Hurd was making his final check before locking the lodge.

"Everybody accounted for?" he asked Jake, who was helping him. "Everybody safely on their way home?"

"Yes, sir, I think they are," Jake said. He knew that Don Francisco and Eleanor Keck were out in the canoe — and he intended to go down to the dock and look for them before he took off — but he saw no reason to mention this to George Hurd.

"Well, fine," Hurd said. "It was a good picnic — except for that one thing."

"Mr. Hurd."

"Yes, Jake?"

"I know it's none of my business, but I happen to be a close neighbor of Howard Snyder, and I just wanted to put in a word for him. He's a swell guy, Mr. Hurd — quiet and dreamy most of the time, but he works hard, and I happen to know he's just had another one of his summer disappointments. I don't know if you heard or not, but he's always planning these trips, and then at the last minute something comes up —"

"Oh, yes, I've heard. It's his wife, isn't it? She balks at the end?"

"Yes, I guess that's about right. Well, anyhow, I happen to know that Howard's trip to Mexico has been called off, and I know he feels pretty bad about it — and, well, I know he hit Doug Schroeder, sir, but I hope you won't be too hard on him. . . ."

"You hope I won't be too hard on him, Jake? Why? Breaking up this party with a drunken brawl! Oh, I know he probably has his troubles; but we all do, and we manage to control them, at least in public. I don't mind telling you, Jake, that I'm pretty angry about this. I haven't made up my mind definitely, as yet, but I may decide to take drastic steps."

"You mean — fire Howard?"

"I don't know. I haven't decided."

Jake sucked in his breath. His heart was beating fast. He was, he knew, at a personal test point of his own. He could stop now. He'd spoken out for Howard; Hurd knew how he felt. It was now really up to the boss to do as he saw fit, but Jake could not stop. He said, "I'm probably out of bounds now, Mr. Hurd. I realize it. But I'm going to say what I feel, if you don't mind —"

"Go ahead," Hurd said shortly. "Everybody's entitled to an opinion."

"If I were running this department, I wouldn't fire Howard Snyder. I'm not going to be a talebearer. But I know what went on in the kitchen before Howard hit Doug, and I'll be frank to say this, if I had been in Howard's shoes, I'd have slugged the guy exactly as he did. Hell, now I'm started, I might as well go the whole way. I think Doug Schroeder's a jerk, and just about everybody else in the department thinks so too. A good layout man, the best you could get — but he's got a nasty tongue and he doesn't care who he hurts. If anybody should ask me to stand up and be counted, I'd say three cheers for Howard Snyder. I only wish he had a better punch!"

George Hurd's eyes were cold. He did not smile. He said, "I'm glad to get your reaction to this, Jake. I'm glad to know how you feel, naturally. Now, if there's nothing else we have to do, I guess I'll be getting back —"

And then, through the trees to the west, the glare of the fire lit the rim of the mountains. The two of them stood motionless, peering at the sky. Jake said, "It's the town, sir. It's an explosion!" He looked up at the sky, hoping with all his might that it would be empty, that it would not be marked with the thin white stripes that bombers make moving in the supercold of high altitude on an H-bomb attack.

Major Ken Carpenter, in his command jeep, held a tight rein on his men by radio. What they did now must be done quickly, but it must be done with as much caution and care as humanly possible. The problem was very clear in his head as Mike Keegan had laid it out. They were dealing, now, with a phenomenon known as a fire storm — a situation where the heat grew so intense that it sucked oxygen from the surrounding area like a giant pump, and force-drafted it into the blaze. It was a bootstrap operation. The bigger it got, the bigger it wanted to get, and could get. Which was why Mike dared not let the fire burn up to Main Street, by itself, and hope it would not have the heat and power, when it got there, to jump the two-lane street and take the rest of the town. If let alone, the blaze would be intolerably hot by the time it had climbed the hill. The fire storm would be towering possibly five thousand feet in the air — not flames, to be sure, but superhot gases which were nearly as hot as flames. The only hope, as Keegan had said, was to backfire — to run a controllable blaze from Main Street downhill, and rob the storm of the houses it was reaching upward to consume, by consuming them with a less hot fire.

"Flatten everything you can flatten," Mike said. "Do that first, before you apply the torch. The wider the lane we can get, before we burn, the better we are. I'll mass all my engines along the other side of the street with their own tank water, and we'll start wetting down the buildings. I'll start right now. You run your tanks through as soon as you can. We haven't got much time."

From the command jeep, Ken Carpenter had laid it out for his tank commanders. Each tank would carry a two-man incendiary team — one man was armed with a forty-five-caliber automatic to enforce evacuation of the houses, at gun point if need be. The other man would carry the flame-thrower. These men would drop off each tank before the demolition order was given. One would run in and check the house to make sure it was empty. The flame-thrower operator would take up his position and wait for the signal. It was now very difficult to see because of the thick pall of smoke which obscured everything, diffusing the beams of portable searchlights. Ken refused to let a single one of his tanks roll until he was assured that power was off, all over town. A tank was steel. A high-tension wire falling on it would electrocute every man aboard, and there would be no way of avoiding such contacts, once the demo began.

Finally, on the radio, Ken got word from Civil Defense headquarters.

"City power off," Herb Johnson's voice said. "You're safe to move, Carpenter, when ready."

"Roger, Mr. Johnson," Carpenter said shortly. Then to his men: "This is Commander Tanks talking. This is Commander Tanks. Start down Main Street on the east side. Knock down everything you can handle. When you come to a stone structure or a brick structure that gives you trouble, bypass it. What I want is the whole first row of dwellings, garages, fences — the whole works — flat as a pancake as fast as you can. If we can do that before we touch off the flame-throwers, we can hold the heat down better. Now give me a read-back — starting with commander of Tank No. 1. There can be no mistakes here. We must do this right. No cowboy foolishness. No unnecessary chances. Now then — Sims, in No. 1. — did you read that?"

"Roger, Major. Read you loud and clear. Sims standing by for demolition, sir."

Quickly, like men sounding off at inspection, the sixteen tank commanders radioed in. In his jeep, Ken Carpenter smiled a little. This was it. The instant when, after months of hard, careful drilling, meticulous maintenance, and close organization, the emergency nobody ever thought would come had come, and the troops were poised, waiting for your word.

"Attention, all tanks," Ken Carpenter said briskly. "Move out!"

The Carey Furnace Memorial Hospital was jammed to capacity and the injured were now filling the reception room and the halls. Dr. Whitehead was in the emergency operating room, which was hazed with smoke that had entered under the doors and windows. There was no public power. The hospital was operating on its emergency generator. The fire on the hillside was plainly visible through the windows of the room, and its light made shifting orange patterns on the walls where the brilliant white light over the operating table left relative dimness. Dr. Whitehead had been operating for three hours without letup. His gown was as red as a butcher's apron, but there was no time to stop and change. There was only time to slip into a new pair of sterilized rubber gloves which the nurse held for him, and to stand back and let a nurse take off one sweat-soaked operating mask and replace it with another. At one time their supply of whole blood, anesthesia, pencillin, and surgical sponges had been running low, but then help from outlying towns had begun to arrive and they had enough and some to spare of these items. Their present great lack was operating facilities. There were not enough proper tables, lights, and, above all, surgeons. From time to time, Dr. Whitehead stopped long enough to drink a glass of water and take a salt tablet. He was wringing wet.

There seemed no end to the influx of burned, maimed and suffering people. Many of them he knew by sight. Not a few of them were high-ranking steel company officials who had taken it upon themselves to try to save some portion of the plant which, by experience, they were uniquely involved with. Old Walter Eberhardt was one of these. He had been blast-furnace superintendent at one point in his career, and he knew the complicated systems, the valves and switches which, if pulled properly, could greatly minimize the spread of the disaster. He had bulled his way through the police lines and had gotten into the plant through the main office building and run through the deserted flame-lit mill to a point between the blast furnaces and the open hearths. He knew that if the fire reached the open hearths, some of which contained tons of white-hot steel waiting to be poured, there would be a repetition of the fury that had taken place in the blast furnaces. If the open hearths exploded, the office building — in fact, the entire mill — would probably go. He had been working in the dark trying to get to the junction box under the Cottrell precipitators, when coke-oven gas from a leaking main had come to him strongly, and he had realized he must get back at once, or die. He made it out, barely, crawling on his hands and knees. He had no recollection at all of breaking his left arm. But when he was finally seized by a rescue team and dragged to safety it was found that he had a compound fracture above the elbow. Now he lay on the operating table under Pop's blinding lights, and Pop was in the process of sterilizing and retracting the bone which had thrust out through the flesh. Walter Eberhardt was under local anesthetic — Pop was giving locals when he could, to save the anesthetists for work in which they were absolutely essential — and so it was possible for Eberhardt to talk.

"Pop," Walt said. "Hell, Pop, never mind this son-of-a-bitching arm. Get me out of the way. Bring in the ones that really got it, Pop. A lick and a promise is all I need."

"Relax, Walt," Pop said, behind his mask. "We'll fix you up. I'll try to set it now, but we'll have to wait until later for the X-ray to see if we've got it just right."

"The hell with the X-ray," Walt said. "How's the plant? Did the fire get over to the open hearths?"

"I don't know," Pop said. "Now just shut your eyes, Walt, and don't talk. For my sake."

"Okay, Pop," Walter Eberhardt said. "I'll shut up and let you work."

Pop worked silently and quickly, sweat pouring down his face into the wet cloth of the mask. He could not remember ever having been more tired. His legs and hips ached and when he delicately maneuvered the splintered bone with his rubber gloves, moving it slowly into place with the sensitiveness and intuition of long experience, his hands felt as if they were holding up heavy weights. He finished the arm to his satisfaction.

"Okay," he said. "Take him now — be careful — keep that traction on — don't jostle that arm. . . . Who's next?"

"Dr. Whitehead!" a voice said sharply from the doorway. "Dr. Whitehead, the fire's coming up the hill. It looks as if it'll take the hospital! Should we start evacuating?"

Pop Whitehead stopped, turned, and looked toward the window. The fire at the base of the hill had now consolidated into a huge furnace which sent its flames hundreds of feet into the air. As he watched he heard a sudden savage thunder and an M-48 tank roared past the hospital toward the corner of Main and Cemetery, swerved off the pavement, smashed down a privet hedge and crashed through the wooden porch of the first house on the corner, smashing it off as neatly as if it had been cardboard. The tank stopped suddenly, backed up, and roared into the building, which shuddered, leaned drunkenly, and the chimney on the near side collapsed in a shower of bricks. Then Pop Whitehead saw another tank race past the hospital, and another and another, moving at full throttle, and swerve hard into the buildings beyond the corner, and into those downhill along the margin of Cemetery Street next to the hospital. The drivers were working furiously, and the night was full of the blurt and bellow of their engines and the crack of timbers and the splinter of glass.

While the newest emergency patient was being wheeled in and prepared for an operation on his leg, Dr. Whitehead stood by the window, drinking a cup of coffee somebody had handed him and watching the tanks as they moved down the street through the swirling smoke, ramming, backing, ramming, backing, flattening everything which would go down under their powerful treads. It was an eerie and yet somehow a thrilling thing — the purposefulness and the discipline of the men buttoned up inside those steel monsters — as if they were all being controlled by one man, pulling the strings. They were, of course, but Pop Whitehead had no way of knowing this.

Ken Carpenter, cruising up and down the no man's land in his jeep, was evaluating the demolition as it progressed on the one side, and listening to Mike Keegan on the other, as Mike reported, by radio, that he had his fire trucks in position and was starting to wet down the buildings in preparation for the backfire. Carpenter had his power megaphone ready now. The demolition was not as complete as he would have liked, but the fire on the hillside was now too close to wait. He lifted the megaphone as he sat in the jeep on the corner of Cemetery and Main, and his voice roared out over the area. "Now, all flame-throwers stand by," Carpenter's voice boomed. "All flame-throwers, this is Major Carpenter. Ignite the knocked-down stuff first — the flat stuff — so it'll have a chance to burn away from the street into the buildings. Okay, boys — give her the torch!"

Inside the hospital, Pop Whitehead's head jerked as he saw the long vicious tongue of flaming gasoline that spurted from the flame-thrower on the corner of Cemetery Street. Instantly he saw other long tongues of flame along Main and down Cemetery, saw the flattened debris burst into flame, saw the fire solidify into a line that came up the hill along Cemetery Street, turned the corner, and went down Main as far as his eye could reach through the smoke. For a moment he did not understand. Then he turned back toward the operating table with a peculiar smile on his face. "They just pulled a pretty cute trick out there," he said — "the Guard boys in their tanks. I don't think we'll have to worry about evacuating, after all. This fire isn't out, by a long shot. But I think the Guard's got a grip on it now."

Jake Abbott and Jack McHugh were standing on the highway at the approach to the Lundyville bridge while George Hurd, sitting in his Cadillac, just ahead of them, was trying to argue the Civil Defense guard into letting them through the roadblock. "I'm Mr. Hurd," Jake could hear him saying. "Head of the advertising department of the steel company, and I have to get through here at once —"

Jake saw the local volunteer, a big farmer in overalls, wearing a shiny white helmet with CD printed on it in blue, bend down in the light of the headlights and say, in a nasal Western Pennsylvania voice, "I don't give a damn if you're Jesus Christ's little brother, Mister — nobody gits acrost this here bridge less'n he's got a job to do —"

"I have a job to do," Hurd's voice said. "I have a family in Carey Furnace and —"

"You got a family in Carey Furnace," the CD man said. "You and everybody else in this here line's got a family in Carey Furnace. If we let you all through, the fire trucks and the ambulances and the other stuff would be flat out stalled. Now look, Mister, wheel it around to the left here —"

"But I'm George Hurd —"

"*Wheel it around to the left!*" the Civil Defense guard suddenly yelled. "Before I drag you outa there and slap you under arrest!"

Jack McHugh touched Jake Abbott's arm. "You heard what the man said? We'll never get across this bridge — but I'm going home, and I'm going right now. Trix may be in trouble, and if she's not, she'll be worried sick. You want to come with me?"

"How?"

"You can swim, can't you?"

"Sure."

"We'll drive back through the Lundy estate and down to the mouth of Black River. It's only about three miles north of Carey Furnace — and there's Catbird Island in the middle. The river is swifter than hell on this side, in the east channel. But if we can reach Catbird Island, we can rest, and the channel on the other side is shallow enough to wade in this low water."

"Okay," Jake Abbott said. "We take both cars?"

"No, let's just use mine — it's easier and you won't have to eat my dust, because, brother, I'm going to step on it." He was silent a moment. "I got another idea in mind for the swim, just in case we get carried downstream past Catbird and have to make it all in one leg. I've got a five-gallon can in the back of my car, in case I should ever run out of gas on the highway. It'll make a dandy life-preserver. We can take turns riding it if we get tuckered out. Okay, boy, let's get moving."

Mary Whitehead had stayed with Eva Carey in the mansion on the mountaintop after both their husbands had left — Pop to the hospital, and John Carey to the plant. The electric power was off, but Eva had a portable radio which worked on batteries, and they were getting what news they could from the local radio station. Their view of the fire was the best possible one. Smoke was heavy now, however, and at times all they could see, below them in the valley, was a caldron of glowing murk in which nothing but smoke and flames were visible. But the radio station somehow remained operational, and reported bulletins as they came in. The dead and injured, according to the radio, would run into the thousands; as yet there was no way of accurately reporting numbers. Help was streaming in over the highways from a hundred miles around in every direction; the governor had called out the National Guard and designated the town a disaster area. And then there came the chilling announcement that the town was under martial law and that all persons not concerned with fighting the fire or conducting rescue operations must stay off the street; looters, the announcement said, would be shot on sight. . . .

It was Mary Whitehead who noticed the flame-throwers begin their action along Main Street.

"Eva — look! They're doing something — over there on Main. See it?"

"Yes I see it. What does it mean?"

"I don't know. But they're starting little fires for some reason, all along the street."

The radio explained it for them, seconds later. The situation had become desperate, the announcer said. Unless something drastic was done, the entire town would burn to the ground. So the firemen and the Guard had selected Main Street as the line they would hold, and had started backfiring from that line.

The two women watched the quickly spreading blaze the flame-throwers had started. As it grew brighter, they could see the white plumes of the hoses playing over the buildings across the street. And then the announcer's voice said sharply, "I have just received word from the police department concerning one of our foremost citizens — Mr. John Carey, head of the Carey Furnace Steel Company. . . ."

Eva gave a little cry, and Mary Whitehead reached out and held her against her. "Now, Eve," she said. "Now . . ."

"The police report that Mr. Carey went through the safety line at the corner of First Street and River Avenue shortly after the fire began, and got across to Knapp's drugstore. He was seen to enter the store, and attempts were made to call him back. He did not heed the calls and it was too dangerous for anyone to try to go across, at that time, to bring him back. He wrapped his face in some kind of cloth and started across the intersection — apparently trying to reach the plant — when No. 2 blast furnace broke out. Mr. Carey was standing in the middle of the street when the molten iron reached him . . ."

"Oh, John," Eva Carey cried sharply. "John! John! *John!*"

Mary Whitehead's arm held her friend tightly, but she did not speak. Eva's body was trembling all over. And then, gradually, she quieted. She felt the sorrow and the loss that had gripped her like savage hands slowly relax, and the feeling she had had when she kissed John Carey goodbye, so short a time ago, expecting that some report like this would come to her, was returning. John was safe now. He was safe from that black leech that had fastened on his body. He had beaten it. He would not die, stinking and helpless, in his bed. He had died on his feet, striding through the flaming town that he and his father before him had built.

Eva Carey turned to her friend, and her eyes were open now, and bright. Tears welled out of them and trickled down her cheeks, but she was smiling. "I'm all right, Mary," she said. "I'll be all right now."

Frances Abbott, Trixie McHugh and the two Abbott children were sitting in the Abbotts' kitchen listening to Trixie's portable radio when there was a sound of footsteps on the gravel of the driveway below, and the low sound of men's voices. There had been reports of looting on the radio, and one case of attempted rape, and all citizens had been warned to be alert. Neither Trixie nor Frances was worried about looting or rape. As the hours had gone by and accounts of the dead and injured mounted, they had both become obsessed with the idea that their men had been killed. Now, at the sound of footsteps, Trixie shut off the radio and they all sat in the candlelight listening, holding their breath.

"There's a candle burning in the kitchen," Jake Abbott's voice said below, in the dark. "You want to come up with me, Jack — or go up the hill?"

"I'll go up the hill," Jack McHugh's voice said. "I want to see Trix."

The two women reacted differently. Trixie smiled, a timid, little-girl smile in the candlelight, and her lips quivered, and then she began to shake, sitting upright, looking at the doorway, shaking violently all over. Frances Abbott twisted out of her chair and pulled the kitchen door open as Jake, covered with river mud, soaking wet and staggering with exhaustion, reached the top of the steps. She went to him in a single quick motion and held him tight against her, kissing him on the mouth, holding him with all her strength.

"Jake — Jake, honey, oh, honey — I thought you were dead."

"Not dead," he said, panting. "Just wet. We had to swim the river to get here."

The two Abbott children, Nancy and Henry, grabbed their father from opposite sides and hugged him. Then, from inside the kitchen, they heard Trixie McHugh calling to Jack, and in the darkness below, Jack's voice saying, "Okay, Trix — okay, baby. I'm coming." The Abbotts stood aside, still holding each other, to let Jack pass as he ran up the steps toward the doorway.

The moon rose above Carey Furnace, serene and white above the massive tower of smoke. It moved slowly across the sky in its accustomed course. Below, the fires burned and smoke coiled upward and merged, finally, into a brown overcast that was like a cloud deck, and the flames grew yellow through it, and orange, and brown, and finally were lost altogether. Air traffic into Greater Pittsburgh Airport was placed under instrument-flight rules, even though the night was clear. No rain was forecast. The entire nation still sweltered under a stationary high-pressure frontal system.

On the ground, at Carey Furnace, fire-control operations concentrated on the Main Street line. The fire storm was sweeping up the hillside faster now, as it moved into the alleys where the houses were mostly dry wooden shacks. But the backfire was in progress. It had burned halfway through its first block, headed downhill, when it met the fire storm coming up, and they merged. The heat at this point was so severe that it blistered paint on houses across the Main Street fire lane. But the hoses were able to prevent actual combustion, and finally, toward morning, the fire storm began to subside, and the heat to diminish. There was no more fuel for the fire to feed on. It was dying — with here and there a last vicious revival, such as the explosion of a thousand-gallon gasoline storage tank under the burned-over Texaco station, which belched flames suddenly over most of a block.

There were casualties among the rescue workers and the firemen.

These were expected. A flame-thrower operator was shot, but not killed, by a home-owner who was trying to prevent the firing of his house. One National Guardsman was accidentally struck and killed by a backing tank. But by four o'clock in the morning, when the first flush of dawn appeared through the smoke, it was apparent that the fire was under control.

In nonaffected parts of the steel plant, repair gangs were already on the job checking gas mains and electrical circuits, and in the area of the blast furnaces, high-pressure hoses, picking up water from the river, were speeding the cooling of the superheated piles of twisted debris. The plant was a chaos which resembled the aftermath of a bombing, but danger of extensive further damage had passed. The drastic backfire on the hillside had saved the rest of the town. The hillside area was still burning — burning brightly in some isolated spots — but nobody was trying to stop these last fires. The town water supply had been exhausted long ago, and anyhow, it was obviously now just as sensible to let the fire complete the work it had begun. Very little of value could be saved, and what the fire burned up now would not have to be torn down and carted away. Clean-up and rebuilding would actually be expedited. As the sun's light grew stronger, somewhere, amazingly, in the smoke-filled air birds began to chirp. The long and desperate night was over.

Friday

SHORTLY before eight o'clock Friday morning, Major Ken Carpenter was officially relieved of his command by a cold-eyed colonel who'd been with the 82nd Airborne, who had flown in from Harrisburg under orders from the Adjutant General of the National Guard. He was the AG's man, and he was here to take over. And Ken, so tired now he was having difficulty staying awake even in the presence of the man who was relieving him, was glad to hand over the responsibility.

"It looks as if you've handled things pretty well," the colonel was saying. "I've got it now. You can take off and go home if you want to."

"All right, sir," Ken Carpenter said. "I think I'll do that."

"I suppose your phone number'll be on the board — in case I need you for consultation."

"Yes, sir. It's on the alert board, sir. I can give it to you now, on a card, if you like."

"No, I'll check the board if I need you. I don't think I will, though. It looks mainly like a mop-up from here on in."

Carpenter stood up and saluted, and the colonel returned it. "I hereby relieve you, Major," he said formally. "Take off."

Carpenter found his car and fell into it, his legs leaden with fatigue, but after he got the car started and rolling, the breeze coming through the ventilators revived him slightly. He drove through the yard, passing his men, some of whom were still standing there discussing the night. They grinned at him tiredly. The violent action of the night had made them close, the way combat made men close. They were a good outfit: he would be sorry to leave them.

He drove out onto the street and turned left and headed downhill into the valley. The roadblock was still there, but no cars were lined up behind it now. He waved to a Civil Defense man, who motioned for him to come through, and drove downhill out of the worst of the smoke. But it hung over the valley, as far as he could see, and when he got down to the valley floor, behind the mountain, smoke lay in low layers over J. P. Detweiler's fields, like brown fog. Cars were parked solidly around Dutch Huber's bar. Nobody had done much sleeping last night and now, in the morning, they were having a nightcap before they went to bed. If he had been a drinking man he would have stopped at Dutch's now and had a drink. But he wanted to find Margaret Fiori, to check up and see if she was all right, before he went to bed. He was not worried about Enid. She wasn't home; she was in Sewickley or some such place, visiting some friend. Enid wouldn't be caught in the fire. People like Enid were never near anything as dangerous and real as a fire. They were sitting in a beauty salon, or on the verandah of a country club, or en route to a beach or a mountain resort or a summer cruise ship. They died, when they finally died, in bed at an advanced age, surrounded by expensive doctors. Maragret Fiori was another sort. After Ken had left her on the hill last night she might have gone almost anywhere, done almost anything. He had to know that she was safe before he could sleep.

He turned off the blacktop road onto the gravel of the Fiori driveway and stopped in front of the house. Nobody seemed to be about. He got out of the car and went to the door and called through the screen. Nobody answered. He called again, and a weak, petulant voice said, "Come in — come in."

He opened the screen door and walked through to the den, where Umberto Fiori lay on the bed looking at him, hollow-eyed. "Oh, it's you, Carpenter. I might have known. Looking for my wife, I guess."

"Is she here, Bert?"

"Don't call me Bert, you bastard. No, she's not here."

"I see. Could you tell me where I might find her?"

"I don't know where you might find her, you bastard, and if I did I wouldn't tell you. Now get out and let me alone."

"All right," Ken Carpenter said. "Look — I don't blame you. I know how you feel. And I want to tell you something. I'm leaving town. I'm leaving the steel company. You won't see me again."

Umberto Fiori's hooded black eyes lit up, briefly. "Good," he said. "I'm glad. When I get up, if you're still around, I'm going to kill you."

Ken looked at the man, and for the first time since he had known him, he felt a sudden respect. He said, "I don't blame you for that, either."

"Never mind the shit talk," Fiori said. "Just get out, will you, Carpenter?"

Ken said no more. The nurse was coming in with the breakfast tray. So he turned and left the room, and as he reached the front door, he saw Margaret Fiori drive in in her car. He stopped and looked at her as she got out. She, too, had obviously been up all night, and he could see her dress was brown with dried blood, and he felt his nerves constrict. "Margie," he said, stepping forward. "You're hurt — you're bloody —"

She smiled at him, her face sagging and lined with weariness, looking like an old woman, yet, in a way, as young and vital as she had ever looked. "It's not my blood," she said huskily. "I've been at the hospital — helping the nurses. . . . How's Bert? Is he all right?"

"Yes, he's all right. But I think both Bert and the nurse had a pretty rough night, not knowing what was going on."

"I was worried about him."

"Sure, I know."

Margaret Fiori looked at him and her eyes were bright. "I saw your tanks," she said. "I saw them from the hospital." She stepped close, lifted her lips and kissed him, quickly, and then pushed past him and hurried inside.

In the early morning, Howard Snyder left Louise Stegmeyer with Carole and went out to look for his wife. He knew from Carole that Ethyl had gone down to buy her some comic books, but there was no way of checking the various stores she might have visited. Most of them were burned. Carole had also said that her mother had been talking on the phone with somebody about an antique. There was no phone service, so Howard was not able to check any of the dealers. He left the yard and walked down Mountain Avenue, asking people he chanced to pass, and whom he knew, if they had seen Ethyl. None of them had. On Grandview Avenue he saw Louise's house and it occurred to him that he should stop and tell them she was safe. Nobody answered the front door, and he walked around through the yard to the kitchen door and tapped.

"Just a minute," a woman's voice called, and the door opened and Vivian Stegmeyer looked out. "Oh — it's Mr. Snyder. Come in."

"I can't come in, Mrs. Stegmeyer," he said. "I'm looking for my wife. I just stopped for a minute to tell you about Louise. She was at the picnic, and she — we came back together, and she's up at my house now, with Carole, absolutely safe."

Mrs. Stegmeyer's eyes filled with tears. "Louise," she whispered. "Safe —" She turned back into the kitchen, opening the door wider, so that Howard Snyder could see in. He saw Herman Stegmeyer sitting at the table in front of a plate of fried eggs. Herman had a piece of toast with a fried egg on it in his hand. As Howard watched, he put it into his mouth.

"Louise is safe, dear!" Vivian Stegmeyer called to him across the kitchen. "She's safe! She's safe after all!"

Herman Stegmeyer went on chewing a moment, then swallowed and ran his tongue around his lips. He said, "That's good, Vivian. That's fine. Ask Mr. Snyder in for a cup of coffee, why don't you?"

"I can't stop," Howard said. "I've got to look for Ethyl. Is it all right for Louise to stay with Carole until I get back?"

"It's all right with us, Snyder," Herman Stegmeyer said. "Keep her up there as long as you like. Vivian, my coffee, please. If Snyder doesn't want any, I do. . . ."

Howard Snyder left the doorway and hurried out of the yard and down Grandview Avenue. What had Herman Stegmeyer said, back there in the kitchen? *It's all right with us, Snyder. . . . Keep her up there as long as you like . . .*

As long as he liked? That would be a long time. It would be as long as they both lived: it would be forever. Except that it wouldn't. It would only be a short while, an hour maybe, until Ethyl got back. He knew Ethyl was alive. She must be. He could not imagine her being dead. He crossed the square, hurrying, looking about him, expecting to see Ethyl at any moment, coming around the next corner.

He could not know, of course, that Ethyl was dead, buried under tons of still smoldering metal on River Avenue. He could not know that his impossible dreams — which he had abandoned — would eventually come true. He would see Tehuantepec, Mexico. He would listen to the slopping of the sea. And the two people he loved most would be with him — Louise, his wife, and Carole, his daughter.

Howard Snyder knew none of these things that terrible morning when he left Grandview Avenue and began crossing the square past the Civil War monument, peering about through the thin smoke, looking for Ethyl. He was sure she was alive. He was sure he would see her, at any moment, coming around the next corner . . . .

Dave Ross had been up all night. He had been at home in Hunter's Valley, having an after-dinner drink, when the glare and the sound of the wreck had rolled in over the mountain. He had tried to telephone at once, to reach the night superintendent at the plant, but the lines had been busy. He had then taken his car out and driven as far as the roadblock which had halted Carpenter.

Dave Ross was not a member of any rescue squad or auxiliary police, but he was a different man from George Hurd. He wanted through, and he got through. But reaching the plant was another story. By the time Ross had left his car halfway down the hillside and run toward the blast furnaces, the fire had jumped First Street and the heat made further advance impossible. Ross had sized up the situation and decided to go to City Hall. He reasoned that the mayor's office would probably be the nerve center of disaster control, and he was right. A policeman stopped him in the hall, but when he recognized him, he said, "Oh, it's you, Mr. Ross. Hold it a second, sir. I'll see if you can go in." The policeman stepped into the mayor's office and came out in a few moments. "It's all right, Mr. Ross. Mr. Mills will speak to you. Mr. Johnson's on the radio, but I guess you won't bother him."

"I won't bother him," Dave Ross said, and stepped past the officer and into the mayor's office. It was a little before ten o'clock. He stayed there, listening, until nearly midnight. Then, when the backfire was under way, and it seemed certain that the fire would be brought under control, Ross left City Hall, crossed Main Street, and went back a block to Spring Street, which he followed for twelve blocks to the intersection of Cemetery. Here he turned back toward the fire and found the hospital, still standing and no longer seriously threatened. He went into the hospital to see if he could help and met Margaret Fiori, who was helping with patients in the lobby. There was a lull in the arrival of ambulances at this time and he had a chance to talk to Margaret for several minutes. He told her about Ken Carpenter's handling of his tanks — and her eyes lit up.

"He did well, then?"

"Yes," Dave said. "In a way, I guess the tanks saved the town."

"I'm glad!" She looked at him. "You're going to fire him, he said. Is that right, Dave?"

"Yes."

"I know what he wanted to do," Maggie Fiori said. "And I was going to help him do it. I guess you know that."

"Yes."

"Did he tell you about the picture?"

"He mentioned he had one," Dave Ross said. "He didn't describe it."

"He had a photograph of Paul Dana and Dottie O'Brien," she said. "They were in a certain position. It was a very damaging picture."

"What's he going to do with it?" Dave asked.

"Nothing. He tore it up."

Outside, suddenly, there was the wail of an ambulance and a rotating red light swept across the walls of the lobby and somebody shouted, "Dr. Weiss — Dr. Weiss — to the emergency entrance . . ."

Margaret Fiori said, "Dave, you'll have to excuse me — I may be needed. . . ."

He watched her hurry away from him through the lobby. Outside, in the distance, he heard the wail of another ambulance. Near him, a voice said, "Hey you — Mister — how about a hand here with these cots?" He glanced toward the voice. He saw that its owner had, indeed, been addressing him, and he said at once, "Sure — be glad to give you a hand."

Shortly before dawn, when the grim influx of burned and broken people slowed up, Dave Ross left the hospital and went back to find his car. He found it, but he could not drive it. It was buried under the caved-in wall of a warehouse. Dave began to walk home. Two miles short of his house, a passing motorist gave him a lift. He arrived as day was breaking, kissed his wife, and sat down in the living room. The first thing he said was: "Where's Duke?"

"He's upstairs sleeping," Virginia Ross said. "He just beat you in by a few minutes. He was working with the volunteer firemen."

"Oh," Dave said. "Fine."

"Yes," Virginia said. "I know."

"You got my message?" Dave asked.

"Yes. A man came on a motorcycle. Thank you — I'd have been out of my mind if I hadn't heard."

"We tried to phone from City Hall," Dave said. "It was impossible, but Johnson said he'd find a way." He leaned back, stretching. "They've got it in hand now — but it was touch and go for a while, before the tanks moved in."

"I heard about the tanks," Virginia Ross said. "Young Carpenter was leading them, wasn't he?"

"He was directing them from a jeep."

"The way the radio sounded, he was doing a very good job."

"He was," Dave Ross said. "He was doing a hell of a good job."

"Had you fired him yet?"

"No, I hadn't." He looked past his wife at the liquor cabinet. "Ginny, honey — would you pour me one — a big one? Never mind the ice. Bourbon, if we've got it."

She rose and went to the cabinet. She found a bottle of Old Taylor, poured from it generously, and brought the glass to her dirty, exhausted husband. "Thanks, honey," he said, and tipped the glass against his lips and drained it. "Boy — that hit the bottom!"

"Any more?"

"No, thanks. That should do it. . . . I stopped at the hospital. Maggie Fiori was there, helping the nurses. We had a little chat when there was a break. She's in love with Carpenter."

"In love? I knew she was playing — at least, I heard she was playing — you mean really in love, though, don't you?"

"Yes. She didn't say it. But I could tell by the way she talked. He told her he was going to try to take over, you know. And she was going to help him. She admitted it. But that's off now. Carpenter's leaving town. Maggie told me something else —"

"Yes? What was it?"

"Carpenter had a picture — a picture of Dana and that little O'Brien woman. Maggie didn't tell me exactly what it was, but it was rough, I guess, about as rough as you can get. Carpenter had shot it himself, up in the pines the night of the Carey party. I don't know exactly what was going on, but whatever it was, Maggie said it would have been pretty damaging if released."

"Would have?" Ginny Ross said. "You said 'would have.' If Carpenter's got a picture like that, Dave, he'll release it, never fear. He's got nothing to lose when you fire him."

"He won't release it," Dave Ross said, "because he can't. He tore it up."

"Tore it up?"

Dave Ross grinned. "He's got a weak stomach, I guess. Ginny, could I change my mind and have another drink? — a short one, this time? Then I'm going to bed. I figure I'll sleep until I wake up, however long that is. Don't let anybody get through by phone, if you can help it, until I get my battery recharged. I don't think I've ever been so bushed."

"You heard about John Carey," she said.

"Yes. We got it on the police radio."

"It was awful," she said, "burning alive, in front of all those people —"

"Awful? No, I don't think so. As a matter of fact, I think he had planned it that way." Dave closed his eyes wearily, then opened them.

She poured the whisky and held it out. He took it. He looked past her into the smoky dawn light. He lifted the glass to his lips. *If you're out there, John,* he thought, *here's to you, boy, here's luck!*

He took the whisky at a single swallow and stood up. He'd go to bed now, and sleep. He'd have an unholy mess on his hands until they dug out, and he'd need every bit of strength he could get from that bed. Walt Eberhardt couldn't help him — not right away;

and J. P. Detweiler was off buying cattle. Damn it, Carpenter had been right about J.P. A man ought to stick at the job he was being paid for. There'd be a hell of a lot of human dry rot to be cleaned out before the company was stripped for action. There'd be a lot more than brick and mortar necessary in rebuilding the Carey Furnace Steel Company the way Dave Ross wanted it built. He'd need fresh blood. It was just as well, he thought, that he hadn't fired Carpenter. He remembered Maggie Fiori, the way she'd looked and talked about Carpenter when she told about his tearing up the photograph of Paul Dana. He remembered the sound of Carpenter's voice on the radio last night, as he directed the tanks. A smile touched the lips of Dave Ross. Young Carpenter was a wild-assed kid, right now, but he had plenty of years ahead of him in which to take on the smooth armor plate of experience which now protected Dave Ross. And Dave Ross knew that if they didn't at least start out as wild-assed kids they weren't worth a damn. You could train a tiger. But you couldn't turn a joyboy or a Company Man into a tiger — not if you worked at it for a thousand years.

He stood up and looked at his wife.

"I'm going up to bed now, Ginny," he said. "If the phone rings, tell them I just left for an extended sea voyage." He smiled wearily. "If they persist, just tell them to go to hell."

He tilted her chin and kissed her lips. Then he turned and walked through the library and began mounting the stairs that led to his bedroom.